CORA OGLESBY AND HER HUSBAND,
BEN, HUNT THINGS — THINGS THAT
SHOULD NOT EXIST.

When the marshal of Leadville, Colorado comes across a pair of mysterious, bloody corpses out in the badlands, he turns to Cora to find the creature responsible.

But if she is to overcome the unnatural tide threatening to consume the small town, Cora must first confront her own tragic past.

A savage supernatural Western with unforgettable characters and dark secrets galore.

"A brilliant, bloody, violent dark fantasy — Charlie Huston turned up past 11."
Andy Remic, author of *Kell's Legend*

"From its opening chapter, The Dead of Winter *lassoed me into its gritty world of gunslingers and demons. A page-turning thrill ride of a novel that could well redefine your perception of the 'wild' west."*
Rio Youers, author of *Westlake Soul*

OCT   2012

LEE COLLINS

The Dead of Winter

ANGRY
ROBOT

ANGRY ROBOT
A member of the Osprey Group

Lace Market House,
54-56 High Pavement,
Nottingham,
NG1 1HW, UK

4402 23rd St., Ste 219,
Long Island City,
NY 11101
USA

www.angryrobotbooks.com
Saddling up anyway

An Angry Robot paperback original 2012.

Cover art by Chris McGrath
Set in Meridien by THL Design.

Distributed in the United States by Random House, Inc., New York.

ISBN 978-0-85766-272-9
eBook ISBN: 978-0-85766-273-6

Printed in the United States of America

9 8 7 6 5 4 3 2 1

For Tori
who never let me give up on
my dreamy little dreams

ONE

The smell of blood was thick in the crisp morning air as Marshal Mart Duggan dismounted, his boots finding solid earth a few inches beneath the snow. Tossing the reins over a nearby branch, he looked at his deputy and pointed to his own eyes. Deputy Jack Evans nodded, pulling his rifle from the saddle scabbard. Satisfied, the marshal drew his revolver and turned back toward the clearing. Behind him, his mare tossed her head and snorted.

Duggan paused at the edge of the disturbed snow and crouched, his breath lingering in front of his nose like a lover's ghost. He ran a gloved hand over the base of a nearby tree. Examining his fingers, he nodded to himself. Wet and cold. Whatever happened here had happened recently.

Standing up again, Duggan surveyed the clearing. Bits of clothing and strips of dripping flesh dangled from the nearby branches, but there was nothing that resembled a body. Blood-spattered snow was heaped against the tree trunks, exposing strands of yellow grass.

Looking up, the marshal beckoned for his deputy. Jack dismounted and approached the scene, his rifle at the ready.

"Keep an eye out," Duggan said in a low voice. Eyes wide, the young man nodded and pointed his gun toward the trees. Duggan walked a slow circle around the clearing, his blue eyes sweeping the snow for clues. Two pairs of boots and a few dogs had entered the clearing from the east. Duggan pictured them approaching, a couple of young men with rifles in hand, laughing as they led their wolfhounds through the snow. That early, the white peaks would have kept the morning sun from spilling into the valley. Maybe the hounds had been nipping at one another as they walked alongside their masters, unable to sense the danger lying in wait ahead.

Danger from what? Completing his sweep of the perimeter, Duggan frowned.

"What's wrong, sir?" Jack asked.

"Something ain't right here," the marshal said, not looking up. "We got us a pair of wolfers killed by something violent, but their dogs got away clean." He pointed to a set of tracks leading away from the clearing. "See there? Them dogs wasn't even bloody when they lit out, meaning they wasn't in the fight at all. They just upped and ran, letting the poor fools with them get torn to bits."

"Can't say I blame them," Jack said. "Whatever killed them fellers did it right quick, and was awful messy about it."

Duggan grunted as he made his way into the clearing.

As he stepped around a broken branch, his eye caught a small silver gleam in a nearby drift. He reached down and his fingers wrapped around the barrel of a revolver. He pulled it free of the snow and brushed it off. A Schofield .45, its nickel shine accented by blood spatters. Holstering his own gun, the marshal snapped it open and looked in the cylinder.

"Two rounds fired here," he said, holding the revolver up. "One of them wolfers saw it coming, at least."

"Don't look like he hit nothing, though," Jack said.

Digging through the snow, the marshal uncovered another revolver and a long rifle, both unused. "Other feller didn't get a shot off, looks like."

Duggan carried the guns back to his deputy and set them down against a tree. "So," he said, giving the clearing another sweep with his eyes, "one of them wolfers gets jumped and goes down before he can get his irons out. The other pulls on the attacker, gets two shots off, then gets torn up for his efforts anyway."

"And their dogs get away clean," Jack said. "Bad day for them, I guess."

Duggan sighed through his nose, the white cloud pouring over his red beard. "That don't seem right," he said. "Ain't seen the wolfhound yet that wouldn't die for his master."

Jack shrugged, but Duggan's scowl deepened. After four years of serving as marshal for one of the rowdiest towns in Colorado, he'd seen more than enough outlaws and criminals with a quick gun and a good aim. He'd also had his fair share of run-ins with wolves, bears, and other man-eating critters. Not a one of them could have taken down two seasoned wolfers like this, even if they didn't have their dogs with them.

Duggan felt Jack tense up beside him. Holding his breath, the marshal turned his head toward his deputy. The young man was alert, his fingers squeezing the barrel of his rifle. Duggan strained his ears, hoping to catch anything out of the ordinary, but the morning was still. After a few moments, he caught Jack's eye and nodded. The two lawmen turned and walked back to their horses. The marshal's mare whinnied, eager to leave. Duggan patted her neck, keeping his eyes on the clearing while Jack climbed into the saddle.

Without warning, a wave of gooseflesh rippled up the marshal's arms. Jack must have felt it, too; his gloved hands curled around the rifle's barrel. Duggan placed his boot in the stirrup and lifted himself into the saddle. Drawing his Colt, he peered through the trees. The air around them felt colder. The horses began fidgeting, stamping their hooves in the snow. Duggan could hear his own breathing and the creaking of the leather saddles, but nothing else. It seemed like an ordinary winter morning in the Rockies, but something still wasn't right. The fine hairs at the base of his neck pressed against the red bandana he wore against the cold. Somewhere, hidden in the trees, something was watching them.

Turning to his deputy, Duggan gave a single nod. The two men pulled their horses around and kicked their sides. The animals needed no encouragement, trotting between the trees toward the edge of the forest. Once clear, they broke into a gallop. As the clearing shrank in the distance behind them, Duggan felt the chill and malice melting away like ice on a spring river.

The marshal didn't say much on the ride back to town. In fact, he didn't say much for the rest of the day, which was fine with Jack. After seeing something like that, the deputy needed time to mull it over. Aside from breaking up a midday saloon fight and sending a dispatch to the county sheriff about the morning's discovery, both men spent the day in silence. Duggan put Jack on the porch of the marshal's station for the afternoon "to keep an eye on things outside." Jack knew the marshal would be keeping an eye on the bottle of whiskey in his desk. The old man was funny about people seeing him hit the bottle. Probably had something to do with being released from his duties a few years back on account of a drunken binge. Or maybe it was because Duggan's reputation had gone downhill since he'd shot a miner outside the Purdy Brothel a few months back for causing a ruckus. Trouble was, folks in town had favored the miner over the marshal, though Jack had never held the shooting against his boss. In a town like Leadville, lawmen learned to shoot first.

A powerful thirst started tugging at Jack's throat. From his post, he could see the front door of the Pioneer saloon down the street. The big two story building called to him, its shiplap walls and glass windows promising shelter from gruesome memories. It wouldn't suit an on-duty deputy to be seen standing at the bar, though, no matter what kind of morning he'd had. Jack tipped his hat toward the saloon, offering a silent promise of the evening ahead.

"See anything, kid?"

Jack leaned his head back to look at the marshal. "Not a thing, sir. Seems everybody's hiding from the cold."

"Just as well," Duggan replied, his voice thick. Jack could smell the whiskey on his breath, but his eyes were still clear. "Don't want folks running about today."

Jack didn't need to ask, but he did anyway. "On account of what we saw this morning?" The marshal nodded. "Never seen you get so wound up over a bear, sir."

Duggan looked down at his boots. "That wasn't no bear that did that, son."

"No?" Surprised, Jack felt a familiar chill creep up his spine and tried to shrug it off. "Pack of wolves, then?" The brim of the marshal's hat moved from side to side as he shook his head, but he didn't look up from his boots.

"You think bandits did it?" Jack asked, incredulous. No outlaw gang, no matter how ruthless, would do that to a pair of lone wolfers. Most outlaws wanted money, not carnage. They wouldn't hesitate to shoot a man for being poor, but they wouldn't spread him across the landscape for it, either.

Duggan looked up and met his deputy's gaze. Jack could feel the marshal taking stock of him, those blue eyes asking themselves if he measured up. The deputy shifted his weight in the chair, waiting for the verdict. A horse whinnied inside the livery across the street.

Finally, the marshal sighed, his breath filling the air between them. "No, that wasn't the work of bandits, either."

"We're running short on suspects, sir."

"I know." Duggan turned to look down the street. A few moments passed. "Fact is, Jack, I ain't got a clue what killed those men this morning."

"Looked like critters to me. Bears or wolves or some such."

"That's what I thought at first, too. Big old grizzly attack, and if anybody asks, that's our story. Between you and me, though, that was one special bear."

The chill started crawling up Jack's spine again. "What's that mean?"

"Whatever killed those men got it done without giving their hounds a scratch. I've known a good number of wolfers in my day, and every one of them trusted their dogs with their lives. Swore up and down that their hounds would jump down a grizzly's throat for them. Them dogs with those men this morning lit out without getting so much as a drop of blood on their coats. Whatever killed them boys must have scared the dogs bad, and a wolfhound don't spook easily."

Jack stared at the livery's sign, pondering the marshal's words. "So what's out there that could spook a wolfhound, then?"

"Nothing I'd care to meet." Duggan stood silent for a moment, fingering the hammer of his Colt. Finally, he stirred himself and looked at his deputy. "Don't worry about it, kid. These mountains are full of strange critters. I'd lay twenty dollars on this being a one-time thing, a story to scare your kids with one day." He clapped Jack on the shoulder. "Go home and get some rest. I'll take the evening shift till the night boys show up."

"If you insist," Jack said, standing up. He pulled his coat closed and tipped his hat to the marshal. "See you in the morning, sir." Duggan grunted and went back into the office.

Jack turned his back on the Pioneer, making clear tracks away from the saloon. He didn't know if the marshal would be watching him or not, but it wouldn't do for Duggan to see his deputy heading straight for a saloon on a day like today. Jack kept his head down, his boots crunching in the snow past the general store and down Main Street.

When he was a safe distance from the marshal's station, Jack ducked into an alley and doubled back toward the Pioneer. He could already feel the whiskey warming his belly. The afternoon sun hung just above the western peaks, turning the clouds a brilliant shade of pink. Jack paused and glanced up, drawing the cold mountain air into his lungs. Evenings like this could be deceptive. Everything seemed peaceful, but the men from the second shift in the mines would be heading out in search of their nightcaps soon. Cold nights and drunken miners meant trouble.

Maybe he shouldn't get all that drunk tonight.

The Pioneer greeted him with a jingle from the

doorbell and a warm rush of air. The familiar smells of coffee, spirits, and sweat blended into a single fragrance as Jack took in the saloon's afternoon lull. A few miners stood at the bar, getting an early start on their drinking. Two had their backs to the door, staring into their whiskey between gulps. Another at the end faced the room, both elbows planted on the bar. Drops of liquor clung to the man's beard like beads of dew on a grizzly's fur. The only other patrons sat around a game of poker at one of the rough-hewn pine tables, talking and laughing as they studied the cards in front of their faces.

"Afternoon, deputy," Boots said as Jack walked up to the bar. "Nothing else to worry about in here."

"I'm off duty, Boots," Jack replied, making sure the others at the bar could hear him.

"Good." The bartender set a glass of whiskey in front of the deputy, a grin on his round face. "This one's on the house. Payment for them thugs you and Mart ran off earlier."

Jack picked up the glass, nodded his thanks, and threw it back. The alcohol left a burning trail through his chest down into his stomach. Eyes closed, he relished the feeling for a moment, then he looked at the bartender and grinned.

"Ain't seen no lawman enjoy his whiskey like you, Jack," Boots said, refilling the glass.

"I deserve it today," the deputy replied. An image from the clearing sprang into his mind, the sight of red guts hanging from a branch, and his face grew serious. He'd seen plenty of gunshot wounds, frostbite, and mining accidents; they came with the territory out here. Hell, he'd seen a man's brains get blown out not more than a month after signing on as a deputy. The sight had turned his stomach, but it hadn't burrowed into his memory like this. Shaking his head, he drained his glass, hoping to burn the images from his mind.

"As I see it, you deserve it most every day," the bartender said, leaning against the rack of bottles behind the bar. "Dealing with this lot day in and day out would drive any man to drinking."

Jack replied with a cold grin. He could see the bartender's bald spot in the mirror above the bar. Despite his age, Boots seemed sure of himself among the miners, thugs, and other residents of Leadville. Then again, he'd stood behind the Pioneer's bar in the same black military-issue boots for longer than Jack knew. No matter how disheveled the rest of him might be, Boots always kept those boots shiny and clean. A proper tribute to his days in the service, he said, but he refused to elaborate whenever Jack pressed him for details. Every once in awhile, the miners would get to speculating on the nature of that service as they drank away the day. Some said he was Custer himself in hiding, waiting for the day when he would announce his return and sweep away the rest of the Indian nations. Others, spurred on by the fact that nobody knew his real name, said that Boots was a deserter hiding from the government. Still others figured Boots had gotten his balls shot off in some battle and resigned in shame. Nobody knew for sure, and the bartender never offered to shed any light on their speculation. Ignorance was good for business, he claimed.

The bell over the door made a pitiful jingle. Glancing over his shoulder, Jack watched the newcomer make his way over to the card table. The man kept the wide brim of his hat pulled low. A few at the table seemed to know him and called out a greeting. The stranger responded with a silent wave and pulled up a chair.

"That one looks like trouble," Boots said, refilling Jack's glass.

"Why's that?"

"No respect. Bastard just waltzes in here and plants his ass for a round of cards without buying so much as a cup of joe."

Jack's third glass flowed down his throat. Potent as it was, the whiskey wasn't going to work fast enough to suit his need. Gray light from the saloon's windows winked at him from the empty glass, pulling him back into the early morning hours and the sharp scent of blood.

"If that's the worst of your problems, you got it easy," Jack muttered, not looking up. "Hell, I'd take a hundred angry miners screaming for my blood and call myself lucky if I never had to cross paths with that monster that did those wolfers in." Catching himself, he drew a quick breath and looked up, afraid he had let the secret slip, but Boots had moved to the other end of the bar. Relieved, Jack let the breath out and glanced at himself in the mirror.

The stranger was standing behind him.

The shock slammed into his ribs. He whirled around, his hand flying to the butt of his six-gun, but the stranger didn't flinch. The man's buffalo hide coat stayed wrapped around his small frame, and his hands rested at his sides. Jack couldn't see any iron on him, although he wore a leather rifle sheath across his back. All he could see of the man's face was his mouth, small and twisted into a mocking grin. Without a word, the stranger stepped up to the bar and rapped it with his knuckles.

Jack let himself relax, his hand dropping away from his gun. This close, he could see the man's rifle sheath in greater detail. The leather was old but well-oiled, marking a long and friendly relationship with the gun-man. The stranger was shorter than the deputy, his profile hidden by the brim of his hat. A dark braid tied with a simple strand of twine ended halfway down the man's back.

The stranger rapped on the bar a second time, and Boots hurried over. "What will you have?"

"Whiskey. The good stuff," came the reply, followed by the clinking of two silver dollars on the bar. The bartender nodded and scooped up the coins. As the black boots disappeared into the storeroom, Jack almost laughed out loud. The voice had been low and quick, but there was no mistaking it: the stranger next to him, who had scared the daylights out of him not a minute before, was a woman. A chuckle escaped his lips as he fingered his glass.

"Nothing funny about an empty glass, deputy," she said as Boots returned with a clay jug.

"No, ma'am," Jack agreed, lifting it up. "Take care of it, Boots."

"Give him a drop or two of the good stuff, Boots," the stranger said, sliding a few more coins toward the bartender. Boots grinned and filled Jack's glass from the jug. Jack brought it up to his nose and drew in the aroma: strong and full-bodied. He'd never had the money to sample the Pioneer's private collection himself, but he never turned down a free drink. Smiling, he lifted his glass to the woman beside him.

"To the good stuff!"

Glass clinked against glass, and the good stuff filled Jack's chest with fire. Eyes closed, he allowed a stupid grin to bloom beneath his mustache. He took a deep breath, then clapped the stranger on the back.

"Much obliged, ma'am! That was a treat."

"Go on, have another," she said, giving Boots a nod.

Jack lifted the refilled glass to his lips. "Well, ain't you generous? Anything I might do to repay the favor?"

"I ain't looking for much," the stranger replied, running her fingers along the rim of her glass. "I'm just a mite curious about that monster you mentioned earlier."

Mart Duggan shut the door of the marshal's office, leaving Victor Sanchez and George Murray in charge of the midnight watch. Pulling his coat closed, he heaved a sigh and stepped into the snow-covered street. The livery's lantern winked at him from across the street, burning a pale yellow against the cold night. He could almost feel his wife's hands on his shoulders, working out the knots in his muscles in front of a crackling fire. Shaking his head against the morning's carnage, the marshal crunched across the snow toward home. The night was crisp and quiet out on the streets, but he could sense trouble brewing behind the town's walls. He would've been up for a good fight any other night, but tonight he hoped his deputies could keep a lid on things. Tonight, all he wanted was a good sleep to put some distance between himself and the day's events.

"You might want to teach that deputy of yours how to keep his mouth shut, marshal."

The voice came from a dark alley to his right. Duggan turned and pulled his Colt in a single motion. The night air resounded with the metallic click of the gun's hammer.

"Hey, now, no need for all that." A slim figure in a wide-brimmed hat stepped into the moonlight, hands raised. "Just wanted to have a word with you before you tuck in."

Duggan's temper flared, but he forced himself to lower his gun. "What about?"

"I hear tell you and your deputy had some trouble this morning." Her voice was calm as she leaned against a hitching post and crossed her arms. "Your man Jack seemed pretty shook up about it, and there ain't much as can shake up a Leadville lawman."

"That son of a bitch," Duggan said, shaking his head. "I tell him to keep quiet and he shoots his mouth off to the first woman he meets."

"Can't say I didn't help loosen his tongue a bit," she replied. "Good whiskey sure works wonders on a man."

"Well, ma'am, I appreciate you telling me about my wayward deputy. Now, if you'll excuse me, it's a bit chilly out and I've had a long day." Duggan holstered his gun. Something about the woman bothered him, and he didn't want to lose his temper. Tipping his hat to her, he turned toward home.

Her voice brought him up short. "I imagine you'd sleep a lot better knowing what killed those men this morning."

"And I suppose you know?" he asked without turning.

"Ain't got a clue."

Duggan's fists clenched as he whirled on the woman. A few strides brought them inches apart. "Then don't waste my time," he said, his breath covering her face.

The stranger met the marshal's cold blue eyes with a calm stare. "Wouldn't dream of it. Fact is, I'm looking to save you some. You're a busy man and ain't got the time to be chasing down spooks, am I right?"

"Who said it was spooks?"

"You ain't no fool, marshal," she replied. "You know damn well that wasn't no bear that killed those men."

Surprised, Duggan took a step back, his gaze falling to the snow on his boots. This woman, whoever she was, didn't seem like a fool, either. He hated drawing in outside help, but she was right. He didn't have time for spook hunting with all of his regular duties as Leadville marshal, and he didn't want to risk sending one of his deputies after something that dangerous. Problem was, he didn't know this woman from Eve. She could have butchered the wolfers herself for all he knew. Still, if she could really take care of the problem, he'd be a fool to turn her down.

After a long silence, his blue eyes came back up to her face. "So what do you want from me?"

TWO

From atop Our Lady of Virginia, Cora Oglesby surveyed what remained of the scene. Above them, the noonday sun filtered through the evergreens, dappling the mare's chestnut coat. Our Lady snorted and flicked an ear. Despite the marshal's warnings of carnage, both horse and rider were unconcerned by the clearing spread out before them.

Then again, there wasn't much to be concerned about.

Cora pounded the saddle horn and cursed. "That Mart Duggan is a damn fool," she said.

"How's that?" Ben asked, nudging his gelding up beside her to see for himself.

"If he'd led us out here when we first asked him to, there might have been something to see," she said. "A trail of blood, or footprints, or some leftover guts, or something. But no, he has us sit in our hotel room a full week while he runs our story past that good-for-nothing sheriff Jim Barnes. 'Can't associate with no criminals,' he says while he lets the real monster just slip away."

"No use worrying about that now," Ben said.

"I'll fret about it if I want to." Cora sighed and dismounted. She gave Our Lady a pat on the neck, then looked up at her husband. "Don't fall asleep, now."

Ben nodded. Cora pulled her rifle from the saddle scabbard and stepped toward the clearing. Scavengers had picked the area clean, leaving only a few rust-colored stains behind. She made a full circle around the area without finding much of anything. Another sigh filled the cold air around her. If only they could have gotten here sooner. Still, even with the scavenger's tracks, she could tell that nothing big enough to kill the wolfers had been through the clearing. It was as if the men just vanished in a bloody mist.

She was intrigued.

A crow's call broke the silence. Cora scowled up at the interruption. The black bird perched about fifteen feet above her head, its feathers gleaming in a patch of sunlight. It crowed again, turning to stare at her through one beady black eye. She considered blowing the smug look off of its face with her rifle, then thought better of it. Her bullets were too valuable to waste on animals, no matter how irritating they might be.

Rocks, however, were much cheaper. She slipped the rifle into her shoulder scabbard, knelt down and began digging through the snow. She rejected several stones before finding one that felt right. Standing up, she was glad to see that the offending bird hadn't moved from its perch. She smiled and drew her arm back, ready to see feathers fly, when she noticed something.

"Hey, Ben," she said over her shoulder, "come have a look at this."

Ben tossed his reins onto a nearby branch and walked up next to her. "What am I looking at?"

Cora pointed at the crow's perch. The branch the bird sat on was broken, jutting out from the pine's trunk like a snapped bone. From what she could see, the break was still white and clean. A single black feather drifted down and settled on the snow at the tree's base. Acting on instinct, Cora walked over and picked it up. It was about as long as her gloved hand and boasted a glossy sheen, but there wasn't anything unusual about it.

Frustrated, she let the feather drop from her fingers. It floated off to her left, lighting on a branch sticking out from the snow. Cora's brow furrowed as she leaned down for a closer look. The scent of pine sap drifted up to meet her from the fresh break in the wood. She lifted the branch out of the drift, grunting from the effort. Shaking the snow from its needles, she hoisted it upright and leaned it against the tree's trunk. The branch was nearly as tall as she was and too thick for the fingers of one hand to wrap around.

"Here's this," she said.

Ben came over to inspect the branch. After a few moments, he nodded to himself. "Something broke this off, and it wasn't no snowfall. Limb's too thick for that." Looking back up at the bird, he took an estimate of the height, then looked back toward the clearing. Smiling, he nodded again. "I reckon our killer was perched right up there, just waiting for those poor fools to wander too close."

Cora crouched down, turning the broken branch this way and that. "Sure didn't leave much by way of sign. Ain't no claw marks or hairs or nothing."

"Guess that means it wasn't no werewolf or hell-hound," Ben said.

"That's too bad," Cora said. "I was hoping for something easy. All them dog monsters is alike: line them up and put them down. Hellhounds is our specialty, besides. How many have we bagged in all?"

"Half a dozen, I reckon."

"Well, we ain't adding to that count today." Straightening up, Cora made to brush her gloves on her coat when a white blob splattered on the branch in front of her. Startled, she took a step backward. The crow let out a satisfied croak, which she answered with a glare. Her hand dropped to her revolver when the bird took wing in a flurry of black. Her heart sank a little as she watched it disappear into the trees.

"We ain't killing nothing at this rate," Ben said, a smile spreading beneath his trim mustache. "You're too old and slow."

Cora glared at him. "I've bagged me more than my share of critters, thank you kindly."

"Guess we're lucky none of them was evil birds." He dodged the punch she aimed at him, his blue eyes sparkling.

"Well, fine," Cora said, crossing her arms. "We got us an escaped crow and a broken branch with no good reason for being broken. Ain't much to go on, but we've made do with less." Her brown eyes swept over the clearing once more, then she nodded. "Let's get on back to town."

Ben followed her back to the horses without a word. Our Lady whinnied as they approached, stretching her neck out for a pat. Cora obliged her and was rewarded with a snort of hot, moist air. She smiled, running her hand down the horse's mane before slipping the Winchester back into the saddle scabbard. She placed her boot in the stirrup and swung herself up. Our Lady tossed her head and nickered, but Cora didn't share her enthusiasm.

"What do you reckon that prickly marshal will have to say when we tell him we ain't got nothing?" she asked.

Ben sighed through his nose. "Five dollars says he'll run us out of town."

"I'll make it ten."

"Think we still ought to find this critter even if he does?"

Cora shook her head. "He can rot along with his little town," she said. "He's already wasted a week of our time. We ought to head for Carson City or somewhere without all this damn snow."

Cora pulled on the reins, turning Our Lady away from the clearing. They trotted through the trees until they reached the meadow. Squinting against the blinding glare of the sun, it took her a few moments to spot the mountain Marshal Duggan had pointed out to her. She finally picked it out, its peak thrusting toward the blue sky like a crooked gunsight. Mount

Something-or-Other, her guide back to the silver boom town of Leadville, Colorado.

Pulling her bandana over her nose, she lifted her boots on either side of Our Lady to give her a kick when she paused. Her breath warmed her face and neck, but she could feel a chill creeping into her fingers through her gloves. She glanced skyward and held her hands out beneath the sun. Clenching her fists a few times, she tried to drive the cold out, but it persisted. She could feel it flowing up toward her elbows. Her fingers became hard to move, a feeling which always gave her a slight panic. Cold fingers meant a slow draw and a slow trigger, and neither was good for staying alive.

Ben rode up beside her. "What's wrong?"

Cora held up her hand, and he fell silent. She pulled the Colt revolver from her belt and cocked the hammer. Turning her head, she looked back into the mess of evergreens. The sunlight still fell in patches through gaps in the branches. Nothing looked out of the ordinary, but the chill in her blood kept moving. It was past her elbows now, working its way up to her shoulders. Uneasy, she lifted her gaze toward the tree-tops, sifting through the branches with her keen brown eyes. The blue sky winked at her from between clusters of green needles. Her fingers began to throb, the chill digging in toward her bones.

A sudden breeze pulled at her hat and caused Our Lady to shift her weight. Cora felt the horse roll and pitch beneath her, but her gaze never left the trees. The branches were swaying with the wind, but something didn't look right. Deep in the maze of prickly limbs, she could see a gray shadow in the branches that lagged behind the motion of the trees. She couldn't make out a recognizable shape at this distance, but that hardly mattered. Maybe it was a bird or a confused bear, or maybe it was something else. Whatever it was, she blamed it for the unnatural chill in her veins.

Forcing her cold arms into action, she leveled her revolver at the shadow. It was a long shot for a pistol, but she didn't want to waste time pulling out the Winchester. The pain in her fingers made it hard to hold the gun steady. She gripped her gun arm with her other hand and closed one eye, sighting down the barrel. The gunshot clapped her ears and rolled through the winter forest. Our Lady flinched at the noise. The kickback stung Cora's fingers, but she forced her thumb to pull the hammer back a second time.

When the smoke cleared, the gray shape had vanished from the branch. Cora's eyes darted to the base of the tree. Nothing. Keeping her gun raised, she checked the surrounding trees. Seconds passed, but the only movement was the breeze through the branches. Her gun hand began tingling. Looking down, she flexed her fingers around the grip. They were still cold, but feeling was returning.

"Did you see anything?" Ben asked.

Cora replied with a shrug. She holstered her revolver, turned her back on the forest and punched Our Lady's sides with her heels. The mare sprang into motion. Ben spurred his own horse after her, giving the trees one last look as they rode across the meadow.

"Refresh my memory, marshal. What time did you and your deputy find that clearing again?"

Mart Duggan looked up from the newspaper, annoyed to find this woman standing in his office. Where the hell was Sanchez? Why hadn't he stopped her from barging in like this? Looking past her into the front room of the station, he could see the deputy's boots propped up on the desk. If Victor wasn't asleep yet, he would be in the next fifteen minutes. Duggan cursed under his breath and looked back at the strange woman, his patience that much shorter.

"Sometime in the morning," he answered.

"I remember that part." Cora helped herself to the chair facing the marshal. "But how early or late was it?"

Duggan folded the paper in a messy heap and leaned his elbows on the desk. "Early. No more than an hour past sunup."

Cora's brow furrowed. "You're sure? It wasn't still night?"

"Yes, I'm sure, Mrs Oglesby. Jack and I was following up on a report we got first thing that morning. Somebody had been out on a morning ride when they came across that spot and high-tailed it back to town to tell us about it."

"Who was it that told you about it?"

"Bill Hicks."

"Who's Bill Hicks?"

The marshal leaned back in his chair and folded his arms. "Look, Mrs Oglesby, I ought to thank you for being so eager to look into this for me, but I ain't got time to discuss the townsfolk with you. I'm a busy man, and Leadville is a busy town. Until you got any real results for me, please leave me to my business."

"Is that right?" Cora stomped her boots on the floor.

"It is."

"Well then, it just so happens that I may have caught me a glimpse of your culprit."

The marshal picked up the newspaper. "What did he look like?"

"Can't say, really," Cora replied. "It wasn't a very good glimpse."

"So it wasn't the spook you thought it was, then?" Duggan said, not looking up.

"I ain't the only one who thinks it's a spook. Your deputy Jack thinks the same as me."

"I can't help hiring idiots from time to time."

Cora snorted a laugh through her nose. "Seems to me you can't help being one, either."

Duggan's boots slammed on the wooden floor as he stood to his feet, the newspaper scattering. He planted one hand on his desk and pointed the other in her face. "Now you listen to me! You and your husband is only here because Sheriff Barnes thinks you're worth a damn. If I had my way, you'd have till sundown to clear out of my town before I ran you out. It still ain't settled in my mind that you ain't drifters looking to turn a quick dollar before moving on to some other fool town. Lord help you if that's true. I won't stand to be made a fool of."

Cora let him finish, a small grin playing at the corners of her mouth. "Ain't no fool I've ever met that needed help being made, marshal. I know you got to keep this town together, and that ain't no mean feat. Last time I was through here, why, you could have thrown a stone from one end of town to the other without hitting a single head. Now the only thing you got more of than saloons and brothels is the miners that use them."

The marshal's finger sank to his desk as she talked, and she took that as her cue to stand. "As I said before, we're looking to make your life a bit easier," she said. "You're a right fine lawman, but you're green when it comes to handling any sort of monsters. Me and Ben happen to be experts in that area, and as experts, we're fixing to lend you our expertise. If you choose not to take it, that's your business. We'll be on our way, no hard feelings. You and that sleepy Mexican in the front room and all your other little deputies can have this town to yourselves."

"But." She planted her own palms on the desk and leaned toward the marshal until their hats touched. "When that thing in the woods finishes picking them wolfers out of its teeth, you can bet your badge it'll come back for more. Creatures like that can't never get their fill. If it can't find any idiots like them wolfers out in the forest, it'll start prowling around your streets. Pretty soon, you'll hear stories of lonely miners disappearing between brothels. Maybe that *vaquero* out there won't show up one morning." She grinned at him, her brown eyes colder than the frost on the windows. "Could be your office here ends up looking like that clearing, only instead of you cleaning up some unlucky saps, it's your wife cleaning strips of you off the windows."

Cora straightened up and rested her right hand on the hilt of her cavalry saber. "Of course, your monster could take a fancy to none of that. Maybe killing the wolfers was a one-time thing. I wouldn't bet an entire town on it, but it ain't my town. Ain't no piss in my soup if Leadville gets torn apart and dragged to hell bit by bit. Me and Ben can kill this thing for you, but not without your help. So it's your call, marshal."

Duggan stood silent for a moment. This woman had a way of getting under his skin that few could manage. The hot-headed Leadville marshal was known for his temper, but it usually took longer than a few minutes to whip him up into a fury. A self-proclaimed woman spook hunter with enough lip to call him a fool in his own office was a new thing for him, and he hated every bit of it.

Her words unsettled him down to his bones, though he would never admit it. In his four years as Leadville marshal, he'd jailed more than his fair share of ruffians, rowdies, and crooks. Most were drunk enough that a good smack on the head and a night behind bars would clear them up, but he'd settled a few high-profile troublemakers as well. He'd even faced down the mayor a time or two, refusing to let a rich friend of his walk free until the man sobered up.

Duggan feared no man, but what this woman described wasn't a man, and he knew it. As much as he
hated to even think it, he couldn't pistol-whip something that could shred two grown men in seconds and
disappear without a trace. He could shoot it, maybe,
but one of the wolfers had done the same thing and
ended up dead anyway.

He rose to his full height and looked across his desk
at this strange bounty hunter. Duggan was not a tall
man, and his eyes were level with hers. As she said,
there was a chance that this thing would keep to the
woods or even move elsewhere, but he didn't trust the
notion. What he had seen in the clearing had been the
work of something savage. He'd never heard of the
animal that was satisfied with just a taste of human
blood. Bears, wolves, and cougars all became regular
man-killers once they'd whetted their appetites for a
man's flesh. That thing out there wasn't any of those,
but it was an animal just the same. Better than any of
them, when it came right down to it. More dangerous.
If this woman wanted to throw herself in its way, he
shouldn't try to stop her. If she actually managed to
kill the thing, so much the better.

"All right," he said at last, extending his hand. "You
got yourself a deal."

Cora took his hand and shook it, another grin bearing the gap in her front teeth. "Glad to see you ain't a
fool after all."

"That Duggan is a damned fool."

A loud bang echoed in the hotel room as Cora

slammed the door behind her. Ben was stretched out on the bed with a book in front of him, a kerosene lamp casting its dim light over his shoulder. He didn't look up or even flinch at the sound of the slamming door.

"Why is that?" he asked.

"I had to sit in his office and tell him that his own wife would be cleaning his guts off his windows before he could bring himself to help us out." Cora's boots thudded her indignation into the worn hide rug as she walked across the room. She set her pistol on the wooden table that stood between the room's two windows and rolled her head around on her shoulders. "Seems to me that a man with any kind of sense would be begging us to chase that thing off after seeing the clearing."

"Didn't seem that bad to me."

"Sure, when we was there," she said, sitting down and pulling off her boots. "Critters had picked it pretty clean by then. Not much left to go on."

"Then what did you shoot at?" Ben finally looked up from his book.

"A gray something hiding itself up in the trees."

The book's spine crackled as Ben closed it. "So you did see something."

Cora told him of the strange shadow she'd seen in the trees and of the chill she'd felt. When she finished, he leaned his head back against the headboard and smoothed down his mustache.

"Ring any bells?" she asked.

Ben shook his head. "Can't say it does. I've never heard of something that can cause a chill like that."

"Sure wasn't no hellhound." Cora propped her feet up on the other chair. Ben nodded his agreement, his eyes tracing the thick pine logs that framed the room.

Cora's gaze settled on her toes, and she gave each set a stretch. Like the rest of her feet, they were thick and hard from long years trapped in boots. The second toe on each foot stuck out beyond the others, the nails worn small. When she was a little girl, her father had told her that having long middle toes meant she was born to ride. Their tiny farm on the Shenandoah hadn't housed more than the two horses needed to plow the furrows. They were big and thick with shaggy brown hair, four-legged giants in her young eyes, but they weren't for riding. Her father had promised that he'd make enough one day to buy her a real riding horse. Then he'd show her how to sit and ride like a real lady, he said.

Of course, that was before the blue coats had come through the valley and burned them out, leaving nothing but blackened earth behind them. She had been a young woman then, gangly and freckled, not the pretty Southern belle she had pictured herself growing into when her father had made his promise.

"Don't seem like a hell beast to me," Ben said, pulling her out of her thoughts.

"What do you mean? Anything that can whip two wolfers that quick sure ain't no angel."

"Course not, but most of the things old Hades spits out have the feel of that place about them, you know? All fire and flames and pain, like the good book says.

That unnatural chill you felt out there don't sound like Hell to me."

"Well, maybe Hell has a patch of cold for those that enjoy the warm," Cora said. "Folks living out in Carson City or Santa Fe wouldn't be all that uncomfortable in the regular parts of Hell, and that ain't no kind of punishment. Maybe Lucifer made some part of his kingdom like Montana in the winter-time to put them off their feed."

"Could be," Ben said. "Still, you'd think the good Lord would've mentioned something like that if it was so."

"If the good Lord wanted us to be prepared for everything in life, He'd have put us in the womb with one of these." Cora picked up her Colt from the table, admiring the nickel shine in the lamplight. She wore her holster cross-style, the butt of the gun pointing toward her right arm from the front of her left hip. Every now and again, some pudding-headed cowboy would call her out for it, saying she carried like a Mexican whore instead of a proper white woman. Most of the time, she was too involved with a card game or a glass of whiskey to pay them much notice, but they'd sometimes catch her in a foul temper and end up in the street with a fresh bruise. If they were still sore about it, she'd challenge them to a shooting contest. Used to be that she could win a month's wages with a few rounds, but her reputation started calling ahead of her, turning the gunmen yellow about facing her. Not much of a loss, really. She and Ben were set for cash from the jobs they did, and the quiet left her more time for gambling. Hearsay still couldn't keep the occasional young buck from trying to make a name for himself by besting her in a match, though.

"I doubt even the Lord's rich enough to give every new baby a silver shooter," Ben said, picking up his book.

"Good thing He ain't, or we'd have to settle for regular work like tilling a farm or digging in a mountain somewhere."

Ben grunted in agreement. "Speaking of, did that marshal say anything useful?"

"Mentioned some feller named Bill Hicks. Said he was the one that told him and the deputy about the killings that morning. Seems this Hicks is one of those retired miner types, like old Jules Bartlett from a few years back."

"Which one was he?"

"He's the one that made Sheriff Jim Barnes jump out of his boots for fear of vampires last time we was through here."

"That's right," Ben said. His memory was sharp except when it came to names. "Took a liking to lurking around at night for his meat instead of during the day like most folk. Good thing he had himself that full beard, or you'd have shot him for a vampire anyway."

"Hunting at night ain't natural for any folk except the unnatural ones."

"You damn near pulled that beard off the poor ass when you dragged him in to the sheriff."

"Shouldn't have been about at that hour, plain and simple," Cora said with a small shrug. The revolver

clicked as she turned the cylinder with her fingers.
"He's damn lucky we found him before something
else did. Never did thank us for that, now that I think
about it."

"Thank us?" Ben raised an eyebrow as he looked at
her. "He looked right ready to put his pick through
your hat with your head still in it."

Cora could still see the miner's face, his eyes blazing
above his gray beard as he stood next to her at the
door of the sheriff's station. The sheriff himself was
disheveled, having been roused from a good sleep by
the pounding on his door. When he opened up, Cora
had Jules Bartlett in one hand and the miner's big
Henry rifle in the other. Marching past the bewildered
lawman, she had set the rifle on the desk before propping the miner up like a prize stag.

Jules had balked when Cora told the sheriff she'd
found his vampire, but Jim Barnes looked as though
he couldn't decide whether to laugh or apologize. The
miner's confusion turned to anger, and he'd demanded that Barnes arrest her for making sport of
him. Cora had laughed at that notion, telling the old
man that he was lucky she'd left Ben with the horses
or he'd have laid him out for such talk. Both men
flushed red, and Cora had left them to it after telling
the sheriff she'd settle accounts with him the next
morning.

"All the same, I reckon we should look him up and
get our due gratitude," she said. "For all he knew,
Barnes could have been right about a vampire in the
area. A sucker would've made a short meal of that old

codger, though I'm not sure it would've bothered. He didn't look like he had more than a pint of blood in the whole of himself."

Ben nodded. He was sinking back into his book when a thought hit him, bringing his head up again. "Maybe Barnes was right all along and we just dragged in the wrong fool. What if there is a real vampire around here, and it's started acting up again? Think a vampire could've done those wolfers in?"

"Not a chance," Cora replied, shaking her head. "A vampire could've done that kind of damage, sure, but the sign was all wrong. Wouldn't do one any good to spill that much blood on the ground. Besides, that fool marshal said the bodies was torn to bits, so much that he couldn't find anything recognizable. Vampires usually leave shriveled stiffs behind, all curled up and panicky-looking."

"At least until the dead folk start moving around again," Ben said. "Still, maybe this is some new kind of vampire."

"They is all the same from what I've seen. Savage, mindless blood-suckers the lot of them. Remind me of them Yankees, to be honest."

"Couldn't be because the first vampire we killed was wearing a Union jacket," Ben said, his blue eyes alight with amusement.

"Well, can't say I was surprised the Union had actual monsters working with the human ones in their army. Damn shame we can't blame their tactics on the undead, but there ain't no vampire that can make battle plans."

"Can't imagine what would happen if there was," Ben said. "We would have a serious problem on our hands."

"Well, that's one of the advantages the good Lord does give us, I guess. He may not see fit to give us all peacemakers and blessed silver bullets, but at least He gave us the brains to make them." She replaced her Colt on the table. Looking out the window, she considered the remaining daylight, then she turned to her husband. "Sun's about set for the night, meaning a shift of miners will be coming through the Pioneer soon. I've a mind to go fleece them for their earnings and get me a few drinks in the meantime. You up for a game?"

A smile bloomed beneath Ben's mustache. "Think I'll stay in. You know I hate to watch you lose half our money in a single night. Besides, one of us needs to come up with a plan for tracking this monster down, and I don't reckon the king of hearts will have any good ideas."

Cora picked up one of her boots and threw it at him. He caught it in one hand without looking up from his book, the grin never leaving his lips. She pulled the other boot over her toes, then step-thumped her way over to the bed and held out her hand. Ben dropped the boot on her palm and looked up at her. She returned his smile as she put the boot on, then leaned over and kissed his forehead.

THREE

Our Lady of Virginia picked her way along the snowy path one hoof at a time. Cora let the mare go at her own pace, taking the time to enjoy the quiet. The two of them were traveling along a rough trail that wound around the base of a mountain. They were near the treeline, giving Cora a clear view of the snow-covered slope rising above her. Somewhere behind her, she could picture the crooked peak rising on the other end of the valley, and her thoughts returned to town for a moment.

She wondered if Ben was having any luck tracking down Bill Hicks. He had wanted to stay in town, leaving her the task of heading out to visit Jules Bartlett. While she was playing cards, Ben had given more thought to the idea of looking up the old hermit, thinking that he might know something about the creature prowling the woods below his house. By the time she returned to the hotel room, Cora had been too drunk to feel stupid for not thinking of that herself. She listened as closely as the whiskey allowed

while he outlined the next day's agenda. Despite the
potency of Boots' private stock, she only had to ask
him to repeat himself six or seven times.

Cora could see a dirty yellow trail flowing down
the mountainside above her, muck belched out by a
nearby silver mine. She smiled at the ugly stain,
thinking of the silver that mine would produce, silver
that she could use for bullets. Silver that had once
been part of a holy relic or symbol was more effective
against Hells' minions – it made a priest's blessings
that much more potent – but any silver would do in
a pinch.

The trail continued to wind its way around the
mountain's base. Through the trees, Cora could see
what seemed like a thousand snowy peaks reaching toward the afternoon sun. The sight made her head
swim, and she soon found the saddle horn in front of
her a much more comforting view. Our Lady was content to find her own way up the slope, snow crunching
beneath her hooves.

Once, a stray limb reached out for Cora from a
nearby tree, its branches groping toward her like a
skeletal hand. Her eyes were still fixed on the saddle
horn when the branch brushed against her coat and
neck, and she jumped at the touch. Her right hand
had already pulled away the leather flap that held her
Colt in place before she realized what had scratched
her. Looking back at the tree, she gave it a deep scowl.
She hated to leave it unharmed for such an offense,
but the mare's steady pace had already put it out of
reach.

After a while, her thoughts returned to Jules Bartlett. Despite the hostility the old miner probably still harbored toward her, Cora wasn't worried about paying him a visit. Age had taken the best part of his strength, leaving him with bony arms and legs. She figured he had spent his youth in California during the big gold rush they'd had back in the early fifties. His beard had been big and brown beneath his floppy hat then. She pictured him sticking his hands into the freezing runoff in some mountain stream, a stubborn set to his jaw as he filled his pan with mud. No gun, no horse, not even a pick to his name. He was just a sprout looking to make himself a fortune and go on to live a fancy life down in San Francisco.

Perched on a rocky outcropping above her head, the miner's cabin crept into view. Cora studied it as Our Lady continued her way up the path. The walls were built of the pine trunks that had once stood on the ledge, lashed into place by old Jules himself. As they rounded the final switchback and made for the cabin, she could see crooked shingles on the cabin's roof. They looked as though he'd cut them from tree bark but hadn't sealed them against the weather. Tanned hides hung inside the window by the door.

Jules had put in a small hitching rail outside his door, though Cora couldn't imagine him entertaining many visitors. It wasn't a fancy one, at any rate: a small log suspended crossways over two upright logs. She guided Our Lady up to it, dismounted, tied the reins off, and made her way to the cabin's door. The string was out, but she was feeling polite, so she knocked. A few moments passed as Cora listened to the mare working the bit in her mouth. Shifting her weight toward the door, she knocked again. Still nothing.

"Well, ain't that odd?" she asked the horse. "Seems old Jules took himself for a walk. Or maybe he's drank himself into a stupor."

Her patience gone, she pulled at the string and eased the door open. It groaned, making a racket in the still mountain air. If Jules hadn't heard her knocking, though, he wouldn't be roused by a creaking door.

The inside of the cabin was dark. Sunlight streaming through the open door gave her light enough to make out the shapes of the miner's furnishings. She propped the door with a stone so it wouldn't close on her and stepped inside. Snow crumbled from her boots onto the wooden floor as she looked around the small enclosure.

There wasn't much to see. An oil lamp hung from a central rafter, dark stains running down its sides. Jules had propped his bed up in one of the far corners, the mattress nothing more than a shapeless bag. An icebox sat in another corner near the fireplace. Several charred logs lay among the ashes. Removing a glove, Cora knelt down and felt one of them. It was long cold.

She pulled open the icebox and looked inside. Nothing but snow and a few strips of what appeared to be venison. She closed it, straightened up, and gave the small room another sweep with her eyes. An impressive assortment of picks, shovels, ropes, lanterns, and other mining gear lined the cabin's rear wall, suspended on rusty nails. Apart from them, the cabin had no other amenities.

Jules lived a very simple life.

Frustrated, she took the few steps back to the door. No miner and no clues about where he might have gone. She had hoped to get some information out of the old man today, but that wasn't in the cards for her. For all she knew, Jules had gotten eaten himself, taken at night just the way she said he would be. Not much to show for all the time she spent getting up here. Hopefully Ben had tracked down Bill Hicks and learned whether or not Jules had gone missing. If not, they'd be shooting in the dark when they tried to come up with a plan for bagging this monster.

Cora hated not knowing what they were up against. She never took to books the way Ben did, but she liked knowing what she was hunting before she started hunting it. Even regular hunters took the time to learn what they could so they'd know what to expect. Those unlucky wolfers had probably learned a thing or two about wolves before deciding to go out and start collecting bounties. Stupid hunters could end up getting gored by an elk or torn apart by a bear, and those were just regular animals. Folk in her line of work were lucky to end up as a pile of scat after a bad hunt. She'd heard stories of turned hunters, those who went out looking for something and came back as the very thing they were looking for.

Such tales had always chilled her blood a little. Death was easy enough to accept, but she didn't want to lose her soul to some lucky monster and start going about as one of its children. One time, after a priest had given them the unpleasant job of killing a former hunter, she'd made Ben swear to put her to rest should that ever happen. He had gone all teary-eyed when she said it, but he'd made the promise.

Shaking her head, Cora turned to leave, then noticed something. A flat wooden board, like a table without legs, sat in the far corner of the room. From the look of things, Jules didn't seem the type to worry about formalities like a table. Intrigued, she walked over to examine it, then shook her head in amazement.

"Jules, you crazy bastard," she muttered.

It was a trapdoor. Cora gripped the rusty handle with both hands and heaved upward, but the door refused to budge. Determined, she kept pulling at it, her curses almost as loud as the shrieking hinges.

The door suddenly gave way, causing Cora to lose her footing. She fell backward, landing on her back with a loud thud. When her breath returned, it came with a string of profanity. As she got to her feet, she thought of how Ben would be laughing at her expense if he was there. First the crow, now the door. She stretched her back and grimaced, thankful that he was back in town.

Putting the thought aside, Cora returned to the task at hand. The door's hinges had been bent by her efforts, and it stood open at an odd angle. She ignored the damage, peering into the dark hole it had covered. A wooden ladder descended into the inky depths, vanishing after the first two rungs. Frustrated, she looked around the cabin. Jules had a few lanterns hanging from the back wall, but she didn't have any matches. He might have some stashed away some-where, but finding them would take too long. Instead, she went to each of the cabin's four tiny windows and tore away the hides. Cold afternoon light streamed in. It did little to cheer up the old cabin, but as luck would have it, a beam of sunlight fell across the top of the ladder. She went back over to the hole and looked down.

Pick-marks and scratches in the stone suggested that old Jules had carved this tunnel out himself, or else he'd found it and built his cabin on top of it. Cora guessed it connected to the larger mine she'd seen on her way up here. She couldn't blame him for wanting to work for himself instead of for a big mining com-pany. She'd always liked doing things her own way, too, even if that meant doing them herself.

Despite the added light from the windows, she still couldn't make out the bottom of Jules's mineshaft. Lowering herself onto the floor, she stuck her head in the hole and took a deep breath. A mixture of aging pine and ancient rock filled her nostrils.

"Hello!" she yelled into the hole. "You down there, Jules? Can you hear me?" Her voice echoed into the inky darkness, giving her an idea that the tunnel went deep into the side of the mountain.

She paused to listen for a response. Nothing. She called out again, but only received echoes in reply. Cursing, she raised herself to her hands and knees. Old Jules may be having fun with his disappearing act, but she didn't take to it much, not when she needed information out of him.

Cora brushed her gloves on her cowhide chaps and made to stand up, then paused. Still kneeling, she cocked her head and listened. There it was again: a faint groaning. She lowered her head back to the opening. It was soft and deep, like a horse's snoring, magnified by the echoing tunnels. It could have been nothing more than rocks grinding against each other somewhere in the mine's bowels. Then again, it might be the groans of an old miner caught in a cave-in.

"That you, old timer?" she called into the hole. This time, a moan answered her. "All right, then, just sit tight. I'll be down in a jiffy." She walked over to the old miner's tool wall and poked around until she found a book of matches. Selecting a promising lantern from the wall, she set to work. Sparks flashed and faded as she struck a match, throwing shadows around the cabin. After a few attempts, she managed to get the flame to catch, and the lantern sputtered to life.

Satisfied, she tucked the matches into a pocket of her flannel shirt and pushed her hat off her head. The white streak in her raven hair glowed in the yellow light as her hat settled between her shoulder blades, the stampede string tugging softly on her throat. She picked up the lantern and stepped over to the mine's entrance.

"I'm coming down, Jules!" she yelled into the darkness before placing her boot on the ladder's top rung. The wood was old, but it held her weight as she descended into the cold, stale air of the mine. Shadows danced on the rough stone walls to the rhythm of the lantern's swaying.

After no more than twenty feet, her boots set down on solid rock. The tunnel extended downward into the mountain at a gentle slope. She could see the first of what she guessed were many support beams lining the mine. She stepped closer and ran a hand over the beam. It looked to be made of the same wood as the cabin above. Jules must have cut down half the forest setting up his claim out here.

The lantern's halo of light only extended a few feet, so Cora made her way one step at a time. Ahead of her, she could still hear the groaning echoing off the walls, almost as if the stones themselves were in pain. She felt as though she was walking down the throat of a dying giant.

"Where are you, you old fool?" she called. Her words fell flat in her ears, the shadows swallowing the sound of her voice. Jules must have heard her, though: the moans grew louder. At least that meant he was still alive and awake. Encouraged, she continued deeper into the mine.

After a few hundred yards, she came to a junction and stopped. She couldn't tell which direction the old miner's noise was coming from. She took a few steps down the right-hand tunnel and listened. The moans echoed in the darkness around her. Maybe he was down there, maybe not. She would take a look and come back if she couldn't find him.

Cora rolled her eyes as she started down the right-hand fork. All this work just to pull some old man's leg out from under a rock. In all likelihood, Jules hadn't found more than a few hundred dollars' worth of silver in here, just enough to pay for the cabin and the mine. Miners had always eluded her understanding, though. She couldn't fathom what would drive a man into spending years of his life in a tiny tunnel like this, swinging a pick at a rock until his arms fell off. She preferred wide open skies and endless trails, but she'd always loved being outdoors. Even as a girl, she'd spent more time playing in her father's fields or swimming in the river than learning needlework with her mother.

A shiver ran through her body. Even needlework would have been better than mining. At least you could do it next to a fire instead of in a chilly, cramped tunnel. She flexed her free hand, trying to fight the chill that was growing in her fingertips.

A chill she'd felt before.

A wave of dread washed over her, sending tingles down her spine. Her instincts told her to run, but she forced herself to think. Jules could still be down here somewhere. Maybe the monster hadn't found him yet. If she was quick, she might be able to get him out.

Another groan rolled through the tunnel, bringing with it an image of the old miner lying in the dark, torn apart and left to die. Even if she did find him, she wouldn't be able to save him. She had to assume the creature could see like a cougar in the dark, meaning her lantern would draw it in like a giant, bloodthirsty moth. The sooner she got topside, the better.

She drew the Colt from her belt and began backing out of the tunnel. The walls echoed with the metallic click of the revolver's hammer before another moan swallowed the sound. She felt a small twinge of guilt for leaving the miner to die, but better one death than two. The chill had already overtaken her elbows, and she could feel it starting in on her toes. It was spreading faster this time.

Her boots ground against the pebbles on the tunnel floor as she made her way back to the ladder. Keeping the barrel of her gun pointed into the darkness, she fought the growing urge to run. The lantern's flickering light played tricks on her eyes, and she nearly shot one of the tunnel supports when its shadow jumped out at her.

Then, without warning, the groaning fell silent. Cora halted her retreat. Panic squeezed at her lungs, and she tried to quiet her breathing to listen. Silence pressed in on her from all sides. Her breath curled around her face in short-lived white clouds.

Then, somewhere beyond the lantern's halo, a new sound crept into her ears. It was quieter than the groaning, but she knew it right away: the soft padding of skin on stone. A faint scraping of pebbles along the tunnel's floor. It was slow but constant, the quiet sound of a predator stalking its prey. Whatever it was, it was following her.

Cora forced herself to face the approaching menace as she resumed her exodus. With each step, she hoped to feel the ladder against her back, but the tunnel seemed endless. The shuffling stayed with her, lingering just out of sight. By now, the monster's chill had spread through her limbs and was starting to send cold fingers snaking across her chest. In this state, climbing the ladder would be slow and painful, but it was either that or charge headlong into the thing's waiting jaws.

After an eternity, she bumped into the ladder. Stealing a quick glance upward, she could still see the sunlight at the top of the shaft. The glare left a blind spot in her eyes. She let out a quiet curse as she tried to blink it away.

As if in response, a moan echoed up the tunnel. It sounded close, almost close enough to see. Keeping her revolver aimed at the sound, she waited. She thought she could see two points of light floating in the darkness. She squinted against the purple blotch in her vision, straining to see.

Then, at the very edge of the lantern's tiny halo of light, something emerged from the shadows. It was a human hand. Elongated fingers settled on the floor of the tunnel, their tips cold and black. Loose skin hung from the wrist like white curtains. As Cora watched, a second hand appeared, followed by a thin arm. Blackened veins wormed their way beneath the sickly flesh as the hand settled onto the tunnel's floor.

The first hand moved again, long fingers curling as the arm flowed into the dim light. It was long, too long to be human. The pale limb stretched from the edge of the light almost to her boots, yet she still couldn't see the creature it belonged to. She kept her revolver pointed into the darkness, at where this thing's body must be. As much as she wanted to shoot the hands as they approached, precaution demanded that she wait until she had a clear shot. Besides, she wanted to know what she was shooting at.

A round shape edged its way into the lantern's light, and Cora swallowed back a cry. It was the face of a frozen corpse. Ashen skin hung from the cheeks like old leather. Wisps of a gray beard still clung to its jowls, framing a row of pointed teeth that glinted at her from black lips. Between the yellow eyes was a pit, lined by cracked skin, where a nose had once been.

Only the eyes were alive, burning from within their dark pits. They regarded her with murderous intensity, and the teeth clacked together in anticipation.

Cora had seen enough.

A bright flash erupted from the barrel of her Colt. The gunshot filled the tunnel with thunder as the silver bullet found its mark between the creature's eyes. Cora pulled back the hammer and fired a second shot into the cloud of smoke, then holstered her revolver and turned toward the ladder. Her cold limbs sent spikes of pain shooting through her body, but she forced them into action. The lantern dangled from her left hand as her boots slammed into the wooden rungs. With each step, she expected to feel the grip of those long black fingers closing around her ankles. The gunsmoke burned her lungs, and she began gasping for breath.

She reached the top and pulled herself out of the mineshaft. The sunlight was still streaming through the cabin's tiny windows. She rose to her feet, pulled her gun, and aimed at the smoke-filled opening. Thinking better of it, she set the lantern on the floor and pulled her saber free of its scabbard as well. Then she waited.

The hands were the first to emerge from the smoke, grasping at the cabin's floor with black fingers. Long white arms followed. When the creature's body lurched into view, a shaft of sunlight caught its ribs, outlining them in hideous detail.

Yellow eyes turned toward her. Cora fired, the bullet punching a smoking hole in the creature's cheek. It wailed in anger, mouth yawning open far wider than seemed possible. Cora unloaded her remaining three shots. Her bullets struck it in the neck and chest, sizzling through icy flesh. It cried out at each impact, but the silver rounds didn't seem to slow it down.

By now, she could see the entire creature. Its head and torso were man-sized, but the limbs were long and grotesque. The cabin's low ceiling forced it to crouch like a giant, four-legged spider. Its wounds seeped a thick black fluid that pooled in the ragged beard and ran between its ribs like tar. It was injured but far from dead, and her revolver was empty.

With a sinking feeling, she realized that she'd let it get between her and the cabin's door. No way out but through the creature now staring at her with demon eyes. She returned its gaze in the dim light, listening to the clacking of its teeth as she gripped her saber. Then a flash of recognition washed over her, and the air left her lungs in a rush.

The monster had the face of Jules Bartlett.

A pale arm shot toward her, black fingers outstretched. Cora slashed with her saber, carving a deep gash across the creature's palm. The force of her blow knocked the hand away, and it smashed into the cabin's wall. Picks and shovels rattled on their hooks. Her saber flashed in a beam of sunlight as she brought it down on the creature's forearm. The blade bit through the thin flesh but stopped cold at the bone, the jolt sending a spike of pain through her arm. The sword fell to the floor with a clatter.

Cora jumped backward as the black fingers came for her again. Her boots landed on a fallen mining pick. She stumbled for a moment, lost her balance, and fell heavily on her back. Knowing those fingers were closing in, she flailed her arms in a panic. Her hand found what felt like a metal handle. Thinking it was her saber, she swung it with all her might at the ghastly face as the monster bore down on her.

To Cora's surprise, the monster recoiled as the lantern shattered against its face, spilling flame onto the cold skin. Taking advantage of its distraction, she grabbed the pick near her boots and came up swinging. The crunch shook her bones as the pick buried itself in the creature's skull. A wail of anger filled the small cabin as the creature stumbled under the impact, and Cora saw her chance. Leaping over a flailing leg, she rolled across the floor and made for the open door.

Once outside, she sprinted for Our Lady, who was pulling at her reins in a panic. Laying a hand on the mare's neck, Cora whispered a few words in her ear before drawing the Winchester from its saddle holster. She chambered a round and swung the rifle back toward the cabin. The hideous face gnashed its teeth at her through the open door. It seemed hesitant to follow her into the sunlight, which suited her just fine. The rifle butt kicked against her shoulder as she fired, and another wail of pain erupted from the cabin's interior.

Cora pumped the action and prepared to fire again, but when the smoke cleared, the creature was nowhere in sight. Keeping the gun raised, she approached the cabin. Mindful of the reach of those pale arms, she kept her distance from the open door and strafed back and forth, peering into the dark building.

Nothing.

Cora crept back through the cabin's door, rifle at the ready. The room was empty except for a trail of dark sludge leading back to the trap door. Cora allowed herself a small smile of victory. Whatever Jules Bartlett had become, she had driven it back into the cold darkness of the mines.

She recovered her saber and revolver from where they lay and emerged back into the sunlight. Her frightened mare was still fighting with the hitching post. Cora kept an eye on the cabin's door as she stroked Our Lady's neck, quieting her. She slid the rifle into the saddle sheath, untied the reins, and swung herself across the horse's back.

The mare needed no prompting to turn away from the cabin. Cora kept a steady hand on the reins to keep her from breaking into a gallop. Looking back over her shoulder, she thought she could make out a dark shape looming in the doorway. Her cold fingers pulled fresh rounds from her belt, ready to reload her revolver in the blink of an eye, but the shadow did not follow her into the mountain air.

When the cabin disappeared from sight, the chill started leaving her body, and Cora gave Our Lady more slack. The mare picked her way down the mountain as the hunter began kicking herself. She should have figured out that something was wrong long before the chill started digging into her bones. None of the lanterns in the cabin or the mine had been lit. None of her calls out to what she thought was an injured miner were answered. She had been so irritated by the thought of saving Jules from his own stupidity that she had nearly fallen victim to her own.

Our Lady descended further into the trees. Cora gave the mare's sides a soft punch with her heels, urging her to hurry back to town. She was sure she could hear the sounds of a warm fire and a bottle of whiskey calling her name.

FOUR

Ben Oglesby found his wife planted at a table in front of the Pioneer's big stone fireplace, her fingers wrapped around a near-empty bottle. Cora looked up as he approached, her face flushed from the liquor. In the firelight, he could see the thin scars running down her left cheek, white stripes on red. Her brown eyes squinted at him for a moment, then she broke into a lopsided grin.

"Well, ain't you a sight for sore eyes."

He sat in the chair next to her. "I hope I'm a sight better looking than old Jules."

To his surprise, she burst out laughing. "Time ain't made him no prettier, that's for damn sure."

A group of miners at a nearby table glanced their way. Ben offered them a small smile, then turned back to her. "So you saw him?"

"You could say that," she replied, then laughed again. "Saw him, shot at him, nearly got ate by him. We had ourselves a grand old time."

Ben stood and reached for her hand, a cautious

smile beneath his mustache. "Let's get you back to the hotel."

"Ain't no fire there."

"We'll make one, then," Ben said. "Now come on."

She struggled to her feet, still clutching the bottle. "We got a fireplace in our room?"

"Yes," he lied.

"All right, then, let's go." She took a few steps, then paused for a swig from the bottle. When Ben offered her his hand, she slapped it away. "I can help my own self, thank you kindly. I ain't as drunk as all that yet."

Behind them, Boots looked over from where he was wiping down the bar. "You OK, Cora?"

"Yes, I am," she declared in a loud voice, her braid whipping around as she turned to face the bartender. "What is it with all you men thinking I'm too weak to find my way back to my own damn room?"

"Well, I just thought—"

"You thought nothing," she said. "I'll have you know I went all the way up to the Bartlett place and came face-to-face with something or other in the mountains today, and that thing wanted to eat me, but I shot it up and made it run back into its tunnel. What'd you do today, Boots? Huh? Can you top that?"

The bartender's round face flushed as he looked down at the rag he was holding. "No, but you've had quite a bit from that bottle tonight, and maybe you'd want—"

"What I want is to go back to my room and have myself a good sleep," she said. "I can't get that with you all pestering me about whether I'm fit to do it."

"Just take care of yourself." Boots found some bottles behind the bar that needed straightening and turned his back to them.

"Just thank your lucky stars that I ain't got that Mart Duggan's temper," Cora said, more to herself than Boots. Her own boots started making a crooked line for the door. "That mick's got a short fuse on him. Why, he'd probably shoot you in the mouth just for saying howdy if you happened to catch him in a bad way."

"Glad I ain't had the pleasure yet," Ben said. He moved to open the saloon's door for her, but she crashed into it before he could. Bouncing back from the impact, she stared at it in confusion for a moment. A stream of curses flowed from beneath the wide brim of her hat as she reached a shaking hand toward the doorknob.

The knob pulled away just as her hand reached it. She fell face-first on the wooden floor, the bottle spilling from her hands. Ben heard an exclamation of surprise from the other side of the door. Looking up from his fallen wife, he saw two men standing in the doorway, their boots inches from Cora's head.

"Well now, ain't this a sorry sight." Mart Duggan crouched down, his wrists resting on his knees. Recognizing Cora's braid, he tossed Jack Evans a look. "Not even quitting time at the mines yet and here we got us a drunken disorderly."

"I ain't disorderly," Cora said, pushing herself up on her hands and knees. The floor seemed to pitch and heave under her. "And who's asking, anyway?" She raised her head and squinted at the marshal. "Why, speaking of Mr Satan himself. Look here, Ben, it's the marshal."

Duggan kept his attention on her, a scowl knitting his red eyebrows together. "I don't take too kindly to drunkenness in my deputies, Mrs Oglesby."

"Good thing we ain't your deputies, then." She tried to roll back onto her heels, went too far, and fell into a sitting position. "I never did take to wearing no badge, anyhow."

"Can't say that's a shame," Duggan replied. "The way I see it, no law outfit would benefit from having you with them. I'm ashamed to be working with you myself."

Cora laughed. "That's what they call gratitude here in Leadville?" Her boots scuffed across the floor as she tried to pull them under her. After a few attempts, she managed to rise to her feet. A wave of nausea rolled through her, but she swallowed it down. "Maybe we should just leave you to get ate by that monster out there."

"Can't do us much good from inside a jail cell," Duggan said. "I've more than half a mind to take you there right now."

Jack spoke up. "Maybe she just needs to be walked back to her room, marshal."

"By God, I will shoot the next man who says that," Cora said, pushing her way past the two lawmen. Her breath puffed out in white clouds beneath the evening sky. "The hotel is just down the street here. I can find my own way."

"All the same, I think Jack here will walk you back," the marshal said. "I'd hate for you to fall and not be able to find your feet." With that, Duggan turned and disappeared into the saloon, leaving Jack standing next to her, looking awkward. Ben waited for the marshal to pass, then slipped through the door and went to stand by his swaying wife.

"It's for your own good, Mrs Oglesby," Jack said, his voice hopeful. "We don't want no trouble."

"You boys already got more trouble than you can handle." She gave the deputy a smile that revealed the gap between her teeth. "I seen what's up there that killed those wolfers, and it ain't a pretty sight."

Her words brought Jack's thoughts back to that clearing, and the sinking dread returned. He ran his tongue over his lips. "You've seen it?"

"Sure as Satan's hooves," she replied, then beckoned him with a lazy sweep of her arm. "Come on, boy. Since you're walking us back anyhow, I might as well let you in on it, too."

They walked her back, one man on each side, as she told them about her encounter in the cabin and the mine below. Ben remained silent, his face thoughtful, but the fear became plain on Jack Evans's face as she gave them a detailed description of the monster. The deputy had joined up with Mart Duggan as a way of making peace with himself for running out on his family back East. He figured that the good Lord would look more kindly on him on Judgment Day if he did his part to keep some of the world's troublemakers under control.

What this woman described wasn't just another troublemaker, though. He wanted to write the whole thing off as a drunken fantasy, but he'd seen that clearing and what was left of those men. If the creature had managed to escape from her, who claimed to have fought things like it before, what chance did he have against it? He hadn't joined a law outfit to fight monsters, and he doubted that even Mart Duggan would know how to fight one. By the time Cora Oglesby staggered into the Northern Hotel, he was already on his way back to the Pioneer in search of his own bottle.

"Well, I'd say you scared him nice and good," Ben said after the deputy left. "Wonder if he'll skip town."

"Oh, he'll pull through," Cora replied. The mattress crackled as she collapsed on the bed. "That sprout has got some guts in him, I think. He needs them to work for a man like Duggan."

Ben sat on the edge of the bed and pulled off his boots. "Not really our concern, anyway. We need to work out how we're going to stop that thing you saw."

Cora sighed. The bed felt far more comfortable than she'd expected. The whiskey began pulling at her eyelids, and she gave in after a brief struggle. "I think it can wait while I catch a few winks."

"Looks like it's going to, at any rate," Ben said. He settled himself at the table and stared out the window. Down the street, he could just make out the shutters covering some of the Pioneer's second-story windows. Snow covered the gables crowning the saloon, reflecting the evening sunlight in a sheet of tiny sparkles. Soon, soft snores began coming from the bed.

Cora opened her eyes, then immediately squeezed them shut again. The morning sunlight glared through the open shutters, flooding her head with pulsing pain. She rolled over and pulled the sheet over her face with a moan. After a few seconds, the pain subsided enough for her to remember where she was.

Ben's side of the bed was empty. She called out for him, wincing against the redoubled throbbing in her temples, but there was no answer. Where had he disappeared to? Gathering her strength, she forced herself to peek out from beneath the sheets.

The room was empty, and the door was open. Ben must have left to get something to eat from the common room downstairs. Her stomach rumbled at the thought, and she hoped he remembered to bring her a plate or two. She pulled the sheet back over her head, closed her eyes, and waited.

Soon, footsteps in the hallway announced Ben's return. She opened one eye expectantly, but to her disappointment, his hands were empty when he came through the door.

"Where's my breakfast?" she demanded.

"Downstairs," he replied.

"Why didn't you bring anything up?"

"I wasn't sure if you'd be awake yet," he said, sounding irritable.

"Well, I am. Go get me some flapjacks or something." He ignored her, and dug through the small trunk he used to carry his books. She wanted to pester him more, but her head was still pounding. Grumbling in protest, she curled herself into a ball and shut her eyes.

Ben's boots thumped around again, followed by the scraping of a chair along the floor. She could hear the soft sound of turning pages as she tried to go back to sleep. The blood pounding in her ears began to ebb, taking the pain with it. A patch of warm sunlight fell across the bed, and she dozed off.

"What exactly did that creature look like?" Ben's voice cut through the haze of sleep. She whined in reply, but he persisted. "Come on. We need to figure out what it is if we're going to kill it."

"No, we don't," she said. "We just need to shoot it until it stops moving."

"You tried that already, didn't you?"

She didn't answer, hoping that he would give up and go back to his reading. After a few moments, she heard his boots thump on the floor again, and she smiled to herself.

The smile vanished when she felt the sheet disappear. She curled into a tighter ball, opening one eye just wide enough to glare at her husband. The sheet hung from his hand. "Get up, Cora," he said. "We need to work on this."

"I already told you. My plan is to shoot it until it stops moving."

"Worked like a gem yesterday, I hear."

"Sure as hell did," Cora said. "Drove that bastard back down his hole right quick."

"After how many shots?"

"Enough," she replied, rolling on to her other side.

"Cora, stop it." Ben seldom raised his voice, but he did now.

"Who shoved the sand up your craw?" She matched his tone and regretted it as her head throbbed in protest. Lifting a hand to her brow, she continued in a softer voice. "Why is you being so ornery about this?"

"Because it's our job to kill this thing, and we don't know how to do it."

"You still ain't said what's so wrong with my plan."

Ben sighed through his nose. "How many times did you shoot it yesterday?"

"A lot," Cora replied, giving in. There was no deterring him when he got like this. "Six rounds from my Colt and one from my Winchester."

"Where did you hit it?"

"In the head, mostly. Maybe one or two in the chest."

Ben nodded. "So we know this thing ain't an ordinary spook."

"Ain't one we've seen before, but that don't mean it's some kind of super spook."

"Well, I've never heard of anything that can take that many silver bullets to the head and not go home to the devil."

"There was something else, too," Cora said, her face clouding from more than just the hangover. "My sword didn't so much as scratch it. I was all set to chop off one of them spindly arms, but it was like taking a swing at a rock. Just bounced right off."

Ben frowned. "The blessing is still on the blade, ain't it?"

"Of course it is. Father Brown blessed it before we left Dodge, and I ain't killed a damn thing with it since."

"So it resisted a blessed blade?" Ben asked. Cora nodded. "And you still think it's just an ordinary monster?"

"Of course I don't," Cora said. "I just wanted you to shut up so I could get back to sleep."

Ben grinned at her. "You know better than that."

"Hey, a girl can hope, can't she?"

"Only if she's aiming to be disappointed."

"So I reckon it's too much to hope for that you'll go and get me breakfast."

"Yep," Ben replied. He dropped the sheet on the floor and sat back down at the table. He opened his book, crossed his legs, and proceeded to ignore her.

Sighing, Cora tossed her feet over the edge of the bed and sat up. Her eyes closed on their own as her head started pounding with renewed vigor. Her muscles ached now, too, but that's what she got for passing out with her clothes on. Ben had pulled her boots off for her, giving her the trouble of putting them back on. Her fingers fumbled with the leather, refusing to cooperate. She'd have to remember to tell Boots that his rotgut had given her more trouble than she was used to. Knowing him, he would take it as a compliment, and she supposed it was. Most whiskey wouldn't have given her more than a small ache behind the eyes, but Boots's suppliers knew how to distill their liquor.

After a few minutes, she won the battle with her boots. Bracing herself, she rose to her feet, then leaned against the wall as her head punished her. She waited out the worst of the storm before picking up her coat and moving to the door.

"They got eggs down there?"

Ben grunted.

"Think I'll have me a prairie oyster with breakfast, then. Might do me some good."

Ben grunted again, but she had already left the room. Her shaky legs carried her through the hallway and down the stairs. A hearty breakfast greeted her when she stepped into the Northern Hotel's big common room: fresh sowbelly, long strips of crackling bacon, steaming sourdough biscuits, and several large tins of coffee. The hotel's early risers hovered around the fare like flies buzzing around a week-old carcass. Several others sat at nearby tables, wolfing down their first meal of the day.

The sight was enough to make her sick.

She worked her way past the crowd of hungry guests and grabbed a nearby bellhop.

"You got any fresh eggs?"

"Of course," he replied, prying her fingers from his shirt. "How many would you like?"

"Just one, with some whiskey and pepper in a glass."

"Fried?"

"Raw."

Confusion flickered across the little man's face for a moment before his head bobbed and he disappeared into the kitchen. Cora made her way to an empty table and collapsed. She folded her arms on the rough wood, rested her forehead on them, and waited. Her shoulders muffled the sounds in the room enough to allow her to doze for a few minutes before she heard a voice at her elbow.

"Your egg, ma'am."

Picking her head up, she stared at the concoction he had brought. Dark flecks of pepper dotted the egg yolk as it floated in the whiskey. Taking a deep breath, she picked up the glass. Her other hand pinched her nose shut, and she downed the mixture in one gulp. She could feel the egg slide down her throat and drop into her stomach like a lump of mud. She smacked her lips a few times, set the glass down, laid her head back down on her arms, and waited.

After a short while, Cora felt well enough to join the other guests. Taking the empty glass with her, she walked over to the big table. She grabbed a couple of sourdough biscuits, stuffed them in the glass, then picked up a handful of sowbelly. Satisfied, she made her way back to her table and set to.

The sowbelly, heavily salted, was the first to go. The biscuits followed, one after the other. They were warm, not steaming like they had been when she first walked in, but they were good. Halfway through the second, her thirst caught up with her. Picking up her glass, she looked around for a pitcher of fresh water. There was plenty of coffee, but the tiny bellhop seemed to have forgotten any other drinks. Not wanting to bother with him again, she threw her coat around her shoulders and stood up. She made her

way through a small side door and found herself in
an alley. The snow was still fresh and undisturbed, so
she sank to her knees and began to shovel handfuls
into her mouth. The cold numbed her throat, but it
was water.

Cora wiped her mouth and rose to her feet. Stepping out from the alley into the street, she squinted
in the sunlight and cursed her hat for being back in
the room. She considered going up to fetch it, but
that might mean another talk with Ben. Another talk
meant another argument, and she didn't want to sit
around doing nothing while he read through his
books. He hadn't been there to see that monster
bleed and hear it squeal as she unloaded on it, so he
didn't know it could feel pain. Sure, it was tough, but
so was she.

Her breath curled around her face as she looked
down at her boots. He was right, though. Nothing
they'd fought in the past had taken that many silver
bullets to the head and kept coming. Knowing it was
still up in that mineshaft made her uneasy, but what
could she do about it?

Get some advice, she answered herself. She wasn't
sure if Leadville had a proper priest, but maybe Father
Baez was still in Denver. They could get some information from him before charging headlong back into
the woods.

She'd met the Denver priest only once, nearly ten
years before. She and Ben had been hunting a vampire nest in the area and needed information on its
whereabouts. Father Baez had been eager to help,

telling them several times that the occurrences had centered around an estate northwest of Denver. The little priest had even offered to consecrate their weapons before they set out. They hadn't needed the blessings renewed, but he had so wanted to give them more than just information that they couldn't bear to disappoint him. He had spoken the prayers in his quiet voice, beseeching Saint Anthony to shield the hunters as they sought to silence the servants of the devil. His prayers were answered a few days later when they found and burned out the vampire lair.

The sound of raised voices pulled Cora out of her reverie. Looking down the street, she could see a group of men milling about near the center of town. They were fingering picks and guns at their belts and pacing as if waiting for some action. Maybe fifty strong, most of them miners, the group tracked over the snow-packed streets like cattle waiting to board a train. More men trickled out from the surrounding saloons, adding to the herd until it filled the square.

Cora made her way down the wooden sidewalk toward the angry mob. As she approached, they began calling in whiskey-slurred voices for somebody named Elkins. She couldn't make out what this Elkins had done to rile such a crowd, but now she was curious. She crawled up on an overturned rain barrel outside a brothel, folded her arms, and settled in to watch.

The grumbling and hollering of the men soon shed some light on what had stirred them up. From what she could make out, two miners named Elkins and

Hines had turned violent while settling a card game the night before. Elkins had knifed up Hines pretty good before running out. Duggan's deputies had picked him up just outside of town and locked him up, but that wasn't good enough for Hines's mining buddies. They'd spent the rest of the night drinking themselves into a frenzy, and now they were demanding justice at the end of a rope. She heard the words "darkie" and "nigger" being tossed around, so she figured that Elkins was a black man, which slimmed his chances.

Despite her Southern birth, Cora had never held much against black men. Her family had never been rich enough to afford slaves, but they'd lived close enough to the Yankee states that freed slaves weren't all that unusual in town. Her parents told her to stay well away from them, and she had obeyed out of fear. Since coming west, though, she and Ben had met a good number of black men. They seemed like regular folk to her, saints and sinners just like anyone else, and she couldn't figure out why her parents had been so scared for her. Still, she knew a black man wouldn't have much hope of justice at the hands of a white mob, and Cora found herself hoping that this Elkins was on good terms with his maker.

A voice rose above the crowd. Looking up, Cora saw a heavyset miner with a full beard and thick arms. He waved those arms at the crowd, moving his hands in exaggerated motions.

"Are we going to sit by and let that blackie go unpunished for what he done?"

"No!" the crowd roared.

"Old Hines is laid up in a doctor's bed with a cut that might end him any minute. If we don't string that nigger up for it, he'll ride out of here tomorrow without facing his music. We can't trust the marshal to do justice, so if we want it done, we got to do it our own selves."

The crowd roared again, swirling along after the big miner as he started marching toward the marshal's station. Shutters winked open at the noise, then pulled shut again as the miners passed. Trailing behind the mob, Cora saw the shutters creak open again, and she smirked. The onlookers didn't want to get involved, but they sure weren't going to miss anything, either.

As the mob approached the marshal's station, Cora could make out the solid shape of Mart Duggan standing in the doorway. She could picture his blue eyes watching them, fingers hooked through his belt loops. The mob stopped in front of the station, still chanting their victim's name.

After a few moments, the big miner stepped forward. "Marshal, you let that black boy out so we can do him proper justice." Behind him, the miners yelled and hollered their agreement, fists and bottles waving.

Duggan watched them carry on, his face calm. After they had quieted a little, he took two steps forward. The brim of his hat hid his face in shadow, but his beard glowed red in the sunlight. The marshal pulled twin peacemakers from his belt and pointed them at the crowd. In the following silence, Cora heard two distinct clicks as Duggan pulled the hammers back.

"You're welcome to try," Duggan said, his words clear in the morning air, "but I will shoot the first man that steps forward."

The miners exchanged nervous glances and shuffled their feet. The big one at the head of the group found something to stare at on his boots. Cora folded her arms across her chest and grinned. She hoped poor old Hines wasn't watching from a window somewhere, or he'd be mighty disappointed to see that none of his friends were willing to take a bullet for him.

After a tense minute, the miners began to disperse, breaking into smaller herds and ambling down the street. A few squinted at the morning sun with red eyes before deciding to go in search of a bed. The ringleader, now abandoned by his friends, stared at the barrels of Duggan's guns for a moment before turning away. He shuffled through the snowy street, unsure of where to look or where to go.

Duggan watched them all leave. Only when the street was empty did he thumb the hammers back to rest. Catching sight of Cora standing in the street, he holstered one revolver but kept the other in his hand.

"Morning, marshal," Cora called out as she approached, her buffalo coat swirling around her legs.

"Morning, Mrs Oglesby. Glad to see you've recovered." Duggan turned and walked through the station's door.

She followed him into the station. "Amazing, what a prairie oyster can do for you. Them things is truly the mercy of the good Lord for the drunkard."

"I wouldn't know," Duggan replied, annoyed that the woman was standing in his station again. At the deputy's desk, Jack Evans sat staring wide-eyed at his boss. Duggan turned his attention to him. "What's wrong with you, deputy?"

"I ain't never seen anything like that before, sir," the deputy said. "You faced down a entire lynch mob all on your own."

Duggan nodded. "Ain't like I had a deputy on duty to back me up."

Jack flushed bright red and lowered his head. "Sorry, sir. It just happened so fast."

"Lots of things do," the marshal said. "You got to act just as fast or you'll end up shot. Worse, somebody else may end up in a box that don't deserve it."

"Ain't met the man yet that didn't deserve it," Cora said.

The marshal didn't look at her. "I don't reckon you'll find him at a card table or a bar."

Cora ignored the remark. "Once met a cowpuncher not a day over eighteen years down in Santa Fe. Told me he ain't done a single sin his whole life on account of his being cooped up on his ma's farm for all of it. I says to him that we're all equal sinners in the eyes of the Lord, but he shook his head and proclaimed his innocence. Said he once saw angels flying about his farm, and how could he have seen them if he wasn't a good boy? The good Lord was watching out for him, he said."

Duggan rolled his eyes, but Jack was curious. "What happened to him?"

"Poor fool went and got himself ate by a werewolf, I think," she said, shrugging. "Ben could tell you better than me. He's got the memory for that sort of thing."

Duggan turned on his heels and started toward his office, intent on the bottle stashed in the top drawer. This woman's nonsense brought out his thirst like nobody else.

"Hold up a tick," Cora called after him. "I got something for you."

"What might that be?" Duggan turned and looked at her from his office doorway.

"My own personal sighting of your monster."

A spark of anger flashed in the marshal's blue eyes. "This another one of your 'glimpses'?"

"No, sir," Cora said, shaking her head. "Got all up close and friendly this time around."

"How close?"

Cora stepped up to the deputy's desk and looked at him. "About like this. To his head, anyway. Couldn't really tell how close the arms got, seeing as I was busy not getting eaten."

Duggan took a step toward her, the glimmer of anger replaced with curiosity. "What did it look like?"

"Like old Jules Bartlett. You remember him? That miner hermit out west of town?" The marshal nodded. "I reckon it's what's left of him after some kind of evil thing took hold. Kept his human shape, at least, though his arms and legs are all spider-like now."

"Ain't he the one from before?" Duggan asked. "Sheriff Barnes said you dragged in a miner once to prove he wasn't a monster."

"One and the same."

"Guess you was wrong about that, then."

Cora laughed. "Marshal, if I'd been wrong back then, you wouldn't have no Jim Barnes to grump about no more. This here development's new. Probably happened within the last month or so."

"What makes you so sure?"

"Too few dead folk," she replied. "Whatever that old miner has turned into, it ain't got no reason left. Thing's like an animal, only looking for food. You said them wolfhounds fled the scene, right?"

Jack nodded before the marshal had a chance.

"So I'll warrant this monster only takes to human flesh. Don't know if it remembers anything that old Jules knew, so it's anybody's guess if it knows how to find its way into town. Can't imagine it would take long for it to figure it out, though. You'll have it breathing down your necks before you know it if we don't whip it." Cora paused for a moment as she thought. "Actually, I don't think it breathes, or needs to, anyway. It makes a moaning noise, though, so listen for that."

Jack couldn't believe what he was hearing. "You're expecting this thing to come after us?"

"Why not?" Cora said. "Like I told your boss a few days ago, monsters don't never get their fill. For all we know, it could have tracked me back here yesterday."

"Well, if that don't beat all," Duggan said. "We got us a man-eating critter out there and a halfwit bounty hunter in here. I don't suppose you got a plan worked up?"

"First thing today, Ben and I are catching the train for Denver."

"What?" the two lawmen said in unison.

"Yep," Cora said. "We got a priest down there that knows a thing or two we don't, so I reckon he might know what we're dealing with."

"So we're supposed to just sit here and wait for you to get back?" Duggan asked.

"That's about the size of it."

"What if this thing comes around while you're gone?"

"Fight it off. Ain't that hard."

Duggan clenched his fists, restraining himself from striking her across the face. "If it ain't that hard, what do we need you for?"

"There's a difference between fighting it off and killing it, marshal. Ben and I will figure the killing part out, but even you boys should be able to hold it off for a few days."

"How would we go about that?" Jack asked, not liking her dismissive tone. The thought of the monster lurking in the streets made him uneasy, but he didn't consider himself a coward.

"Well, can't say, exactly," Cora said. "Seemed to take a mighty disliking to my silver bullets. Didn't seem too fond of fire, neither."

"That's easy, then," Duggan said, rolling his eyes. "We just need to find us a silver arsenal of our own and we'll be safe as a bear cub with its ma."

"Finding silver is hard work in a mining town, ain't it?"

The marshal glowered at her. "I ain't exactly got a mine of my own."

Cora folded her arms. "Can't you just ask one of the mining companies to loan you a mess until we get this settled?"

Jack burst out laughing, and even Duggan cracked a smile. "I'll get right on that, Mrs Oglesby, as soon as you pull the sun down out of the sky."

"I take your point," Cora said. "You ought to make do with fire, though."

"Don't have much choice," the marshal said. "If we're lucky, we may even settle this while you're gone."

It was Cora's turn to laugh. "I never figured you for a sense of humor, marshal."

FIVE

"Well, ain't this a regular mess."

Cora and Ben stood on the train station platform, watching the steady stream of people flow around them. Men in dark suits and waxed mustaches paraded into passenger coaches bound for San Francisco, Saint Louis, Chicago, and New York. On their arms, ladies in calico dresses peered from beneath lace-trimmed hats. Their perfume lent the scent of flowers to the stench of smoke, oil, and human sweat.

Following the swell of the crowd, they stepped out into the street and started walking. The afternoon sun glowed on the brick buildings, its reflection in their windows blinding them at regular intervals. The murmur of voices all around them blended with the clopping of horse hooves on the street.

After a few blocks, Cora paused and stamped her feet. "I hate walking," she said. "Just our luck to catch the only train left in the world that ain't got a livestock car."

"Don't you worry none," Ben said. "Them boys at the hotel livery will take right fine care of Our Lady."

"Ain't her I'm worried about, it's me. Won't do to show up at the good Lord's house all worn out and ragged. Old Father Baez might take us for vagabonds or some such."

Ben started walking again. "He'd be more than half right if he did."

They made it to the church just before dusk. Red sunlight made the golden cross atop the bell tower shimmer, and Cora paused for a moment to admire it. As pretty as it was, she'd never understood why some churches chose gold over silver. Sure, the gold was more valuable, but no demon or monster had succumbed to a golden bullet through the heart.

"Well, let's go see if the old man can help us out." She pushed her hat off her head. The white streak in her dark hair glowed as she smoothed down her braid.

"You go talk to him. I think I'll go scare us up a room for the night." Ben's book was tucked under his arm as his blue eyes looked up and down the street.

"Make sure it's got a good view," she said. "You know how I like to see the mountains."

Ben nodded and started on his way down the street. Cora watched him go for a moment before ascending the big stone steps. The church building, though modest, was still new, having only been built in 1865. The Vatican had commissioned it in honor of Denver's appointment as the capital of the Colorado Territory. Before its construction, Father Baez's congregation had met in a small Spanish mission on the eastern end of the city. Cora had never been there, but the way

Father Baez had spoken lovingly of the new church on their last visit, she figured it hadn't been very nice.

She challenged the big front door to a brief Indian arm wrestle before earning her way inside. The smell of stained wood and resin incense drifted out of the shadows to greet her in the darkened foyer. Candles winked at her from their stands on either side of an archway that opened into the small sanctuary. Beneath her feet, thick carpet muffled the sound of her boots as she made her way inside.

Once past the arch, she looked to her right. A small marble basin stood at attention behind the first row of pews. She reached over, dipped her finger in the cool water, and crossed herself. Satisfied, she began walking down the center aisle. Solemn saints watched her progress from their painted windows of red and purple and yellow. Their rich colors were fading with the daylight, shifting from a dazzling display of light to a soft evening glow. Candles burned atop iron stands at either end of each row of pews, casting their pale light toward the rafters. In front of her, a crucifix hung above the altar, illuminated by rows of candles on either side. A purple sash hung down from the Savior's arms as He looked skyward in pious agony. To the left of the altar, the water in the baptismal font reflected the orange candlelight.

The smell of incense grew stronger, mixing with the sweet scent of candle smoke as she approached the altar. She knelt before the crucifix and crossed herself again, bowing her head in reverence. The carpet was soft on her knees, so she lingered for a bit, savoring the silence.

"What can I do for you, child?" a voice behind her asked. A grin blossomed on her lips as she turned to face the voice's owner.

Father Baez stood in the aisle, his hands clasped in front of him. His white hair and beard were bright above his black vestments, making him look a little like a candle himself. The look of concern on his face melted into a wide smile when he saw her face.

"Ah, Cora," he said, stepping forward and holding out his arms. "It is good to see you again."

She accepted his embrace, stooping a little in the process. Father Baez was one of the few men in the world shorter than her. "I'm surprised you remember me, Father."

"Well, I don't get the chance to meet many vampire hunters," he replied, a twinkle in his dark eyes. He stepped back and looked her over. "The years have been kind to you, I see."

"You'd sing a different tune if you saw me in the daylight," she said. "You look the same as you ever did."

Father Baez smiled. "Not much changes when you reach my age." Despite his years, he still stood upright, not stooped like so many old men. He sat down in a pew and motioned her to sit beside him. "So what brings you here?"

"Well, I'm in a fix," she said, taking the offered seat and crossing her legs. "Got me a monster up near Leadville that I can't lick or even put a name to."

The priest's white eyebrows drew together. "You've never seen one like it?"

"Not a one," Cora replied.

"Tell me what it looked like."

"Well, it looked like a cross between a frozen corpse and a spider. It had black skin like frostbite on its fingers and hands and lips. And it was missing its nose. The head and chest was normal-sized, like the kind you'd find on anybody, but the arms and the legs were a good sight longer than they ought to be." Cora settled into the pew as she continued. "If I had to guess, I'd say the arms were half as long again as the torso, and the legs maybe another half or so. It made a kind of moaning sound, which I first took to be the sounds made by a miner who done hurt himself something fierce. Imagine my surprise when the miner I was searching for turned out to be the monster what tried to eat me."

"Did you notice anything else about it?" Father Baez asked.

"It made my hands and feet go all chilled, like I was standing outside in a blizzard without gloves or boots. Had itself a big old mouth, too. Bigger than it should be." She paused, thinking for a moment. "Didn't smell like much of anything, which is rather irregular. This thing has a taste for people, so it should have the smell of death on it, but it just smelled cold."

"I see." The priest stroked his beard with one hand as he considered her story. "And you said it looked human?"

"Yessir," Cora said. "Was human at one point, in fact. The body belonged to Jules Bartlett, a hermit-style miner that lived near town. I ran into him before a few years back when the sheriff of those parts thought he was a vampire."

"A vampire?" The white eyebrows arched. "What gave him that impression?"

"His own cowardice tossed in with the old coot's habit of hunting for his keep at night. That sheriff felt a mighty fool when I dragged the hermit into his office, but he was grateful all the same." She grinned at the priest. "Or maybe the sheriff's instincts were spot on and it just took the miner a bit to catch up."

Father Baez shook his head even though he knew she was joking. "No, not unless the sheriff himself turned the miner into what he is. Might that be a possibility? The sheriff may be looking for revenge on the man who humiliated him."

Cora laughed at the thought. "Ain't no way old Jim Barnes would go and do a thing like that. The man is as yellow as they come. He might have been sore about it awhile, but he wouldn't go making trouble for himself. The only reason he's kept his seat as long as he has is thanks to the toughs he's got working for him. They take care of the dirty work while he cools his heels wherever he sees fit. Without Mart Duggan and that herd of deputies he's got, there'd be no Sheriff Barnes."

The priest's dark eyes reflected the candlelight as he stared at the crucifix hanging above them. Vampirism, curses, necromancy; none of the usual suspects matched what the hunter was telling him. He supposed it could be some new creature, but that seemed unlikely. Evil had been crawling all over the face of the earth since its creation, and most of the demons in the world were as old or older. They always found new bodies, new servants, and new lairs, but their nature never changed. Yet whatever Cora Oglesby had encountered was a creature he had never heard of before.

He thought of something else and turned back to her. "You fought this thing, didn't you?" She nodded. "How did you manage to escape when you encountered it?"

"A number of ways, really," Cora said. "For one, it didn't seem to appreciate my silver bullets. I shot it full in the face half a dozen times and made it bleed some black molasses. It carried on a good deal about it, but it didn't roll over and die like it should have. Seemed right scared of fire and sunlight, too, from what I could see."

"Most creatures of the darkness are."

Cora nodded. "One thing was funny, though. I tried to cut it up with my saber, the one I have a blessing on, but it was like trying to cut through a cannon. Blade just bounced right off."

"The blessing was still good?"

"Yep. Had Father Brown over in Dodge see to it not four weeks ago."

Cora's news troubled the little priest. What sort of evil creature could defend against a blessing placed by a servant of the Most High? Unless she had crossed paths with Lucifer himself, he didn't see how it was possible.

The priest looked at Cora and spread his hands out. "Well, I'm sorry, my dear, but I really don't know what it could be."

Cora's shoulders slumped. "Not even a hint?"

"I'm afraid not," he replied. "It is clearly a powerful creature, and very dangerous, but beyond that, I can't say much."

"All right, then," she said. "Ain't sure what I'm going to do now, though."

"Not to worry, my child," the old man said, patting her hand. "I will send telegraphs to some of my friends back East. They have a lot more experience dealing with these sorts of things than I do. I'll send it first thing in the morning, so it should only take a couple of days to find your answer."

Cora smiled. "My thanks, Father."

He smiled back at her, then his face grew serious again. "Have the years been hard since our last meeting?"

"Oh, ain't got much to complain about," she said. "Still living with my virtues and building on my vices, just like always."

"It's been a long time since you fought the vampires here," Father Baez said. "Have you found your peace with it?"

"I reckon so," Cora said, finding the question strange. "I ain't the type to let myself get all in a sulk on account of shooting a few monsters, Father."

"No, I suppose not," the priest replied. "I'm glad to hear you say that."

"Me too." Cora stood to her feet and offered her hand. Father Baez accepted it and accompanied her to the front door.

"Well, as I said, I expect to hear back from New

York or Philadelphia within a day or two, so stop by tomorrow evening." He patted her on the back and smiled. "Maybe I'll even have time for a confession."

"The good Lord knows I need one," she replied, "but I don't think it does any good if you ain't looking to change your ways. If I didn't have whiskey and poker, why, I'd have to take up reading like Ben does just to pass the time."

A shadow passed over the priest's face, but it cleared within the span of a breath. "Well, if you change your mind, I will be here to listen."

Cora nodded, smiling as she pulled the door open. Father Baez watched her saunter down the front walk, a prayer coming to his lips.

"Heavenly Father, lover of all and defender of the weak, bless Cora in Your love. Accept her offering of dedication and service, and help her to give You praise, to pray for Your church and the world, and to serve Your people in peace and joy. I ask this grace through Christ my Brother and my Lord, amen."

Jack Evans lowered his head as he walked by the Pioneer. Despite the powerful thirst in his throat, he kept his eyes pointed straight ahead down the dark street. He could hear the piano plinking away at some classic tune, accompanied by a chorus of miners well past their first drinks. Picturing a row of glistening beards on either side of the old upright, Jack broke into a grin. He longed to toss his arm around the shoulders of the last man in line and sing along, all his worries of monsters in the woods forgotten.

His boots slowed down as his thirst began overpowering his will. He came to a stop and had started to turn back when he heard a tinkling crash and a stream of shouting. More voices rose in answer, drowning out the piano in an avalanche of slurred cursing. They rose in pitch until the roar of a 12-gauge cut them off. The shot echoed in the street, causing a few to duck for cover, and Jack knew Mart Duggan and his on-duty deputies would soon arrive to break up the fight. As a lawman, he knew he should fetch the marshal himself, even if he was off-duty. It was his responsibility and might earn him another free drink from the bartender. Had it been any other night, he might have done just that. Duggan could probably use another hand in keeping the rowdy miners under control. Still, that's what he had the on-duty deputies for. Let them deal with the situation.

He had somewhere else to be tonight.

His boots crunched through the dirty snow, leaving footprints in a straight line away from the Pioneer. He wondered how many times he'd left a sober trail from the saloon since he and the marshal found that clearing. No more than the fingers on one hand could count, he was sure.

The thought of what Cora Oglesby had said about the monster wouldn't leave his mind. She seemed sure of herself, and was probably as good a shot as she claimed to be. If she, a self-proclaimed expert at dealing with monsters, could be bested by this one, what chance did the rest of them have?

He glanced over his shoulder, more in response to

his thoughts than to any sound or sense of danger. The street behind him stretched out into the shadows of the night. Lanterns and candlelit windows floated in the darkness, strongholds of warmth in the cold expanse. He imagined the creature watching from its mountain. To those hungry eyes, the town would shimmer like a glowing feast in the dark night. It was a wonder it hadn't started making a habit of preying on lonely men wandering the streets.

Men like him.

His pace quickened as he tried to put thoughts of the monster out of his mind. Cora Oglesby had told them she would take care of it, and he had no choice but to trust her. She was gone now, though. Off on a train ride up to Denver with her husband. It occurred to him that he'd never actually met the man married to such an unusual woman. He would have thought that her husband would have been as loud as she was, but maybe he was the quiet one of the pair. Jack couldn't figure out how that would work for a married couple, but he'd never been married himself, so he couldn't call himself an authority on the subject.

The thought of marriage put a bit of a bounce in his step. He was on his way to visit the girl he intended to marry one day, and maybe tonight would be the night he would win her over. He had stayed out of the Pioneer because he knew she didn't take to the smell of whiskey on a man's breath. Staying sober was a strain, especially with the thoughts of Leadville's local terror running through his mind, but she was worth it.

Annabelle Rose. He whispered her name, enjoying how it felt on his tongue. He could picture her bright blue eyes looking his way, a smile on her lips. Honey-colored hair spilled down around her face in gentle waves. Her cheeks would be flushed, their red blossoms standing out against the creamy whiteness of her skin like the sunrise peeking over the mountains. She would say his name in her soft voice, extending a small hand for him to kiss.

Yellow lamplight spilled across the snow on his boots. His thoughts of Annabelle had carried him all the way to her. He adjusted his hat and smoothed down his mustache, planning out what he would say in his head. His nervous hands, having made him as presentable as they could, began fingering the bullets in his belt. Taking a deep breath, he tried to stop them from shaking and reached to open the front door of the Purdy, one of Leadville's finest brothels.

A rush of warm air enveloped him, carrying the scent of flowers and the plinking of another piano. Red carpet flowed up the central staircase of the house like a trail of rose petals. Elsewhere, the floor's polished shine reflected light from dozens of candles hanging in ornate candelabras. Around the room, paintings of gray-haired men watched him from the walls. Jack had never taken to such paintings himself, but most people seemed to think they were in good taste. He didn't figure he'd ever earn enough money as a lawman to put such things in his own home, so he didn't pay them much attention.

A handsome black man in a porter's suit walked up

to him. "Good evening, Mr Evans." Jack nodded in response and removed his hat and coat. The porter bowed as he took them, then vanished through a side door. A few of the house's ladies lounged on overstuffed couches, wisps of hair draped across their faces. Bosoms strained against corsets of red and white and black while thick dresses covered dark stockings. Their red lips smiled at him, but he only answered with a polite nod. Each girl had her charms, but none were for him. He was here for Annabelle.

The porter returned, his smile wide and white. "If you'll follow me, Mr Evans."

Jack nodded, trying to keep a silly grin off his face as he followed the porter. It was all he could do not to shove the man aside, take the stairs two at a time, and gallop down to Annabelle's room. The porter's footfalls were slow and deliberate, as if he knew of Jack's mounting excitement and wanted to make him sweat. Jack took a few deep breaths to calm himself.

When they finally reached Annabelle's door, the porter bowed with another smile before taking his leave. Jack stared at the door, listening to the sound of the porter's retreating footsteps. His stomach felt like it was going to jump out of his mouth and go flopping down the hall. Closing his eyes, he gave his head a shake, then turned the knob.

The aroma of perfume and scented candles filled the steamy air, inviting him into the room. He stood in the doorway instead, wishing he'd kept his hat so his hands would have something to do. He let them fidget around his ammo belt for a moment before shoving them in his pockets.

He could hear the sound of splashing coming from the room, and although he couldn't see the bathtub from where he stood, he knew exactly where it was. He could picture Annabelle in that tub, soapy bubbles climbing up to perch on her bare shoulders. Hot blood flooded his cheeks at the thought, and he looked down at his boots.

"Is that you, Jack?" Her voice floated out to greet him.

"Yep, yessir, it's me," he said.

"Well, why don't you come on in?"

"OK, then." Shutting the door behind him, he walked down the short hallway, his boots sounding to his ears like a herd of buffalo. When he came around the corner, his foot caught on the floor, tripping him up. He recovered himself before he fell, but he could feel his cheeks burning. The burn grew hotter when he looked up to find her blue eyes watching him.

A smile played about her full lips. "You might want to take them boots off."

He nodded and sat down in the nearest chair. His feet, still cold from the walk through the snow, throbbed in protest as he wrenched his boots off. The sour tang of his sweat cut through the sweetness in the air. He shoved his feet as far as they would go under the chair, hoping she wouldn't notice.

"Are you going to stop there?" she asked, her smile lingering. "You're welcome to, of course, but you might not enjoy yourself quite the same." She rose to her feet and stepped out of the tub, water running down her white sides. "Come on, let's get you out of them clothes."

Jack's gut lurched in excitement at the suggestion, but he just stood to his feet and walked over to her. Up close, she smelled clean, like fresh water from a mountain stream. He was all too aware of his own stink, but she didn't seem to notice as she began working the buttons of his shirt. She untucked it from his pants, pulled his arms through the sleeves, and tossed it on the floor. She gave him a coy smile as she stepped behind him and reached her arms around his body. Her palms pressed into the coarse hairs on his chest.

"You smell like a man ought to," she said, her fingers tracing tiny circles on his skin. He blushed again, glad she couldn't see.

Soon, he was seated in the bathtub. Annabelle knelt by the edge of the tub, cupping water in her hands and pouring it over his head. The warmth made his skin tingle. He wanted to lean back, close his eyes, and let her keep pouring handfuls of water over him, but the nearness of her naked body made it impossible to relax. He sat in nervous silence, the water running through his hair, into his eyes, and down his mustache.

She reached over to a small stand behind him, picked up a scrubbing brush, and dipped the bristles into the soapy water. Placing a hand on his back, she gently pushed him forward. He bent at the waist, his back stiff as the brush scrubbed his shoulders, his neck, and his back. Annabelle smiled, watching his skin turn from fishbelly white to the rosy pink of sunset.

After a few minutes, she declared him finished and stood up. He splashed his way out of the tub and into a towel she was holding. She rubbed him down with it, stopping a few times to kiss his exposed skin. Her lips were soft, but he still jumped as though she was poking him with a needle. She giggled when he did, a lilting sound that made his knees feel weak.

Grasping his hand in both of hers, she led him through an archway into the bedroom. The smile never left her lips, even as she began kissing him. She lay back on the sheets and pulled him on top of her. The heat of her seemed to set him aflame, and he felt his arms quiver as he held himself above her.

It was over all too quickly. He crawled up next to her and collapsed, still catching his breath. Annabelle's smile widened as she draped an arm over his stomach.

"So tell me about your week," she said.

He swallowed, his mouth suddenly dry. "Oh, it was pretty normal, I reckon." Pillow talk was one of her services. Most of her clients probably enjoyed talking about themselves and their work, hoping to impress her with stories of strength or riches, but Jack's tongue always tied itself in knots. Her breath on his cheek made him want to best them all, to tell her a tale grand enough to make her eyes shine. His mind raced, searching for something, anything to say.

A thought came to him. He opened his mouth to say something, then closed it again.

"Go on, sugar." Her voice felt like silk on his ears. "Say what you want to say."

"You can keep a secret, can't you?"

"Secrets are my trade," she said, giving him a look that made him want to crawl under the bed.

"Well, then," he said, "I got a secret to say."

"I'm all ears," she murmured, kissing his.

Her kisses sent shivers down to his toes. "Well, me and the marshal went out riding one morning, and we come across this clearing, right? Well, some poor fellers met with a bad end there. Real bad. I don't want to tell you the details, so I'll just say I've never seen worse in my two years of upholding the law."

Her hand traced circles around his belly button. "Did you find out who done those fellers in?"

"Of course I did," he replied, trying to make his voice sound strong. "I tracked him all the way through the woods and up a mountain. Cornered him in a mine and made ready to do what I had to do."

"Did you lick him proper?"

"Well, turns out the culprit wasn't exactly a man or even a gang of them," he said, turning his head to face her.

Her thin eyebrows pulled together. "What was it, then? A grizzly?"

"Nope, not that, neither." He swallowed and looked her in the eyes. "It was some sort of monster. A monster that used to be a man."

"I don't follow," she said.

"Can't say for sure my own self," he said. "It had a man's shape, see, but its legs and arms was all stretched out like a spider's." Jack could see her interest growing, and his heart started beating faster.

"Anyway, like I said, I got it cornered in a mine, but it lashed out and knocked my gun right out of my hand. Took a leap at me, so I had to roll to get clear and nearly bashed my brains out on a big old rock. I picked myself up and pulled my other gun. The monster was coming back at me pell-mell, its big arms reaching to tear off my head. I stood stock still, waiting for my shot. When it came, I took it. Hit the thing square between the eyes, but even that didn't put it down. It howled something awful and lit out down the mine tunnel. I tried to run it down, but it gave me the slip on account of the darkness."

"My heart," Annabelle whispered. She gazed at him in disbelief for a moment, then a thought came to her. "You best not be pulling my leg, or so help me, I will end you right here."

He could see that she was impressed, and for the first time that night, a smile spread beneath his mustache. "On my word," he said, then tried out a new word, "darling."

"So you really faced down a monster?" She curled a long white leg around both of his and leaned in to him. "They should make you the marshal and run out that old drunkard Duggan."

Jack swallowed, uneasy. "You think so, do you?"

"Why, sure," she replied. "Ain't much of a feat to toss drunk miners in jail for a night, but running off a man-killing monster? That ain't nothing to sneeze at."

"I reckon so," Jack replied. His thoughts jumped back to that morning, when Mart Duggan had whipped over a hundred miners without firing a single shot. Jack himself had been scared spitless, sure that the mob would tear the entire station apart and him with it. He'd been making his peace with the Lord when the marshal marched past his desk and into the morning sun. In the space of a few minutes, Duggan had called every mother's son of them a coward and watched them slink away in shame. Jack Evans had never seen anything like it, and Annabelle's casual scorn for the marshal didn't sit right with him.

He could feel the heat from her body as she pressed into his side. Maybe she was right, though. Sure, Duggan could whip a crowd of miners, but he hadn't done much by way of whipping that thing in the forest. Now that Jack thought on it, the marshal had seemed downright scared that morning in the clearing, looking over his shoulder like the trees themselves were going to grow teeth and eat him. Jack had felt the same chill but stayed calm. He'd been the marshal's eyes that day, and if he hadn't kept a sharp eye, they could've both been eaten. That was almost the same as saving Mart Duggan's life, yet the marshal never said a word of thanks. If Jack was marshal, he'd be sure to give his deputies a hearty thank-you if they did something as thoughtful as saving his own life. He'd also make sure no man-killing creatures were welcome in his town, even if that meant chasing them up a mountain and into an old mine. If that crazy Cora Oglesby could do it, there wasn't any reason why he couldn't, either.

Jack's grin returned. He could make a fine marshal if given the chance. The first thing he'd do would be to take this beautiful woman as his bride and move her out of the brothel. He looked into her deep-blue eyes, eyes that reminded him of the sky, and she smiled back. Maybe she really could come to love him if he became marshal.

Jack pulled Annabelle closer. She came willingly, lowering her lips to his. The soft skin of her back felt warm on his cold hand. Her fingers combed through his hair, sending thrills skittering down his spine. Waves of goosebumps rolled over his skin, and he shivered.

A scream echoed from the street outside. Startled, the lovers turned toward the window. Annabelle pulled the bedsheets over her body as a second scream rattled the glass. Jack scrambled to his feet and ran into the other room. He fumbled with his pants, nearly falling over as he pulled them on. He threaded his arms through his shirt sleeves, grabbed the pistol from his belt, and ran to the window. All he could see was a steamy outline of his reflection. Several gunshots cracked in the darkness, followed by another scream.

The deputy pulled on his boots, gave Annabelle a quick nod, and ran downstairs. He crashed through the Purdy's front door into the night. The cold air hit him like a slap in the face. Blinded by the darkness, he could hear shouts and shots coming from somewhere on his left. A few heartbeats later, his vision cleared, and he could make out several figures down the street, outlined by the Pioneer's glowing windows. Imagining Annabelle's big blue eyes watching him from her window, he ran toward them, revolver at the ready.

As Jack ran, he saw several flashes as the figures fired into the shadows across the street. He looked where they were firing, but couldn't see anything except a row of lights winking in the darkness. When he reached the other men, he crouched down next to them and pointed his pistol in the same direction.

"Glad you could join us, deputy." The voice belonged to Mart Duggan.

"What's going on, marshal?" Jack asked, winded from the sprint.

"Seems that crazy bitch was right. Murray and me got the thing cornered, but–"

Duggan fell silent as a shadow lurched into view across the street. It stood on two legs like a man, but it was far too tall. Long arms hung down from a ten-foot height, brushing across the thing's knees as its fingers curled and flexed. Jack squeezed the trigger, adding the crack of his Schofield to the roaring of Duggan's Colt. On the other side of the marshal, he could hear the clap of a Winchester rifle in the hands of Deputy George Murray.

The creature reeled from the impact of the bullets, but it kept its feet even after Jack's revolver was empty. Shells skittered across the snow as he snapped the gun open. He reached down to pull more bullets from his belt, then cursed at his own stupidity. His ammo belt still lay on the floor in Annabelle's room.

The marshal's fingers reloaded his own gun with

practiced ease. Across the street, the shadow crouched, its knees and elbows rising above its back as it lowered itself toward the snow. It watched them for a moment, swaying like a giant spider. Then, as the marshal slammed the Colt's cylinder back into place, the creature sprang toward them with a piercing screech. Jack flinched at the sound, his gun falling from his hand. He heard Duggan fire once before a long white arm slammed into him, knocking the lawman backward into the saloon's wall. Pain exploded in Jack's head, followed by a wave of nausea. Through the ringing in his head, he heard a choking scream and looked up.

Black fingers curled around Deputy Murray's neck as a pale arm lifted him off his feet. The marshal's gun roared in Jack's ears. Every one of Duggan's shots found its mark, but the creature didn't flinch. Instead, it turned a death grin at them, its teeth clacking between bloodless black lips.

Duggan fired again, and sparks flashed in the creature's face as the bullet ricocheted off its fangs. The monster answered with a sharp hiss. Jack heard the distinct click of an empty gun followed by Duggan's curse. Murray's boots dangled in midair as he clawed at the dead hand around his throat, desperate for a breath. Paralyzed, Jack watched the helpless deputy struggle for a moment before he felt something clamp onto his leg. He only had a moment to register the long black fingers gripping his boot before the creature hoisted him into the air. Hollering in panic, he twisted in the powerful grip, arms flailing. His fingers caught the cold, clammy skin hanging from the creature's ribs. It stretched like rubber, pulling away from the frozen bones, but it didn't tear.

The monster reared to its full height, releasing Jack's leg as it did. He fell headfirst onto the packed snow and lay dazed, his stomach reeling and his head foggy. Shadows danced across his vision. He lifted his head and squinted upward through the pulsing in his eyes.

The long arms cradled Deputy Murray like a child. Murray wrestled against the black fingers and kicked at the creature's ribs, but it held him fast. A stream of prayers poured from his lips. The creature hissed in reply, black lips pulled back. Long teeth sank into the deputy's neck, and his prayers ended in a gurgling scream. Jack felt something warm splash against his face, blinding him, but he didn't turn away. The sounds of crunching bone and grinding teeth filled his ears.

Only when the creature turned its eyes to him did Jack awake from his stupor. He rolled onto his stomach and scrambled to his feet. Before he could take two steps, icy fingers clamped around his stomach, bringing him up short. Hoisted skyward, he came face-to-face with those wicked teeth, now covered in fresh blood and bits of flesh. The creature seemed to grin at him, its yellow eyes alight with savage hunger. A wave of frigid air covered him as the jaws opened, revealing a pit as black as Hell itself.

Jack screamed.

A flash of orange light caught the monster's attention, and its eyes left the deputy's frightened face. In that moment, Jack heard the most welcome sound he could have imagined: the roar of Mart Duggan's voice.

"Back, you devil, or I'll set a fire in your hide!"

The black fingers let go of Jack's leg, and the deputy landed head-first on the packed snow. Stunned, he lay still as the world pitched around him in a swirl of black and orange.

Mart Duggan stepped over the fallen form of his deputy, a burning branch in each hand. He waved them in the creature's face, the flames brilliant against the night. The monster reeled backward with a loud wail. It beat at the fire with its long hands, but the marshal kept the branches just out of its reach. Duggan advanced, flames crackling, and pressed it back into the night. Finally, the creature turned and loped down the street, its long legs disappearing into the shadows.

Duggan stared after it for a moment, branches held high. With a final shout of triumph, he lowered the flames and turned back to his fallen deputy. The marshal prodded Jack with a boot until he rose to his feet.

"Where's Murray?" Duggan asked.

Jack opened his mouth, but the words didn't come. He could only look at the splattered blood and crushed bones that had once belonged to Deputy Murray. Duggan followed his gaze, then lowered his eyes to his boots. Only a handful of decent men called Leadville home, and George Murray had been one of them. The marshal swallowed the hard lump in his throat and whispered a prayer for his fallen man.

"Well, can't be helped now," he said aloud. "At least he don't have a wife or kids to give the bad news to."

Jack nodded. A man had just been eaten before his eyes, and he'd have followed in like kind had the marshal not returned when he did. His hands trembled, but he didn't have the wits to put them on his hips. Instead, he just looked at the bloody snow around them, thinking back to the clearing and wondering what those wolfers had felt in their last minutes.

"Well, come on, son," Duggan said, handing him a flaming branch. "We best make sure that thing has run off for good."

Jack took the branch from the marshal. It shook in his hand as he stared into the flames. That woman had said the creature was scared of silver and fire, but he'd forgotten. If the marshal hadn't remembered, it would have torn both of them apart. He could still see that gaping mouth and feel the icy breath on his face. Taking a deep breath, he tried to pull himself together enough to meet Duggan's eyes.

"What in God's creation was that, sir?"

SIX

"A wendigo."

"Wendigo?" Cora's brow furrowed. "Can't say as I've ever heard of one of them before."

"Neither have I," Father Baez said, his hands folded in his lap. "Apparently, they are quite rare in these parts. A priest in Boston, Father Davidson, was the one to find the information we were looking for."

Cora leaned back in the pew, wishing Ben could have been here to hear this. She had kept her word to Father Baez and returned to the church the following evening, but Ben hadn't followed. He had chosen to spend the time in the library near their hotel. His decision irritated her, but it wasn't a surprise. He'd always been the bookish type, shy and quiet, not at all suited to the military life that the war had forced on him. Duty was duty, though, so he'd marched off with his gray coat on his shoulders and a rifle in his hand. His engagement ring had been around her finger as she watched him go, his promise to return still echoing in her ears. That ring had gone with her to the local church every day during those four long years. She had lit a candle and knelt beside other women, both young and old, as they prayed for sweethearts and husbands and sons. As the years passed, their numbers dwindled. Some received word of the worst kind and lost the will to keep praying. Others just gave up hope, but Cora kept her faithful vigil. Each time a gray-coated rider appeared in town, Cora's breath would catch in her throat, but they would always ride past her door. Her heart had ached to see so many faces hidden behind black veils, but she couldn't help feeling thankful that hers was not one of them.

"What did Father Davidson say about it?" she asked.

"Well, he was a little vague. He hadn't heard of this wendigo himself, but as it turns out, several members of his congregation are from an Indian tribe."

"Indians?"

"Yes," Father Baez said, nodding. "According to them, the wendigo is a mythical beast from their own folklore. From what I understand, it's a cannibalistic ghoul that devours the flesh of humans due to a never-ending hunger in its own belly."

"I figured that much. How did old Jules get himself turned into one?"

"It seems a wendigo is created when one person eats the flesh of another person to avoid starvation. The moment they swallow their first bite, a demon begins to twist them from their natural shape, slowly turning them into the creature you saw in the mine the other day."

"So you're saying that old miner was a cannibal?"

"At some point, yes." Father Baez glanced at his hands for a moment. "You said he had a habit of hunting at night, correct?" Cora nodded. "I suppose he must have shot someone one night, mistaking them for an animal. Wanting to cover up his mistake, he took the body back to his cabin and cooked it anyway. Then, when he ate it, he began turning into the monster."

Cora shook her head in wonder. Jules Bartlett a cannibal, and now some kind of cannibal demon. She wondered what Sheriff Jim Barnes would say when she told him about it. Probably that he had known it all along.

"Did these Indians happen to know how to lick the wendigo after it's changed?" she asked.

The priest nodded again. "Yes. Wendigos are vulnerable to silver weapons, but the silver must have the blessing of an Indian shaman."

"No, that ain't right," Cora said. "I filled that thing full of my blessed silver bullets, but it ain't dead yet."

"Your bullets were blessed by a Catholic priest," Father Baez replied. "Although the silver in them was able to injure the wendigo, without the proper blessing, they couldn't finish it off."

Cora made a face. "Why's that? Ain't a blessing a blessing?"

"Apparently not." Father Baez shrugged. "Father Davidson's parishioners said that only the blessing of one of their shamans could make a silver weapon effective against the creature."

"So I couldn't get one of the tribes around here to do the blessing?"

"Most likely not. Even if you were able to find a willing tribe, I doubt it would be effective. The wendigo isn't common in these parts of the country. Too warm, from what I understand. It's a demon of the cold and the snow, and this part of the country is too hot for them to flourish."

"You clearly ain't been to Leadville during the winter," Cora replied. She pondered this new information for a moment, then sighed. "I reckon I ought to make my way out to Boston, then."

Father Baez smiled. "No, that won't be necessary. Father Davidson promised to send out a shipment of blessed bullets as soon as possible."

"Really?" Cora's eyebrows arched in surprise. "What makes him so generous?"

"The Indians in his congregation were very upset by this news. The wendigo is one of the most feared creatures in their society. When Father Davidson told them of our problem, they immediately asked one of their shamans for help. The shaman wanted to come out and deal with the problem himself, but Father Davidson managed to convince him that there was a perfectly qualified hunter already working on the problem."

"And this shaman already had him some silver bullets?"

"Well, no," the priest replied, "but Father Davidson had some spares on hand. Not many, mind you; maybe two dozen at most. You'll have to use them sparingly when they arrive."

"Well, don't that beat all." Cora folded her arms. "Did this shaman happen to mention how many it should take to kill this wendigo?"

"No more than one or two, I understand. The blessing is quite powerful."

Cora nodded, marveling at the innovations of evil. No matter how many monsters she and Ben put to rest, something new always managed to spring up. It was almost as if the Devil took it as some sort of challenge. They had battled his minions for well over fifteen years now, yet he still managed to toss something new their way every once in a while. This wendigo was certainly a fair sight different than anything they'd seen before, even needing its own special type of blessing. Still, a spook was a spook, and she was sure they could whip it all the same.

"So how long did Father Davidson say the shipment would take?"

"No more than a week, I imagine." A smile spread within the priest's white beard. "Still enough time for a confession if you feel the need."

Cora snorted a laugh. "Thanks for the offer, Father, but I reckon I'll slide back into my sinful ways before the night is over, so I can't say I see much of a point."

The priest sighed and tossed up his hands, but the smile never left his face. Cora rose to her feet and offered her hand again, but Father Baez was already rising. They walked down the aisle together, the priest with his hands clasped behind his back.

"I expect you'll send the bullets on to Leadville when they arrive?" Cora asked.

"No need," Father Baez replied. "Father Davidson said he would ship them directly to Leadville in your care."

Cora nodded in satisfaction as they reached the wooden doors. Turning to face the little priest, she held out her hand. Father Baez clasped it in both of his and smiled. "Take care of yourself, Cora."

"You too, Father. Thanks for all your help."

"Of course, my dear. If you ever need anything, please do not hesitate to ask."

"Oh, I reckon me and Ben will be just fine, but thanks anyway."

The priest's smile faltered. "Yes, well, my offer is always open. Go with God, my child." Cora nodded, gave his hand a firm shake, and left

In the darkness of the foyer, Father Baez closed his eyes. The hunter's unexpected visit had brought back the memories of ten years before. A lingering sorrow crept into his heart when he thought on them, but it encouraged him to see the brave huntress still fighting the servants of Hell. Some of the things she'd said worried him, but it was not his place to pry He could only entrust her to the good Lord's care and wait for her to come to him when she needed his guidance.

"How long do you reckon we'll be waiting for them bullets?" Ben asked. He was stretched out on one of the benches in the passenger car, a newspaper covering his face.

"Father Baez said no more than a week," Cora replied.

"I hope he's right. We don't have time to wait for some priest back East to count his tassels."

"Ain't got much of a choice in the matter," Cora said, annoyed by his flippant attitude. "Besides, that Father Davidson is helping us out of the kindness of his own pockets. Silver bullets ain't cheap."

"Ain't that pricey, neither." The newspaper rustled as Ben spoke. "Most of them ain't even pure silver, but you'd think they were diamonds, the way some priests carry on."

"As I recall, you're the one that claimed that them silver alloy rounds worked better."

"Well, they certainly didn't work no better on that wendigo thing."

"Neither did you." Cora crossed her legs and looked out the window. "You're just cranky because you had to leave your precious library behind."

"That was a damn fine library. Best I've seen in a powerful long stretch. We really should spend more time in proper cities and stop dumping around in the sticks."

"No kind of living for us in a city," Cora said. "Monsters prefer living in the sticks, so that's where we have to hunt them."

"Not arguing that point, missy. Just saying we might find ourselves a bit more civilized if we took some time to read every now and again."

"Who's saying we ain't civilized?" Cora asked.

"When was the last time you opened a book?"

"You know I ain't much for letters. Even so, I still read my Bible at least once a week."

Ben snorted a laugh through his nose. "Reading the bits about wine when you've had your fill of whiskey hardly counts as reading."

"Oh, go to sleep, you old grump," Cora said. "Your bellyaching is like to drive me to the drink before we even get off this train."

Ben grunted and pulled the newspaper down a bit farther. After a few minutes, Cora could hear his even breathing. She stared out the window, watching the canyon walls roll by as the train pulled them deeper into the Rockies. The great gray stones seemed to swell and fade like the waves of the sea as they passed by the windows. Pine trees clung to the sides of the boulders with tough roots, their green tops reaching toward a bright blue sky.

The West was so different from her farm back home that Cora sometimes felt she lived in a dream world. The plants out here lived much like the people did, somehow pulling life and water out of the red clay that covered the ground. She remembered the rich, dark soil of the Shenandoah Valley, how it felt almost like cotton in her fingers. Her hands had been smaller then, the hands of a young girl. Mother would scold her for dirtying her stockings and her dresses, but Cora had loved being close to the earth. She knew her father worked with his own hands in the soil, growing food for the three of them and their small lot of animals, and she wanted to be a part of it. Her mother told her not to bother with such things, that she would grow up and find herself a proper husband to work the earth for her. Cora would always reply that she wanted to help her man when the time came, and her mother would shake her head and sigh.

She turned her eyes from the window to consider the sleeping form of her husband. Ben was the son of a printer, not a farmer, and it was from his trade that he learned his love of books. She'd met him in the town nearest her farm while she was running errands for her mother. Rounding a corner, she had collided with him as he had been walking the other way, his nose buried in a book. The impact knocked her down and sent the book flying. Ben had stooped to recover his lost treasure before offering his ink-stained fingers to her. She had taken his hand with a coy smile, enjoying the feeling in her stomach as he pulled her to her feet. The feeling didn't go away once she was standing, so she kept her eyes on the cobbles beneath her shoes as he apologized.

The train rounded a sharp corner in the tracks. A muffled thump echoed in the near-empty passenger car, and Cora turned her head around to search for the source. A small, round man in a bowler hat and suit sat across the aisle from her, fumbling with a small suitcase next to him. The trunk must have fallen over during the turn, causing the thump. Red-faced, the man grunted with the effort of pulling it upright again. Cora watched in amusement as he strained. When he finally succeeded, he smacked it with a pudgy fist, put a hand to his forehead, and took a deep breath.

"That's a mighty fine trunk you got there, sir," Cora said.

"Isn't it, though?" the stranger replied, turning to her and smiling. "I purchased it from a quaint little shop in Sussex. Burgess Hill, if I remember correctly. Though I must admit I rather neglected to consider its size when picking it out. It holds a fine number of texts, but I'm afraid it gets rather cumbersome as a result."

"Is that right?" Cora said, unable to contain a smirk. "Maybe you could find yourself a servant to haul it around for you and save yourself the work."

"Oh, I'm afraid I'm not quite that high in station. Yet, anyway. I hope one day to afford a nice staff of my own, perhaps even a valet, though of course one must own a buggy for that." He laughed, a rich sound that made his round belly jiggle. "Until such time, however, I must resign myself to my burden." He thumped on the trunk and laughed again.

"Well, at least you're cheerful about it," Cora said.

"The fine cider back in the city may have something to do with that, I think."

Cora's eyebrow arched. "Cider's your drink, is it?" When the man nodded, she shook her head. "Can't say I care for it much myself. Not when there's whiskey handy."

The man's round face twisted into a grimace. "Awful stuff, if you ask me. I honestly can't fathom who first took a sip and decided it was fit for human consumption. Most likely an Irishman."

Cora couldn't believe what she was hearing. "A man who don't drink whiskey? How can you even call yourself a man?"

"Quite easily, actually. Of course, I could call myself a roasted ham for all the good it would do. The names a man gives to himself aren't worth tuppence if he can't stand behind them, I say."

"And what's the name you call yourself?"

"James Townsend, if you please." He tipped his hat to her, and Cora nodded in reply. "To whom do I owe the pleasure?"

"Name's Cora Oglesby." She kicked the bench in front of her, but Ben just grunted. "That sorry sack of sod there is my husband, Benjamin Oglesby."

"Always a pleasure, to be sure," James said.

"Ain't so often we see a Brit out here in the West. What brings you to our little corner of the world?"

"Business, as one might expect." James smoothed down his ruffled shirt. "I'm on my way to a place called Leadville to see to my employer's affairs."

"Well, ain't it a small world?" Cora said. "So happens Leadville's our stop, too."

"Splendid!" James clapped his hands together. "You will have to give me the proper tour! I've always harbored a desire to see the legendary American West firsthand!"

"You ain't been up there before?"

"Oh, good heavens, no! Do I look like the sort of man who frequents such backwoods places?" He sat up straighter. "As it happens, I'm recently come from London herself, and she's where I lay my head when I'm not running about in the wide world."

"How does that work out?" Cora asked. "I mean, what with your boss out here in the States and all."

"Oh, Lord Harcourt would never dream of getting the dust of such a rustic place on his jacket. No, he resides at court and takes his tea with the finest nobility. He's even been called before the Crown a time or two, or so he's told me. A proper lord, he is, and wealthy enough to keep his investments halfway around the world."

"Investments? He deal in liquor or ladies?"

"Neither," James replied. "Lord Harcourt deals in silver. He owns a mine to the north of the town of Leadville."

"Fine trade, as far as it goes," Cora said. "Whole reason for the town's existence, or so I'm told. Not that we ever had the money or gumption to dig for our own."

"I thought not."

"You thought not?" Cora asked, leaning toward him. "What's that supposed to mean?"

"Nothing! Nothing at all!" James waved his hands in surrender and leaned away from her. "I only meant that you don't really look the sort to dally about all day while others do your work for you."

"So you're saying we ain't fancy."

"No! Well, yes, but I don't mean to offend! I only meant to imply that you have the look of a gunfighter or an outlaw. A roguish look, if I may be so bold."

"How do you know we ain't? Maybe we're fixing to rob you blind and dump your corpse off the next bridge."

The blood drained from the British man's face. It was clear he hadn't considered such an option. He swallowed once, then looked down at his hands. They rode in silence for a few moments, listening to the clacking of the wheels beneath them.

Finally Cora laughed. "You look a sorry sight, Mr London. No, we ain't planning you any harm. Why, we'd just as soon save your hide for the right price."

"I shall keep that in mind," he said. His hand reached for something beneath his shirt as he muttered something under his breath. Cora could make out the shape of a cross through the cloth.

"You're a religious man, I take it?"

"Well, yes. As much as I need to be, at least."

"Is that right?" Cora crossed her arms. "How much does that come out to, do you find?"

"Enough to keep me alive."

"Well, ain't that an oddity? Most folk I met says they're into religion for what happens after death, not what happens before. What is it about religion as keeps you alive?"

"I can't see how it's really any of your business."

"Fine, have it your way," Cora said. "Just a mite surprised to hear a man give an answer that may as well have been mine."

James gave her a sidelong glance, then pretended to find something on his shirt that needed his immediate attention. Cora watched him fidget, a smirk on her lips. After a few moments, her gaze fell to the trunk. "Say, why do you carry all them books with you, anyhow? Ain't it a pain to lug that old trunk everywhere?"

"Well," James began, his eyes looking around the

coach for words. "You see, I am something of a scholar, as you may have gathered."

"A scholar?" Cora asked. "So you're a doctor, then?"

"Well, not exactly. To tell you the truth, my area of expertise is somewhat... unusual."

"What's that?"

A furious blush crept across the British man's cheeks. "I expect you will find it rather odd, and I did so myself when I first learned of the discipline. It was a Dutchman who let me in on the secret, actually." He took a deep breath, then turned to face her, his dark eyes small in his round face. "I am what some might call a vampire scholar."

"You don't say?" Cora said.

"Yes," James said, nodding. "I know it sounds absurd, but it really is a valid area of study. As I said, it was a friend of mine, a Dutch physician, who opened my eyes to the existence of vampires. He is quite well-versed in the Occult, especially where the undead are concerned. He's actually hunted them in the past, and taught me some of his art."

Cora burst out laughing, nearly falling out of her seat. The Englishman waited for her to stop with an unhappy look on his face. When she finally regained her composure, tears glistened in the corners of her eyes.

"I hardly think it's a laughing matter," James stated.

"I'm sorry," Cora said, wiping her eyes. "It's just the thought of a round little feller like you hunting down vampires."

James lifted his chin. "I've battled my share of the undead, thank you kindly."

"I'm sure you have," Cora said, suppressing another laugh.

"Anyway, what would a simpleton like you know of such matters? You probably spend your days gambling and drinking, blind and stupid to everything around you."

"No need to get a bee in your bonnet," Cora said. "As it happens, I've bagged me a few vampires in the past."

"Ah, of course," James said, folding his arms and looking away. "And how long ago was this?"

Cora thought for a bit. "Last one was about ten years ago, I'd say. Me and Ben here ran a vampire nest out of Denver. Ain't been none since then, though. Maybe they all got scared and hid away."

"You ran a vampire nest out of Denver, you say?"

"Well, burned it is what we did. Had to shoot a few of them in the process, though."

"Hmph," James snorted. "A likely story. A real vampire hunter knows that a vampire can only be killed by running a stake through its heart and removing its head."

"Maybe that's true where you come from," Cora said, "but out here in the West, we're right smart about it. All it takes is a bullet to the heart or the head."

"Nonsense–"

"Let me finish," Cora interrupted. "All it takes is a bullet, but it's a special bullet, you follow? Made of a silver alloy and blessed proper by a priest. Most of my bullets are even made out of silver that once belonged to crosses."

James scoffed. "I've never heard anything so preposterous. What sort of vampire hunter travels without a stake? You must be mad to think that you can just shoot a supernatural creature and expect to live through the encounter. I expect you simply mistook some poor old man for your vampire and shot him.

"If I did, I reckon I'd be rotting in some jail somewhere. We do got laws out here."

"Yes, well, what did this vampire of yours look like?"

"Like a proper one," Cora said. "Had him a pale face what looked like bread dough and a mouth full of nasty fangs. What was left of his clothes just hung off his body in tatters. Hated sunlight, had a thing for blood, and carried himself like a badger."

"A badger?"

"All fangs and drool and growling."

"Ah!" James's face lit up with recognition. "I don't suppose he seemed to possess any notable reasoning faculties?"

"If by that, you're asking if he could think, I'd say no."

"Exactly as I thought, then," James replied, looking satisfied with himself. "What you encountered was a *vrykolakas.*"

"Pretty sure it was a vampire, King George. I happen to be an expert in spook hunting myself, and I know me a vampire when I see one."

"To be sure, and you are correct, after a fashion. The creature you described is correctly termed *vrykolakas,* and it is indeed a type of vampire."

Cora's brow furrowed. "A type?" she asked. "You mean to say there's more than one type?"

"Naturally," James said. "If the ranks of the undead only consisted of the *vrykolakas*, I daresay they wouldn't command nearly as much respect and fear as they presently do."

"I'm afraid I don't follow."

James turned to face her, his earlier animosity forgotten in his scholarly delight. "Much like moths, vampires have two distinct stages of life. The first stage, *vrykolakas*, is by far the more common type, so it is little wonder you are ignorant of any other. These vampires are exactly as you described: powerful and fearsome, yet feral. This is due to the possession of the reanimated corpse by a blood-drinking demon."

"Right," Cora said. "Vampires don't have souls like regular folk."

"A common belief, but only partially accurate. As I said, the *vrykolakas* is the more common variety of vampire, so it follows that most folklore concerning vampires is primarily influenced by its characteristics and behavior. The *vrykolakas* has the intelligence level of a high-end mammalian predator, such as a wolf or your American grizzly bear. Smarter than your average cow, but by no means able to reason or strategize. In addition, they are usually solitary, which makes incidents involving them relatively simple to resolve."

"Except when they gang up, like in Denver," Cora said, shifting her weight. "You ain't telling me anything new. If you've got a point, best be getting to it quick."

"Yes, yes, of course," James replied, not skipping a beat. "So, if the *vrykolakas* is the only kind of vampire in existence, why has the vampire been feared above all other supernatural creatures for so many centuries?"

"I reckon it's because they're scary. Watching a man get his throat torn out by a walking corpse tends to shake most folk up a good bit."

"Quite true, but no more so than watching, say, a werewolf perform the same feat."

"Just say what you're going to say."

"Right. My point is simply that, left to its own devices, the *vrykolakas* would be no more fearsome than any other creature of the night. So, in order to garner the terrifying reputation the race of vampires possesses, they must have another ace in their hole, so to speak."

"Another kind of vampire?"

"Yes! Exactly!" James exclaimed, holding up a finger.

"Just like you said awhile back." Cora shook her head. "Is all you Brits this prone to gabbing? It's a wonder you all ever get around to anything else."

"I should be glad of the opportunity to learn my trade if I were in your position."

"I would be if I'd learned anything. All you've done is talk my own knowledge at me."

"Establishing context, my dear," James replied. "Without context, any further knowledge is useless at best, dangerous at worst."

"Can't imagine it being no worse than not being shared at all."

"Americans," James said with a hint of exasperation. "I don't know which is worse, your ignorance or your impatience."

"We tend to get impatient when people as can relieve our ignorance take too long to get it done."

"Not exactly the most welcoming attitude for those seeking to share their knowledge and insights with you."

"You know, I think I changed my mind," Cora said. "I think I will throw you off a bridge."

James went pale. "Of course, some might say your impatience possesses a certain roguish charm all its own." Cora glared at him, and he answered with a nervous smile. "I'll get right to it."

"Glad to hear it."

"Of course." He took a breath. "The second type of vampire, and by far the more fearsome, is a creature we call the *nosferatu*."

"And what do they do?"

"Quite simply, a *nosferatu* is a vampire whose human soul has been restored to his body."

Cora frowned. "Ain't having a soul a good thing?"

"One would think so, but it's actually quite dreadful. You see, the human soul may be restored, but the creature still possesses all of the characteristics of the *vrykolakas*, such as enhanced strength, enhanced speed, and the need to consume human blood. It's also theorized that they gain some new powers as a result of this unholy ascension."

"What sort of powers?"

"Transformation, for one thing. Most of the *nosferatu* recorded in history have had the power to assume other shapes, such as animals. This allows them to move undetected through a population to single out victims."

"I ain't following you," Cora said. "Wouldn't the human soul make them go all soft on killing folk?"

"Initially, yes, and I imagine there are some that never recover from discovering what they are. If any such vampires exist, however, they keep entirely to themselves." He leaned toward her and lowered his voice. "Although, between us, it is my belief that those who can't live with the burden of vampirism simply choose to end their own lives."

"Maybe so, but why are you whispering? You trying to keep it from this snoring sop?" She kicked at Ben's bench.

"My apologies," James replied, sitting upright again and adjusting his hat. "It's just that my theory isn't particularly popular among most vampire scholars."

"There are other vampire scholars? And here I thought only us hunters and them musty old priests went in for such tales."

"Oh, my, no." James shook his head. "Why, there's an entire fraternity of scholars at Oxford dedicated to unveiling the secrets of the undead. A secret fraternity, mind you, but very knowledgeable."

"So that's your story, is it? You're running errands for this educated group? What, did they take a special interest in American spooks all of a sudden?"

"Hardly," James said indignantly, "nor am I here at

their behest. As I said earlier, I am in the employ of Lord Harcourt."

"You never did say what you do for him. You some kind of property minder?"

"Not at all. My services follow my interest."

"So you tell him about vampires?" Cora asked, raising an eyebrow.

"Essentially, yes. Actually, my line of work is remarkably similar to what I imagine yours might be. We're both mercenaries of sorts." Cora failed to hold in another gale of laughter, much to James's annoyance. "You've not much experience with manners, have you?"

"All kinds," Cora replied. "I just never learned none."

"So I see," James said, standing to his feet. "Well, I shall leave you to reflect on those encounters in the hope that you may learn from them still. Our tickets make us traveling mates, so I suppose I must leave my trunk here, but I believe a rather lengthy stroll about the train is in order."

Cora watched him leave before resuming her vigil at the window. She'd met Englishmen before in her travels, but hadn't had the opportunity to speak much with one. The last one she'd run into had been in a St Louis sheriff station. He'd been bound for San Francisco when his train ran afoul of the James Younger Gang. Lost all his possessions, he'd said, and he was mighty angry about it. That sort of thing wouldn't have happened on a British rail, he'd said. Cora and Ben had been there chasing after a spook that ended up being another misunderstanding, so she'd stopped by the station to inform the lawmen there that they'd be moving on. The foreigner hadn't appreciated her cutting in on his time with the sheriff and made sure she'd known it. He could have been speaking Blackfoot for all the heed she paid him, which only made him angrier.

This James Townsend was different. Cora had never given much thought to the possibility of actually studying vampires as a hobby. Leave it to a bunch of old English codgers to think that such a thing would be interesting. What little schooling she'd received in her life had come from Ben when he'd taught her to read. She liked it well enough, though she'd never taken to it like he had. She couldn't fathom someone devoting an entire life to reading books. Her back got itchy if she sat too long in one place, and besides, nobody ever did anybody else any good by reading. It was much better to ride through the world doing good for those as needed it. Better money, too.

Cora glanced skyward through the window. A thick mat of cold, heavy clouds covered the peaks ahead. Old Man Winter was setting up for a tantrum, it seemed. She loathed the idea of hunting that wendigo creature in a blizzard. If Father Baez was right, the blizzard would only make it stronger. Still, when the special bullets arrived, she and Ben would hunt it, snow or no snow.

Leaning her head against the wall, she pulled her hat over her eyes. Best to rest up before reaching

Leadville. She closed her eyes and let the swaying of the car relax her, hoping she would be asleep by the time James Townsend returned to the cabin.

SEVEN

Mart Duggan's cold blue eyes bored into Cora as soon as she stepped off the train. "Where in the hell have you been?"

"Where I said we was going," Cora said, taking a step backward.

"Well, you should have been here doing what I'm paying you to do," the marshal replied.

"You ain't paid us nothing yet."

Duggan ignored the comment. "We had a run-in with that creature right here in town, and I lost me a good man to it."

"See now, didn't I tell you that, marshal? I said it would start eating up your townsfolk. It's called a wendigo, if you want to know."

"I don't give a damn what it's called." Duggan pointed his finger in her face. "What I want is to see it dead."

"All in good time," Cora said. "Thanks to our little trip, we've got the means to do exactly that. Should be arriving in a few days."

"A few days? What the hell are we supposed to do until then?"

"What I done told you to do," Cora said. "Get yourself some silver bullets and fire."

The marshal's fury waned a little. "You were right about that. I'll say that much."

Cora nodded. "Tell me what happened."

"Me and George Murray were settling a fight down at the Pioneer when we heard a scream from out in the street," Duggan said. "We ran outside to see this spindly-looking thing lurking about in the shadows. Somebody screamed again, and we saw it was a woman in the thing's hands. That scream was the last sound she ever made before the creature bit her head right off. The rest of her body was quick enough to follow it down that thing's gullet. Hell, we didn't even get a chance to fire before she was all ate up."

Duggan paused for a moment to gather his wits. The memory still unsettled him. Not even a grizzly could have killed the woman so quickly. This monster, this wendigo, was far more savage than he ever imagined any creature could be. He could still hear the woman's screams and see her blood on the creature's jaws as it devoured her whole. Those images had even worked their way into his dreams, and he was not a man given to nightmares.

He took a deep breath. "By that time, me and George was dug in by the saloon. George had his rifle handy, and I had my pistol. Between the two of us, we put enough holes in that thing to bring down half the Cheyenne nation, but we might as well have been pissing on it for all the good we did. Jack Evans even came up and helped out, but it still wasn't no good." The marshal paused again. "I've been a lawman for a good number of years now, but I ain't never seen such a thing. That bastard done swept up my deputies and made to eat them both when I recalled what you said about the fire. I humped it into the Pioneer and pulled out a handy pair of burning logs from the fire. By the time I got back out, George had already been ate and Jack was staring down its gullet. I waved the fire at it, and it made tracks right quick. Once it cleared out, Jack and I scouted out the rest of town, but it must have run on back to its cave."

Cora took a minute to ponder the news. "Well, marshal, I have to say I'm impressed. I never figured you for facing down the wendigo like that."

"Did what I had to," Duggan replied, surprised by the compliment. "Damn thing was fixing to eat my men, and you wasn't around to stop it."

"Won't say I'm sorry I wasn't," Cora said. "You routed it well enough, and what we learned in Denver was well worth the people that got ate."

Duggan's temper flared. "George Murray was a right fine deputy, little missie. I won't have you or anyone else say he wasn't."

"Never said no such thing," Cora said, holding up her hands. "All I said was that our trip to see Father Baez was worth his life. You see, while George was getting ate, we was learning how his killer could be killed."

"So it can die." The marshal's eyes lit up with vengeance. "What's the trick?"

"Well, seems this wendigo is an Indian monster."

"Indians?" Duggan asked. "There ain't been any Indian threat in these parts for years. They trying an uprising of some sort?"

Cora shook her head. "No, they didn't cause it or call it into being or nothing. They're just the ones who know what it is and how to lick it."

"Which Indians? The Utes?"

"No, some tribe back East. Father Baez had to send out a telegram to his friends in Boston, and they told him the whole story on the wendigo."

"So how can it be killed?"

"Well, as I said before, silver and fire are weak spots, but to put it to rest proper, the silver needs the blessing of an Indian shaman."

Duggan's shoulders slumped. "We ain't got one, and I can't imagine any of the local tribes would be too willing to loan us one."

"Don't you worry your head about that," Cora said. "The priest in Boston's agreed to settle the whole matter for us. He'll be sending out some silver bullets blessed by one of the tribes in the area."

"So all we have to do is shoot it with them and it'll die?"

"As I understand it, yes," she replied.

"Good," Duggan said, clapping her on the shoulder. "I trust you'll come calling when they arrive, then?"

"Don't see how we'll need your help, but I won't keep you in the dark."

The marshal nodded and left without another word. Cora watched him go, her arms tucked inside the sleeves of her buffalo-hide coat. Hearing how he'd managed to route the wendigo had surprised her. The marshal was made of tougher stuff than she'd thought, even after watching him stand down that group of miners. Drunken miners were easy enough to predict, but it took real guts to go up against a true creature of the night.

Feats like that always began out of desperation, either for yourself or someone else. Nobody in their right mind ever took a supernatural creature head on unless they knew what they were doing, and nobody ever knew that the first time around. It was a wonder anybody lived to tell such tales, but some people just had more luck.

"Ben!" she shouted, turning back toward the train. "Where you at? Let's get them bags and get back to our room!"

Cora sat on the cornshuck mattress and sighed. She was glad the same room was still available when they'd arrived back at the Northern Hotel. Staying in the same room in a city was a sort of tradition for them. It helped them feel more at home when they arrived at each place, and every new city they visited soon had a room they liked to call theirs.

Ben would apologize for it from time to time, saying he felt bad for not being able to provide a real house for his wife. She would always wave him off, saying she preferred the roaming lifestyle, anyway. Wandering from town to town, turning in local bounties, and moving on had seemed romantic, the sort of lifestyle most every woman they met grew to envy. She wasn't tied to children, a cooking stove, or a washboard. They were free to go where they pleased, sometimes sleeping under the summer stars for several nights in a row while on a hunt, sometimes bedding down for a month at a time in a city while investigating rumors and playing cards. Some folk called them heroes when they finished a job, even as they were collecting their pay from the local law. The life seemed to fit them like a well-tailored coat.

Or at least it had. As Cora sat on the bed, she could feel a dull ache in her feet and her fingers. Even a day of nothing but sitting in a train coach had left her slightly stiff. Getting up on a cold morning hurt more than it used to, and her draw wasn't as fast or as sharp as it was when they'd turned in their first bounty. Age. She'd felt it, fighting the wendigo in the mineshaft; the monster's chill had hurt her more than it should have.

She looked over at Ben, who was stretched out on the bed next to her reading a book. If time took its toll on him, he certainly never showed it. His brown mustache, a shade lighter than the hair on his head, showed no signs of graying, and his sky-blue eyes were still clear and bright. The pains of a long day of travel seemed to slide right off his back as they walked to the hotel from the station. Of course, that could have been because she'd carried the bags.

"You know, I sometimes wonder if we ought to retire soon," she said, leaning back against the headboard.

"Why's that?" Ben asked, looking up from his book.

"Seems to me we're about used up is all," Cora said. "Worn out like a pair of old pack mules. Somebody's bound to tie us to a tree and shoot us before too long."

"Not so long as we're useful, I reckon."

"But how long until we run out of useful? Take the situation here: we was nearly outdone by a fool of a marshal, and we had to go see a priest to even understand what it is we ought to be experts at fighting."

"Ain't nobody got to be an expert without learning something."

"But now they got experts that do nothing but sit around and study things like vampires." The meeting with James Townsend upset her more than she liked. She'd told Ben about the eccentric British scholar when he'd awoken from his nap, but he'd been unimpressed. Still, she didn't like that a man in a tweed suit could tell her things about vampires she'd never heard.

"Maybe so," Ben said, "but I'll be damned if that feller on the train could even stand in a vampire's shadow without pissing himself."

Cora chuckled at the image of James Townsend soiling his drawers. "Maybe not, but that ain't the point. Point is, we're coming up against things we ain't never heard of before. Used to be we could lick them right quick anyway, but I'm feeling slowed up lately. One of these days, I may not come back from a hunt at all."

"You ain't giving me much credit."

"Of course you'd be there to lend a hand," she said, giving him a playful shove. "But suppose we meet something else new in a week or a month, and nothing we shoot at it slows it down a whit? I mean, I reckon I was always aware of the risks, but I ain't never given them serious thought. Just kind of rode along and let come what may."

"Can't see a better way of doing what we do," Ben said.

"Ain't like I've thought of one, either," Cora said. "I'm just wondering what happens to us when we meet up with something we're too old or too dumb to whip."

"I expect we'll get our own whipping and head on to glory everlasting."

"You're awful casual about it."

"Ain't much I can do about it," Ben said, shrugging. "Either we whip it or it whips us, like any other time."

"But don't you think we should have a care to stay alive? If not for us, then for all the folks counting on us to keep them safe."

"Well, sure. Ain't no point in riding around looking for your death. You're bound to find it quick if you do that."

"Seems to me that the older we get, the closer we are to doing just that." Cora flexed her fingers. "Give it a few more years, and I won't be able to draw my gun without dropping it on my boots. A fine place to be when there's a wendigo or one of them new vampires fixing to make a meal of me."

"You sure they'd want to eat you? I don't reckon old woman tastes all that nice."

She shoved him again. "Some help you are."

Ben closed his book and set it on the bed. "I wouldn't

waste much thought on fretting about it. We're still spry enough to handle whatever the Devil sends, and when we can't draw our guns no more, why, we'll find ourselves some other means to make our way. This old world is stuffed full of things a pair of bodies can busy themselves with."

"Is that so?" Cora asked, raising an eyebrow. "Can't think of a single one myself."

"We could go back into my family business," Ben said. "Ain't too much work to print a newspaper. My pa could have kept that old shop running for twenty years or more if them bluecoats hadn't burned him out."

"A printer?" Cora's shoulders slumped. "I'd go plumb stir-crazy if I was trapped in a dark, smelly little room all day. My eyes would probably shrivel up and fall out from not seeing the sun."

"It ain't half as bad as all that," Ben said. "Why, once you're used to it, you barely even notice the dark."

"Any other ideas?" Cora asked.

"Maybe we can get a job with the railroad. Can't take much to sit in them engines all day."

"I suppose that's better than print work, but it still ain't my idea of living." Cora sighed and folded her arms. "I reckon I'll have to get used to it, though now the idea of getting killed by a monster is looking a sight better."

Ben put his arm around her shoulders. "Getting old ain't that bad."

"How do you know? You ain't aged a whit since we left Virginia."

"Ain't seen the need yet is all." He ran a hand along the shock of white running through her dark hair. "Besides, unlike you, aging won't make me any prettier."

Cora felt herself blush. "Oh, hush up, you big sweet-talker. You're just trying to make me all soft so I forget about all this and stop badgering you."

"I ain't, either," Ben said.

"Right, and I'm General Lee," she replied, kissing his cheek. "You keep on dripping molasses if you like, but I got me an itching for a game of cards. Age brings knowhow, at least, and I can still make them sprouts a sight poorer for it."

Ben smiled at her as he picked up his book. Cora smiled back, then rose to her feet with a groan. She lumbered down the stairs and out into the street. A soft gray light glowed from behind the thick mantle of clouds. Pulling her coat closed against the snowflakes drifting through the air, she made a new set of tracks in the fresh powder leading from the Northern Hotel down to the Pioneer.

The familiar aromas of the saloon greeted her as she pulled the door open. She blinked a few times, then took off her hat to shake off the snow. Surveying the room, she was disappointed to find only one promising table. She sighed, preparing to move over and claim a seat at it, when she saw Boots out of the corner of her eye.

"Howdy, Boots," she called. "I think you got something of mine."

The bartender turned toward her, his expression blank. "What might that be, Cora?"

"A full glass of rotgut, my good man," she replied, grinning. Boots didn't return the grin as he shuffled into the back room. Cora waved her hand in dismissal and made her way over to the card game. She dropped into an empty chair to a chorus of mumbled howdies from the other players.

"Cut me in, boys," she said.

An older miner with a full salt-and-pepper beard nodded. "Soon as we finish this hand."

Cora nodded and settled in to watch. It was a small game, only four players. The man who had spoken to her seemed to be the oldest as well as the dealer. Two younger men, their mustaches still thin and dark, sat on either side of him. The fourth player wore a well-trimmed, sandy-colored beard that he stroked as he looked at his cards. He spoke in a quiet voice when making bids, and he didn't join in the conversation with the other three. His sharp blue eyes flashed at Cora from beneath the brim of his hat.

The hand finished with the quiet man scooping his winnings into his pile. Cards flew around the table. Cora picked hers up and was trying to make sense of them when Boots appeared over her shoulder, drink in hand.

"Took you long enough," she said, taking the glass.

"My apologies, Cora," Boots said with a slight bow. He turned and marched back to the bar, the polish on his boots reflecting the flames in the big fireplace.

"Who jammed a boot up his ass?" Cora asked.

"He ain't been the same since the other night," the

dealer replied. "The attack has him all shook up, I reckon."

"Ain't nobody who ain't," one of the younger miners said.

"Hell, I ain't," the other replied.

"Then you're a damn fool," the blue-eyed stranger said, his eyes still on Cora. "I got a notion that Cora here ain't scared, though."

"How'd you know my name, stranger?" she asked, taking a gulp of whiskey.

"Heard the barkeep say it twice now," he said.

"Mind sharing yours, then?"

"Washington Jones is my proper name," the man replied. "Most around here call me Wash."

"What's your line of work, Mr Jones?"

"Rather dull compared to yours, I reckon," Wash said.

Cora gave him a hard look. "What do you mean by that?"

"Word travels fast out here." Wash tossed a few coins into the pot. "Most of these miners is too crusty to poke their heads up above ground long enough to hear rumors of the world outside, but I like to keep my ear to the ground, and she tells me you're a bounty hunter and a loon besides."

"I reckon I'm enough of both, but can't say neither is spot on," Cora said. "I'm in for ten."

The other men anted up. "So there ain't any truth to the tales of the Mad Madam?" Wash asked.

"Well," she said, unfazed by the nickname, "as I said, I'm a good sight crazier than some, but I ain't fit to be tied yet, neither."

"Hunting bounties ain't really a woman's work."

"Can't say that ever bothered me." She drained her glass and set it down with a thunk. "My ma always said I wasn't no proper lady. As for that Mad Madam bit, I ain't got no say in what folk take to calling me."

"They ain't exactly playing on your good points."

"Ain't too many good points to play on." She leaned forward and showed her hand: three queens. The others tossed their cards on the table as she swept the take into a pile of her own. She handed her cards to the old miner to shuffle and leaned back in her chair. "Speaking of points, I ain't following yours."

"Just pleased to meet a legend like yourself," Wash replied. "Some folk go their whole lives without cutting a deck with Cora the Mad."

"Lucky them," Cora said. She tilted her head back and shouted for Boots.

"Yes?" the bartender replied from behind the bar.

"I got some winnings that need spending," she said, holding up her empty glass. Boots nodded and walked over with a bottle in hand. Glass clinked against glass, and Cora leaned back with the whiskey burning her throat.

"You're an odd one yourself, Wash Jones," she said, peering at him over the top of her glass. "Ain't got much by way of manners, at least."

"I got a few to help me get by," Wash said, "but not so many as get in my way."

"Well, you might want to find one that stops you from asking strangers questions. Some of them might take offense."

"I ain't worried none about that. Why, I'm the one most folk should take care not to rile. I've ended more than a few as did in my day."

"A gunfighter, I take it?"

Wash nodded. "Some would say I'm a braggart."

"Well, I ain't one of them," Cora said, sliding two cards toward the dealer.

"Never said you was." Wash traded in three cards. "Of course, I reckon you have the same sort of troubles."

"How's that?"

"A lone gunfighter roaming the West with a reputation as big as yours."

Cora laughed. "Hell, I know Ben ain't much of a fighter, but it ain't fitting to leave him out of the legend all through. He's shot him up some bandits, too."

"If he don't make the tales, he ain't worth the fame," Wash said.

"You really is hurting for manners, ain't you?"

"Did I give offense?"

"Could be," Cora said, leaning forward. "Could be you're just lucky."

"How so?"

"Lucky shot, lucky stars." Cora shrugged. "Lucky Ben ain't here to put you in your place."

A small grin spread beneath the man's beard. "I don't suppose you'd care to take it up for him."

Cora blinked at him, then howled a laugh that startled the other players. Wash's grin soured. Behind the bar, Boots leaned on his elbows and watched her.

"So that's what this is about, is it?" Cora asked when

she regained her breath. "You're fixing for a fight and figured licking me would add to your own tale?"

"What if I am?" Wash asked, scowling at her from beneath his hat. "Ain't that always what happens when two legends meet?"

That earned him another good laugh. "I ain't sure about my own legend, Wash Jones," she said, "but I know I ain't never heard of you before. Ain't the two legends supposed to be legends before they have their showdown?"

The gunman's blue eyes burned with anger. "I'll lay you out right here for that!"

He jumped to his feet, his hand reaching for the pistol at his belt. Before the barrel could clear the holster, Cora placed her palms on the edge of the table and shoved. The table fell toward Jones, catching him just above the knees. Coins clattered to the floor as he toppled forward, his head slamming into the tabletop. The revolver fell from his hands as Cora jumped over the table. Before Wash Jones could pull himself together, she gave him a solid smack behind the ear with the butt of her Colt. He collapsed in a heap.

"Damn pups," Cora said, holstering her gun. The other players stared at her as she bent over and recovered a few coins from the mess on the floor. Walking over to Boots, she tossed them on the bar. "Here's for the mess, Boots."

"Thank you, Cora," the bartender replied.

"While you're at it, have yourself a drink," Cora said. "You look like you got a bear standing on your toes."

"A drink, yes," Boots said, favoring her with an odd

grin. Cora paid him no mind as she headed for the door with a wave to her fellow gamblers. Stepping out into the street, she breathed in the cold smell of falling snow, then turned her boots toward the marshal's station. Duggan needed to know that there was a new roughneck in town looking for trouble. If nothing else, sorting Wash Jones out would keep the lawman busy while she and Ben took care of the wendigo.

There was a slight bounce in her step as she walked to the station. Her bones might have protested the cold air, but she could still lick a young sprout when one needed licking. Maybe she and Ben had a few more years left in them before they had to start that print shop of his.

Wash Jones came to on the floor by the Pioneer's big fireplace, his head ringing from that woman's pistol butt. Groaning, he sat up and took stock of his surroundings. The saloon was still quiet, waiting for the evening flow of miners to bustle through the door. Boots stood behind the bar, diligently wiping it down with a cloth. Wash pulled his feet under him and stood up, gripping his forehead as it throbbed in protest.

"Tough day," Boots said without looking up.

Wash nodded, his eyes closed. He stood with his head down until he heard the sound of a glass being placed on the bar. Opening an eye, he watched Boots fill it with whiskey and nod at him. Wash smiled his thanks, walked over, and tossed it back.

"That Cora Oglesby made a fool of you."

The young gunman didn't appreciate the remark,

but his head hurt too much to teach the bartender a lesson. He could only nod again, fingering the empty glass. To his surprise, Boots refilled it. Wash shot him a questioning look.

"I can't imagine that sits very well with you, Mr Washington Jones."

"Ain't you a sharp one," Wash said.

"I pay attention." Boots leaned on the bar. "As it happens, I have an interest in her myself."

"What sort of interest?"

"An interest in seeing her dead."

Wash looked up at him in surprise. The bartender returned his gaze, eyes gleaming as a grin spread across his round face. "You see, she once made a fool of me as well. I've been looking for her for a long time so I might settle the score. Now I've found her at last, but I will need help in bringing her down. As you may have noticed, she is a formidable opponent."

Wash stared into his glass, not sure if the whiskey or the smack on the head was causing him to hear what he was hearing. He looked at the bartender again. The same gleam burned in that red face, regarding him with a sinister intelligence.

"You ain't just a bartender, are you?"

The grin widened. "Not anymore."

EIGHT

"Well, we wasn't expecting much, anyway."

Cora stood in the post office, a small box in her hands. The letter attached to it was from Father Davidson in Boston. Ben picked it up and read it aloud.

To Cora Oglesby,
Greetings in the name of our Holy Father and His Son Jesus Christ. I have enclosed with this letter twelve bullets blessed by the shaman of our local Indian tribe. I will send more if I am able. Until then, please take these weapons and use them to strike down the unholy abomination plaguing the town of Leadville. I will pray for your success.

Yours in Christ,
Father Abraham Davidson

"Only twelve?" Cora opened the box. A dozen points of light glimmered from their bed of crumpled newspaper. "That priest must want us to die."

"Maybe he just has a lot of faith in us," Ben said.

"A little too much, I reckon." She picked up one of the rounds and rolled it between her fingers. "Oh, hang it all. These are .45s."

"Are you sure?" Ben leaned over to look.

"Of course I'm sure," Cora said. "Shot them for years, didn't I?"

"You still got that old gun?"

"Sure, in a box in San Antonio. I left it back there when I got the new .38." She dropped the bullet back into the box. "You ain't got your .45 with you, do you?"

"Back in the room," Ben said.

Cora led the way back to the hotel room. Once inside, she knelt by the bed and pulled out their traveling trunk. After a few moments of rummaging, she finally found what she was searching for. A moan that was half disgust and half dismay rose from her lips as she picked up what the rust had left of Ben's revolver. Grimacing, she tried to pull the hammer back. It was locked in place. The cylinder refused to rotate.

She glared up at him. "Ain't you been oiling this regular?"

Ben looked sheepish. "Well, I thought I had been."

"You should go see the priest about this. Why, this is profane, treating a weapon of the Lord's work like this." She tossed the rusty Colt back in the trunk and stood up. "Well, now we're in a fix. We got a monster we can't kill unless we use bullets we can't shoot."

"Maybe the marshal could loan us one of his pistols," Ben said. "He's got plenty."

"If he doesn't, you're buying me a new gun," Cora said. "Let's go."

Cora stormed down the stairs and through the snowy streets. She burst through the door to the marshal's station, giving Deputy Victor Sanchez a fright. His pistol was nearly clear of his belt before he saw who it was and stopped himself.

"Ah, *señora*, you scared me," he said, sitting back down at the desk. A moment later, he jumped to his feet again when another bang echoed from down the hall.

"Sanchez, what the hell was that?" Mart Duggan stood in the doorway of his office.

"Just us, marshal," Cora said. "We got a favor to ask."

"What might that be?" Duggan asked.

"Well, we're in a bit of a fix. That priest from Boston sent us those special rounds like he said he would, but they're too big for my gun. Ben here don't keep his up, so we're looking to borrow a .45."

The marshal's eyes flicked over her shoulder. "Is that right? I thought you had a peacemaker same as me."

"Sure do, but it's a new one," she said, pulling her revolver from its holster. "This here's a .38. Easier to handle, though she don't pack as much of a punch."

Duggan walked over and took the gun from her. "Since when did Colt make lady guns?" he asked, turning it over in his hands.

"Since recently," Cora said. "I picked me up one to make my life easier. She don't kick like the .45, so aiming's easier. The size of the bullet ain't what kills what I shoot at, so I figured why not."

"Well, I'll be damned," the marshal said, handing the gun back to her.

"She's a lady, all right, but she can't handle what we need to shoot this time," Cora said.

The marshal placed a hand on the gun at his hip. "You sure your new bullets will whip this thing?"

"Ain't no guarantee, but they're better than what I got."

Duggan pulled the Colt from his holster and dumped the bullets out onto the deputy's desk. He snapped the cylinder back into place, twirled the gun in his fingers, and handed it to her, grip first. She took it from him and spun it once. "Funny how quick you forget their weight."

"I expect that gun back on my desk by tomorrow sunrise," the marshal said.

"With any luck, you'll have it, marshal," Cora said. "Even better, you'll have us on the next train out of here."

"All the better," Duggan said, turning back toward his office. Cora turned to leave as well when his voice stopped her. "Oh, by the way, that feller you mentioned the other day?"

"You mean Wash Jones?" she asked, turning back to him.

"That's the one." Duggan crossed his arms. "I stopped by the Pioneer this morning, and Boots told me Jones had already lit out of town."

"Is that right?" Cora asked with a snort. "Boots say where that sniveling little weasel was headed?"

Duggan shook his head. "Not a word about it," he said, tugging at his beard as he thought. "Boots seemed a mite touched his own self, though."

"How's that?"

"Kind of cold and mean," the marshal said.

"I heard tell he was shook up from the other night when the wendigo paid you all a visit."

"Could be." Duggan didn't sound convinced.

"Well, after tonight, he can sleep easy," Cora said, rotating the Colt's cylinder and grinning at the tiny clicks it made.

"You'll be heading up the mountain, then?"

"Maybe." Opening the door, Cora stuck her head outside and sniffed the air. "Maybe not," she said, turning back to the marshal. "Smells like another storm's brewing. If the path up to the cabin ain't snowed in yet, it will be soon. I'd rather not get stuck up there with nothing but a dead wendigo and my fool of a husband for company."

"He'll be riding with you?"

"Well, I reckon he's welcome to tag along," Cora said, throwing Ben a look. He grinned back at her. "Like I said, though, I think we'll be staying in town tonight. Wait for the spook to come to us."

Duggan's brow drew downward. "If it comes back here, it will kill people."

"Could be," Cora said, "but there's also more fire and less frost here. Father Baez said this thing was a creature of the cold, so I figure riding out into a snow-storm at night to face it by ourselves ain't the best way to lick it."

"By yourselves," Duggan repeated. "So you'll be wanting our help in town, then?"

"Don't fret about it," Cora said. "I just figured you

could tell the townsfolk to keep a bit of fire handy, just in case. Never hurts to be prepared."

"This town's scared enough as it is," Duggan said. "I don't want you bringing that thing back here."

"Well, we ain't riding out into the cold night to fight it," Cora replied. "We've only got the twelve bullets, and if we run out or it kills us, your townsfolk will be a sight worse off than just scared."

Duggan scowled at her, not wanting to give in to any more of her outrageous demands. His refusal was on the tip of his tongue when he reminded himself that she would be gone as soon as she killed the wendigo. Whatever helped her toward that end was worth it, he figured. After a moment, he nodded. "I trust you'll do your best to keep it from eating too many townsfolk."

"Well, of course," Cora said. "We're in the business of helping people, not getting them killed."

"Don't forget it," the marshal said.

Cora tossed her hands up and headed for the door with Ben at her heels. "Next time we help a town," Cora said as they walked back to the hotel, "let's find one where the local law ain't as ornery as the monsters we're killing."

Cora swayed atop Our Lady of Virginia as the mare plodded along the dark streets. Snowflakes drifted down from the black sky to settle in Our Lady's mane. The horse seemed indifferent to the nighttime excursion, but the hunter's eyes were alert, peering into every shadow as they rode. Her right hand clutched the marshal's big Colt, the hammer at rest for the moment. The revolver's cylinder held six of the blessed bullets from Father Davidson, and the other six were tucked into her ammo belt.

Ben rode beside her in silence. He'd wanted to bring a torch along, but she'd insisted that the flames would ruin her ability to see in the dark, so he'd settled for her Winchester. The rifle sat in the crook of his arm, the magazine filled with the Catholic-blessed silver rounds. Cora had thought to bring it along as a backup if she needed to reload her revolver during the fight.

Around them, the town of Leadville slept restlessly. From time to time, Cora saw a curtain draw back and a worried face peer out into the darkness. Mart Duggan had his deputies spread the word throughout the town that citizens should keep a torch or firebrand within easy reach. News of the wendigo's attack had already been whispered on every doorstep and in every room, making the people eager to follow the marshal's advice. If she and Ben failed to bring it down, at least it wouldn't find many easy meals tonight.

Of course, there was no promise that the creature would even make an appearance. It had been nearly a week since its last attack. She figured that would be enough time for it to work through the scare Duggan had given it and come out on a hunt, but she could have been wrong. If she was, they'd have no choice but to head back up to Bartlett's mine to root it out. Cora groaned inwardly at the thought.

As they passed the Purdy brothel, Cora noticed a figure seated on the hitching rail, his back against the wall. A torch mounted above him cast his face in shadow. Curious, she nudged Our Lady over toward him.

"Evening, Mrs Oglesby." It was Jack Evans.

"Evening, deputy," Cora said. "Enjoying the weather?"

The shadow shook its head. "No, ma'am. I'm standing watch."

"On the marshal's orders?"

Jack shook his head again. "No, the marshal done told us to patrol on horseback with torches."

"So why ain't you on horseback with a torch?" she asked.

"He's got enough men doing that, but ain't nobody protecting the Purdy till I come," Jack said.

Cora grinned. "So you're holding the line for the whores."

"Yes, ma'am. Way I figure, they ain't set to look after themselves, so somebody's got to do for them."

"Maybe so," Cora said, leaning over the saddle horn. "Or maybe you're sweet on a whore yourself and are looking to make an impression."

She couldn't see his face, but she knew he was blushing. "Well, what if I am?" he asked.

"Then you'll get your heart broke," Cora said, "but that ain't my business." She tapped her heels into Our Lady. The mare shook her head and plodded back into the street. Behind her, Cora could hear Jack Evans muttering to himself.

After a short distance, she turned a grin on Ben. "I reckon I upset him."

"The boy's a fool if he thinks he can win over a whore," Ben said.

They rode in silence for awhile. Occasionally, one of Duggan's deputies would ride by with a torch held high. Each would call out to them as they rode past, and Cora returned each greeting with a silent wave.

After over an hour, Cora pulled back on Our Lady's reins outside the Northern Hotel. The mare came to a halt as another deputy rode past, his torch throwing orange shadows along the street.

"If that thing don't show, it's the fault of them pudding-headed deputies," Cora said. "Ain't they ever laid a trap before?"

"Maybe Duggan is trying to drive it away, make us chase it down."

"It takes a fool to lead more fools, I guess," Cora said. She watched the snowflakes fall in silence for a minute. "Why don't you get back upstairs and sleep for a spell?"

Ben's brow furrowed. "Why?"

"To keep fresh," Cora said. "I'll stay out for another hour or so, then come fetch you so you can take a turn at it."

"What if it shows while I'm asleep?"

"Then I'll whip it." Cora pulled the Winchester from the crook of his arm and slid it into Our Lady's saddle scabbard. "Go on, now."

"I don't like leaving you out here by yourself," Ben said, setting his jaw.

"The longer you fret about it, the less sleep you'll get," Cora said. "No need for both of us to wear out at the same time. Now, if the wendigo shows, I'll run fetch Duggan's boys right quick and send one of them to rouse you."

Ben sighed through his nose. "You got the extra rounds from Father Davidson?" he asked.

"Right here," Cora said, patting her ammo belt with a gloved hand.

"All right, then," he said, swinging himself off his horse. He tied the reins loosely so he could ride again at a moment's notice. "You come fetch me if you're close by when it shows."

"You hear me start shooting, you come running," Cora said. She reached down inside her boot, produced a small silver knife, and tossed it to him. "Sleep with that on the stand. If it happens to come in through the window while I'm away, that ought to slow it down enough for you to light out."

He nodded, sliding the knife into his belt. "God be with you, then."

"And with you." She watched him go, then took a deep breath of cold air and blew it out over Our Lady's ears. She slapped the reins across the mare's neck, rode back into the street, and resumed her patrol.

Snow gathered on her gloves and the horse's mane as she circled through the streets. The torch-bearing deputies became fewer and fewer as the night wore on, and lights began to wink out in the windows. Soon, the town of Leadville slipped into a deeper sleep, leaving her alone with the cold and the night. Only Jack Evans remained at his post by the brothel's front door, his chin on his chest, snoring softly.

Finally, Cora judged a good hour had passed and turned Our Lady's head toward the Northern Hotel. Her fingers were stiff and cold inside her gloves. She holstered Duggan's gun and rubbed her hands together as Our Lady crunched along the street. Time for Ben to come back out into the cold for awhile. There were only a few hours before dawn, anyway, so he could patrol until then. If the damn thing still didn't show, they'd have no choice but to hunt it at the old Bartlett place. She muttered a curse as she rode through the snowflakes, promising the wendigo a few hours of suffering to make up for hers.

Light streamed through the windows at the marshal's station as she rode by. At least Duggan was still awake. She considered stopping by for an update, then decided against it. The marshal wouldn't be pleased to see her, and the feeling would be mutual enough. Better to wait until morning.

She was about to ride on when a small movement on the station's roof caught her eye. Squinting away the glow from the windows, she peered into the shadows above the building's false front. Something up there didn't look right. She drew the big Colt from its holster and nudged Our Lady's head around.

There, just behind the upward curve of the shiplap wall. She thought she could make out a head peering down toward the station's upper windows. Her eyes stole to the base of the station. The building butted up right next to its neighbor, a general store, leaving no alley where she might take cover. Cursing silently, she remained where she was, praying that Our Lady wouldn't snort or do anything to make their presence known.

The shadow remained where it was, the dark knob of the creature's head twisting slightly. After a few minutes, a long, sinewy arm flowed into the dim light of the street. Cora could see the black tips on the fingers as they probed the front of the station, finding purchase on the outer sill of an upper window. The second arm followed, its fingers coming to rest on the porch roof. Gray skin glimmered in the pale light as the wendigo lowered itself toward the window like a giant, misshapen spider.

The monster paused in front of the window. Cora could make out the thin locks of hair still clinging to its scalp as she leveled her revolver. Scarcely daring to breathe, she pulled the hammer back. The wendigo's attention remained on the window, searching the interior of the station, oblivious to her presence, and she allowed herself a small smile. All kills should be this easy.

At that moment, the door to the station burst open. The noise made her jump, and her finger squeezed the trigger. The shot went wide, slamming into the wall near the creature's torso as the Colt's thunder rolled through the silent streets. The wendigo's head snapped up, and its yellow eyes gleamed at her. A wailing moan escaped its black lips.

"Goddammit, Sanchez!" Cora yelled. The deputy stood in the doorway, torch in hand, looking startled by the gunshot and her curse. Cora punched her heels into Our Lady's sides, spurring her into a sudden gallop as the dark shape leapt toward her. It crashed into the snow where she had been a moment ago. Looking over her shoulder, she could see the frostbitten fingers clawing at the snow as the wendigo righted itself and gave chase. She couldn't hope to hit it firing backward from the back of a galloping horse. Turning back around, she gave Our Lady another punch with her heels. The terrified mare pounded down the street, snow flying in chunks from beneath her hooves.

A row of buildings loomed ahead of them, marking a street corner. Cora cursed, knowing they would have to slow down to make the turn. Stealing another glance over her shoulder, she realized they wouldn't make it that far. The wendigo was closing the distance. Keeping her eyes on the approaching monster, Cora clenched the Colt in her hand and thumbed the hammer back. It would be on them in a matter of seconds, and she might only get one shot. She prayed she would be fast enough. Her hands and feet throbbed from the cold.

A shout echoed ahead of her. Turning her face into the stinging wind, she could see another rider charging toward them, a torch blazing in his hand. One of the marshal's deputies. Her heart lifted at the sight, and she glanced backward again. She could see the wendigo's teeth clacking together in savage hunger beneath those demonic eyes. Holding her breath, she bent down, bringing her face close to Our Lady's lathered neck. The oncoming rider swept past them, the torch passing just above her head as he swung it toward the monster's face. The wendigo let out a hiss and veered away from the flames. Cora turned her head as she sat upright in the saddle. The dark, spindly shadow was circling back toward the deputy. She pulled on the reins, slowing Our Lady as quickly as she dared. The mare kept her footing on the snow-packed road, rearing her head as Cora turned her back toward the monster.

The wendigo circled the rider, lashing out at the torch with long arms. The deputy kept his saddle, fighting both monster and mount as his horse stamped in terror beneath him. A smaller flame flashed from the pistol in his other hand, the gunshots echoing down the street.

Laying a hand on Our Lady's neck, Cora urged her into a trot. It wouldn't be long before the creature managed to knock the torch from the lawman's grip, but she was too far away to have a clean pistol shot. Our Lady fought against her reins, trying to turn away from the scene before them, but Cora guided her forward with a firm hand. The gunshots from the deputy fell silent.

Then, just as the hunter and her mount rode into range, black fingers struck the deputy's upheld hand, and the torch flew out of his grasp. It sailed end-over-end through the falling snow before landing in a nearby drift. The wendigo wailed in anger and lunged at the lawman, knocking him to the ground. Cora heard a terrified shout from beneath the sinewy body as man and monster wrestled. She brought Our Lady to a halt and raised the revolver. The man's cries rang in her ears, but she pushed them away. If she missed, those cries would be his last.

The Colt leapt in her hands. A piercing shriek filled
the air as emaciated limbs recoiled in pain. The monster wheeled around to face her, eyes blazing. Cora
pulled back the hammer and fired again. The sacred
bullet missed its mark as the wendigo leapt at her in
a blind fury, mouth open, fingers grasping. Her third
shot caught it in the shoulder, but the impact wasn't
enough to stop it from crashing into her. Our Lady of
Virginia screamed in terror as they fell beneath the
monster's weight.

Cora managed to get her boots clear of the stirrups
before the mare went down. Our Lady let out another
whinnying cry, righted herself, and bolted into the
night. Coming to rest with her boots beneath her, Cora
realized her hands were empty. The wound in the
wendigo's shoulder belched a thick grey smoke into
the winter air. It struggled to get the wounded arm beneath it, to put weight on it and attack her again, but
the limb seemed useless. Air hissed between its teeth
as it floundered in the snow.

Taking advantage of the monster's pain and confusion, Cora searched frantically for her fallen revolver.
Snow flew in her face from the wendigo's flailing
limbs. She ducked under the sweep of a twisted arm,
then jumped over a kicking leg. As she landed on her
hands and knees, her fingers felt the butt of her Winchester. It must have fallen out of the saddle scabbard
before Our Lady of Virginia ran off. Cora picked up
the rifle and turned toward the wounded monster.
The gunshots drowned out the eerie wailing pouring
from the blackened lips. She pumped round after

round into the living corpse, emptying her magazine. Once the rifle started clicking, she flipped it around, gripping the barrel in her gloved hands. She waited until the wendigo's yellow eyes turned toward her again, then swung with all her might.

She heard the crunching of bone as the stock buried itself in the blackness where Jules Bartlett's nose had been. The wendigo jerked its head backward, wrenching the Winchester's barrel from her hands. Rising to its full height, the creature gripped the rifle with its good hand and pulled. After a few seconds, the wooden stock slid out of its face with the sound of grating bone. It tossed the rifle aside with a hiss of hatred, then dropped down onto its good arm. The wicked head lowered as it swept its yellow gaze across the snowy street, searching for the troublesome woman.

The demon eyes came face-to-face with the big Colt.

Cora squeezed the trigger. The revolver bucked in her hands as the consecrated bullet struck the wendigo just above the left eye and burrowed deep into the undead skull. Its wail sent gooseflesh rolling up her arms as it pitched backward, grotesque limbs flailing. Cora pulled the Colt's hammer back and circled around the fallen monster until she could see its face again. The evil eyes were pale, fading to the color of ash, but they still saw her. A faint hiss bubbled from between its teeth. The wound in its forehead trailed smoke like a dying fire.

Cora raised the pistol and fired again. When the smoke cleared, the great beast was silent.

Holstering the revolver, Cora took a deep breath. The wendigo lay dead at her feet, snowflakes gathering in the gray wisps of its hair and beard. Her saber rang faintly in the stillness. Gripping the hilt in both hands, she brought the blade down on its neck. There was no splashing of blood as the sword cut through the mottled flesh and frozen bones.

Firelight flickered over the pale corpse. Looking up, Cora saw Marshal Duggan and Deputy Sanchez approaching on foot. Sanchez still had his torch, and the marshal held a rifle at the ready. She waved them over. Together, the three of them looked down at the lifeless head, its face still locked in a black-lipped snarl.

"So it's dead?" Duggan asked.

"I do believe," Cora said, poking at its cheek with the toe of her boot. Smoke still seeped from the holes in its forehead. "If it ain't, you'll need these." Cora pulled the remaining six rounds from her belt and held them out.

Duggan passed his rifle to Sanchez and cupped his hand as she poured the silver bullets into it. He rolled them around on his palm, watching them shimmer in the torchlight. "That's it, then?"

"Well, aside from the matter of our payment, yes," Cora said. She swung the Colt's cylinder open and dumped out the spent shells. They bounced off the wendigo's ribs in a series of clinks. She gave the revolver one more spin and handed it to the marshal.

"I reckon my riding the torch into this thing's face warrants us a discount," Duggan said.

"That was you, was it?" Cora asked. "Wish I'd known. I wouldn't have been so careful with my aim."

The marshal ignored the comment. "You looking to settle right this minute?"

"No, I reckon I've earned a little shut-eye," she said, stretching her arms toward the sky. "You could probably do with some yourself. How does tomorrow afternoon strike you?"

Duggan nodded and slid the empty revolver into his belt. Still holding the silver bullets in his hand, he took the rifle back from Sanchez. Together, they turned toward the station. Cora watched them go for a moment, then crouched down and looked into the wendigo's lifeless eyes. Now empty of the demon animating it, the face looked like any other frozen corpse. Were it not for the grotesque limbs, anyone would have mistaken it for the body of an old miner who froze to death on a mountainside. And they wouldn't be wrong.

Cora stood up and looked back at the two lawmen. "Hey!" she called out. They paused at the station door and turned back to her. "You should probably burn this thing before folks start waking up." Without waiting for a reply, she recovered her Winchester from the drift where the wendigo had thrown it and set off for the Northern Hotel.

After a short walk, she rounded a corner and came into view of the hotel. Ben's horse still stood tied to the hitching rail, snow covering its mane. The sight of the nameless creature made her realize that she was on foot. Cursing, she stopped in her tracks. Snow layered the brim of her hat as she debated with herself. She could almost feel the warmth of the big fire in the hotel's lobby and the bed in their room. Her bones ached from the cold, and she longed to warm them in a hot bath, but her horse was wandering through the cold streets somewhere, just waiting to be stolen.

Her sigh filled the air in front of her in a swirling cloud. She turned on her heel and started back the way she had come. A few lights gleamed in windows above her head, illuminating the shadows of worried citizens as they peered out into the night. They could all rest easy now. Tomorrow afternoon, she and Ben would board an eastbound train, stop by to thank Father Baez in Denver, and go wherever the mood took them. She clenched her aching hands into fists. After this, she figured the mood would call for someplace warm.

Lost in her thoughts, she rounded the corner and ran into something. Startled, she looked up. There stood Our Lady of Virginia, blowing steam from her nose. The mare seemed as startled as her owner. Cora grinned and took the reins in her gloved hand.

"Glad to see you came around," she said, leading her back toward the hotel. Our Lady tossed her head in reply. "Yeah, I know it's cold out. But, since you was such a good girl coming back, I reckon I'll bed you down myself tonight."

The mare didn't reply. They walked in silence through the falling snow until they reached the hotel. Cora untied Ben's horse from the hitching rail. The animal looked at her with sad eyes, cold and dejected.

"I know, boy," she said, patting his neck. "We wasn't expecting you to stand all by your lonesome for so long."

Keeping his reins in one hand, Cora climbed into Our Lady's saddle. Gently slapping the rawhide strips over the mare's neck, she started for the stable. Ben's horse, used to following Our Lady's lead, came without a fuss, his head down.

"You know, we ought to give you a name," she said, looking back at the gelding. "Ben's too damn finicky about it. Been almost six months since we bought you, and he ain't settled on nothing yet. Course, you know that already." The horse didn't interrupt, so she went on. "You know, I think I'll call you Book. Maybe then he'll pay you more attention. And, if he don't like it, maybe he'll pick one he does fancy." She nodded to herself, and the matter was settled.

After bedding the horses down, she pulled the stable door closed and made her way back to the main building. As she walked, fatigue began settling on her shoulders like the falling snow. Her joints ached, making each step painful. Were it not for the cold, the ache would have been pleasant, a fitting reward for the end of a hunt. Tradition dictated that she and Ben share a bottle of whiskey and talk about the kill. Things they did right, things they did wrong, what they should remember for the future. It was their way of settling the matter in their minds.

Tonight, however, she didn't figure it was worth it. Ben was probably sound asleep, and the nearest saloon felt half a world away. There would be plenty of time for drinking and talking on the train.

Warm air smothered her cold limbs as she pulled the hotel door open and thumped up the stairs. She softened her step in the hallway, then eased open the door to their room. The hinges creaked as she slipped through into the darkness. She shrugged off her coat and tossed it into the shadows, followed by her hat. Her groping hand found a bedpost, and the cornshuck mattress rustled as she sat down.

Breathing a sigh of contentment, she began wrestling with her boots. Her cold feet burned in protest as she pulled them out. The smell hit her like a wall, and she covered her nose with one arm as she set the boots on the floor. She rolled onto the mattress, shoving her feet under the sheets. As soon as her head landed on the pillow, the bed seemed to grip her with invisible hands. She could feel her muscles twitching with each heartbeat, her blood carrying away the cold and the tension. Her fatigue was even great enough to forgo the need for a nightcap from the bottle she kept under the pillow. Instead, she let Ben's even breathing guide her into a deep, dreamless sleep.

NINE

It was well past noon when Cora opened her eyes. Sunlight glowed behind the window curtains, filling the room with a warm light. From outside, she could hear the sounds of horses and wagons rumbling through the street. Ben was already awake and planted in a chair by the window, reading. Cora blinked a few times to clear away the blur from her eyes, then lifted herself into a sitting position.

Ben looked up. "How was it last night?"

"Just dandy," she said, her voice thick from sleep.

"Did the wendigo ever show his face?"

"Yessir," she replied, nodding. "Got that face all shot up, too."

"So you licked it?"

Cora nodded again and recounted the previous night's events for him. As she spoke, she could feel the deep ache in her muscles that she knew would be there. Today's train ride would be uncomfortable. Ben listened intently as she told him about the final fight with the wendigo and how it took a full six shots to bring it down, even with the special bullets.

"Well, I missed twice," she said, "so it was really only four shots."

"Still," Ben said, "that was one tough critter. Tougher than the ones we usually sort out, anyway."

"We'll have to ask Father Baez to send a nice note out to Father Davidson for us. Or maybe you could write him one."

Ben's face lit up. He loved any excuse to put his vocabulary and penmanship to use. "I think I'll do just that."

"While you do that, I think I'll have myself a bath." Cora swung her legs over the side of the bed and stood up. "By the way," she said, "I named that horse of yours for you."

"You did?" Ben looked concerned. "What did you name it?"

"Book," she said, then unlocked the door and stepped out into the hallway.

Her muscles creaked as she made her way toward the community bathing room. Poking her head in, she was pleased to see it was empty. The hotel's bell-hop had placed a kettle of water next to the stove that stood against the far wall. The fire in the stove burned low, so she added a few pieces of kindling before placing the kettle on top. She grabbed two more kettles in fingers that ached with every movement, made her way down to the kitchen, and filled them from the pump that stood next to the big Dutch oven.

Soon, she was reclining in the tub, everything but

her head, elbows, and knees submerged. Little wisps of steam rose from the water's surface, fading into the air like ghosts at the coming of dawn. Outside, she could still hear the muffled sounds of an ordinary day, and she smiled. Those people could continue about their ordinary days and nights free of the wendigo's terror. Mart Duggan could collar his rowdies, Jack Evans could court his whore, and Boots could serve his whiskey.

The thought of Boots made her smile widen. She'd have to stop by the Pioneer before they left town and inform the bartender of her victory so he could go back to being his jolly old self. Seeing men tense up with fear wasn't anything new for her, but it rarely happened to the local whiskey slingers. Such men were usually the ones who kept brave faces on while a town's citizens were vanishing or being eaten by some spook.

Maybe Boots just had a sensitive spirit, too sensitive for that kind of carnage. She'd pegged him as an Army deserter when they first met. She and Ben were on the first Jules Bartlett case then, and word had already spread through the town that a vampire was loose in the woods. The Pioneer was the new watering hole in the growing boom town, and she'd stopped by to wet her whistle. Boots had greeted her warmly despite the general gloom, and his mood had only improved when she ordered from his private stock. The thought of a vampire didn't seem to bother him then, but nobody had been eaten alive outside of his saloon that time, either.

The bath water began growing cold. Reluctantly, Cora roused herself from the tub. She wrapped a rough linen towel around herself, gathered her discarded clothing, and made her way back to the room. Ben hadn't moved from his seat. He glanced up as she entered, and she could feel his eyes lingering on her as she shut the door and knelt beside the bed and pulled out her trunk. She indulged him a little, taking her time as she removed the towel and pulled on her traveling clothes. He watched her all the while, only returning to his book after she fastened her belt.

Cora sat on the bed as she rummaged through her trunk, keeping her head down so he wouldn't see her flushed face. Ben's attentions, silent though they were, always made her feel beautiful. She knew she wasn't. She had looked into a mirror enough times in her life to know that. Her face was too thin, her teeth crooked, and her hair stringy. As a young woman, she would often stare at the pretty girls in town, sick with envy. She'd wanted nothing more than to be a proper Southern belle for a while, even if her family had been far too poor to afford fancy dresses and bonnets. It seemed cruel that the good Lord hadn't even blessed her with a pretty face.

When Ben looked at her that way, though, she felt different. His gaze was intense, almost reverent. She'd seen that look on his face when he watched a desert sunset or read a poem he was fond of. It had been reflected in mountain lakes and stained-glass windows. When he turned it on her, she felt as beautiful and majestic as any of them.

Everything was accounted for in their trunk except one thing. "You still got that knife on you?"

"Right there," Ben said, pointing to the bedside stand.

She picked it up and pulled it out of its sheath. The silver blade shimmered in the faint light. Grinning, she walked over to Ben and knelt in front of him. "You want to do the honors?"

Ben's blue eyes darkened. "You know I don't like that."

"Fine," Cora said. She ran her fingers along the scars on her left cheek, searching for the last one. When she felt it, she raised the knife to her flesh and pressed. The sting made her eyes water, but she drew the point of the blade down her cheek, carving a shallow gash.

Pulling the knife away, she showed her cheek to Ben. "How's that?"

"Fine," Ben said, not looking up.

"You ain't looking," Cora said, poking him. "How many we got now?"

Ben sighed and looked at her bleeding cheek. "With the new one, we got twelve."

"Only twelve?" Cora said, shaking her head. "Seems like we've run twice that many spook jobs since we started this business." She clapped him on the shoulder. "Let's go settle up with the marshal."

Outside, the day was warm and bright. They pulled their hats low to ward off the glare from the snow and walked to the marshal's station in silence.

Ben paused outside the door. "I reckon I should check the times at the train station."

"Go on, then," Cora said, waving her hand. "I'll take care of our tab."

She pulled open the station door and stepped inside. Jack Evans sat behind the deputy's desk. "Howdy, Mrs Oglesby."

"Howdy, Jack."

"The marshal told me about last night," the deputy said. "That must have been quite a sight."

"Sure was ugly as hell," Cora said.

"But you killed it!" Jack said. "You shot it square in the head."

"Seemed like the best place to shoot it." Cora shifted her weight toward the marshal's office. "Is Duggan about?"

"Sure is," Jack said. He hollered for the marshal, who emerged a few moments later.

"Afternoon, marshal," Cora said, tipping her hat.

"Mrs Oglesby," Duggan replied.

"You got our money?"

Duggan nodded, motioning for her to follow him. Once inside his office, he closed the door and sat behind his desk. "Please, take a seat," he said.

Cora remained standing. "Ain't got time for chat, marshal. Our train pulls out soon, and I still got to swing by and see Boots."

"All right, then," Duggan said, his courtesy spent. He pulled open a drawer and produced a small wad of bills. "Five hundred dollars."

Cora picked up the money, surprised. "Mighty generous of you."

"After last night, I figured it was worth it," Duggan

said. He pulled up his sleeve and showed her his fore-arm. Dark bruises in the shape of long fingers colored his fair skin. "That thing had me pinned and would have ate me if you hadn't drawn it off."

"Just doing my job, marshal."

Duggan nodded. "Maybe so, but I never forget a man who saves my life. Or a woman."

"Glad to be of service, then," Cora said, extending her hand. The marshal rose to his feet and shook it. "Maybe you'll repay the favor one day." She tipped her hat and let herself out of the office. As she passed Jack, she shot him a grin. "Good luck with that whore of yours, deputy."

Jack blushed, pulling his hat down over his face. She chuckled to herself as she stepped out into the street. Her boots had turned toward the Pioneer when Ben's voice stopped her.

"Ain't got time for that."

She turned toward him. "Train's about to leave?"

Ben nodded. Cora looked toward the saloon with a sigh. "They better have whiskey on board, then." She picked up the trunk. "Let's fetch the horses."

Fifteen minutes later, they stood on the station plat-form. Their horses were already dozing in a livestock car, none the worse for the previous night. Ben exam-ined their tickets, then walked down the length of the train, looking for their car. When he found it, he waved her over. She hoisted the trunk with a grunt and started toward him.

"You! Cora Oglesby! Wait a moment!"

The voice came from behind her. Even before

she turned around, she knew who was hollering for her.

"Well, if it ain't King George himself."

There stood James Townsend, looking winded in his tweed jacket and tie. After taking a few moments to catch his breath, he stood upright and adjusted his glasses. "Might I request a moment of your time?"

"We're a bit tight on time," Cora said. "Train's about to leave."

"Exactly the reason for my rush," James replied. "I have a business proposition for you."

"Is that right?" Cora set down the trunk so she could fold her arms. "Well, we just settled with the marshal, so I think we're set for awhile."

James mimicked her posture, his elbows resting on his belly. "Don't misunderstand me, Mrs Oglesby. Had I a choice in the matter, I would gladly let you board that train for parts unknown. I am, however, here at the behest of Lord Harcourt."

"Your boss, huh? What's he want with us?"

"Well," James said, lowering his voice, "I'm afraid there's been something of an incident inside Lord Harcourt's primary mining interest." He adjusted his glasses and peered at her. "I have reason to believe that a nest of *vrykolakas* may have taken up residence there."

"Vampires?" Cora asked. "Ain't they your specialty?"

"Precisely so," James said, looking indignant. "However, this infestation is rather extensive, and Lord Harcourt believes it would be prudent to seek outside assistance."

Cora burst out laughing.

"I hardly find this amusing," James said. "My lord's mining investment is in grave danger. We've already lost at least a dozen workers to these monsters, and the rest of his miners are refusing to return to work for fear of being killed or turned. Unless we take action, and quickly, the vampires will overrun the entire mining complex."

"Quite a fix," Cora said, "but I don't see how it's any of our concern. We ain't in the business of saving silver mines."

"Well, there is the matter of Lord Harcourt's generous offer. In addition, it is highly likely the vampires will continue multiplying until the entire town is overrun and destroyed."

Cora sighed. "What's the offer?"

"Lord Harcourt insisted on negotiating with you personally," James said. "He's waiting at his manor north of town."

"I thought you said he was still in England. Don't want to get his coat dusty or some such, right?"

James looked down for a moment. "Yes, well," he said, "he doesn't wish for the knowledge of this misfortune to become public. I'm not at liberty to discuss his doings with strangers."

"You just told me about the vampires."

"Lord Harcourt heard of your exploits with the monstrosity last night. He's quite intrigued by your ability to contain and eliminate supernatural threats."

Cora could feel Ben staring at her back from the train car and sense his impatience. They'd already bought their tickets, their horses were already on board, everything was set to go. Ben hated the cold as much as she did, and they had enough money to spend a few months in San Antonio drinking and gambling before they took on another job.

But the uptight Englishman standing in front of her had an even bigger deal for them. Smoking out a nest of vampires was easy work, and this Lord Harcourt would probably reward them handsomely. Maybe enough to start Ben's print shop when they finally grew too old to smoke out vampires. What was a few more weeks of cold compared to a large sum and a future like that?

"Ben," she called, turning to look at her distraught husband, "get over here."

Ben walked up to her. "What is it?"

"Well," Cora said, nodding at Townsend, "this man here has another job for us."

TEN

The butler graced them with a low bow. Cora grabbed
a handful of her buffalo-hide coat in either hand and
responded with a curtsy. She straightened out of it before he came back up, her hands clasped demurely in
front of her.

"Please, come in," he said, standing to one side and
waving his hand.

James Townsend led the way into the front hall of
Lord Harcourt's private retreat. Cora followed him,
and Ben brought up the rear. The butler closed the
door behind them, shutting out the cold mountain air,
then turned to them with a polite smile.

Cora didn't see it. Her gaze was sweeping around
the hall, taking in the overwhelming if not unexpected opulence. The ceiling sloped upward above
them in graceful arches of richly stained wood. To
the right of the front landing, a carpeted staircase
ascended along one wall, bordered by a carved rail-
ing. Paintings of garden parties and old men in fine
suits dotted the walls. Above their heads, candles

winked down at them from behind clusters of star-cut glass.

"If you'll follow me, please," the butler said, passing through the group to take the lead. His shoes made no sound on the thick carpet. As they walked, Cora became acutely aware of her buckskin pants and worn flannel shirt. Most of their jobs came from men as rustic as they were, so she never felt the need to dandy herself up. She didn't even own a dress anymore. However, judging from the look of this place, Lord Harcourt wouldn't be overly impressed with her riding boots and hand-stitched gloves.

The butler opened a set of brass-knobbed doors and ushered them into a large sitting room. A small fire popped in a marble fireplace as they entered. In the flickering shadows, Cora could see rows upon rows of books lining the room, gold titles glimmering. Windows bordered by heavy red curtains peered out into the winter night. Two high-backed chairs faced the fire, casting long shadows across the carpet. Flanked by a number of smaller glasses, a bottle filled with a dark liquid stood ready on a small table between the chairs.

Ben immediately lost himself in the books on the nearest shelf, his fingers hovering near their spines. Cora rolled her eyes, then noticed that the butler had vanished. She looked around the room, hoping he would reappear with a glass of whiskey.

James kept his back straight as a rod as he walked over to the fire and began to warm his hands. "Lord Harcourt will be with us shortly. Please, make yourselves comfortable."

"I ain't sure about that," Cora said, advancing into the room. "I ain't never comfortable in a place where my boots don't make noise." She stamped her feet several times to illustrate.

"Hardly a reason not to enjoy yourself," said a voice from the corner of the room. Cora spun toward it, drawing her pistol. A tall figure in a well-tailored suit emerged from the shadows, a brandy snifter in his hand. "Mrs Cora Oglesby, I presume."

"My lord," James said, bowing his head. "I didn't hear you come in."

"I was here before you arrived, Mr Townsend," Lord Harcourt replied. "Now, if you don't mind, I believe I was introducing myself to the lady."

"Of course," James said, bowing again. "My apologies, my lord."

"Accepted," Lord Harcourt said. "Now then, my lady?"

"You presume right," Cora said, holstering her gun. The exchange between the two Englishmen was already boring her. "I'm Cora Oglesby." She looked for her husband, but Ben had already disappeared into the shadows. "My husband's taken a fancy to your books here. You'll meet him once he's done drooling."

Lord Harcourt offered a slight bow. "I am Lord Alberick Harcourt." He took her gloved hand in his and brought it up to his mouth.

"A pleasure," Cora said, retrieving her hand. "I hear you've got yourself a slight problem."

"Straight to business, I see," Harcourt said. "I believe James has informed you of the basic situation."

"I have, my lord," James said. "Cora has agreed to assist us with the matter."

"I said I'd hear you out," Cora said, shooting James a look.

"More couldn't be expected at this juncture," Harcourt said. "Might I offer you a glass of brandy?"

"Well, I suppose, if that's all you got," Cora said.

Lord Harcourt looked at James, who shuffled over to the small table. He filled a glass from the bottle and brought it to her. "Here you are, Cora."

"Thanks, George," she said. She took a gulp and swallowed, grimacing. "This is the best you got?"

"It is," Harcourt replied, arching an eyebrow. He shot a quizzical look at James. "Did she call you George?"

"Yes," James replied, attempting to smile. "A nick-name."

"How pleasant," Harcourt said, sitting in the nearest chair. "Please, Mrs Oglesby, come and have a seat."

Cora accepted his offer and felt herself sink into the cushion. She cautiously leaned against the back, unsure if she was committing some offense, but Lord Harcourt seemed unconcerned. The firelight gleamed off of his silver hair as he turned toward his retainer.

"James, might you stoke the fire for us?" Harcourt asked.

James blinked, then stepped over to the fire. He picked up a gold-handled poker and poked at the dying flames. Unsatisfied, he tossed a few logs on the fire, sending a flurry of sparks up the chimney. The fire sputtered back to life, and James took up a post next to Lord Harcourt's chair, his hands clasped behind his back.

"Now, Mrs Oglesby," Harcourt said, crossing his legs. "As James has already told you, I have a rather urgent predicament on my hands."

"Yeah," Cora said. "You got yourself a nasty pack of vampires eating your miners."

"Yes, to put it bluntly." Harcourt took a sip of brandy. "Ordinarily, I could rely on James to handle this situation. He's quite knowledgeable about these creatures, which is why I keep him on as a retainer."

"Is that right?" Cora asked.

"Indeed," Harcourt said. "Of course, this isn't to imply that we attract an unusual amount of attention from the undead. It's a rare occurrence, actually, but remarkably inconvenient. Typically, we only have a solitary perpetrator, which James is certainly capable of handling. However, this particular infestation is quite extensive, so I deemed it prudent to request outside assistance."

"And George told you about us?"

Harcourt nodded. "He mentioned meeting you on the rail from Denver, where that reprehensible orator kept him overlate."

"Who's that?" Cora asked.

"Oscar Wilde," James replied before Harcourt could. "He was giving a lecture in Denver and I thought to stop by on my way here. I must admit, I'm a fan of his work."

"Inexplicable, if you ask me," Harcourt said. "I do not understand what you see in the man."

"I appreciate his wit, my lord."

"As compensation for your lack of it, I imagine," Harcourt said with a wave of his hand. "It's not pertinent to the matter at hand."

"I reckon we should set a deal, then," Cora said, draining her glass. James reached over and refilled it.

"Of course," Harcourt said. "I'll get right to the point, then. I am prepared to offer you a total sum of four thousand American dollars if you manage to eliminate this threat to my investment."

Cora's glass paused on the way to her lips. "Come again?"

"I take this matter quite seriously, madam. If word of this were to reach the Court, I would become the laughing stock of Buckingham."

"Really?" Cora asked, her right eyebrow arching. "You all take vampires lightly over yonder?"

"Vampires are not considered a proper topic for discussion among nobility," Harcourt said, his tone indignant. "I am not so daft as to complain of my problems with the undead to the House of Lords. No, madam, the source of my humiliation would be the failure of my venture here. There are some who believe speculation in the American silver panic is foolhardy, and the loss of my mine would provide them with ample reason to question my judgment."

"OK," Cora said. The word hung in the air for a second. "What's the matter with that?"

Harcourt lifted his chin. "The problem with that, my dear, is that the political situation at court is remarkably delicate. Were my judgment in financial matters to be called into question, it might upset the balance of power in the House of Lords and destabilize the British government."

"You've got that much clout, huh?"

"I may be flattering myself, but yes, I believe so." Harcourt took a sip of brandy, staring into the fire. Cora watched the firelight play in the old man's spectacles. She shifted in her chair and emptied her glass, but he didn't stir. The fire snapped and sparked. She glanced at James, but he just returned an even gaze.

Harcourt finally took a deep breath and looked back up at her. "Regardless of my reasons, Mrs Oglesby, I want those monsters out of my mines so my workers can return to their jobs. Are you willing to help me or not?"

Cora grinned at the British lord as she set her empty glass on the table. "Cleaning out a nest of vampires is powerful dangerous work, Mr Harcourt, so I'll tell you what: throw in another thousand dollars and I'll make sure your boy George there is still alive and well when the job's done."

"I doubt he's worth that much," Harcourt replied.

"I must respectfully disagree, my lord," James said, his face breaking out in red spots.

Harcourt regarded Cora with narrow eyes. The fire popped. James Townsend quietly cleared his throat. "Very well," Harcourt said at last. "A bonus of one thousand American dollars if you keep my retainer alive."

"Glad to hear it," Cora said. "Now, what exactly are we up against?"

"James can explain the particulars of the situation," Harcourt said.

James cleared his throat again. "The first victim was discovered three weeks ago in one of the recent expansion tunnels. After eliminating all known natural causes of death from the list of possibilities, the foreman contacted me, requesting my expertise to confirm supernatural involvement. In the time it took me to travel from London to Leadville, an additional seven miners were discovered diseased, and all of the victims had become reanimated.

"Upon my arrival, I immediately recognized the signs of a *vrykolakas* attack and took appropriate measures. The infected wing of the mine was quarantined, I erected crosses and cloves of garlic at each access point, and equipped the crews working the other wings with holy water."

"Sounds right so far," Cora said. "So what went wrong?"

"Well," James said, looking down at his hands, "what I had believed to be a single *vrykolakas* turned out to be an entire nest of them. I haven't determined the exact number, though I believe their ranks to have grown since the attacks began. Several more miners disappeared in the mines after my arrival."

"Why is that?" Cora asked. "Don't matter if it's one or a hundred vampires if you've got the crosses and other truck in place."

"That was exactly my line of thinking," James said. "I was at a loss to explain their constant advancements into the other areas of the mine despite my efforts."

"So what was the problem?"

James looked at Lord Harcourt, who nodded. He

took a deep breath and looked back at Cora. "I have reason to believe a *nosferatu* is at the heart of this infestation."

"That's one of your special vampires, right?"

"Yes, an intelligent, powerful being," James said. "The *nosferatu* possess the ability to control the lesser *vrykolakas* like extensions of their own bodies. I believe this control is what allowed them to bypass the wards I set up in the mine."

"Ah," Cora said, "so they're too tough for stuff like that when they've got a big bad at their heels."

"Essentially, though it is more accurate to say that they are simply no longer frightened by them," James said. "Contact with these elements can still injure and kill them, but the *nosferatu*'s influence may be capable of overpowering their instinctive fear of death."

"Good." Cora nodded in satisfaction. "I hate fighting monsters I can't kill." Her face clouded over as a thought struck her. "So why do you need my help, again? You got it figured out what's causing this, and you know how to kill it. Where do I come in?"

"Well," James said, looking at his hands again, "I'm afraid I am unable to contain the *vrykolakas* through my efforts alone. Their lack of inhibition is quite problematic, and..." He trailed off.

"Spit it out, George," Cora said, waving her hand in a circle.

"I've never actually killed a vampire myself." He continued staring at his hands, waiting for her laughter, but it never came. He peered over his glasses at her, surprised.

"What?" Cora asked. "Ain't no shame in that. Not many folks can make such a claim, and even less that are telling it true."

"Yes, well, I suppose you're right," James said. "Anyway, as I told you on the train, my primary interest in vampires is scholarly, so I'm not much for actually combating them. I can contain and exorcise ordinary infestations, but this situation is beyond my capacity for either." He spread his hands to either side, palms upward. "To put it another way, we require a sword, but all I can offer is a shield."

Cora leaned back in her chair, the empty glass back in her hand. She stared into the fire, watching the sparks flutter each time it popped. Taking on a nest like this wasn't going to be as easy as she'd first thought. From what James said, there could be as many as a dozen vampires in Harcourt's mine, and one of them was as intelligent and cunning as any human. She wasn't sure if these *nosferatu* existed or not, but they were as good an explanation as any for a bunch of the lesser vampires to form a nest like that.

She looked at Lord Harcourt and his loyal vampire scholar. They were both waiting for her answer. If she and Ben took this job, they might very well not come back from it. If they did, they could retire with the reward and set up a quieter life for themselves. These two British gentlemen were offering them the chance of a lifetime: to brave impossible odds and either emerge victorious with a king's ransom in their pockets or perish in a vicious struggle that would earn them places among the pages of James Townsend's books. They would be the General Custers of the vampire hunting world.

"All right, then, you've got yourselves a deal."

"So we're just supposed to march into a dark, crowded mine and pick a fight with a dozen vampires?" Ben asked.

"That's the general idea," Cora said, "which you would know if you wasn't so damn taken with Harcourt's books."

"That man's got an amazing collection," Ben said. "I reckon we could make a living just printing books for him."

"Well, if we live through this, we may end up doing just that. Five thousand dollars could set us up proper for the rest of our lives if we had the notion."

They were back in their room in the Northern Hotel, the sheets pulled up to their shoulders. A single flame danced on the lamp wick near Cora's head.

"I don't reckon you'd be apt to just sit on your rear and work a press all day," Ben said. "I know you better than that."

"Maybe so," Cora said, "but I've been thinking." She rolled onto her side and looked him in the eyes. "This new job will see us rich or see us dead. If it sees us rich, I don't see no reason why it can't be our last."

"What do you mean?" Ben asked.

"I ain't a fool, Benjamin," she said. "I seen how you don't care much for this work."

"That ain't true," Ben said. "You know I ain't no coward, shying away from them demons that we fight."

"Never said you was," Cora said. "All I said was you don't care for it." Ben was about to protest again, but she put her hand over his mouth. "Don't you argue with me. You ain't no soldier or fighter. You're a reading man, just like that James Townsend feller."

"Well, I am partial to my books," Ben said, "but that don't mean I don't enjoy our work. Fact is, I enjoy it a good deal. Doing the Lord's work always makes me happy."

"There's plenty to do in the Lord's service that don't involve shooting and riding into trouble," Cora said. "We could print out Bibles or some such."

Ben smiled at her. "You'd never be happy doing that and you know it."

"No, but we've done what I like for a long time now. It's only fair we do what you want for a change."

"You really mean that?" Ben asked.

"Wouldn't say it if I didn't," she said. "I reckon I can put up with ink and machines for a spell if we do this job without getting ourselves killed. Running a press ought to give these old bones a chance to rest, anyway."

Ben searched her face for a moment, then smiled and kissed her. "Well, if you're serious, I ain't saying no."

Cora smiled and kissed him back. "Good. I wasn't above knocking you on the head and dragging you along if you was going to be stubborn about it." Without another word, she rolled over, blew out the lamp, and settled in for a sleep.

ELEVEN

The next morning, Cora met James Townsend at Lord Harcourt's retreat, where he had prepared a coach to take them to the infested mine. He offered her a cup of tea before they set out, but she declined.

"Suit yourself," he said as the coach jerked into motion.

"I hope this ain't far," Cora said, watching tea splash on the floor of the carriage despite his best efforts to hold the cup still. "You're like to be baptized in Earl Grey before much longer."

"I've never quite mastered this art, I'm afraid," James said, drinking what little liquid remained. "I've always taken tea around this time of the morning, however, and old habits die hard."

Cora smiled briefly, then turned her attention out the window. The carriage rumbled along a wide road overlooking a meadow. The morning sun glinted off the snow in a thousand tiny rainbows. In the distance, a dark green carpet of trees draped across the lower slopes of the mountains. Above them, stony peaks towered toward the cloudless sky.

Watching the perfect landscape roll by, Cora had to remind herself that evil slept beneath it somewhere, waiting for the cover of nightfall to pour out. She tried to imagine how much damage a dozen vampires could do to a small place like Leadville, and all she could picture were bloody streets and shrieks of terror.

"That reminds me," she said, turning back to James. "Why ain't these vampires taken over the town yet?"

"I'm sorry?"

"Well, from what you said, these suckers ain't scared of crosses and garlic and what have you, so why ain't they swarmed all over those helpless folks in town?"

James looked out the window for a moment. "To be honest, I can't say for sure," he finally said. "It's confused me as well. My best explanation is that my efforts have frustrated them, if only somewhat. Even the *nosferatu* are pained by the presence of such wards, though they possess the cunning to avoid or circumvent them."

"But they can't actually get rid of them?"

"Not to my knowledge, no," James said. "In fact, such weapons are still effective at combating a *nosferatu*."

Cora blinked. "Is that right? I thought you said they wasn't scared of them."

"I said they are capable of mastering their fear of them and driving the lesser *vrykolakas* to do the same. You'll find that touching a *nosferatu* with a crucifix will produce as satisfying a result as it would on their lesser kin."

"Well, that's good," Cora said. "From what you said last night, I was starting to think they was unkillable."

"Don't misunderstand me," James said, looking her in the eye. "They aren't to be taken lightly. The foe we face is possibly the most dangerous one you will encounter in your life. If you approach it with the same jocularity you have displayed thus far, you will end up dead or one of his minions."

"Don't you worry, King George," Cora said. "I aim to do this one sober."

"Do you typically fight the supernatural while intoxicated?"

"It's been known to happen," Cora said, grinning at him.

James shook his head in wonder. "I find it remarkable that you're alive, Mrs Oglesby."

"I could say the same, James. People that take this kind of thing too serious end up killing themselves with worry before the spooks get the chance."

"In order to combat this powerful a menace, one must be methodical and careful in the execution of one's tactics. A single mistake could mean the difference between life and death, or life and unlife, as it were."

Cora rolled her eyes. "That only works until your prey catches wind of your plan. Then it's all up in smoke."

"Which is precisely why you keep your own counsel," James said. "Speaking out of turn is one of those missteps that can lead to your undoing."

"Well, that's the difference between you and me, I guess," Cora said. "I ain't never fought nothing that

could think better than a mongrel, so I never had to
worry about them figuring out what I was up to."

"You'll need to accustom yourself to the idea if you
intend to survive this encounter."

Cora nodded, and they spent the rest of the ride in
silence. The carriage rumbled and bounced along the
snowy road for another fifteen minutes before coming
to a stop. She felt the cab shift as the driver climbed
down from his perch. A few moments later, the door
swung open, letting in a stream of cold air.

James motioned for her to exit first, and she obliged.
Her boots crunched on the fresh snowfall as she
stepped into the morning air. The sun hung just above
the eastern peaks. She squinted into its glare, her gaze
sweeping over the valley below them.

"Mrs Oglesby?" James asked. "This way, please."

Turning away from the sun, she followed James
toward the great frowning wall of the mining complex. A single tower dominated one end of the
building, fed by a long ramp built on aging trusses.
The roof sloped back toward the mountain's peak
in a large black slab. Along the far wall, a low row
of windows lingered in the shadow of the over-
hanging roof.

James unlocked a windowless door at the base of
the tower and disappeared into the darkness beyond.
Cora noted the large cross nailed above the doorway.
Looking closer, she saw that it was made of broken
trusses. James Townsend must really be worried if he
was making makeshift crosses out of scraps. She
wasn't sure what the vampires would make of it, but

she wasn't all that impressed. Still, any shelter in a storm, or so her father used to say.

Cora followed her guide into the shadows, leaving the door open behind her. In the dim light, she could see the back of James's tweed jacket as he busied himself lighting lanterns for their trip into the mines.

"You ain't got them fancy electric lights up in here yet?" she asked.

James turned, a surprised look on his face. "Why, no, we don't. I wasn't aware America had electric power in remote locations like this."

"I don't reckon we do," Cora said, "but I figured Lord Harcourt could money up his own if he had a mind."

"There are some things money can't purchase, my dear," James said, "and civilization in America is one of those things."

"I reckon so," Cora said. She waited in silence while James lit a pair of lanterns. In their glow, she could make out the details of the room. It looked like an office, though it was clear it hadn't been used in a few weeks. A thin layer of dust had already settled on the large desk standing in one corner, covering abandoned papers and coffee tins.

"Here you are," James said, handing her a lantern.

"So what exactly is your plan?" Cora asked. "Just charge down there with these lanterns and our good looks and hope they run off?"

James offered her a tight smile. "Hardly, Mrs Oglesby. I will be taking you into the secure area of the mine to show you the environment and the precautions I've already taken."

"You're sure that area is still secure?"

"Of course," James replied. "I make daily rounds here to ensure that Lord Harcourt's property doesn't fall further into their control."

"And I'm sure he's thankful," Cora said. "Let's go, then."

James nodded and led her through another door into a large room. The halos of light from the lanterns glimmered on silver rails. The angular shapes of mine carts lurked in the darkness like sleeping beasts. Stray shafts of sunlight filtered through grimy windows, doing little to cut through the shadows. Cora peered upward, but the ceiling was lost in the darkness. The air was stale and cold, filled with the smell of earth and grease.

James didn't give the processing room a second glance as he stepped over the rails. Cora followed suit, keeping her eyes on her boots in the dim light. The British scholar passed over several tunnels before pausing in front of another. He took a few steps into it, lifted his lantern, and looked around. Nodding to himself, he motioned for her to follow.

This mining tunnel was much more developed than the small one beneath Jules Bartlett's cabin. Wider and taller, it had been carved by dozens of skilled hands. Instead of pine trunks holding up the roof, Harcourt's workers had lined each wall with boards. Archways boasting lanterns loomed at regular intervals. James lit each lantern they came across as they worked their way deeper into the mine. He didn't say why, but Cora was grateful enough for his foresight.

The last time she'd been in a tunnel, she hadn't had it, and it had almost cost her her life.

After a short while, the tunnel began opening into a larger space. The light from their lanterns faded into the shadows, as did the cart tracks they had followed. They stood for a moment in silence, the light glinting on the scholar's glasses. From somewhere deep in the cave, Cora thought she could hear the sound of dripping water.

"The miners found this cavern fairly early on in their excavations," James said. Even though he spoke softly, his voice seemed to travel for miles. "They don't know how far it extends, and they didn't much care until recently."

"So you think them vampires came from in here somewhere?" Cora asked.

"No, actually," James replied. "As I said before, this tunnel is still secure, or it was as of yesterday morning, so I can only conclude that this cavern doesn't connect to the other tunnels."

"You've still set up crosses and such, though, right?"

"Of course, my dear. I'm not daft." In the dark, she couldn't make out his expression, but she could picture his indignant look. "I'd rather not lose any more of the mine."

"I didn't see nothing when we came through."

"The wards are further in," James said, his tone patient.

"Good," Cora said. "So when do we see to getting the other areas back?"

"All in good time," James said. "I thought familiarizing

yourself with the combat environment would be useful before jumping into the fray."

"Right, a dark, dank mine. And here I thought it was going to be pistols at high noon." She clapped him on the back with her free hand, then reached down to her belt and drew her revolver. "Now let's go jump into that fray."

The lantern light glinted on James's glasses as he shook his head. "Such haste will only get you killed."

"Maybe," Cora said. "Could be that we take them by surprise right here and now and flush the whole lot."

The shadows around them swelled and danced as James turned back toward the tunnel. Cora followed, lantern in one hand and Colt in the other. The tunnel closed in on them and the shimmer of the rock walls returned to the dull brown of boards. James extinguished each lantern as they passed, cloaking the tunnel behind them in shadow.

They stepped out into the ore processing station, the sound of their footsteps fading into the large room. Without a word, James turned to his left and headed back for the office. Cora stepped over a few sets of tracks before pausing and peering into the inky blackness of another tunnel.

"Hey, what's down this one?"

James turned. "That leads deeper into the mountain."

"I figured that much, thanks," Cora said. "I mean, what else is down there?"

"A nest of vampires, most likely. Possibly some silver ore."

"Let's find out," Cora said, stepping into the tunnel.

"Wait, Mrs Oglesby!" James cried, but her lantern had already disappeared from his view. Panicked, he high-stepped over the rails and looked after her. All he could see was her shadow, still crowned by her wide-brimmed hat. "Mrs Oglesby!"

"Don't wait up, George." Her voice echoed down the tunnel. "I aim to bag me a vampire before the day's out."

Wash Jones stared at his reflection in the Pioneer's big mirror. The whiskers on his face had grown shaggy, and his blue eyes were dulled by the whiskey, but he still looked the same. He still looked normal.

"Goddammit, Boots!" he yelled, looking around. The bartender was nowhere to be seen, but a group of miners playing cards glanced over at him. He slammed his empty glass down and staggered his way up the back stairs. They led him to a hallway with doors along both walls. Door after door revealed nothing but storage rooms or empty bedrooms. He slammed the last one shut, roared another curse, and turned back toward the stairs.

Boots was standing in the hallway, his hands clasped in front of his apron.

Wash cursed in surprise as he tripped over his own boots. Sprawled out face-down on the wooden floor, he let out a groan. He opened his eyes to see the bartender's polished boots standing above him.

"Perhaps I have made the wrong choice," Boots said.

The gunman pulled himself up onto his knees. "No, sir, I assure you you ain't. I'm your man."

A grin flickered across the round face. "We shall see."

The polished boots thumped past him. Wash turned to see Boots opening the door he had just slammed. The bartender looked over his shoulder and motioned for the gunfighter to follow. Wash pulled himself to his feet and reeled for a moment before following his host into the darkened room.

"Close the door," Boots said. Wash obeyed, then stood in the semi-dark, his hands fidgeting with the rivets on his pants. The room was empty save for a few large wooden crates. Sunlight seeped in between the cracks of the boards covering the two windows, catching on the floating dust. The bartender stood in the shadows, watching Wash sway.

"Sit down before you fall down," Boots said, pointing to one of the boxes.

Wash stumbled over and sat where the bartender pointed. "What's this about?"

"I sense that you grow impatient with my offer," Boots said.

"With an offer like that, what'd you expect?"

"More self-restraint, for one." Boots stepped closer to the gunman. "This is not a decision I make lightly."

"Me neither," Wash said, "but somebody's got to put that bitch in her place."

"Quite so," Boots said. "However, you are not yet ready to face her."

"I sure am," Wash protested, pulling his gun. "You just point me at her and I'll lay her low."

"Yes, like you did last time." Boots smirked, shaking his head. "No, Mr Jones, you will need more power.

Power that only I can give you. But first, you must prove yourself worthy of that power."

"How's that?"

"A simple task," the bartender said. "All I need is for you to retrieve something for me and bring it here. Are you familiar with the Harcourt mine?"

"No."

"It is a large mining interest located north of Leadville. A British lord owns it, though he seldom deigns to visit."

"OK," Wash said. He couldn't care less who owned it. "So what you want me to get?"

"Inside the mine, deep in one of its many caverns, there is a coffin."

"What's inside?"

"Nothing that concerns you yet," Boots replied. "All you need to do is bring that coffin to this room."

"What for?"

"Because it is in danger." Boots closed his eyes for a moment. Wash thought he saw the bartender's form start to fade, but before he could be sure, Boots opened his eyes again. "Yes, she is in the adjacent tunnel, though I don't believe she knows of the coffin's existence."

"She? You mean Cora Oglesby?"

Boots nodded, his eyes glinting in the shadows. "Yes. If she manages to find the coffin before you do, I won't be able to fulfill my end of the bargain, leaving you weak and mortal should your path cross hers again."

Wash rose to his feet, holstering his gun. "All right, so where do I go?"

"Ride north from here, following the railroad. A few miles out, you will come to a fork in the road, and there you will turn west. This road will lead you to the mine."

"Seems simple enough."

"The British aren't known for their love of complexity," Boots said.

"Right," Wash said. "Where do I find the coffin?"

"Follow the first set of mine car tracks into the mountain. You will find it hidden behind a row of large boulders near the end of the rails."

Wash nodded. "Anything else?"

"Yes," Boot said. "You may encounter some objects blocking the tunnel on your way in. Please make sure to dispose of them before you leave."

Wash nodded again, turning toward the door. "I'll see you in a few hours with your pine box."

"I will be waiting for you," Boots said. "Oh, and if you should encounter Cora Oglesby while you are there, please try to contain her in the mines. I won't be able to help you if you don't."

Wash gave him a funny look, then took his leave. Boots watched the door close behind him, then turned his gaze toward the narrow shafts of sunlight and smiled.

"What the hell is this, George?" Cora's voice rang out in the darkness.

"Please, Mrs Oglesby, do keep quiet," James said, looking around. "We don't want to draw them down on us."

"Then please explain what I'm looking at."

In front of them, several large beams stood upright in the tunnel. A horizontal board was nailed to each one, forming a crude set of crosses. Withered cloves of garlic hung from the wooden arms, filling the air with their scent.

"This is my barricade, madam," James said. "It keeps the vampires from leaving this tunnel and gaining access to the mine entrance."

"I see," Cora said. "And what's to stop them from just stepping around them?"

"Their unholy fear of a holy God."

"Well, couldn't they just throw rocks or something from further back and knock them down?"

James paused in mid-step. "Well," he said after a moment, "perhaps they haven't thought of it yet." Another pause. "I believe the scent of the garlic would keep them from passing through even if they managed to destroy the crosses."

"Good for us, then," Cora said. Careful not to disturb the crosses, they worked their way to the other side of the barricade. The rails beneath their feet continued on into shadows. "Any more farther down?"

"I'm afraid not," James said. "After all, they were rather hastily constructed."

Cora lifted her lantern and peered forward into the darkness. This tunnel was much like the other, stable and straight. James had continued his habit of lighting the lanterns along the way, allowing them a visible retreat if things turned sour.

She turned to him. "Here, take this," she said, offering him her lantern.

"Why?" James asked, taking it in his free hand.

"I need my other hand," she replied. With a fluid motion, she drew her saber and turned back toward the darkness. "Come on, George, let's find us a spook."

Her boots crunched along the sandy floor as she advanced into the shadows. James followed, the light from his lanterns playing along the length of her saber. Aside from their footsteps and his nervous breathing, the mine was as silent as a tomb.

Soon, the tunnel widened, opening up into another cavern. The rails snaked off ahead, vanishing into the bowels of the mountain. To their left, a small wooden platform led to a series of stairs descending down a steep slope.

"Which way should we go?" Cora asked.

"Back," James replied in a whisper. "We're quite unprepared for this."

"Suit yourself," Cora said, "but I'm going this way."

She thumped across the wooden platform toward the stairs. Taking them one at a time, she listened for any new sound, but all she could hear was James muttering to himself. The stairs bottomed out on the rocky floor of the cavern, which was strewn with sand and pebbles. Cora motioned for James to hold his lanterns higher. In their glow, she could see the floor slope upward into the cave wall. At regular intervals, square beams braced the rocky surface, holding back potential cave-ins. Several picks and a small shovel lay on the floor, evidently dropped by panicked miners in their retreat.

"You boys sure are sloppy," she remarked.

"Yes, well, it's hard to remain organized while your comrades are being eaten alive," James replied.

"If you say so," Cora said. "I still ain't seen no sign of these vampires."

"With the way you keep yammering, I expect they will show themselves shortly."

"Maybe they're all asleep."

"I suppose that's a possibility," James said, "though without the threat of sunlight, I don't see–"

Cora held up her gun, cutting him off. In the silence that followed, she could only hear the sound of the blood rushing through her ears. Yet she thought she had heard something else, a faint shuffling. Her gaze swept over the blackness surrounding them. Maybe it was nothing, just the echoes playing tricks on her.

No, there it was again: the soft sound of skin on stone. She pictured cold flesh stepping across the cavern floor, and she tightened her grip on the revolver.

Another step. The echoes and the darkness made it impossible to know where it was coming from. She strained her eyes against the shadows, searching for a telltale glow of undead eyes or the glimmer of the lamplight on glistening fangs. Even if she couldn't see them, she could sense them. The hairs on the back of her neck stood on end.

They were being hunted.

Cora looked at James. His eyes were white behind his spectacles. Pointing with the barrel of her revolver, she first indicated a lantern, then the staircase they had just descended. He nodded and tiptoed over to the wooden stairs. He placed a lantern on a step about chest high and looked back at her. She nodded, then pointed to a large rock just in front of her. The scholar set the second lantern down and stepped back to stand beside her.

The sound of the approaching footsteps was un-even, like a drunkard's staggering walk, but it was drawing nearer. Cora turned her back on James and tapped the butt of her Winchester with her pistol. After a moment's hesitation, the rifle's weight lifted as James pulled it from the scabbard. Twisting to face him, she saw him turning the weapon over in his hands. She nudged him and with her saber mimicked pumping the action. A loud click echoed through the darkness as he chambered a round. Nodding, she pulled back the hammer of her Colt. They took up stations with their backs as close to the cavern's wall as they could, the light from the lanterns glowing on their guns.

They waited.

Cora's pulse thundered in her ears. From the sounds, it was only a single creature, but that would be enough. Vampires were fast and strong, able to tear off an arm or a head in seconds. If it caught her off-guard, they would both die. James was just as likely to shoot himself or her as he was to hit the monster. She crossed herself with her pistol, praying that he at least had the sense to carry some sort of ward with him.

The sound changed, shifting to the dull thud of footsteps on wood. The creature was following their trail. Soon, she could hear hesitant steps on the wooden stairs. She turned to face the lantern James had placed there, raised her pistol, and waited for the creature to show itself.

A shadow erupted from beyond the lantern's glow, hurtling toward James with blinding speed. James toppled backward with a cry, the monster on top of him. Cora could see the pale fingers tangled in the scholar's hair, pulling his chin up. With a howl of hunger, the vampire sank its teeth into the soft flesh of his exposed neck.

A moment later, another howl shook the cavern as Cora's saber clove the undead flesh. She brought her sword arm around for another strike, but the vampire's clawed fingers gouged at her face. The impact knocked her backward as the saber clattered to the stone floor. Before she could recover, the vampire's weight slammed into her chest. A cold hand clamped onto her skull like a bear trap, forcing her head backward. In desperation, she dropped her pistol and wrapped her fingers around the vampire's throat, pushing against it as needle-sharp fangs snapped inches above her throat.

The strain on her arms suddenly lifted as the vampire let out a bellow. It staggered to its feet and turned toward James, hissing in anger. As it turned, Cora could see a small wooden cross protruding from its back. The flesh around the wound smoked and sizzled as the monster crouched, preparing to launch itself at the frightened scholar.

A brilliant flash blinded them all for a moment as the thunder of Cora's Colt filled the cavern. The sacred bullet punched through the vampire's leg, and the monster let out a screech of pain. Cora pulled back the hammer. When the vampire turned toward her, she fired again, aiming for its heart. The impact blew it backward over James's prostrate form and into the stone wall. Cora hauled herself to her feet, recovered her saber, and drove the tip into the vampire's chest. The life faded from its eyes, and the empty body tumbled to the floor of the cavern.

Cora holstered her revolver, rolled the body over, and pulled the still-smoking cross from its flesh. She wiped both the cross and her saber on the vampire's ragged pants, then looked over her shoulder at James.

"You still with me, George?"

"I'm not sure," James replied. He rose on unsteady legs and braced himself against a boulder. Once on his feet, he pulled a handkerchief from his pocket and tied it around his bleeding neck.

She grinned and tossed him the cross. "Not bad for a greenhorn."

The Englishman fumbled with the cross, and it clattered to the stone floor. He retrieved it and tucked it away inside his tweed jacket. "Yes, well, I figured it was safer than my trying to shoot it."

Cora nodded. Her blade shimmered in the lamplight as she raised it high and brought it down on the vampire's neck. The head tumbled away, and she grinned again. "I'd say today was a good day."

"Only if we leave before the rest of the brood arrives," James said, picking up a lantern. As he turned, his foot accidentally kicked the vampire's head toward Cora. He stumbled and nearly fell. Even in the dim light, Cora could see his pale face. She bent over, picked up the vampire's head by one ear, turned it toward the light for a good look at its face, and felt her own knees go weak. She slid her saber back into its scabbard, took the head in both hands, and turned it right side up. Her breath caught in her throat as she stared into the lifeless eyes of the creature she had just killed. The jagged mass of fangs protruding from its red lips turned the dead face into a nightmare mask, but she would have recognized those round cheeks and that bald patch anywhere.

It was Boots.

Her throat worked at swallowing for a few moments. "Hey, James," she finally said, "I don't suppose you can tell me how long this one's been a vampire?"

"Perhaps, but not here," James said, picking up the second lantern from its place on the stairs.

"Right," Cora said. Holding the head in one hand, she retrieved her Winchester from where James had dropped it. She kept it in her hand as she followed James up the stairs and into the mining tunnel. The Englishman set a brisk pace, slowing only for the barricade in the tunnel. He didn't turn back to her until they were in the foreman's office.

"Now, then," he said, setting down the lanterns, "let's have a look."

Cora set the head on the desk, and James bent over and looked into the dead face. He grimaced as he took it in one hand and rotated it from side to side. Cora waited by the door to the processing station, keeping an ear open for any sound of pursuit. Finally, the scholar nodded to himself and stood upright.

"Well, I'm no physician," he said, "but I'd say this fellow's been dead for at least a week."

"You sure?" Cora asked, coming to take a closer look.

"Well, this isn't a fresh kill, by any account," James said. "Once a human has its blood drained by a vampire – *vrykolakas* or *nosferatu*, it makes no difference – the transformation into an undead will occur at the next sunset. The corpse must be shielded from sunlight during that time, or the change will not take place." He pointed to the dead man's jumble of elongated teeth. "However, this specimen exhibits an advanced degree of mandibular development, though not as advanced as some I've seen. Still, I'd say this man has been a vampire, and a well-fed one at that, for at least five days."

"So you're telling me Boots had been dead for five days?" Cora asked. James nodded as he extinguished the lanterns and prepared to close up the mine. He picked up the bartender's head with his handkerchief and tossed it through the open door, where the morning sun reduced it to a flurry of ashes. Taking one last look around, James motioned for her to follow him.

Cora didn't say a word as they climbed back into the coach and started for Harcourt's retreat. James contented himself with staring out the window at the passing scenery. Cora tried to enjoy it, too, but her mind kept returning to Boots. She'd stood at his bar, drank his private stock of rotgut, and played cards in his saloon. Boots, who was always so carefree and happy, a man too soft for the army. A man whose body had just tried to drink her neck dry.

What James had said troubled her, too. Mart Duggan had mentioned speaking to Boots about that Wash Jones character only two days ago, but if the bartender had been dead for at least five days, that couldn't have happened. Either James was wrong about the time it took to turn into a vampire, or Duggan hadn't actually spoken to Boots.

"Hey, George," Cora said. The scholar turned from the window to look at her. "You're sure about the five days thing? Boots couldn't have turned vampire any later?"

"Well, my estimation wasn't precise," James replied, "but I would stake my life on at least three days. A freshly-turned vampire would not have exhibited such an extent of fang growth."

"Right," Cora said, "so here's a stumper for you. What if I said the marshal in town, Mart Duggan, talked to Boots, the dead feller, two days ago?"

James blinked a few times. "Well, I would say you were mistaken."

"There's no way for that to happen?"

"None," James said. He opened his mouth to continue when the coach pitched to one side, slamming his head into the wall. At the same time, a shadow swept past the window. James fell back into his seat, holding his palm to his head and cursing. Despite her worries, Cora laughed. James answered her laughter with a tight grin, then looked out the window, careful not to get too close. After a moment, he leaned back again and shook his head.

"What is it?" Cora asked.

"I think someone just passed us," James said.

"Passed us?" Cora asked, sitting upright. "You mean they're heading back toward the mine?"

"Yes," James said, then shrugged. "Perhaps Lord Harcourt has sent the foreman to retrieve something."

They fell back into silence as the coach continued to sway and rumble along the road. When they arrived back at the retreat, Cora headed straight for the stable to collect her mare. She cinched up the saddle, led Our Lady around to the front of the retreat, and swung herself across the horse's back. As she turned back toward town, James emerged from the front door and called to her.

"What is it?" she asked.

"I just spoke with Lord Harcourt," James said, approaching her. "He hasn't ordered anyone aside from us to the mine."

"Any reason one of your boys would head out there on his own?"

James shook his head. "They know of the dangers. Most of them think we should just abandon the mine altogether."

"Maybe some fool heard about the rout and thought to swipe himself some silver while you're away."

"Perhaps," James said. "If such is the case, he'll have a nasty surprise in store for him." He allowed himself a small smile. "I suppose the vampires are good for that much, at least."

"At least until they eat so many bandits that they start to outnumber the townsfolk," Cora said.

James pondered that for a moment. "Well, if we act quickly, they won't have the chance to grow their numbers. How soon can you make your preparations?"

"Well," Cora said, watching Our Lady's ears twitch, "I ought to let the marshal know that his bartender ain't his bartender no more. After that, all I'll need to do is round up a few things from the hotel and fetch my husband."

James consulted his pocket watch. "Can you return in an hour?" Cora nodded. "Very good. I shall see about recruiting some volunteers to accompany us."

"Not too many, thanks," Cora said.

"Of course not," James said. "Just enough to provide some backup."

"Good enough." She tipped her hat to the scholar, gave Our Lady her heels, and headed south. Above her head, the sun was nearing its noonday summit. Glancing up at it, she prayed they could settle the vampires and make it back out of the mine before nightfall. She pulled her hat down over her brow and urged Our Lady forward.

Wash Jones thundered up to the mine in his stolen wagon, pulling back on the team's reins at the last minute. The horses reared in protest, but he didn't care. He'd nearly rammed that coach on the narrow road, and he knew when he saw it that he'd missed his chance to trap the bitch in the mine. That put him in a sour mood, and the fear that she'd found and stolen the coffin only made it worse.

Slapping the reins over the team's back, he nudged the wagon up to the door and climbed down. He didn't bother to hobble the horses, instead checking on the burlap sheets in the back of the wagon. He'd added them as a last-minute consideration, thinking that it wouldn't do to ride into town with a coffin in plain sight. The sheets were still tucked beneath the seat. Satisfied, he made his way to the door. It was locked, but his pistol reduced the knob to a smoking hole. Once inside, he found a pair of lanterns sitting on a desk, still warm to the touch. He lit one and held it up in front of him. A door stood at the other end of the room, and he walked through it into the processing station.

Wash found the first set of rails easily enough. He started making his way into the tunnel when he paused. Finding the coffin would be simple, but hauling it out to the wagon by himself would be damn near impossible. He walked back, following the rails, until he found a mine cart. It was empty except for a discarded pick. Grinning at his own cleverness, he set the lantern down inside and gave it a good pull. The metal wheels groaned in protest, but the cart moved. He retrieved the lantern, got behind the cart, and began pushing it down the tunnel.

A hundred yards into the tunnel, he brought the cart to a halt. Something was in his way. Squeezing past the cart's rim, he lifted the lantern above his head and peered at the objects in the tunnel. These must have been what Boots had been talking about. Not much by way of barriers; just a few beams of wood nailed together standing upright along the tracks. Crouching down, he saw that each of the three contraptions stood on a misshapen wooden base held together by a few nails. He noticed a strong smell, like garlic, and wrinkled his nose in disgust.

Wash set the lantern down and picked up the closest roadblock. It was lighter than it looked, but awkward in the small tunnel. He maneuvered it over to the mine cart and dropped it inside. After wiping his hands together, he lifted the second one and deposited it on top of the first, then crossed his arms and looked at the third. The mine cart wasn't big enough to hold it, but he couldn't just leave it after what Boots had said.

After a few moments, he thought of a solution. He leaned the cross against the wall of the tunnel and began smashing it with the heel of his boot. The pounding echoed throughout the tunnel as the boards cracked beneath his blows. He kept it up until the entire thing had been reduced to kindling. Wash tossed a few pieces into the cart, picked up the lantern, and continued down the tunnel.

As he walked, the gunman began wondering what on earth he was doing. He had blasted his way into a locked mine and spent the last half hour pushing a mine cart down a tunnel so he could steal a coffin and bring it back to a touched bartender. This wasn't the sort of fame and glory he wanted. To win a shooting match or even a duel against Cora Oglesby would earn him bragging rights for years to come. For the second time that day, he cursed his bad luck for letting her slip away. If he hadn't needed that stupid wagon, he could have made it in time and not be bothering with this little errand.

The cart's wheels continued to groan along the tracks, sending echoes bouncing off into the shadows. He just had to be patient. Boots had promised to give him power beyond what he could fathom if he could bring back the coffin. Wash wasn't sure what he meant by that, but he knew he could feel something strong and sinister whenever the bartender was around. If the bartender's promise had something to do with that power, Wash would gladly take it and show the Mad Madam who was the better fighter.

At long last, the tunnel opened into a cavern. The sounds of the cart's wheels and his own footsteps faded into the blackness around him. Wash lifted the lantern and peered to either side of him as he pushed the cart. He couldn't see anything except shattered rock and pebbles, but a tinge of fear twisted at him in the pit of his stomach. Something was lurking in those shadows; he could feel it.

The mine cart jerked to a halt, and he nearly toppled forward into the ruined crosses. He caught himself with his free hand and swung the lantern forward. The rails ended in a metal wall right in front of the cart. Wash grinned. Boots had said the coffin was near the end of the cart tracks. All he had to do now was find it and haul it out of here.

He lifted the crosses out of the cart and tossed them into the shadows. Holding the lantern in front of him, he started looking for the row of boulders Boots had mentioned. Unseen eyes, glistening with hunger, watched him from shadowy perches as he wandered. A will stronger than their own held them in check, whispering promises of feasts to come.

TWELVE

Cora tossed the reins over the hitching rail outside the marshal's station. Our Lady's breathing came in noisy gasps, her nose blowing clouds of steam into the cold mountain air. Cora gave her a pat on the neck and burst through the station door. Deputy Sanchez dropped the deck of cards he'd been holding, scattering them on the floor. He slid off his chair and began collecting them without bothering to see who had come through the door. Cora could hear a stream of Spanish curses coming from beneath the desk. Despite her hurry, she cracked a smile.

The deputy's head finally popped up behind the desk. "*Si, señora?* What can I do?"

"I'm looking for your boss."

"*Señor* Duggan is at the hog ranch."

"Which one?" Cora asked.

"The one with the *puta* Evans loves."

"The Purdy it is, then," Cora said. She clapped Sanchez on the head. "*Gracias.*"

The deputy's head disappeared behind the desk.

Outside, Our Lady was still recovering from the hard ride. She tossed her head in protest as Cora climbed into the saddle, but the hunter rode her easy over to the brothel.

Once inside the Purdy, Cora had no trouble finding the marshal. He was standing over the crumpled form of a man, revolver in hand. He glanced up at her as she approached. "Afternoon, Mrs Oglesby."

Cora tipped her hat. "Trouble?"

"Not much," Duggan said, looking back at his fallen foe. It was a young miner, his beard still thin and scraggly. "This sprout was making rough with one of the ladies here."

"Jack Evans's girl?"

"Jack's girl?" The marshal looked surprised. "Evans is sweet on a whore?"

"So I figure," Cora said. "He was out in front the other night when I whipped the wendigo. Said he was watching out for the whores here."

"Well, ain't that something," Duggan said, holstering his pistol. "I reckon I'll have words with him about that."

"Don't waste your breath," Cora said. "Poor bastard is so sick with love he was freezing his pecker off for that girl. Ain't no words have been said that could break him of that."

The man at Duggan's feet groaned and rolled onto his back. The marshal rewarded him with a kick to the ribs. "I reckon not. I got better things to do, anyhow, like locking this lump away."

"I got something for you after that," Cora said.

"How's that?"

"You got a citizen in your own town that ain't human no more."

Duggan looked at her, silent for a moment. "What's that mean?" he finally asked.

"You remember Boots, the barkeep from the Pioneer?" she asked. The marshal nodded. "Well, I just shot him up in the Harcourt mine."

Duggan cracked a smile. "You been at your bottle, ain't you?" he asked. "I seen Boots just this morning when me and Sanchez settled some rowdies."

"That ain't Boots," Cora said. "Can't tell you who or what it is now, but it ain't him."

The marshal gave the man at his feet another kick before stepping over him. He drew Cora aside and spoke in a low voice. "I ain't looking to play games, Mrs Oglesby. Now, I paid you your due for licking that monster the other night, but don't think I won't put you away for a spell if you start causing trouble for me."

"I ain't causing no trouble, marshal," Cora said. "I'm just doing my duty and warning you of it. You know Lord Harcourt, right?"

"Ain't a man in Leadville who don't," Duggan said.

"Right. Well, turns out him and his man Townsend got themselves a problem with vampires up in that mine of theirs. Me and Townsend was up there this morning poking around when we got jumped by one of them. We settled it up proper, but when I got a good look at his face, I realized I'd just put my sword through that bartender's heart."

"You killed Boots?" Duggan asked. His blue eyes blazed as he reached for his gun.

Cora raised her hands. "Calm yourself down," she said. "Ain't like that."

"You better tell me what it's like, then."

"I will if you give me half a space," she said, stepping backward. The marshal let her move, but his hand never left the butt of his gun. "Now, what do you know about vampires?"

"Not a damn thing," Duggan said. "Ain't my specialty."

"I'll make it quick, then," Cora said. "A vampire is a blood-sucking demon that's made when a man has his blood drained by another vampire. They keep the form of the dead man, but there ain't nobody inside no more, just a monster hell-bent on killing."

She paused, taking a look at the marshal. He didn't seem put off so far, so she went on. "When somebody gets made into a vampire, ain't no saving them. Best you can do for them is kill them quick."

"And you're saying Boots got himself turned into one of these things?"

Cora nodded. "Yessir, and that's what I killed this morning. Not Boots, but the thing that took over his body."

"You're sure it was him?"

"Sure as shit, marshal. Got a good look at his face when I cut his head off. He had himself a fine new set of mean-looking teeth, but it was Boots."

Duggan looked down, dropping his hand from the revolver. He took a deep breath. "So what's that make the feller who's running the Pioneer?"

"Wish I could say," Cora said, "but it ain't human. Don't you worry, though; me and Ben will get to the bottom of it."

"So you're looking for more work, I take it?" Duggan asked.

"Well, as your luck would have it, Lord Harcourt's the one picking up my tab this time," Cora said. "All you need do is cooperate with me and Townsend, and you get these vampires smoked out of your town free of charge."

The marshal nodded, a small smile on his face. "So what can I do?"

"Not much just yet," Cora said. "Just keep an eye on the Pioneer and let us know right quick if anything funny happens."

"That's all?" Duggan asked. "I ain't the type to just sit and watch, especially when something's fixing to kill folk."

"Me neither," Cora said, "but somebody's got to, and me and Ben can't."

"Why not?"

"We're looking to root out the boss," Cora said. She clapped Duggan on the shoulder. "With a spot of luck, we'll settle this before sundown, and you can sleep easy again."

"Ain't having no trouble with that," Duggan muttered, but Cora had already turned toward the door. As he watched her go, he found himself hoping that she was right and they could settle everything before dark. Having that wendigo creature in his town, a threat he couldn't fight, jail, or string up, had made him uneasy.

Being uneasy made him jumpy, which was no way for a lawman to be. If there was some other unnatural monster around, he might get uneasy again.

He heard a groaning behind him and turned. The young buck was on his hands and knees, trying to stand. Mart Duggan walked over and swept the man's arms out from beneath him with his boot. The man fell on his face with another groan. Shaking his head, the marshal grabbed the miner's wrists and hauled him to his feet.

Cora walked into their hotel room, pulled the trunk out from beneath the bed, and started digging through it. Slipping a few vials of holy water into her belt pouch, she looked up at Ben, who was seated by the window, book in hand.

"You seen that big old crucifix of ours?" she asked. Ben pulled it from his belt and held it up, his eyes never leaving the pages. Cora nodded and picked out a few silver bullets before closing the trunk. She set the rounds on the bed, pulled out her revolver, and opened the cylinder.

Ben watched her empty the chambers of the spent rounds. "Any luck?"

"More than I thought," Cora said, loading fresh bullets into the pistol. "Turns out Boots was a vampire."

"What?" Ben asked, setting his book down.

Cora nodded. She filled him in on the events of the morning and her conversation with Mart Duggan. When she finished, Ben sat silent for a few minutes, tugging on his mustache.

"I just can't buy that Boots ain't Boots," he finally said. "Why, I had myself some of his whiskey just this morning while you was up in the mine."

"How did he act?"

"Well, he was quiet and liked to glare more than he used to, but I just figured he was working though a bad drunk himself. Never thought he wasn't human no more."

Cora stood to her feet. "Enough jawing. I aim to get to the bottom of this and find out who he really is. Let's get moving."

Ben rose and followed her down the hotel stairs. Stepping out into the cold air, they squinted against the glare of the snow. Cora untied Our Lady's reins from the hitching rail and led her around back to the hotel's small livery, where she gave the mare's reins to the stable hand and helped Ben saddle up Book.

"You still got that knife?" she asked. Ben nodded, pointing to his boot. "Good. You keep that and the crucifix since you ain't got your guns working yet. I reckon George and I will be making enough of a racket that them suckers won't bother much with you."

Ben looked at his boots, embarrassed. "You know I'm looking to get my irons cleaned up."

"Right, but until you do, you got to be careful," Cora said. "I won't have you getting killed by no vampire."

Ben kept his head down as he led his gelding out of the stable and mounted. Cora reclaimed Our Lady and followed him back to the main street. Together, they nudged their horses into a trot, pointing them

north toward Harcourt's retreat and the infected mine
that lay beyond.

Across the street, cold blue eyes watched her go.
Wash Jones kept his hat pulled low as she rode by.
Once she vanished into the bustle of horses and carts,
he flicked the reins over the team's back and started
the wagon moving again. He'd been riding by when
he saw her come out of the hotel. His fingers had been
reaching for his gun when he remembered that there
were probably lawmen about. Forced to content himself with watching, he'd stopped the team and waited
until she had ridden on.

His fingers squeezed the reins as he drove the wagon
over to the Pioneer. He ached to turn around and follow her, to draw his pistol and settle the matter where
the law couldn't stop him. Mounted as she was,
though, the wagon couldn't hope to catch up. He
guided the team up behind the Pioneer and jerked the
reins back. The horses snorted and stamped in protest.
Ignoring them, he checked to make sure the coffin was
still covered by the burlap sheets before barging
through the rear door.

He hadn't taken two steps before he stopped short
as Boots came around a corner, wiping his hands on
his apron. "Glad to see you, Mr Jones. Did you bring
the item?"

"Wouldn't be here if I didn't," Wash said. "It's in
the wagon."

"Good," Boots said, a grin twisting his pleasant face.
"Bring it up to the storage room. You may use the
back stairs."

Wash was about to protest, but the bartender turned and vanished around the corner. Grumbling to himself, the gunman went back outside and tossed the burlap back, revealing the pine box. He grabbed the end of the coffin and pulled, lowering it into the snow. He stepped around the lower half, wrapped his arms around the wider part, and began dragging it toward the door.

The coffin was too heavy to be empty, but Wash didn't want to know what was inside. There was no stench, so it couldn't be a dead man, but it still smelled a little off. Musty, perhaps, like it had been tucked away in some rich man's closet for a long time. Whatever it was, Wash made sure to keep his arms wrapped around the box as he dragged it along the ground. The lid wasn't nailed shut, and he didn't want it falling open.

Grunting with effort, Wash maneuvered the coffin through the narrow doorway and began pulling it up the stairs. The bottom edge banged against each step as he went, making a racket, but he didn't care. If Boots wanted it to arrive in good shape, he could damn well give him a hand with it.

Wash finally made it to the storage room, panting from the exertion. He looked at the skid mark behind him and grinned to himself. He threw open the door, dragged his burden through, and let it drop to the floor with a loud bang. He wiped his forehead with the back of his hand.

"A little more respect might be in order," said a voice behind him. He jumped and spun around, pulling his gun. When he saw the bartender's eyes looking back at him from the shadows, he relaxed a little but didn't lower the revolver.

"Yeah, well, you want it treated nice, you can haul it yourself," Wash said. "Now where's my reward?"

Boots smirked at him. "All in good time. Were I you, I would savor the veil of your innocence while you can. It will be torn from your eyes before you leave this room."

Another twinge of fear twisted Wash's gut, but he stood his ground. "Tear whatever you want to as long as I get what I want from this deal."

"As you wish," Boots said, the smile never leaving his face. "If you would kindly open the lid of the coffin, I will begin."

"What's that?" Washed asked, casting a worried look at the box. "You want me to open it?"

"Yes."

"Why can't you?"

"Because you must master your fear of the unknown if you are to learn what I have to teach you," the bartender replied. "The choice is yours. However, I should warn you: if you turn back now, I will kill you before you reach the door."

Wash swallowed. His instincts were screaming at him to run, to leave this unsettling man and his coffin in the dust and get out of Leadville as fast as he could. If he shot Boots quick enough, he could do just that. He could steal one of the horses still hitched to the wagon downstairs and light out before the law could catch up to him.

His finger drifted toward the trigger as his thoughts raced. Boots watched him, still grinning. The bartender seemed to know his thoughts and was challenging him, waiting to see what he would do. Shooting him would be easy enough, but something told Wash that getting shot would only amuse the bartender. The muffled sound of the piano filtered up through the floorboards as the two men stared at each other.

Finally, Wash slipped his revolver back into its holster. He gave Boots a long look before kneeling down next to the coffin, wondering for the second time that day what he'd gotten himself into.

The coffin's hinges groaned as Wash opened it. He expected them to be stiff and hard to move, but the lid gave way easily, letting the dim light trickle into the coffin's interior.

What he saw made him jump to his feet and take a few steps backward, his hand over his mouth. He bumped into a crate and almost fell, but he didn't take his eyes off the coffin. His stomach threatened to heave his breakfast onto the floor.

Reclining in the coffin, eyes closed as if in sleep, was a man.

As Wash regained control of himself, he approached the coffin for a better look. The man appeared young, no older than thirty years. A black, well-trimmed beard circled his red lips, perfectly matching the fine suit he wore and the raven locks that lay on his shoulders. Clean white gloves covered his hands as they rested at his side. The only bit of color about him aside from his lips came from a blood-red necktie at his throat.

What struck Wash the most, however, was the man's face. Despite having been in that coffin for who knew how long, the man hadn't started rotting. Indeed, the face was rather handsome. It wasn't the face of a dead man, but Wash couldn't imagine anyone enduring the ride from the mines and the trip up the stairs trapped in a coffin. He looked up at Boots with questions in his eyes, but the bartender only stared back at him. Neither man spoke, and Wash suddenly realized that his breathing was the only sound in the room.

"Rather dashing, wouldn't you say?" Boots said, stepping up to the coffin and looking down at the man. "I always think so, but it doesn't mean much coming from me."

Wash's mouth worked in silence for a few moments. "What is this?" he managed.

"This is your future," Boots said, eyes glinting in amusement. "This is what will empower you to kill Cora Oglesby."

Wash shook his head, not understanding but frightened half out of his wits. Boots favored him with a look fitting for a lame dog. "How often I forget the fear mortality strikes into the heart. Very well, Washington Jones, I will explain. I do hope you won't mind if I do so in my own voice, though. After a good sleep, I enjoy nothing so much as a long talk."

Before Wash could react, Boots faded into the shadows, leaving the gunman alone in the room. Startled, Wash turned in a slow circle, hoping to see the bartender hiding behind a crate or standing by the window, grinning his grin, but the room was empty.

A moment later, he heard a soft rustling behind him. Turning his head, he saw white gloves gripping the edges of the coffin. The dead man pulled himself upright, his eyes sliding open. Wash Jones let out a yelp and scrambled backward, only to trip over a crate and fall on his back. The impact knocked the air from his lungs. He rolled over onto his belly, pulled his arms and legs under him, and tried to get to his feet.

The man was standing in front of him.

Before Wash could move, a hand gripped his shoulder like a bear trap, hauling him to his feet and holding him until he could stand on his own. Wash found himself looking into the man's eyes. They glowed a soft golden color in the dim light.

"I had hoped you were made of sterner stuff," the man said, "but perhaps you will learn in time."

Beneath his fear, Wash felt his pride stir. "I ain't so yellow as all of that. You just startled me is all. Never had no experience with spooks."

"And I suppose you believe you would have acted differently if you had known what I am," the man said. His voice resonated from deep within his chest, making the air around them vibrate.

"Well, sure," Wash said, his own voice small in his ears.

"A show of bravery, perhaps?" The man's tone was mocking. "A valiant attempt to destroy me before I snapped your neck like a twig?"

"Not exactly," Wash said, looking down at his boots.

"I thought not. Such displays of bravado and prowess are best saved for mortal enemies."

"So what should I do to you, then?"

"Kneel," the man said. "Kneel before me and acknowledge that I hold your very life in my hands. Kneel before me that I might show you mercy."

Wash's legs stiffened. Never in his life had he knelt before another man, and he didn't want to start now. He looked into the man's eyes, trying to drum up his usual defiance, but the intelligence and raw power burning in those golden orbs melted his resolve. He felt his legs buckle beneath him. Looking up, he saw a grin spread across the man's handsome face.

"You should consider yourself fortunate, Washington Jones," the resonant voice said. "Few mortals have ever survived so long in my presence."

"Who are you?" Wash asked.

"I am a master of life and death. I hold eternity in my palms. I am a true child of the night, chosen by those before me to carry our dark standard forth into this great, untamed land." His eyes flashed in the shadows. "I am the one that will grant you eternal life and the power to slay your enemies. You will walk the night as one of us, immortal, omnipotent, a dark god upon the face of the earth."

"What should I call you?" Wash asked.

"I am *nosferatu*, a king of the undead. My name, such as it is, is Fodor Glava."

"Fodor Glava?" Wash tested the name on his tongue. "That's an odd one."

"I make no apologies."

"Shouldn't need to, I say," Wash said, looking at the vampire's polished shoes. His mind was racing. This man, whoever or whatever he was, hadn't killed him yet. Even more, he was offering to make Wash into something he'd never heard of before. It sounded powerful, like he would truly become a god among men. Nobody, not even Cora Oglesby, could stand up to him then. She would be the first of many defeated opponents, many helpless victims swept away by his power.

He looked back up at Glava. "So you're going to make me into one of you?" The vampire nodded. "Why?"

"It is our law," Glava said. "The line of *nosferatu* must not go extinct, so upon each awakening, we must select a mortal to receive our gift, raising them above mere slaves to join the ranks of the true undead. In that way, we ensure that the world will never see our end."

"But ain't you immortal?" Wash said. "What's this talk about keeping the line going?"

"We are not impervious," Glava said, his face placid. "We are powerful, intelligent, and cannot die of old age or disease, but we may still be killed."

"How's that?" Wash asked. If a vampire could still be killed, maybe he didn't want to waste his time becoming one after all.

"You will learn in time. For now, be content to know that there are those among your kind that actively seek our ruin." A hint of anger crept into the vampire's voice. "They study our weaknesses. They pursue us like hounds. They prepare traps and lie in waiting, eager to claim our lives should we take but one false step. All this because they refuse to accept the truth."

"What truth?"

"That we are the future," Glava said. "It may take a thousand years or more, but we will overcome their pitiful weapons, their paltry schemes, and their powerless gods. We will assume our rightful place as rulers of the earth."

The golden eyes flashed at Wash's upturned face. "Do you wish to have a seat among us on that day, Washington Jones? Will you cast aside the weakness of your humanity, your mortality, and embrace true power?"

Wash jumped to his feet. "Yessir, I will!" His blue eyes were bright with lust. This was better than he could have imagined. He would never grow old, never die of pneumonia or tuberculosis. He would be free to do whatever he wanted, and eventually, he would become a king. Maybe these *nosferatu* would let him rule over Colorado or even all of the West. He could have the best whiskey, the finest cuts of beef, and all the women he wanted.

A smile spread across Glava's handsome face, revealing a pair of pointed teeth. "So be it." The vampire's cold hand clamped onto the back of Wash's neck. Glava pulled him close, twisting his head back to expose his neck. "Prepare yourself for the taste of death."

Wash felt the man's teeth punch through the skin on his neck, and fear seized him. He flailed his arms and legs, trying to break Glava's grip and escape, but he might as well have been trying to pry open a grizzly's jaws. Searing pain coursed through him as his lifeblood flowed out of his body. A scream erupted from deep within his lungs.

The burning in his limbs began giving way to a warm haze. His muscles relaxed, and he even managed a smile, his eyes closing on the last light he would see as living man.

Fodor Glava let the corpse fall to the floor with a thud. He pulled a handkerchief from his jacket pocket and wiped lingering beads of blood from the corners of his mouth. As he tucked the handkerchief away, he sneered at the fallen gunman.

"When next you wake, Washington Jones," he said, "you will be one of us. You will share our power and our lust." He crouched down next to Wash's head, black locks framing the pale skin of his face. Leaning over his victim's ear, he whispered, "And you will share our curse."

THIRTEEN

Cora leaned back in the saddle and surveyed the motley bunch assembled before her. The men slouched in their saddles, shoulders hunched against the cold wind blowing down from the mountain. Snow swirled around them in silvery whirlwinds, catching the sunlight like a thousand glass shards. Next to her, James Townsend sat atop a brown stallion, looking unhappy.

Sighing, Cora lifted her Colt from its holster and dropped it back into place. She didn't like bringing this many men, but it couldn't be helped. They were riding against a small army of vampires; they needed all the help they could get. Standing up in her stirrups, she pulled the bandana down to her chin.

"All right, gentlemen, this is how it is," she yelled over the wind. "We're about to charge into a dark, dusty mine that's filled with undead monsters." The men exchanged glances. "I know King George here filled you all in on what's going on up there, so don't act like you ain't in the know. I see your crosses and your garlic, so I know you're prepared.

"The good news is you ain't going to be doing much of the fighting your own selves. That's what me and George are here for. All you boys need to concern yourselves with is keeping them from rushing us all at once. Ben here will stay with you and show you how it's done, so keep your wits and you'll do fine.

"But," she added before the men could relax, "that don't mean it ain't going to be dangerous. We're riding into a nest of demons, and maybe not all of us will be riding out. Stay frosty, stay loose, and above all, stay where you can hear me." She looked each of the ten men in the eye, one at a time. "As far as you're concerned, I'm the Queen of England. What I say is law, on account of I know what I'm doing and you don't. I'm the big damn hero here, and don't you forget it."

Cora drew her saber and let it flash in the afternoon sunlight. "Now then, let's go win us back a mine."

The men gave a half-hearted cheer through their bandanas, raising their crosses in the air. Cora waved her saber in a circle over her head, then sat down and turned Our Lady of Virginia toward the mines. Ben and James rode on either side of her, and the rest of the men filed into two columns behind them.

"Ten men is the best you could scare up?" Cora asked, giving James a sidelong glance.

"It isn't as though Lord Harcourt keeps a standing army of vampire hunters living at his private retreat, Mrs Oglesby," James said. "I had to make do with what I could find."

"What did you find?"

"Stable hands. Butlers. Whoever had a free after-noon," James said.

Cora turned her head to stare at him. "You ain't serious?"

"Of course," James replied, returning her gaze. "Why wouldn't I be?"

"Because we can't take a bunch of stable boys into a nest of vampires. Ain't you got hunters or hounds or something a little more able? Ain't you and Harcourt into hunting like that other British lord feller up there in Estes Park?"

"Oh my, no," James said. "Lord Harcourt finds hunting rather distasteful, and I must say I share the feeling. We both find scholarly pursuits much more rewarding."

"That don't sound familiar at all," Cora said, tossing Ben a look. "I swear, I don't know why I came out here without my bottle. Killing vampires with a pair of uptight schoolteachers ain't sober work no matter how you cut it."

"Ain't like you done it before," Ben said. "When was the last time you hunted sober?"

"In the farm fields when I was just a sprout," Cora said. "Hunting grasshoppers for my pa."

"What's that?" James asked.

"I was just reminding Ben here that I ain't been sober since I was about ten."

"Are you serious?" James asked, the shock in his voice clear even through his scarf. "You've been a tippler since you were a child?"

"Why, sure," Cora said. "I learned good and young

that there ain't no point to fighting sober. I shoot straighter after I've had me a few, anyhow."

"At least until you start seeing double," Ben said.

"Why, I'll still hit both of them between the eyes," Cora said.

"Both of what?" James said.

"Hush up if you ain't going to pay attention, George," Cora said. "Just keep riding that pretty carriage horse of yours."

"I beg your pardon," James said. "This is a thoroughbred hackney from pedigree stock, I'll have you know. The Prince of Wales himself couldn't ask for a finer horse."

"I don't reckon he could," Cora said. "Them's a fine breed for hauling rich folk around all day, but it ain't no riding animal. You'd be better off on a mule."

"Forgive me if I'm not accustomed to riding the same commonplace animals you content yourself with, madam, but my standards happen to be slightly more refined than all of that. It's hardly my concern if you're so consumed with jealousy that you must fall to insults."

"Let's stop fighting, girls," Ben said. "We got other things to worry about."

"You heard what he said about my horse," Cora said. "You think I can just let that go?"

"You will if you want me to hold them boys together," Ben said. "I ain't riding into no mine with a pair of hunters that can't get along for more than half a tick."

"All right, have it your way," Cora said. "I just figured

old George would be more grateful for my pulling that vampire off his neck this morning. He ain't said a word of thanks."

"A vampire that we never would have encountered had you not ventured past the barricades," James said.

"Enough!" Ben said, his voice rising.

Cora shot him a look, but rode on in silence. James dropped the argument as well, and pushed his hat down over his ears. The hackney brown held his head high as they rode, his mane shining in the afternoon sun.

Cora turned her head and looked at the line of men following them. They were silent, their eyes forward. She felt a twinge of pity for them. Here they were, a ragtag gang of butlers and stable boys riding toward a nightmare of terror and death. She hadn't been bluffing when she'd told them that not all of them might be riding back out of the mine, but that was before she'd known they weren't even fighters. She thought James could have found a more capable army, even if that meant pulling from the mining crews. Miners were tougher, at least, and they would have known the tunnels better than Harcourt's house staff. The thought had probably never crossed James's mind, though.

Soon, the dark face of the mining facility crept into view. Cora pulled back on Our Lady's reins before she crossed into the building's shadow, looking the place over as James dismounted. It seemed as though nothing had changed since the morning, yet she felt uneasy. A gust of wind blew snow down from the roof into her face. She cursed and raised her arm, trying to shield herself from the freezing shards. She nudged her mare forward, keeping her head low as she rode toward the front door.

"Cora," James called. Something in his voice made her look up. He was standing by the door, bent over so his face was level with the knob.

"What is it, George?" she asked, dismounting.

"Have a look at this," he said.

Cora approached the door. "Well, I'll be damned," she muttered, looking at the shattered ruins of the lock. "Looks like somebody had a hankering for some of your silver, after all."

"So it would seem," James said. He pushed the door open and peered into the darkness. "I wonder if the poor soul is still alive."

"As something, no doubt," Cora said. "I doubt that poor soul of his is still here, though."

James gave her a correcting look, then turned and took a few steps into the building. "Fetch me a lantern, would you, dear?"

"Get your own," Cora said, pushing her way past him. She went over to the desk and picked up one of the lanterns from that morning. She lit it and surveyed the office. "Nothing looks different here."

"Are you sure?" James asked. "I could have sworn I placed the two lanterns side by side when we left this morning."

"Ain't much of a thief that comes through a silver mine and only takes a lantern," Cora said. "Maybe he didn't even get past the office before he got spooked and humped it back to town."

"I reckon he was too busy dragging something through it," Ben said from the doorway. He crouched down and ran his fingers over the floor. "Floor's all scratched up."

"Let me see," Cora said, moving over to crouch beside him. In the yellow glow of the lantern, she could see several parallel scratches along the wooden floor of the office. "Wasn't that big, whatever it was."

"Whatever what was?" James asked.

"Whatever that fellow dragged out of your mine," Cora said.

"You found something?"

"Ain't you been listening?" Cora said. "Somebody dragged something out of here."

"Are you sure?" James asked. He stepped around the desk and knelt down to inspect it himself. "Well, isn't that interesting?"

"Anything in there that could make tracks like this?" Cora asked.

"Not that I'm aware of," James said. "Of course, these tracks don't mean anything was stolen."

Cora looked at him. "The evidence is right under your boots."

"I see the tracks," James said, "but they could have just as easily been made by something being dragged inside."

Cora blinked, then looked back down at the scratches. "Never thought of that."

"I know," James said. "It would also seem that you haven't yet thought to invite the rest of the team inside."

She looked at Ben. "Ain't those boys your responsibility?" she asked him.

"Hardly," James replied before Ben could say a word. "You're the combat expert, and we are taking them into combat."

"Button your lip," Cora said, glaring at the scholar. She turned toward the door and cupped her hands around her mouth. "All right, boys, pile on in here!"

The men shuffled through the door in single file, their faces red from the cold. Once inside, a few of them pulled their bandanas down and blew into their gloves. One volunteer almost looked too young to shave. Cora shook her head as she watched them, praying that they would live to see the next morning.

"You boys ready?" she asked.

They nodded, shuffling their boots. Some of them had lanterns hanging from their belts. Cora held up hers and pointed to it. They took the hint, holding them out for her to light. She lit each in turn, and the small office was soon awash in the warm glow.

Suddenly, something slammed into Cora's back, knocking her forward into the group. The lantern fell from her hand and smashed apart on the floor, spilling flames into the dust. A chorus of surprised hollers filled the room as the men instinctively covered their heads. Cora fell face-first into their boots, the weight behind her pinning her down. She felt cold hands grab her elbows and yank her arms backward. Pain exploded in her shoulders, sending waves down her arms and across her neck. Her spine popped as the creature pulled. Each breath became a battle. A moment later, she heard a sharp hiss and felt the scraping of razor-sharp fangs against her neck.

The hands suddenly released her. She flopped forward, but caught herself before her face smashed into the floor. Forcing air back into her lungs, she pushed herself onto her hands and knees. Somewhere behind her, she could hear banging, scraping, and hissing. Her fingers curled into fists as she pulled herself to her feet and turned toward the sound.

James was grappling with the vampire against the far wall. His right hand held a wooden cross in a death grip, and he kept trying to press it against the monster's chest. The vampire growled and snapped at him with jagged fangs, trying to shove the cross away without getting too close to it. James pressed his attack, always keeping the cross just beyond the reach of those cold fingers.

Seeing an opening, he thrust the cross into the undead face, and the vampire recoiled in fear. James took advantage of the brief respite and reached for something at his belt. Not feeling what he was looking for, he glanced down. The vampire seized its chance, throwing itself into him. He tumbled backward, and the cross flew from his grip. He fell to the floor with a heavy thud and screamed as the monster pinned his arms down. Pale lips drew back from the mouthful of jagged teeth. With a hiss of anger, the vampire's head descended on the scholar's neck.

Thunder filled the small room, causing dust to stream down from the rafters. The vampire reeled from the bullet's impact, and Cora fired again. The second round punched a smoking hole clean through the undead skull, and the monster collapsed.

Everyone stood in silence for a moment, waiting for the harsh ringing in their ears to fade. Blue smoke hung in the air. After a few seconds, Cora lowered her revolver.

"Anyone dead?" she asked.

"Just this fellow," James said, struggling beneath the corpse. Cora gave the body a solid kick with her boot, and it rolled aside.

"Seems we got a problem," she said, looking at the scholar. "I guess they ain't scared of them contraptions in the tunnels no more."

"A disturbing development, certainly," James replied, "but not one I fully understand."

"Don't take a genius to figure it out," Cora said.

"Yes, it's clear they've gotten past the barricades, but the question is, how?" James stepped over to his fallen cross and picked it up. "You saw it for yourself: the vampire was still weakened by this cross. They clearly haven't developed an immunity to holy items, so they must have discovered a way around the ones in the tunnels."

Cora was about to reply when Ben cut in. "Meaning that the rest of the nest could come galloping through that door any minute. Let's get a move on."

"Yeah, you're right," Cora said.

"Of course I am," James said, tucking the cross into his belt. "Now, let's get a move on." He motioned for the rest of the men to follow him, but they remained in place, staring at the fallen vampire. Rolling her eyes, Cora drew her saber. There was a wet crunch as the blade sliced through the monster's flesh. Holding the head aloft by a tuft of hair, she waved it at the group.

"See, boys? It's dead." She tossed the head onto the desk. "Can't hurt you no more."

The head rolled off the edge of the desk and thumped to the floor. They flinched as one, then began shuffling toward James. Cora grinned as she watched them go. With a little luck, a few of them might close the day out with a kill of their own.

She wiped her sword clean on her coat sleeve and sheathed it. She stepped over the headless corpse and went to retrieve her lantern. A curse fell from her lips when she found the shattered remains. The struggle with the vampire had snuffed out the small flame, leaving her without a light. In a flash of anger, she kicked the broken lantern against the wall, shattering what remained of the glass casing. She cursed again before following the group into the mine.

"Keep them crosses handy, boys," Cora called out as she stepped into the large processing room. "Never know when a big ugly is going to fly into your face with them fangs snapping." She reached into her belt pouch and pulled out a small rosary. She rolled the beads between her fingers and smiled. Two kills for the day so far, and night hadn't even fallen yet.

James stood at the mouth of the first tunnel, peering forward into the darkness beyond the edge of his lantern's halo. Behind him, Ben faced the silent collection of mine carts, his silver dagger in his hand.

Cora was glad he'd remembered to bring it. A crucifix was a handy tool against vampires, but nothing could top sticking them with a length of holy silver.

Walking past the nervous group of men, Cora joined the two of them by the tunnel entrance. "Any good ideas, boys?" she asked in a low voice.

"I found what I believe to be the vampire's tracks," James said, pointing to the dirt covering the floor of the tunnel. Something had clawed at it, leaving narrow streaks through the pebbles. "It would appear he came at us on all fours."

"Ain't the only one come through here, either," Cora said, pointing at another spot. "If that ain't a boot print, I'm the Queen of Sheba."

James bent down for a closer look. "Could have been made by one of the miners."

"No, it's a riding boot," Cora said. "Heel's too high for a miner's boot."

Before James could reply, the sound of scraping gravel echoed from deep within the tunnel. They both looked up, but the shadows blocked their view beyond a few yards.

"Look sharp, boys!" Cora called over her shoulder. "Pack in tight and watch our rears." The men obeyed, forming a semi-circle around the tunnel entrance. They fingered their crosses as they peered at the vast darkness around them.

"Keep them steady," Cora said to Ben. "I don't want them spooking and running off to get themselves killed."

Ben nodded and stepped back to join the circle. As she stared into the tunnel, Cora's fingers closed around the rosary. She thumbed back the Colt's hammer with her other hand as the echoes grew louder.

When the first vampire broke into the lamplight, time seemed to slow to a crawl. She could see the pebbles flying from beneath the vampire's hands and feet as it rushed toward them, fangs bared. Cora took aim at the soulless face, a psalm coming to her lips.

"Save me, O God, by Thy name."

She squeezed the trigger.

"Judge me by Thy strength."

The cylinder clicked as she pulled back the hammer.

"Hear my prayer, O God."

She took aim at a second vampire.

"Give ear to the words of my mouth."

The vampire tumbled to the ground.

"For strangers are risen up against me."

Another flash.

"Oppressors seek after my soul."

Thunder. The empty pistol fell from her hand.

"Behold, God is mine helper."

Her saber flashed in the light.

"He shall reward evil unto mine enemies."

She charged forward over the ruined corpses and into the oncoming rush. Human shapes lurched out of the shadows, and she cut them down, the sanctified blade carving smoking gashes in the unholy flesh. A thrust through an undead heart, a slash across a rotting neck, a cry for the joy of battle, and the tunnel was silent once more.

"For He hath delivered me out of all trouble: and mine eye hath seen His desire upon mine enemies."

Cora's voice echoed off of the stone walls. Head bowed, she stood amid a pile of smoking corpses. The rosary hung from her left hand, her palm pressing the beads into the hilt of the saber.

Taking a deep breath, she turned back to the group. Her eyes glittered in the lamplight. "You boys OK?"

They stared at her in stunned silence.

"We ain't got all day, now," she said. "I reckon these ones here was only half their numbers, and we still ain't found the big bad pulling their strings."

"My heart, Cora," James said. "What just happened?"

"I was earning my pay," Cora said. She cleaned off the blade and slid it home. "You was expecting something different?"

"You've just slain over half a dozen vampires, and in a matter of seconds," James said. "I've never even heard of such a thing being done by one person."

"You ain't reading the right books, then," Cora said as she retrieved her fallen revolver. She dumped the spent shells on one of the corpses and pulled fresh rounds from her belt. "Hell, we've done this plenty of times. Granted, we was hunting a pack of hellhounds, not vampires, but you still go about it the same way: trap them in a small space, line them up, and cut them down."

James just shook his head, speechless.

"All right, Ben," she called. "Bring them boys on through."

James looked back and waved at them, then turned back toward Cora and began picking his way around the lifeless arms and legs littering the tunnel floor.

Cora fell in behind him, her boots cracking ribs with a sound like a popping fire. She could hear the shuffling of the men's feet as they followed them deeper into the tunnel.

After a few minutes, the party reached the ruined cross. James and Cora crouched down and inspected the damage.

"Not the work of a vampire," James concluded after a few moments.

"No, sir," Cora said, "No way they could get up close enough."

"It looks as though our intruder had a similar revulsion for holy objects," James said. "The damage is quite extensive." He stood up and looked around. "Come to think of it, he seems to have made some of them vanish. I distinctly remember erecting three crosses here."

Cora looked at the dirt covering the floor. "Didn't drag them out, neither."

"This would explain how the vampires escaped, at least," James said. "That's a comfort."

"Ain't much of one," Cora said, "but I reckon it'll have to do."

She waved James forward, and he took up his position at the head of the line. They continued down the tunnel, silent except for the shuffling of their boots. The light from their lanterns kept the shadows at bay, and James continued his habit of lighting the tunnel lamps as they moved forward.

Soon, the tunnel walls gave way to a cavern. Cora called for a halt. The men formed a cluster behind her, their lanterns throwing long, human-shaped shadows in every direction. The echoes of their footsteps died away. In the following silence, Cora strained her ears, listening for the slightest sound from beyond the ring of light, but nothing came. After a few minutes, Ben stepped up beside her.

"Anything wrong?" he whispered.

She shook her head. "No, and that's the problem."

"What is?" James whispered.

"Ain't nothing here," Cora said. "If them vampires is really in here, they're being more quiet than they ought to."

"Perhaps they're frightened of us," James said.

"Right," Cora said, throwing him a look. "Nobody's waving their crosses or garlic in the air, so they don't know to be scared of us. Dumb as we look, any vampire would take us for a proper feast. You said there was at least a dozen of them suckers in here, right?" James nodded. "Well, we ain't killed that many yet, so the rest of the nest should be fixing to drink us dry to replace the losses."

The men overheard her, and shuffling began echoing through the cavern. Cora waved her hand, and they quieted down. She listened for a few more moments, then sighed.

"Hey!" she yelled, startling the group. "You suckers in here?" Her voice bounced off the invisible stone walls. "Come on out! We're plumb dripping with hot, juicy blood!"

"What on earth are you doing?" James whispered.

"Proving a point," Cora said. "Now hush."

They stood in silence for a minute, their ears ringing from Cora's shout. Finally, the hunter nodded in satisfaction.

"Yep, this place is as empty as Jack Evans's head."

James stared at her in stunned silence, but Ben laughed. "You've proved your point."

"Damn right I have," Cora said. "Now let's get out of here."

"I beg your pardon?" James asked.

"We're leaving, George. Ain't nothing else to be done here."

"Surely you aren't serious," James said. "We haven't eliminated the remaining vampires."

"They ain't here," Cora said, "and frankly, that makes me a good sight more worried than if they was."

James blinked at her. "Whatever for?" He smiled then, showing his teeth. "We've reclaimed the mine! Our job here is done."

"No, it ain't." Cora turned and started walking through the group. "It just got all kinds of messy. Instead of a nest of vampires trapped nice and pretty in a mine, we've got a nest of vampires free to roam about as they please. And, if you're right about how vampires work, we've still got a big bad to burn out somewhere."

James scrambled after her, and the rest of the men followed. Ben brought up the rear, keeping his crucifix pointed behind them as they entered the tunnel.

"You're a real boost to the morale, you know," James said when he caught up to her. "I'm beginning to understand why you work alone."

"Ben don't seem to mind," Cora said. "I reckon the rest of you is just too soft."

"Or perhaps we're of sound mind and you're barking mad," James said. "Still, I suppose even that has its advantages, especially in your line of work. It makes you stronger, more reckless and unafraid of the horrors you face."

"I may be crazy, but that ain't why I'm good," Cora said. "I'm good because I've had plenty of practice. Me and Ben been doing this job for near about twenty years now. When you been at something that long, you find your knack for doing it."

"Twenty years?" James raised his eyebrows. "It truly is a miracle that you're still alive."

"By the grace of the Lord," Cora said, crossing herself.

"How did you first get into the business?"

Cora glanced at the ruined cross as they passed. "You know of the war between the states?" James nodded. "Well, that's how."

"I'm afraid I don't follow."

"Ben and I was raised and married in the South. Virginia, to be exact," Cora said. "Once the war was over, we didn't have much by way of anything. No homes, no family, no nothing." She spat in the dirt. "Damn Yankees took all that away from us when they came through and burned out our town. On top of that, they went and made a law that said we couldn't head west and claim our own land to start over. Our hands was tied everywhere we turned, so we had to think of something else.

"We was plain stumped for a spell before Ben came up with the idea of bounty hunting. He figured since he'd trained some with guns and swords in the Confederate army, we could come out west and round up crooks and rustlers. Being raised on a farm, I already knew my way around horses. I taught him to ride and he taught me to shoot, and we sold what little we had left to buy some tickets out to Saint Louis."

"I'm with you so far," James said, stepping around the fallen vampires in the tunnel, "but it's still a big leap from arriving in St Louis to hunting the supernatural."

"Hold your horses for a tick and I'll get there," Cora said. "As I said, we showed up in St Louis with our guns, our horses, and not a damn clue as to going about hunting bounties. Ben figured we could just check in with the sheriff and he'd set us on our way, but turned out it ain't that easy. Back then, the James gang was just getting their start, Indians was still a big threat west of Dodge, and the railroad didn't go all the way through to the Pacific yet. You couldn't take ten steps without falling afoul of somebody or other."

"Sounds like an ideal set of circumstances for bounty hunters," James said.

Cora nodded. "So it was, which was exactly why we was in a fix. Saint Louis was crawling with folk hunting bounties and folk with bounties on their heads. Couldn't make sense of which was which, and the sheriff wasn't no help to us. We was penniless and in a strange city, so we turned to the Church. A priest called Father Higgins took us in and gave us a place to sleep for a few nights. He asked us why we was in Saint Louis, and we told him. When we did, he got a funny look on his face, and he says, 'What kind of bounties you hunt?'

"'Just about any we can find,' Ben says.

"'Can you spare some help for an old priest like me?' he says.

"Me and Ben looked at each other for a moment. 'Why, sure,' Ben says. 'We owe you, anyway.'

"Father Higgins got a big grin on his face then. He started telling us how he had himself a problem with a local coven of witches. Seems they was set on calling demons out of hell into this world. The local law and bounty hunters couldn't help him none, not wanting to dirty their hands with anything unnatural and all. Father Higgins was up a tree about it, and had nobody to help him out. Ben and I talked it over, but we really didn't have no choice. This nice old man had taken us in, and he needed help.

"So we took the job, and soon we found where the witches was hiding. They'd managed to conjure up a hellhound that they kept in a big cage in this old abandoned schoolhouse on the outskirts of the city. We saw that and figured it'd be suicide to fight them with what we had, so Ben gets the idea to ask the priest if he had any sort of holy weapons we could use. Father Higgins asked a blacksmith to melt down one of them silver crosses from his altar, mix it with lead, and make us some bullets. Once he had them, the priest gave them a blessing and handed them to us.

"We took them holy bullets back to the school-house with us and set them witches to running. They set their pet hellhound on us, but Ben shot it square in the head with the special bullets and killed it stone dead. I managed to round up a good number of the witches, and we dragged them back to Father Higgins so he could set them straight.

"When we got back, the priest was so happy to see that we did the job that he near burst out crying. After he pulled himself together, he said we could find work doing that sort of thing if we wanted. Lots of folk out here had trouble with hellhounds and witches and whatnot, but there wasn't but a few folks in the business of killing such critters. The priesthood does what it can, but most priests ain't fighters, so they was looking for some more heroes. We enjoyed the job we did well enough, so we figured we'd try it out for a spell. Father Higgins let us keep the rest of the bullets he made for us and sent word to the other priests that we was in the business now.

"Now, a score of years later, here we are, still doing the same business. Hasn't all been glory and high spirits, but we stayed alive and made a living besides."

"A fascinating story, certainly," James said. They had arrived back in the foreman's office, and the rest of the men were waiting by the door, looking anxious.

"I like to think so," Cora said.

"One thing puzzles me, though." James set his lantern on the desk. "You say your husband has accompanied you all these years, yet I don't seem to recall ever meeting him. Do the two of you work separately?"

Cora looked at him in shock. "Why, he's been with us all afternoon." Looking over at the group of men by the door, she searched through their faces, but couldn't find Ben's. "He must have gone out to see to the horses just now. I swear I introduced the two of you when we talked to Harcourt, or even on the train back from Denver. He was asleep on the other bench, remember?"

"I'm afraid I don't," James said, "though I must admit I wasn't entirely sober that day. Still, you must introduce me when we get outside. I feel rather sheepish for having ignored him all this time."

"Well, he's easy to ignore," Cora said. "Why, I forget he's in the room half the time when he's into one of his books."

"Books, you say?" James asked, a smile spreading across his face. "Your husband is a bibliophile?" Cora gave him a blank look. "A book lover."

She laughed. "You got that right."

"I beg your pardon." The voice came from the cluster of men by the door. "Might this conversation be continued elsewhere?"

James turned and looked at the man who spoke. "Getting impatient, are we, Edward?"

An older man nodded. "Yes, actually."

"I suppose it is getting late," James said, examining his pocket watch. "I hope Constance remembered to put the kettle on, or tea will be late."

"Can't have that, now," Cora said. "All right, boys, go get your horses. Let's get out of here."

The men jostled one another as each fought to be the first out the door. Cora took one last look around the office. The rest of the vampires could still be lurking somewhere in the shadows beyond the door, watching them leave. They could rot there for all she cared. Night would bring them swarming out of the mine like ants. Leadville was quite a few miles away, and she didn't think they'd roam so far after losing half their numbers. Still, if they had a mastermind driving them, predicting their movements would be impossible. They wouldn't behave like normal animals.

"Shall we?" James asked.

"Shouldn't we put up a cross or something?" Cora said. "Try to keep them bottled in?"

James shook his head. "They have a human accomplice now. We'll need to find and eliminate him before we can move against the *nosferatu*." He turned and walked out the door.

"Whatever you say," Cora said, tossing up her hands and following him outside. Although she walked in the shadow of the building, she still had to squint against the afternoon sunlight glimmering on the peaks around them. Most of the men had already mounted and were facing the road leading back to Harcourt's retreat. The sight brought a smile to her lips. At least they were all making it out alive.

Cora looked skyward, trying to gauge the remaining daylight, but all she saw was a dark shape plummet from the roof onto the British scholar. James didn't have time to holler before the vampire drove him into the ground. His legs thrashed against it, tossing snow into the air, but the vampire held him down. The snow muffled his cry as the fangs sank into the back of his neck.

"*In nomine Patris!*" Cora's boots pounded across the snow as she drew her saber. Diving into the undead monster point-first, she knocked it clear of James's prostrate form. Vampire and hunter rolled over the ground, snow sticking to the gray flesh. The monster ended up on top, Cora's sword lodged in its side. Smoke poured from the wound, but the creature ignored it and wrapped cold fingers around her braid. She spat curses and struggled against the iron grip. It seemed to mock her, baring its fangs in front of her eyes instead of sinking them into her throat.

Then, without warning, the vampire turned and leapt away.

The rushing of cold air into her lungs drowned out the screams at first. When they reached her ears, she picked her head up and squinted at the sound. The dark shape of the vampire crouched on the snow, pinning a writhing pair of legs beneath it. Beyond it, a riderless horse stamped in fear among the rest of the mounted men, who were backing up into the sunlight. Cora struggled to her feet before realizing that her sword was still stuck in the monster's side. She pulled her pistol from her belt and forced her legs into a run.

The vampire heard her approach and raised its head, blood soaking its matted beard. Even at this distance, Cora could see the gleam in its eyes as it reveled in the fresh kill. She pointed her revolver at that gleam and squeezed the trigger. The gunshot echoed against the wall of the mining complex. Smoke erupted from the vampire's forehead as it pitched backward into the snow.

Cora didn't check her stride, her boots kicking up small chunks of snow. She could sense the line of men on horseback staring at her, but she ignored them, keeping her revolver trained on the fallen vampire. It lay sprawled on its back, one hip jutting toward the afternoon sky. She pressed the toe of her boot into the mottled shoulder, pushed it over, pulled her sword free, and lopped off the monster's head. She considered it for a moment, then looked up at the line of mounted men. Before they could react, she raised her boot and kicked the head straight at them. A number of them hollered, holding up their arms to protect their faces, but the head left the mountain's shadow before it reached them and disintegrated into a fine dust.

"That isn't very amusing," one of the men said.

Cora's smirk widened, but she didn't reply. Instead, she turned and inspected the vampire's victim. It was an elderly man clad in a tweed suit beneath his wool coat. Puncture wounds lined both sides of his throat. Dark streaks of blood trailed down his neck into the snow, but no fresh blood flowed.

Footsteps approached, and she glanced up. James looked disheveled, his glasses crooked and his tie loose around his neck. His face contorted with sorrow when he recognized the fallen man.

"Ah, poor Edward," he said. "I knew I shouldn't have brought him."

"He is kind of old for this work, ain't he?" Cora said.

James nodded. "I even told him as much back at the retreat, but he insisted on coming. Old fool kept blathering on about his duty to House Harcourt and all of that, so I finally agreed. Now look where I got him."

"Ain't your fault, James," Cora said. "Why, you should be thanking your lucky stars that it ain't you where he is right now."

"I suppose you deserve the majority of the thanks," James said.

"Well, then, I reckon you owe me a drink," Cora said. "Anyhow, this feller's already working his way toward becoming a vampire himself, so unless you got any pressing business with him, I'll get right to taking his head off."

James sighed and nodded, turning his face away as Cora's saber came down on the old man's neck. She wiped the blade clean on the snow next to the body, then dried it on her coat and slid it home. James turned back toward the old man and knelt. He reached into his pocket, produced a small clove of garlic, and stuffed it into the victim's mouth. He muttered a brief prayer, then stood and looked at Cora. "Shall we?"

"I reckon so," Cora said. "You want to bring him back for a proper burial?"

"I'll send a wagon for him in the morning," James said. "The *vrykolakas* will have no interest in his remains."

"If you say so," Cora said. "You got to get the retreat ready, anyhow."

"Ready?" a young man from the group asked.

"Ready for what?"

James looked skyward at the waning daylight. "For the coming darkness."

FOURTEEN

Ben and Cora rode back to town under the afternoon sun. She had wanted to stay and help James fortify Harcourt's retreat against the vampiric attack, but the scholar would have none of it. He had stood beneath the archway leading to the front door, refusing her passage.

"I can prepare my own home," he said. "It's more important that you return to Leadville and make what preparations you can. You will need all the help you can get should we fail to hold them back."

Cora finally relented, but not before informing James just how much of an old fool he was. Shaking her head, she walked down the path to where Ben stood with their horses. When he saw her approaching, Ben climbed on Book's back and turned the gelding's head toward the road. Cora followed suit, Our Lady swaying beneath her as she mounted. She readied her heels for a punch to the mare's ribs when the scholar's voice echoed back to her.

"You will remember to bring your husband next

time, won't you?" James called, waving his hand. "I should so like to meet him."

Cora raised her hand without responding, then gave Our Lady her heels and followed Ben down the road. They rode at a good clip, bandanas pulled up against the frigid air. The town of Leadville was nothing but a dark gray shadow in the distance, ignorant of the menace that threatened to swallow it whole. Above their heads, the eastern sky was beginning to give way to the darker blue of evening.

After awhile, Cora broke the silence. "That James Townsend is a mite touched, if you ask me."

"Why's that?" Ben asked. "Cause he's set on making a stand all by his lonesome?"

Cora shook her head. "He just wants to be a hero, and I can't blame him on that account. There's plenty of times we've made dumb moves just to make the kill that much more fun. You remember the time we cornered that werewolf down in Santa Fe?"

"That's the one them Indians said was a skinwalker, right?"

"One and the same," Cora said. "There I was, set to put a silver bullet in its head while it was still human when you come barging in and tell me to wait. 'It's a better time if you let it change,' you says. So I held my fire until them hungry-looking eyes were staring holes through me. Fool thing nearly tore my neck out before I put that bullet in it, but at least we looked like the heroes we is."

Ben chuckled. "I only said that to get you to hold off on the killing until it didn't look like a man no more," he said. "They'd have hung us right quick if you'd shot it before it changed."

"That ain't so," Cora said. "They knew that boy was a monster. Why else did they call us in?"

"All they knew was that something kept killing their sheep," Ben said. "As I recall, the Mexicans in town thought it was one of them chupacabra critters."

"That notion had us chasing through that desert scrub for near two weeks before we came to our senses."

"We?" Ben shot her a smirk. "Ain't that giving yourself too much credit? You never did have no sense, not then and not now. I was the one that figured we was chasing the wrong spook and turned us back out of the desert. Without me, you'd have been nothing but buzzard chuck."

"You should have left me out there, then," Cora said. "That way, you could have gone off to San Francisco and started up your print shop."

Ben's brow furrowed. "Come on, now, you know I'd never do such a thing."

"Sure you would," Cora said. "Why, you'd leave me to rot in a vampire nest if it meant pulling one of your books out of a fire."

Her husband didn't reply. His shoulders slumped as he sank into a sulk. A silence settled between them, and Cora watched the distant buildings draw nearer. Every so often, she would turn in her saddle and check behind them for any sign of pursuit. She didn't figure James and his men would have fallen yet, but nothing would stop the vampires from bypassing Harcourt's retreat and attacking the town. If they did, she and Ben would have their work cut out for them. If not, it would be a dull evening. Cora sighed at the thought. Another long night of alternating watches that might not even be necessary. It always irked her when the monsters they hunted didn't have the decency to show after she waited up for them.

Cora ran out of patience. "Oh, stop your sulking. You know I was just joshing you."

"I hope you don't really think that," Ben said. "You know I'd face down a whole pack of hellhounds with my bare hands if it meant saving your life."

"Of course I know that," Cora said. "I wouldn't be in this business with you if I didn't."

Ben smiled. "Me neither."

Once they made it back to Leadville, they made straight for the Northern Hotel. They tied the horses to the post out front, giving them a much-needed rest. Back in their room, Cora began digging through their trunk for cloves of garlic while Ben started sprinkling holy water on the door and windows.

After a few moments, Cora cursed.

"What is it?" Ben asked, looking over at her.

"No nails," Cora said. She held three garlic bulbs in her hand. "How are we supposed to hang these above the door with no nails?"

Ben thought for a moment. "No way that I can think of. I guess we'll have to make do with setting them out around the room."

Cora tossed one at the table. It rolled along the top and came to rest against the wall near the far window.

She set another on the bed between the pillows, then slipped the last one into her pocket. Her face grew serious as another thought came to her. "You'll need to leave that crucifix here."

"Why?" Ben asked, his hand dropping to where it was tucked into his belt.

"We'll need something stronger than garlic if that chief vampire feller shows himself," Cora said. "From what we saw in the mines, he don't seem the type to be squeamish around garlic."

"I don't see how you figured that," Ben said as he handed over the wooden cross. "James said it was a human that broke down the crosses in the tunnel."

"Just a feeling I got," Cora said, taking the crucifix. She pushed the trunk shut with her boot and propped the crucifix up against it so it faced the door. She looked around the room, then nodded to herself. "I reckon that's about all we can do for it."

"So what's the plan?" Ben asked.

Cora thought for a moment. "You run on down to the marshal's station and let Duggan know what's happening. I don't know what he'll be able to do, really, but at least he won't be surprised when them vampires start killing his townsfolk."

"You said he was an Irishman, right?" Ben asked. "Could be he's a religious man. Might have a cross or two of his own to lend."

"The more the merrier," Cora said. "While you're seeing to the marshal, I'm going to stop by the Pioneer."

Ben frowned. "This ain't the time to be drinking."

"I spent all afternoon sober, and look where it got

us," Cora said. "That poor old man got his throat torn out, and James got all his crosses smashed."

"Ain't neither one of them on account of your being sober," Ben said. "I don't want to ride against no vampires with a drunk partner, even if it's you. You'll get us both killed or worse."

Cora laughed. "Take that bee out of your bonnet. I just feel like getting me a drink or two and having a word with old Boots is all."

"Boots?" Ben asked. "You sure that's a good idea? We don't even know what he is."

"No, but that ain't no reason not to find out," Cora said. "The way I figure, no matter what he is, he's tied in to this whole mess. Maybe he ain't no more than a ghost now, but he can still talk, and I aim to make sure he does."

Ben looked puzzled. "How do you plan to make a ghost talk that don't want to? Ain't like you can smack him across the head or shoot off his fingers."

"I'll work something out," Cora said. "If nothing else, I'll challenge him to a drinking competition."

"Can't you be serious about this?" Ben said.

"Never said I wasn't," Cora said. "We ain't getting nowhere fussing like a pair of old fools. Run along and help the marshal and leave Boots to me."

Ben looked at her for a long moment, then turned and left. Cora counted the silver bullets in her ammo belt before taking one last look around the room. Everything was as ready as they could make it. If the vampires attacked tonight, they would at least be able to fall back here and fight. If they were singled out, that is. She had no reason to think they would be, but it never hurt to be prepared.

Cora put the horses to bed in the hotel's stable before walking over to the Pioneer. Overhead, the sun drifted toward the western peaks, lighting the few clouds in the sky aflame. Her fingers curled into fists as she walked, remembering the unearthly chill of the wendigo. The lesser vampires and their leader, the *nosferatu*, were powerful and deadly, but at least they couldn't freeze her limbs like that. They preferred the blood of their victims hot and spurting. That thought brought an uneasy chill of its own, and she pulled her coat close around her.

The Pioneer was in full swing at this time of night. Every table was crowded with miners and businessmen playing cards for their day's wages as ladies from the Purdy hung on their arms. Through the din of voices, she could hear the plinking of the saloon's piano. A row of miners in denim pants and thick coats stood along the bar, their backs to the door. Serving girls threaded through the clouds of cigarette smoke with trays of whiskey, coffee, and cider.

Cora stood at the door, her arms folded across her chest. This place would be easy pickings for a pack of vampires, and the Pioneer was only one of dozens of saloons in Leadville. Even if they had all of Duggan's deputies and all of James Townsend's servants-turned-hunters, they couldn't hope to defend everyone in town. If the vampires attacked tonight, people would die. They could only hope to find the bodies and dispose of them before they turned.

Heaving a sigh, she began sifting through the many faces, searching for the round red one that belonged to the bartender. Having no luck, she tapped on the shoulder of a man standing by the door.

"You seen Boots?" she asked, raising her voice over the noise.

"I'm sorry, I didn't quite catch that," the man said, betraying a crisp Irish accent. His brown hair hung in wavy locks on either side of his face.

"Boots," she said again. "Have you seen him?"

"Quite a few pairs in my day," he said, "and all of them dishonest." He smiled at Cora's puzzled look. "You've never met a boot that lies?"

"Can't say I have," Cora said, looking around for someone a little less drunk to help her. She was about to step away from the odd Irishman when he caught her arm.

"Men are like boots, miss," he said. "Don't you trust them. If you must trust anything, trust that." He pointed to a sign hanging above the piano, which read *Please do not shoot the pianist. He is trying his best.* "That is the only sensible piece of art criticism I have ever seen," the man said with a chuckle. With that, he let go of her arm and settled back against the wall. She offered him a polite smile before retreating into the crowd.

As she searched for the bartender, she reflected on the eccentricities of foreigners. James Townsend was bad enough, with his tea and his fancy speaker down in Denver, and even he had never talked about art criticism or dishonest boots. Cora had never had time

or money for any sort of art, and her taste in music
was limited to whatever instruments the local saloon
happened to own. She couldn't imagine anyone bothering to write criticism about either one.

After a few minutes of searching around the gambling tables, Cora made her way over to the bar and
ordered a drink. When the woman set the whiskey
down in front of her, Cora spoke over the din. "You
seen Boots around?"

"Boots?" the woman asked. "Yeah, I seen him upstairs a bit ago. Said he was going to get off his feet
for a spell."

"Do you think he'd mind some company?" Cora
asked, handing over a silver dollar.

The woman looked her over. "Maybe so, but not
from you. He tends to like his women a bit younger
and more ladylike."

"I ain't looking to take care of his pecker," Cora
said. "I just need a few words with him is all."

"He looked a sight testy when I saw him," the
woman said, "so you might want to buy him a drink
to lighten his mood."

"I'll be damned the day I buy a bartender a drink
from his own bar," Cora said. She tossed back the
whiskey and handed the glass to the woman. "Thanks
for the drink."

"Anytime, honey," the woman replied, moving
down the bar to refill glasses from the bottle in her
hand. Cora headed for the big staircase that ran along
the bar's wall. A breath of cold air blew over her as
she passed by the front door. She noticed that the

Irishman had vanished, probably in search of a saloon
with a better pianist. Shaking her head, she made her
way up the stairs. At the top, she turned the corner
into the hallway and almost collided with the bartender. Cora took a step backward, startled, but Boots
didn't seem alarmed.

"Ah, Cora Oglesby," he said, offering her a thin
smile. "What can I do for you on this fine evening?"

Cora grabbed the front of his shirt and pulled him
down the hallway. He went along, the smile never
leaving his face. When they were out of sight of the
saloon, she pushed him against the wall and shoved
the barrel of her Colt into his belly.

"I want some answers, spook," she said, her voice low.

"My, my, such hostility," Boots said. "Whatever
have I done to deserve this treatment?"

"Hush your mouth," Cora said, twisting the gun.
"You can't fool me. I know you ain't the real Boots
because I done put a silver bullet in his brain just this
morning."

"Did you, now?" the bartender said. "Well, isn't that
a disappointment. And here I was, planning my entire
strategy around that bloated corpse. It looks as though
you have foiled me again, Cora Oglesby. If you'll excuse me, I must see to the licking of my wounds."

He placed a palm on her chest and shoved. Cora
slammed into the wall behind her and slid to the floor.
Sucking in a breath, she raised her pistol and fired at
the bartender's grinning face. The gunshot clapped
her ears as she pulled back the hammer and waited
for the smoke to clear.

Boots remained on his feet. Cora's bullet had punched a hole just above his right eye, carving a gouge in the wallpaper behind him. As she watched, the wound closed in on itself as if it never had been there. She tried to fire again, but the bartender was too quick for her. His fingers wrapped around the Colt's barrel and wrenched it from her hand. He tossed the revolver aside and clamped his other hand around her throat.

"No more hostility," he said. "If you don't calm down, I will knock you out and deny you the honor of looking into my face when I kill you."

Cora struggled against his grip, but she couldn't hope to overpower him. After a few moments, she let her hands fall away from his fingers. Boots rewarded her with a sneer.

She spat in his face.

A look of surprise flickered there for a moment before the sneer reclaimed control. "Really, Cora, I would have expected such behavior from a common cur, but not from a lady such as yourself."

"Sorry to let you down," she said, curling her lips to spit again.

Boots clamped a hand on her mouth. "I would advise you not to test the limits of my courtesy, even if you are an old friend." Her eyes reflected her unspoken question. "You don't remember? I suppose it is only natural, what with my wearing this face. In my vanity, I assumed I had left such an impression when last we met that you would discern my poise and wit even through this mask."

Cora rolled her eyes at him. He hauled her to her feet, pulled her saber from its scabbard, and tossed it aside, then started pushing her down the hallway. As they walked, Cora suddenly noticed that Boots had no smell. This close to the man, she should have been overwhelmed by his usual aroma of sweat, smoke, and alcohol, but all she could smell was the faint scent of the pine floorboards.

Boots opened a door at the end of the hall and shoved her inside. A whiff of rotting flesh greeted her as she stumbled and fell in the semi-darkness. Behind her, the door slammed shut. She picked herself up and turned to face her captor.

"I would apologize for the smell, but I rather like it," Boots said, his face invisible in the darkness. "I have faith that you come to love it as well, given enough time."

"I reckon I'll love it just fine when it's coming from your bloated corpse," Cora said. She tried to take stock of her surroundings. Her nose told her that something nearby had died recently, but she could only see gray shadows. The afternoon sun glowed around the boards covering the windows, but no beams of light cut through the darkness. Despite the stench, she took a deep breath to calm herself. She'd been cornered before and managed to work her way out of it. She could do it again. Besides, Ben would come looking for her once he'd told Mart Duggan about the vampires. All she had to do was sit tight until he showed up or Boots let his guard down.

"Still so unrefined, especially for a woman from the

American South," Boots said. "Although, if you relish the scent of an enemy's death, this aroma should be to your liking. The corpse rotting in this room once belonged to a Mr Washington Jones, who I believe made your acquaintance recently."

"Wash Jones?" Cora asked. "You mean that upstart card player?"

"I can't speak for his gambling habits, but he certainly seemed to bear a grudge against you. One strong enough to encourage the sacrifice of his humanity to see it avenged."

"Seems you did the world a favor, then," Cora said. "That boy was fixing to be a bandit, so you just saved some lawman a lot of work by culling him early."

"I doubt the world of humanity has much to thank me for," Boots replied, "and the murder of Washington Jones certainly isn't in their interest."

"Then why'd you kill him for?" Cora asked.

"To turn him, of course." Footsteps echoed in the darkness. "Replacing fallen soldiers is always a difficult task for a general. Not that you would understand such harsh realities yourself. Life is simpler when you are alone."

A cold wave of dread washed over Cora as she put the pieces together. "You're the big bad that James was going on about."

"The word is *nosferatu*," Boots said, "and you are correct. Frankly, I'm disappointed it took you so long to realize it. Perhaps I've been too subtle."

"Or maybe you just ain't no good at being evil," Cora said. "Me and Ben already wiped out a full half-dozen of your boys without breaking a sweat, and I don't see no reason why we won't do the same to you."

"You and Ben, you say?" The bartender's voice took on an amused tone. "He has been of some use to you these past ten years, then?"

Cora blinked. "Why, sure. We've been riding together hunting the likes of you for a good long while now. Fine work for a man and wife, if you ask me, though some may find it unusual."

"Unusual indeed," Boots said. "Tell me, when was the last time you saw your husband?"

"Not thirty minutes ago, fresh from killing your vampires."

"Is that so?" There was a bright flash as Boots struck a match. The tiny flame sputtered in his hand as he reached over and lit a lantern. A warm glow filled the room, illuminating large crates covered with dust. Strange shadows danced across his round head as he approached her.

"You inquired earlier as to how I am able to wear the body of the former proprietor of this saloon, whom you so decisively killed." Boots stepped closer, and Cora backed away. "I don't suppose your illustrious scholar could enlighten you?" Cora shook her head. "I thought not. Such men pride themselves on their knowledge, but they are only grasping at shadows. Shadows that will one day devour them." His grin deepened at the thought. "I shall relish the taste of his blood, and I imagine he will prove himself a useful servant, just as this portly bartender has."

"Till we came along, anyhow," Cora said. "Boots ain't no servant of yours no more."

"You destroyed his body, yes, but men are more than mere flesh and bone." The bartender's eyes sparkled in the light. "Sometimes, their true usefulness lies in their other natures."

"Your usefulness sure ain't in getting to the point," Cora said. "I didn't figure you'd try to kill me with talk when you dragged me in here, or I would have ate my own gun to spare myself the misery."

"Such spirit in you," Boots said. "It will make the breaking of it so much the sweeter."

"I reckon I'll have a better time breaking your neck."

A single laugh shook the bartender's shoulders. "Such unpleasantness as well. Still, if you would only stop interrupting, I might get to the point you are so eager to hear."

Cora opened her mouth to reply, then shut it. If she could keep this creature talking, it would give her more time to think of a way out. Ben could come crashing through the door at any minute, too, which would solve things nicely.

"That's better," Boots said. He raised the lantern and walked behind a set of crates. "Come over here."

Cora stepped around the crates and looked down. The dead eyes of Wash Jones stared up into the darkness between them. His jaw hung open as if in shock, and his arms and legs were crumpled beneath him.

"Look well, Cora Oglesby," Boots said. "Look at the early stages of vampiric metamorphosis. When the sun sets tonight, Mr Jones will arise anew, a soldier in an unholy army."

Sickened by the glee in his voice, Cora nonetheless found herself drawn to the corpse at her feet. Kneeling down, she looked at his open mouth. His teeth still looked human, not sharp and elongated like those of the vampires she'd killed that day. No blood seeped from the puncture wounds on his neck; his body was completely dry. Cora shook her head. Wash Jones had been an arrogant fool, but he hadn't deserved this. She made the dead man an unspoken promise that she would see his body put to rest.

"Don't waste any thoughts of pity for Mr Jones," Boots said. "He chose to become one of us so he might settle his score with you. I merely provided him the means by which he could achieve such power."

"So you're as honest as the serpent in the garden," Cora said. "Can't say I'm surprised."

"I assure you, I am a man of my word. I did have every intention of allowing him the pleasure of ending your life, but it seems he will not wake up in time. I had not counted on catching you so easily. Still, I suppose I might save some of your blood to serve as the first meal of his new life."

Cora was getting bored with such threats. "Ain't like he'll be around to enjoy it. James already told me that the weaker vampires ain't got their own minds."

"I have reason to believe he will be present." The bartender's voice changed as he spoke, becoming deeper and raspier. Cora looked up at him, and her breath caught in her throat.

In front of her, where Boots had stood a moment ago, the cold blue eyes of Washington Jones looked back her.

Cora fell back against the wall as the living image of the dead man leaned toward her. His sandy-colored hair framed his face, and the same mocking smile spread beneath his beard.

"You seem surprised, Cora," the voice of Wash Jones said. "Surely your Mr Townsend informed you that a *nosferatu*'s power is far greater than that of a lowly *vrykolakas*."

Cora glanced at the corpse, then back up at the living image of Wash Jones. "He did say that your type could do different things, but he didn't mention taking on a dead man's body. Mostly just that you had your human soul."

"Correct on both counts," the vampire said. "Let us explore the first mystery, then." Cora was silent, so he continued. "As you know, sunlight is fatal to a *vrykolakas*. We *nosferatu* find it rather uncomfortable as well, so we prefer to use more indirect means to influence the sunlit world. To accomplish this, we have learned to use the souls of those we drink as familiars."

"The souls?" Cora asked. "Ain't the soul of a vampire stuck in hell?"

"A common belief, but one I find rather insulting," Wash said. "I prefer to think being subject to my will is more of a divine privilege than an eternity of torment."

"I think I'd prefer hell," Cora said. "So you take in the soul through the blood, then?"

"Precisely, and it follows our every command, just as the newborn *vrykolakas* made of the body does. We can conjure these souls to enact our wills during the day, when we ourselves are somewhat more restrained."

Cora nodded, feigning indifference while her mind raced. The danger of her situation was finally sinking in, stoking the fires of her panic. She was now balancing learning more about her enemy with being devoured and enslaved, and the longer she lingered, the less likely her escape seemed. James needed to know what she knew so he could share it with his friends back in England. If Ben didn't show soon, she would have to make a break for it and hope for the best. Better to go down fighting than to let herself be taken without a struggle. Still, as panicked as she was, she couldn't resist asking one more question. "You all can't drink blood through them souls, right?"

Wash shook his head. "No. Some *nosferatu* even regret this shortcoming, though I can't fathom why. The thrill of feeling your own lips on a person's pulsing neck, the sweet flow of their lifeblood down your throat, and the screams ebbing to whimpers as you drink them dry simply cannot be replaced."

"You really are a monster," Cora said.

"Words spoken in ignorance," the vampire said. "At times, I try to recall my life before my immortality, when my mind was small and my body frail, but the memories always elude me. I imagine it is what the butterfly feels when it tries to remember its life in the chrysalis: fear and confusion and limitations. I suppose

I had a clearer memory when I was still young in un-death, but even an immortal mind cannot hold all the history of the universe."

"Yours sure can hold a lot of bullshit," Cora said.

Wash's blue eyes grew hungry in the dim light. "And what will yours hold, I wonder?"

Cora crossed her arms. "Nothing but my own self till the day I die, which will be well after I put you in your grave."

"Defiant even in the face of certain defeat." The vampire bared Wash's teeth in a smile. "Such willpower is far too valuable to waste in such a miserable shell. I had thought to make you my slave, but you have moved me."

Quicker than a striking diamondback, Wash's hand shot out and grabbed her throat. He pushed her against the wall, his eyes burning with hunger. "No, I shall usher you into the ranks of the *nosferatu*, and you shall learn to walk the shadows as a true ruler of the night. In time, you will understand the weakness of humanity and their puny gods. We are the gods who shall rule the world, Cora Oglesby."

Cora didn't answer, and silence filled the room. She knew her time had run out, and she struggled to quiet her frantic thoughts enough to prepare for a last stand. Overpowering the vampire was impossible, but it couldn't use the body of Wash Jones to turn her, meaning it would have to come in its own body. When it did, she might be able to get the jump on it and escape. If it left her conscious.

In the silence, she thought she heard footsteps in

the hallway. They were slow and intermittent, as if searching for something. She heard a door creak somewhere nearby, and she grinned. She looked into Wash's cold blue eyes and lifted her chin.

"You hear that, spooky?" she said. "That's the sound of my husband looking for me. I hope you got a plan for when he comes through that door and sticks you with a silver dagger."

"Your husband?" the vampire asked. "Surely you don't mean Benjamin Oglesby?"

"The one and only," Cora said. "Even the big bad vampire is scared of him, I see."

"He was never the threat you are," the vampire said.

"Well, that's about to change."

Confusion flickered in the borrowed eyes. "You truly believe he is in that hallway looking for you?" Cora nodded, and the confusion melted into glee. "How absolutely delicious! I heard tales of your madness in the wake of our previous meeting, but I never imagined I could have so thoroughly broken your mind."

"I ain't the one with the touched mind," Cora said. "You ain't hearing me spouting nonsense."

"Oh, but you are," the vampire said. "I cannot begin to tell you the joy that this moment brings me. It will be like reliving ten years past and our first fateful encounter. To break the same hunter twice in one lifetime is a rare thrill even among the immortal." He looked down at her, his face ecstatic. "Cora Oglesby, Mad Madam, scourge of the unholy West, I believe I have some bad news for you."

As he spoke, the face in front of hers changed. The sandy blond beard faded into a well-trimmed brown mustache, and the deep blue eyes of the young gun-man gave way to a lighter shade of blue she knew as well as her own brown eyes. The mouth below the mustache twisted into a sadistic grin she had never seen on those lips. All of her fight and spirit evaporated in a single flash of recognition.

"Your husband," said the voice of Benjamin Oglesby, "has already found you."

FIFTEEN

Cora's knees gave way. Had it not been for the hand clamped around her neck, the hand of her own husband, she would have collapsed to the floor. Her heart screamed that she was seeing an illusion, some sinister trick played by the vampire, but as the seconds passed, the man standing before her never wavered or disappeared.

"What's wrong?" Ben's voice asked. "You haven't seen me in ten years, and you don't have anything to say? Not even some pithy sentiment about how you've missed me so?"

"No," Cora said.

"How about an apology, then?" The face of her husband leaned in until their noses almost touched. "Can you at least apologize for just letting me die like you did?"

"Who are you?" she asked.

"Who am I?" Ben's other hand grabbed her gun belt. He spun her around and hurled her across the room. "I'm your husband."

Cora slammed into a large crate with a bone-jarring thud. She fell to the floor and hugged her knees to her chest as the monster wearing Ben's face came to stand over her. She shook her head, her eyes squeezed shut. It wasn't possible. Ben hadn't been killed by this creature. He was with Mart Duggan right now, making preparations for the coming wave of vampires. She would meet up with him later to defend the town.

"Maybe I was wrong about you," Ben's voice said as the creature knelt next to her. "Maybe you are only suited for life as a slave. I still have time to decide. Perhaps the taste of your soul will tell me what I need to know. Either way, I've grown tired of this conversation." He reached out and grabbed her jaw, pulling her face toward him. "Look at me."

Cora opened her eyes. Ben's face loomed above her, his kind features twisted with hatred.

"I want the last thought of your mortal life to be of your failure," he said. "I want you to look upon the enslaved soul of your husband and carry that sight with you into eternity. Not the eternity of bliss your foolish god promised you, but an eternity as the very thing you most despise."

The hand gripping her jaw let go and cracked across her face. The blow knocked her back into the crate. Her head swam from the impact, and she felt as though she might vomit. She fought the sensation as she lay on the floor, her mind repeating the same thoughts. Ben couldn't be dead. She had just seen him in their room. He was with the marshal. He would come through the door any second. They would kill this vampire just as they had killed so many other monsters.

Standing above her, the image of her husband faded into the gray shadows of the room. A few seconds later, a slow creaking came from somewhere in the darkness. Glowing golden eyes fixed themselves on the fallen hunter.

Fodor Glava stood over his fallen enemy, relishing her suffering and confusion. He always marveled at how easily mortals could be rendered helpless with mere words. It was such a handy tool if used right, but to use it on the Mad Madam herself, one of the most feared hunters in the West, was a special thrill. He could never have predicted her delusions, of course, but he was still pleased with himself for driving the knife through her heart. Her tears would sweeten the taste of her blood, and bringing her into the fold of the undead would make him a legend among *nosferatu*.

Today was truly a great day.

Glava knelt down and pulled the hunter's head toward him. She seemed only halfway conscious, her eyelids fluttering as the occasional sob escaped her lips. He brushed her disheveled braid off her neck like a lover, caressing her skin with cold fingers. The thirst screamed from every inch of his body, demanding that he drink his fill, but he held it at bay. Holding the helpless form of Cora Oglesby in his arms was intoxicating, sweeter than the taste of any blood. He wanted to savor the moment.

Finally, he gave in to the demand and lowered his face to her neck. Her skin popped beneath his fangs like gossamer. The ecstasy filled his being, spiraling through his limbs, and he surrendered to it. No mortal sensation, no matter how powerful or beautiful, could ever approach the pleasure he now felt.

Lost in his delirium, the vampire didn't hear or feel the shattering of glass against his forehead. A moment later, the bliss in his veins evaporated, replaced by a searing pain that tore across his scalp. The sensation was so alien that for an instant he remained motionless, trying to understand it. Then his instincts kicked in, and he gripped his head in both hands. The pain spread to his palms, and he cried out. Rolling away from his victim, he rubbed his hands on his suit, trying to wipe the unseen fire away, but still it burned.

An impact in his side tore open another torrent of pain. The scent of his own searing flesh filled his nostrils. He rolled onto his back and squinted through the agony at the form of the hunter standing over him. Her brown eyes bored into him with seething hatred.

"Enjoy the pain while you can, you bastard," she said. "It will seem like bliss after you get to where I send you."

Cora's spurs chimed in a brisk rhythm as she left the room to reclaim her weapons. Her head still swam, but she forced herself to remain on her feet. Her saber gleamed a few yards away where it had fallen. She grabbed the hilt in her fingers, relishing the feel of the cold steel against her palm. This sword had been given to Ben during his days in the Confederate army. It was only fitting that it would behead his murderer.

Gripping the saber with white knuckles, Cora smiled. She could already feel the impact of the blade on that bastard's neck and hear the sweet crunch as it bit though the bone. More torture would be in order first, though. Another vial of holy water to the face, perhaps, followed by a few more kicks from her silver spurs. She would see the mighty vampire beg for death before Ben's sword pierced his unholy heart. Cora stormed into the dark storeroom, ready to administer her holy justice.

Her determination quickly turned to confusion. The room had filled with a thick white mist, and the vampire had vanished. As she stood dumbfounded, the mist flowed around her ankles and out the door, forming a river of white cloud down the hallway. Before she could react, it vanished down the stairs, leaving her alone.

Cora stared after the cloud for a moment before turning back into the room. She searched through it, but only found the body of Wash Jones and the vampire's coffin. She gave the pine box a few kicks with her boot before the sword fell from her shaking fingers. She collapsed to her knees and held her face in her hands as powerful sobs shook her body. The memory of Ben's eyes filled with contempt and murderous rage filled her mind. She kept telling herself that it hadn't really been him, that it was just his image being used like a puppet by that monster, but that thought only reminded her that he was gone. His sweet words, his banter, and his smile had been stolen from her, and she would never find them again.

After a few minutes, the storm subsided, and she struggled to her feet. Metal rasped in the silence as she sheathed her saber and walked back into the hallway. Her pistol still lay where the apparition of Boots had thrown it. She slipped it back into its holster, wiped her eyes, and began a slow descent down the stairs.

Halfway down the stairway, a thought brought her up short. What if the vampire had been lying? Maybe Ben wasn't really dead after all. She hadn't found his body when she'd gone through the room, and she would have if the vampire had killed him before capturing her. The image of Ben must have been a trick, some black magic used to catch her off guard and make her easy prey. He had to be with Mart Duggan, setting up defenses for the town.

Her boots pounded down the stairway and out into the cold afternoon. The street bustled with the citizens of Leadville, miners and bankers and whores. Several passersby gave her odd looks as she darted between carts and around slow-moving horses, but she paid them no heed. She needed to see her husband with her own eyes, to touch his face and assure herself that it had all been a cruel trick.

The door to the marshal's station barely withstood her entrance. A deputy she didn't recognize sat at the desk, looking as though he had just soiled himself. He pointed a pistol at her, but the barrel wavered in his hand.

"Where's Duggan?" Cora demanded. The deputy just blinked at her. She stormed past him and threw open the door to the marshal's office.

Duggan was seated behind his desk cleaning his big Colt. "Something I can do for you, Mrs Oglesby?"

"Where's Ben?" she asked.

"Ben?"

"My husband," Cora said, panic and irritation welling up inside her. "Ben Oglesby. A few inches taller than you, blue eyes, neat mustache. He was supposed to drop by and let you know that there's a swarm of vampires that might come calling tonight."

The marshal put his gun on the desk. "Vampires in my town? How many?"

"That ain't important," Cora said. "Have you seen Ben?"

"Can't say I have," Duggan said. He looked back down at his gun. "Come to think of it, I don't think I ever met your husband. You should bring him around some time so we can get acquainted proper."

Cora stood in silence, her mind racing. Had Ben ever met Marshal Duggan? Now that she thought on it, she wasn't sure he ever had. She'd been the one dealing with the marshal most of the time, so maybe Duggan had never actually seen Ben.

"Sir?" a shaky voice said behind her. "Should I arrest her?"

Duggan looked behind her. "Don't fret, Kelley. She ain't no criminal."

Cora turned to see the strange deputy holster his gun. "Ain't seen him before," she said.

The marshal nodded. "Pat Kelley. He's new. Got him to replace George Murray."

"Swell," Cora said. "Hope he can fight vampires."

She fixed Duggan with an intense glare. "You've got some visitors coming, so best make ready. They don't take to crosses or garlic, so keep some handy."

She turned to leave, but the marshal's voice stopped her. "That's it? You ain't helping us?"

"I got to find my husband first," Cora said, struggling to keep her voice calm. "He's gone missing. We can't help nobody like that."

Cora left the office without waiting for Duggan's reply. Ignoring the new deputy, she stepped out onto the street and folded her arms, trying to swallow her increasing panic. Where might Ben have gone? He hadn't made it to the marshal's station, and he wasn't given to wandering about. Maybe he hadn't made it out of the hotel yet. She thought she saw him leave, but maybe he forgot something and had to turn back, or maybe he'd run into one of James Townsend's men and gone off to help them at Harcourt's retreat. The situation must have been serious if he'd joined them before checking in with Duggan.

Her spurs sang her alarm as she ran toward the Northern Hotel. If Ben wasn't there, she would fetch Our Lady from the stable and head out to the retreat. James must need help to hold back the vampires if he was desperate enough to spare a man to look for her and Ben. She hoped she wouldn't be too late.

Cora threw open the hotel's front door and took the stairs two at a time. Their room was empty. She checked to make sure that their wards were still in place, then knelt down by the trunk, set the crucifix aside, and raised the lid. It didn't look as though Ben had taken anything out of it, though there wasn't much left that he could have used. His rusty revolver lay at the bottom of the trunk amid spare rounds and vials of holy water. She tucked a few more rounds into her belt pouch and prepared to close the trunk when something caught her eye.

There, half-covered by silver bullets, lay the silver dagger Ben had carried that morning. The weapon glimmered in her hand as she picked it up. If the blade was here, Ben must be out there with no weapon at all. What possessed him to ride out to the retreat unarmed was beyond her, but the sooner she found him, the better.

Cora slipped the dagger into her boot before closing the trunk and propping the crucifix up against it. She thundered back down the stairs and made for the door. Thinking twice, she turned and walked over to the desk.

"Make sure nobody goes into our room," she said.

"OK," the clerk answered. "Which room is it?"

"Twenty-four," Cora said. "The only ones allowed in there are me and my husband."

The clerk dipped a quill into his inkwell and made a note. "What does your husband look like?"

"You ain't seen him?" she asked. "We came through here about an hour ago. Was you sleeping on the job?"

"No, ma'am," the clerk replied, looking uncomfortable. "I seen you walk in here awhile back, but there wasn't nobody with you."

Cora pounded the desk with her fist. "Dammit, man, you must be blind."

"I'm sorry, ma'am. I must have just missed him. If you tell me what he looks like, I'll be sure to let him into your room when he gets back."

Cora gave him a brief description, then turned to leave. Pausing at the door, she looked over her shoulder. "If he comes by, tell him to head upstairs and stay put. I'll be back after I see to the retreat."

The clerk nodded, but Cora didn't see it. She was already on her way to the hotel stable, her breath streaming in thin clouds as she muttered to herself. What was the matter with everyone? Ben's quiet nature could have him fall by the wayside in any conversation, but it wasn't like he was invisible. She'd make sure to kick him in the pants every so often to make him speak up in the future. People ignoring him like this made him hard to track down.

Our Lady and Book nickered at her when she entered the stable. She shook her head again. Ben was too short-sighted to even take his horse. Panic gave her lungs another squeeze as she saddled up her mare. Ben had to be up at the retreat helping James hold the line against the vampires. Townsend must have sent a wagon, so Ben hadn't bothered with Book. When she finally found her husband, she would show him new ways to commit the sin of wrath before making him buy her a full quart of whiskey to calm her nerves.

Cora fitted Book with a bridle, but there wasn't time to worry about a saddle. Once she made it up to the retreat and took care of the vampires, he could borrow a saddle from Harcourt's stable. It would probably be one of those worthless English saddles, but he deserved to ride back in shame. Maybe it would teach him not to disappear on her.

Once she was clear of town, Cora pushed Our Lady into a full gallop. The mare flew over the icy road, her breath coming in great clouds that streamed out behind them. Book, having no rider, wanted to set a faster pace, but Cora held him in check. Together, the three of them thundered into the winter evening, hoping to reach Harcourt's retreat before time ran out.

As the cold wind pummeled Cora's face, she began working on a strategy to defeat the master vampire. The upcoming fight at the retreat would destroy the rest of his army from the mines, but as long as the *nosferatu* remained alive the army of vampires wouldn't end. She wasn't sure how much damage he could do to the townsfolk while she and Ben were away, but she didn't think Mart Duggan and his boys could to do much to stop them. She and Ben would have to return to Leadville and try to sort out this mess before they could go to bed.

Cora's shoulders slumped at the thought. Her arms and legs ached from the long day of riding, shooting, and swordplay. She longed for a soak in a hot tub and a good night's sleep, but it didn't look like either was in the cards for her tonight. The bottle she would make Ben buy her would have to do.

The last of the afternoon sun glimmered on the manor's windows as she rode up. She dismounted and flipped both sets of reins over a spike in the iron fence. The horses were in a lather from the hard run, though Book still held his head high. Cora pulled her

Winchester from Our Lady's saddle and chambered a round before running for the door.

A young face answered her frantic knocking. When the boy saw her, he seemed to deflate with relief. She clapped him on the shoulder, knocking him to the floor. Other faces peered at her from various doors as she passed. Making eye contact with one, she pulled her bandana down from her face.

"Where's Ben Oglesby?" she asked. The man replied with a blank look. "How about Townsend? You seen him?"

That got her a nod and a finger pointing further down the hall. Cora followed the silent directions, her rifle still in her hands. As she walked, she took note of the retreat's condition. The defenders watching her pass looked tired but still wary, and none of the furnishings looked disturbed. If there had been a fight here, it must not have been serious.

She found James Townsend in Harcourt's study, seated in one of the chairs facing the fire. He looked up as she approached. "Cora? What brings you here?"

"Where's my husband?" she asked.

"Your husband?" James looked confused. "I haven't seen him. I thought I told you as much earlier."

"You did," Cora said, "but now he ain't anywhere." The panic in her voice became impossible to hide. "You're sure you ain't seen him around? I thought he might have come up here to help you out."

"I'm sorry, but he hasn't stopped by," James said. He rose out of his chair, a concerned look on his face. "What made you think he was here?"

"Because he ain't anywhere else," Cora said. "He ain't anywhere, and that vampire said that he…" she trailed off, unable to say the words aloud.

"What vampire?" James said. "Surely you don't mean the *nosferatu*?"

"You know another vampire that talks?" Cora asked.

"Well, I just wanted to be sure—"

"Ain't nothing that's sure now," Cora said, her breath coming in gasps. "My husband may have been killed by that monster, and I need to find out for sure."

"My God," James said. "Are you sure you heard right?"

"I seen it with my own eyes," Cora said, the rifle shaking in her hands. "If it wasn't a trick, anyway. First, I saw old Boots, then he turned into that Wash Jones feller, then he" – she took a breath – "he turned into the spitting image of my Ben."

James raised his hands. "Just calm down for a minute. You're not making any sense."

"Then you ain't listening to me!"

"I assure you, I am," James said. "Take a deep breath and tell me everything that happened."

Cora wrung the barrel of her rifle. Her voice wavered as she recounted the details of that afternoon. The memory of seeing Ben's eyes filled with such murderous hatred nearly choked off her tale, but she took another breath and forced herself through it. When she finished, she looked down at her rifle so the brim of her hat would hide her tears.

James stared into the fire, digesting her story. After a few moments, he turned back to her. "This is quite dire news. You're sure you've left nothing out?"

"Not a thing," Cora said, bringing her head up.

"My colleagues will want to hear this information at once," James said. "Your research has provided us with a critical piece of the *nosferatu* puzzle. With it, we will be able to better equip hunters and protect the innocent from this menace."

"I don't much care about all that," Cora said, anger swelling in her chest. "All I care about is finding my husband. Did anything that bastard said sound like a clue?"

"Of course," James said. "My apologies. Tell me what he said again." Cora did, and he stroked his chin with a thumb and forefinger. "From what you say, he sounded rather surprised that you believed your husband would rescue you from his clutches. That strikes me as more than a little odd."

"Why's that?"

"If the vampire had murdered your husband recently, he couldn't have expected you to know of Benjamin's death." The firelight danced in James's spectacles as he thought. "We must conclude that the creature believed you had prior knowledge of the event."

"How could he?" Cora asked. "I'd seen Ben maybe fifteen minutes before my showdown with that spook." James's words gave her a thread of hope, and she clung to it with everything she had.

"A curiosity, to be sure," James said, "but something else about your account bothers me as well. You say the vampire spoke as if the two of you had previously met, correct?"

Cora nodded. "He must be out of his gourd. I ain't never come across no *nosferatu* before."

"You're sure of this?"

"I think I'd remember it," Cora said. "Ain't every day I get chatted up by a man while he's laying dead at my feet."

"Of course," James said, removing his glasses. Cleaning them with the end of his necktie, he continued. "So then, we have only two reasonable options left to explain these eccentricities. The first of these is to assume that the *nosferatu* mistook you for another of his victims and drew on those memories while taunting you."

"Makes the most sense to me," Cora said, not wanting to hear the other possibility.

James raised a hand. "The second is to conclude that you did indeed encounter this creature in your past and have somehow forgotten the incident."

Cora shook her head. "Ain't possible. Like I said, I'd recollect it if I had."

"There are ways of inducing forced memory loss," James said. "If this *nosferatu* has sufficient knowledge of the Black Arts, he would be able to wipe your memory clean of him." Even as he spoke, James began doubting the idea. "Of course, had he done so, he would not have expected you to remember him. Perhaps the memory loss is due to other influences."

"I don't see how," Cora said, tapping her forehead. "My cracker barrel ain't got no leaks."

"I don't mean to imply that it does," James said. "However, certain traumas can have adverse effects on the memory, causing holes in an otherwise sound mind. Such maladies commonly afflict soldiers on the battlefield, for example. A man may be able to tell you what he ate for his breakfast on the morning of a battle, yet not recall how or when a friend died in that same battle. Given the nature of your work, I don't believe it is too outlandish to suggest that something similar may have happened to you."

"I ain't fought in no battles," Cora said. "At least, I ain't fought no wars. Ben fought the Yankees when we was both sprouts, but he quit the service when General Lee surrendered. We stayed out of them Indian wars, too, so I don't see how I could have lost my memories."

"It isn't only war that can cause such trauma." James looked at her, his eyes kind and sorrowful behind his glasses. "The loss of a loved one may also create a lapse in memory."

Cora began to feel the thread of hope slip from her. "I ain't lost no loved one, either."

James looked back at the fire for a moment, gathering his resolve. "Perhaps there is another way to be sure," he finally said, not looking away from the crackling flames. "You said the vampire made several allusions to your prior meeting occurring ten years ago. Can you remember an incident in your past that might correspond with that time frame?"

Cora studied the Winchester's barrel while she thought. A scream had been building inside of her for the past hour, and it took most of her concentration to hold it in. Part of her wanted to throw the rifle through one of Harcourt's big glass windows, unleash a torrent of obscenities at James, and storm out of the retreat to continue her search. This was all a waste of time, anyway. While she stood here with James Townsend trying to solve riddles, Ben was no doubt waiting for her back in their hotel room, fretting about the growing vampire threat. The longer she stayed here, the harder it would be to find the rogue *nosferatu* and put an end to him before the night was out. Still, James was only trying to help her.

Finally, she looked back up at him. "Sorry, George. I can't come up with a single one."

James sighed. "Perhaps it will come to you."

"Maybe so," Cora said, "but I can't wait here for it to show up."

"Where must you go?"

"Back to town," Cora said. "As you might recollect, there's a vampire on the loose down there, and I don't expect he'll just sit quiet tonight."

"You won't stay to bolster our defenses here?" James asked.

Cora shook her head. "You boys should do all right for yourselves if them critters in the mine come calling. No, I'm more worried about the town. All they've got is that touchy marshal and his band of halfwit deputies. Me and Ben will be more use there, I reckon."

"You and Ben?" James asked.

"Yep," Cora said. "I expect he'll be back at the hotel waiting for me, champing at the bit to get this hunt underway."

James offered her a sad smile. "I pray you're right, my dear," he said, holding out his hand.

"No prayer needed," Cora said, shaking the scholar's hand. She turned and made her way out of the British lord's retreat, ignoring the curious eyes that followed her. A shock of cold air greeted her when she opened the front door. She pulled her bandana back over her nose and stood on the porch for a few moments while her eyes grew accustomed to the fading light. A near-full moon rose above the eastern peaks, bathing the landscape in blue light. The evening stars answered with their own icy glitter. As she walked toward the horses, Cora marveled at how a peaceful night could harbor such horrors in its shadows.

The animals seemed irritated at being left to stand out in the cold. Cora patted Our Lady's neck in apology as she slid the rifle back into the saddle sheath. She swung herself into the saddle, pointed the mare's head in the direction of Leadville, and eased her into a trot. She kept a tight grip on Book's reins, making sure the gelding didn't get it into his head to race them back to town. After a short while, she urged Our Lady into her easy canter and gave Book a bit more slack.

Settling into the saddle, she let her thoughts wander back to what James had said. Surely the vampire had confused her for someone else when he claimed to have killed her husband. The image of Ben that she had seen must have been some black magic spell designed to take the form of anyone's husband or wife. A nasty trick, but that's all it had been. She smiled beneath her bandana, picturing Ben sitting up in their room, buried in a book. A good rap on the head with it and a quart of whiskey would set things right, and then they could go after the vampire bastard that started all of this.

As she neared town, Cora began giving honest thought to the question the scholar had asked right before she left. The *nosferatu* had seemed quite certain that they had met each other ten years before, but she couldn't place when or where. Only a handful of the monsters she and Ben had killed over the years had been any smarter than a cougar, and none of those had been vampires. The clever enemies were always humans dabbling in necromancy.

The answer hit her as she was riding up to the hotel stable, and she nearly fell out of the saddle at her own stupidity. She and Ben had smoked out a vampire nest near Denver about ten years ago with Father Baez. A raucous laugh erupted from her lungs. How could she have not realized it sooner? The vampires in that nest must have been other servants of this *nosferatu*, so of course it was out for revenge. Once they took care of it here in Leadville, they would have to stop in and tell Father Baez the good news. She led the horses into the stable and bedded them down, grinning to herself.

Her grin stayed with her as she entered the hotel and stamped her boots on the entry rug, drawing irritated looks from the few patrons sitting in the front room. She waved at the clerk behind the desk. Making no effort to be discreet, she thumped her way up the stairs to their room, and pulled the key from her pocket. The lock clicked, and she pushed open the door.

"Welcome back," said a voice behind her. She turned, her grin spreading into a genuine smile with the expectation of seeing her husband's face.

Golden eyes gazed back at her.

Hollering in surprise, she fell backward into the room, knocking the crucifix aside. The vampire remained in the hall, a smirk twisting his lips. "You seem surprised to see me, Cora. Were you expecting someone else? Your husband, perhaps?"

Cora yanked the revolver from her belt, pulled back the hammer, took aim at the smirk and fired. Blue smoke and thunder filled the room. When it cleared, her target had vanished. Cora pulled the hammer back a second time and got to her feet. The gunshot still rang in her ears. She strained through it, listening for any sign of the vampire's movements.

After a few moments, the mocking voice echoed down the hallway. "Still as quick as ever. I am glad to see that age and grief haven't slowed your wits."

"I can't see how happy you are," Cora said. "Why don't you show me that pretty smile of yours?"

"And let you draw the curtain before the final act is done? After a ten-year intermission, I should think you would want to relish this performance of a lifetime. Unless, of course, you have forgotten your lines."

"Never gave two shakes for no theatrics," Cora said.

"Not even your own tragedy?" he asked.

"Every life's a tragedy," Cora said. "Only thing that matters is making sure you ain't in the role of the bad guy."

"Ah, but who determines which role is the villain and which is the hero?"

"As I see it, the villain's the cocky bastard that goes around killing innocent folk."

A rolling laugh echoed down the hallway. "'Innocent' is such a human word. Does the fox care for the innocence of the hare? Can a wolf weigh the iniquities of the elk? No, it is only man, burdened by the weight of his mortality, who sews morality into his life as a miser sews gold into his bedclothes."

"Don't matter how you cut it," Cora said. "Them miners you killed didn't deserve it."

"Of course they didn't."

The voice came from behind her. She spun around and swept over the empty room with the barrel of her gun. Nothing. "Then why'd you kill them?" she asked.

"Because the world is unfair," Glava said. His voice seeped in through the window like the cold night air. Stepping toward the sound, Cora tried to make out his shape, but saw only shadows and the lights from across the street.

"Ain't no reason to kill folk," Cora said.

"I was hungry, and they were plentiful. Should I be denied my own right to life because I must kill men in order to live? What are the lives of a few miners? They would have spent them drinking and whoring only to die in a cave-in or a fever. What does it matter that I ended such worthless existences?"

"You ain't God."

"Now you disappoint me, Cora. Have you not yet learned that the *nosferatu* are the only gods humanity need concern itself with? I believe I said as much to you only this afternoon."

"I wasn't listening all that close," Cora said. "Don't put no stock in what a madman says."

"You're one to speak of madness," the vampire said. "Do give my regards to your husband when you see him next."

A well of dread sank into Cora's gut. "What do you know about Ben?"

"The perfect question for that meddlesome priest."

"What priest?"

Cora heard the vampire sigh. "Perhaps your mind has been addled with time after all. I had hoped for a refreshing sparring of wit, the parry and repartee of mortal enemies before the final battle, but here you are, sober and dull. Your husband always was the sharper half of you. I had so looked forward to an eternity of his conversation. It is a shame you cut it short."

The vampire fell silent. Cora leaned toward the window, searching the shadows for any sign of her enemy. All she could see was her own reflection, fogged by her breath. After a few minutes of silence, she holstered her pistol and turned away from the window.

"Tell the priest that Fodor Glava sends his regards." Golden eyes flashed at her from the doorway. Cora pulled her gun again, but the vampire vanished before she could get a shot off. Silence filled the room. After a moment, Cora stepped back to the doorway and peered out into the hallway. It was empty.

Cora kept the revolver in her hand as she locked the door and leaned against it. Fodor Glava. The name didn't ring any bells in her memory, but nothing about him did. He seemed to know who she was, though. Townsend's theory that he had somehow mixed her up with somebody else seemed less and less likely. The vampire knew her name well enough to find the hotel room, and he knew about events in her past that she hadn't told a soul in Leadville.

The mattress rustled beneath her as she sat on the bed, unable to stand any longer. The vampire hadn't called the priest by name, but she knew he meant Father Baez. She and Ben had met many priests in the long years since they came west, but the kind old man in Denver was the one who had helped them with the nest of vampires. Glava's words confirmed her earlier suspicion: the incident near Denver was connected to this *nosferatu* in some way.

Cora looked at Ben's pillow and felt a familiar panic begin twisting her stomach. She hadn't seen him since she left to confront Boots, which already felt like days ago. It wasn't like Ben to simply disappear, so she had to believe he was caught up somehow. Where or by whom, she couldn't begin to guess. He wasn't with the marshal or the Englishmen, and Glava seemed sure he was dead. For all its saloons and brothels, Leadville hadn't seen fit to establish a public library, so he couldn't be there. Her list of possibilities had all but run out, and she wasn't any closer to finding him.

The panic continued to pull at her, demanding

more and more of her attention. She took a deep breath, trying to force it down. Ben would come through that door any minute now. She would give him a good tongue-lashing and then they would be off to take care of Glava.

Minutes passed. In the silence of the room, she could hear her own heartbeat flowing through her ears. She was used to hearing the soft sounds of Ben's breathing and the rustling as he turned pages in one of his books. Without them, each beat of her heart seemed to bring her panic a little closer to spilling over. Her arms and legs twitched, urging her to get up, to stop sitting around and go find her husband, but she ignored them. He had to come back sometime tonight. Waiting in the room was the fastest way to find him.

If he was alive.

Reaching under her pillow, she pulled out a bottle of whiskey. She had to wait for him, but there was no reason she couldn't entertain herself while she did. The brown liquid burned her throat, sending waves of comforting warmth through her restless limbs. After a few swallows, she felt herself beginning to relax. A smile came to her lips as she thought of the things she'd say to Ben when he came through the door. Maybe she would even tie him to the bed all night just to make sure he didn't wander off again. She could untie him once she worked out a strategy for taking care of Fodor Glava. Ben wouldn't appreciate it, but it would keep him out of trouble.

Half an hour later, the bottle fell to the wooden floor with a clunk, its remaining contents darkening the floorboards beneath it. Cora's snores filled the small room. Aided by the alcohol, her fatigue had finally overcome her worry and drawn her into a deep and dreamless slumber.

Through the frosted glass of the window, gleaming eyes watched her sleep before slipping away into shadow.

SIXTEEN

Fodor Glava stood in front of the Northern Hotel, a grin spread across his red lips. The traffic in the street was beginning to thin as the night grew later. Even still, he could feel heat flowing through the veins of the miners wandering the streets and alleys. Their blood called out to him, promising him satisfaction for his desire, but he held the thirst in check. Behind him, the hunter lay in her room, dead to the world. Were it not for the wards she had placed, she would already be his. That she was safe even in her vulnerability irked him, but he refused to let the thought ruin such a beautiful night.

In a corner of his mind, Glava could feel the body of Washington Jones stirring in the storage room of the Pioneer. Unlife spread through the gunman's cold arms and legs, and his dead fingers began flexing. Glava watched through the newborn vampire's eyes as it rose on unsteady feet. He could feel the ravenous hunger searing the belly of the *vrykolakas*, but he commanded the slave to wait for his return. The rebirth of Washington Jones as *nosferatu* would drain Glava's strength; he needed to feed before he could complete the birthing ritual.

The vampire returned his attention to the street, regarding the miners like a butcher sizing up a herd of cows. Any of them would do to satisfy his hunger, but the taste of miner's blood had grown stale in his throat. He longed for younger, sweeter blood.

A group of men stumbled out of a nearby saloon and began ambling off in a common direction. Glava detached himself from the hotel's shadow and followed them. His shoes weren't suited for walking in snow, but wet socks and wet pants didn't bother him. Following the miners was a slow business; the leader kept them more or less together, but their progress was hampered by slips, stumbles, and the occasional quarrel.

After a long walk, they made their way onto the front porch of a building, arguing over who would go first. The vampire grinned again as he looked up at the painted sign of the Purdy brothel. Mortals were so predictable. His unwitting guides struggled through the front door, one of them getting shut out in the process. The straggler hit his head on the closing door and collapsed in a cursing heap. Glava watched the man try to pull himself back up, almost feeling moved to pity. A shadow of a thought to help him flickered through the vampire's mind. Before he could refuse it, a hand reached out into the cold night and pulled the miner inside.

Glava relished the chill of the air for a moment longer before letting himself in. The gaudy lights winked at him as he removed his gloves. A porter moved to greet him.

"Good evening, sir," the man said with a slight bow.

"And to you," Glava replied, offering the man a smile.

"What can I do for you?"

The vampire reached into his pocket and produced a number of bills. "One of your nicer accommodations, if you would be so kind."

"Of course, sir," the porter said, bowing again. "Have you a preference?"

"Something light, I believe."

The young man grinned and turned, leading Glava up the staircase. The vampire followed in silence, reveling in the feeling of so many warm bodies so near to his own. This brothel teemed with life at its most intense, sweaty and passionate, each door glowing with the energy of the men and women within. It was all he could do to keep himself from tearing into his guide as a prelude to a symphony of bloody revelry. All in good time, he reminded himself. Once he'd dealt with the hunter and her smarmy British pet, he would have his pick of the finest morsels this town had to offer.

The porter led him to a door on the second floor, bowed, and returned the way he had come. Glava's eyes lingered on the man's neck for a moment before he opened the door. The walk through the brothel, short though it had been, had worked him into a blood craze.

And there in the room was his first taste. The young woman stood next to a wash tub, her body wrapped in a towel. She glanced up and smiled when he entered. She tossed the towel aside and walked over to him, her body gleaming in the soft light.

"Well, ain't you a fancy one?" she said, running her fingers over his suit. "I reckon you don't even need me to wash you up."

"I do try to keep myself polished," Glava said. The heat from her body called to him. "We can proceed directly to the boudoir if you prefer."

"I just may," she said, lowering her hand to curl around his. When their skin touched, she took a deep breath. "My, but ain't you frozen to the bone! Ain't you got no gloves?"

"My hands prefer their freedom," Glava said.

She giggled. "Well, I hope the rest of you ain't so chilly, or we might have us a problem."

She led him through the archway into the bedroom. Candlelight played on the frosty windows as she laid herself out on the bed. Glava remained on his feet, his skin aflame with lust. She opened her legs slowly, teasing him, but his golden eyes lingered on her neck.

"What are you waiting for, honey?" she asked.

"Just enjoying the moment, my dear," Glava said. "What is your name?"

"Annabelle Rose."

He smiled. "A name as beautiful as its owner."

"Clean, handsome, and sweet," she said. "No wonder I ain't never seen you here before. Your wife probably never lets you out of her sight."

"I doubt she would, if she were alive."

Fine brows arched above her blue eyes. "Oh, honey, I'm sorry. I didn't mean to drudge up the past."

"There is much to uncover," he said, his smile never wavering, "but it is of no concern. She has been gone a long time now."

Annabelle's smile returned. "Well, I'm glad to hear that. No trouble with a jealous old lady, then."

"None at all." Glava lowered himself onto the bed. Annabelle curled up next to him, wrapping a long white leg around both of his. Her breath bathed his neck as her lips hovered by his ear.

"You're a bit over-dressed, honey," she whispered.

"I suppose I am," he said, and he reached down and removed his shoes. She grinned as her hands worked at his tie, the light playing in her blue eyes. Glava returned her smile. It had been many years since he'd been with a woman like this, and he was determined to enjoy it. He hadn't yet decided if he would take her before or after the copulation. Planning too much ahead could ruin the excitement of the moment.

Her fingers began working at the buttons of his suit. "Ain't much of a talker, are you?"

"Your beauty steals my words," Glava said.

"You quit that," she said, giving him a playful shove. "I ain't putting up with no sweet talking, not even from you. I already got me a cart full of miners in love with me, not to mention a marshal's deputy. Don't need no fancy dandy getting sweet on me, too, or I might just up and leave with you."

"Leave with me?" he asked. "Why would you choose me over any of your other suitors?"

She laughed again, a lilting sound. "Maybe you ain't as smart as you look. Why, you're the fanciest feller I seen come through here in a great while. You even got that fancy way of talking that says you ain't from around here, and you said you ain't got no wife. Why wouldn't I run off with you?"

Glava smiled at her. "You are unhappy with your life here?"

"I reckon I ain't," Annabelle said, laying back on the mattress and spreading her arms above her head. "I guess it's an okay living. I got it pretty good here, or better than some in the trade anyway. Men come in steady, and the madam looks after us proper. I expect it's better than doing some man's wash for him or digging in one of them mines." She raised herself up on her elbows and looked at him. "Still, I reckon it'd be a sight nicer living as your wife, what with your pretty eyes and pretty words. We'd best get finished with our business before I decide to do just that."

The vampire looked her over, taking in her porcelain skin and full figure. To think that he would start his conquest of this tiny little town with so pretty a girl. The taste of such women was exquisite; their vitality and fertility sweetened the blood in a way nothing else could. A whore's life stole such happiness quickly, leaving behind a broken and bitter shell. Glava smiled to himself. Taking her now only proved his capacity for mercy. She would live on forever as his servant, ignorant of the disillusionment that would have devastated her.

"What're you thinking, honey?" Annabelle asked, running her hand along his arm.

"Actually, I was considering your proposal, my dear."

"Quit your funning, now," she said, laughing again. "A gentleman like you don't want no whore for a wife. You could go get yourself some fancy lady from the opera house or somewhere."

"On the contrary," Glava said, "high-society women bore me."

"Is that right?" she asked

He nodded. So did all other women, but saying so might ruin her mood. "Would you accept such an offer?"

She blinked in surprise. "Well," she said, "I don't rightly know. Ain't never got proposed to by no rich man before." She looked around the room. "You would take me away from here?"

"Far away," he said, his eyes gleaming. Mortals were so predictable. "Taking you from this place would only be the beginning."

"Is that right?" Her eyes lit up. "What else?"

"Are you afraid of dying?"

Annabelle wrinkled her nose. "What kind of a question is that to ask a girl you intend to marry?"

"An honest one," the vampire said.

She thought for a minute, then looked back at him. "Ain't never given it much thought. Still, I reckon I'm about as scared of it as the next girl. Don't want it to happen tomorrow, if that's what you're asking."

He grinned at her. "An honest answer," he said. "In the interest of maintaining this wonderful honesty between us, I would like to tell you something."

"How about your name for a start?" she asked. "I ain't marrying no man that won't tell me his name, no matter how fancy he is."

"My name is Fodor Glava."

"That ain't no kind of name," she said. "How about I call you Theodore instead?"

"If you prefer," Glava said.

"Now what was you going to tell me, Theodore?"

"That I can give more than you imagine," he said.

"I ain't never been used to riches," Annabelle said, "so I'll be real easy to impress. Why, I expect a real mattress with some of them silk sheets and maybe a maid to clean up after me would be enough to make me happy. You look rich enough to manage that."

"When I wish it, yes." The thirst screamed through his body, but his will was stronger. "However, the value of what I offer you now is not measured in gold or possessions, but in life itself." He paused, admiring the innocent eagerness in her eyes. "Annabelle Rose, I offer you a future in which you may live by my side, undying and eternally young, until the world itself crumbles into dust."

Her musical laugh filled the room again. "Who are you, Jesus Christ?"

"No." He winced at the name, his breath hissing between his teeth.

"Oh, I'm sorry, honey." Annabelle sat up and pulled him into her arms. "I didn't mean no harm."

Glava drew the fresh scent of her skin into his lungs. "I know, my dear." He kissed her neck, feeling the pulse of her warm blood beneath his lips.

Running his fingers through her hair, he brought his mouth to her ear. "My offer still stands. You can have immortality."

Her arms tightened around him. "I'll take it."

The vampire's golden eyes flashed. He brushed his lips across her neck, feeding his appetite with the taste of her sweat. It had been so long since he had tasted human blood sweetened with desire. Most of his victims were filled with fear and loathing, a flavor not without merit, but none the worse for a change. He could taste this woman's lust for his body and his promises on her skin.

Glava ran his fangs behind her ear, taking great care not to pierce the delicate skin. Annabelle giggled, running her hands along his exposed chest and stomach. Pressing his hand into her back, he held her body against his and tilted her head to one side. A sigh escaped her lips as his mouth closed on her neck.

Annabelle gasped, a confused sound born from pleasure and pain. Her sweet blood filled the vampire's mouth and seeped out from under his lips in tiny streams. He leaned into her body, pressing her down onto the bed. Her back arched slightly as the muscles in her arms and legs relaxed.

Soon, the warmth left her body, the last trickle flowing down his throat and into his limbs. Laying her down on the sheets, he brushed a stray wisp of hair from her face. She really was a beautiful woman. The warmth of her blood was pure ecstasy, twisting through his body like ropes of black lightning. His toes flexed as he closed his eyes. Even after centuries of unlife, he still found the flavor of a young woman's desire one of the most beautiful things in the world.

After a few minutes, the peak of pleasure faded into the steady, familiar stream of vitality. Opening his eyes, Glava gazed down at the naked body of Annabelle Rose. He could leave her here for the brothel's mistress to discover, but they might associate him with her death. Having the law after him would compromise his subtlety, and he didn't want to attract any unwanted attention. Cora Oglesby may have been one of the most obstinate and dangerous hunters in the world, but she wasn't the only one. Some of James Townsend's friends might prove troublesome if they caught wind of his activities. No, it was best to conceal the evidence for now and wait until his tide became too powerful to withstand.

Glava stood to his feet and wiped his mouth on a corner of the bedsheet. Moving toward the nearest window, he opened it and looked out. Cold night air rushed into the room, bathing his face and neck. A smile bloomed on his red lips as he turned back to Annabelle's body. He wrapped her in the bloodstained sheet and tossed her over one shoulder as if she weighed no more than an empty burlap sack. Then he stepped into his shoes, walked over to the window, and was about to climb through when he heard a sound and turned.

Jack Evans stood in the doorway, his mouth agape.

Fodor Glava's golden eyes flashed above his bundle. Despite his need for caution, he couldn't refrain from offering the deputy one of his grins before slipping through the window. Keeping his footsteps light, he ran along the sloped roof covering the brothel's porch. A flying leap carried him on to the roof of the building across the street, and he vanished into the night.

Jack remained frozen in place for a few moments, unable to process what he had just seen. A breeze wafted through the open window, pulling at the curtains. The deputy felt the cold air on his face, and it roused him from his stupor. He ran over to the window and looked out. The man was long gone. Cursing, he turned back into the room, trying to calm his thoughts enough to take a good look around.

The bed was empty and stripped of its sheet. The pillows lay against the headboard, undisturbed. Bending down, Jack looked over the rest of the bed for any evidence, but came up empty. In the other room, the bath water was cooling, and a towel lay heaped in the corner.

Jack slammed his hand into the wall. This was Annabelle's room, and somebody had just jumped out of the window holding what looked like a body. He didn't want to believe it. He couldn't. No, Annabelle was still alive. She was probably just downstairs having a drink. Still, just to be safe, he should probably tell the marshal that something was fishy in town. Today was supposed to be his day off, and he thought he'd come pay Annabelle a surprise visit. He cursed this miserable town that couldn't give a lawman even one day of peace.

The cold air burned his ears as he ran through the street toward the station. Bursting through the front door, he gave a brief nod to Sanchez. The seated deputy returned the nod, watching in confusion as his fellow lawman stormed toward the marshal's office.

"Sir, we got a problem."

Duggan looked up from the small wooden crucifix he was holding. "We always got a problem, deputy. I'm stewing about one right this minute, as a matter of fact."

"Well, forget it," Jack said. "We got a worse one."

"You ain't giving me orders, are you?" Duggan asked, raising an eyebrow.

Jack looked down at his boots. "No, sir."

"I didn't think you was," Duggan said. "Now then, what's the new problem?"

"Something's wrong over at the Purdy," Jack said.

"Ain't something you can fix?"

Jack shook his head. "No, sir. Ain't no rowdy drunk this time. I think–" He took a deep breath. "I think somebody might have gone and killed one of them whores."

"Which one?" Duggan asked. When Jack didn't reply, the marshal looked up. Seeing the look on the deputy's face, he groaned. "Jack, tell me it ain't that one you're sweet on."

"Who said I was sweet on a whore?"

"Your face just done told me," Duggan said. "Before that, Mrs Oglesby said she saw you outside that brothel when we was fighting that other monster."

"That bitch," Jack said, shaking his head. "Ain't none of her business where I choose to sit."

"Don't take no big city detective to make the pieces fit." The marshal sighed and stood to his feet. "What makes you think your sweetheart got herself killed?"

Jack swallowed, looking at his boots again. "Well, I went in to call on her. The porter, he was busy with somebody else, so I figured I'd just let myself on up to see her. I went up to her room and I opened the door, and there was this strange feller in the room. He was carrying something that looked like a body over his shoulder. I hollered at him, and he just looked over at me and grinned before jumping right out the window."

Duggan's eyebrows arched over his blue eyes. "You say he jumped out the window?"

"Yes, sir," Jack said, nodding. "It's a second-story window, and he hopped on out like he was jumping a fence rail."

"Well, ain't that odd?" Duggan said, looking down at the cross in his hands. "You didn't find him limping around in the street afterward?"

"Didn't think to look," Jack said. "Ain't heard nobody say nothing about it, though." Jack watched the memory in his mind and shook his head. "It's like he just sprouted wings and flew off into the sky."

Duggan nodded without looking up. Sighing through his nose, he twirled the cross in his fingers. No man he knew could jump out of a second-story window onto a snow-packed street without breaking his legs, and no man anywhere could simply vanish into thin air. If what Jack said was true, their suspect wasn't a man. He didn't want to believe it, but it seemed as though Cora Oglesby's warning was well-founded. Again.

He looked up at his deputy. "You a praying man, Jack Evans?"

The question took Jack by surprise. "Why, I don't attend church regular, but I was raised in the faith."

"Well, that's something, at least," Duggan said. "Don't suppose it matters much which one, neither. My ma raised me Catholic, and I expect Sanchez out there will say the same."

"What difference does it make?" Jack asked. "How will that help us bag this feller?"

"You wasn't here when Mrs Oglesby stopped by," Duggan said, "so I'll give it to you quick."

The marshal summed up Cora's brief visit, explaining what she had said about crosses and garlic. When he finished, Jack's face was pale. "You mean to tell me my Annabelle Rose got killed by a vampire?"

"Ain't nothing sure about it," Duggan said, "but if what you said about him jumping out the window is true, I expect it's at least a possibility."

"Shit, marshal, we got to get moving," Jack said, heading out of the marshal's office. He paused at the front door and looked back. "Well, come on! We got to save her."

"Save who?" Sanchez asked, looking alarmed.

"Annabelle," Jack said, but Sanchez just gave him a blank look.

Duggan's boots thumped on the floor as he walked toward his deputies. "Jack," he said, "I don't reckon there's much we can do for her."

"What do you mean?" Jack asked. "We can't just leave her out there to get killed."

"I expect she's already dead," Duggan said.

"But you ain't sure of that," Jack said. "I didn't see

no dead body, just some sack over his shoulder. Until we know for sure, it's our duty as lawmen to find and protect her."

"There's more folk in this town besides your whore," Duggan said. "I ain't about to run all three of us after some spook just because you was dumb enough to fall for a whore. My duty is to all the people of Leadville, and so is yours. Don't you forget it."

"Hunting down that vampire would make the whole town safer," Jack said. "The sooner we do it, the sooner we do our duty."

"*Madre de Dios,*" Sanchez whispered from the desk. "There is a vampire here?"

"At least one," Duggan said, not taking his eyes off of Jack. "Mrs Oglesby said there might be more. Jack here seems to think one just jumped out a window with his sweetheart over one shoulder."

"What do we do, *señor*?" Sanchez asked.

"We stay right where we are," the marshal said. He raised a hand to halt Jack's outburst. "Won't do no good to charge off after a vampire at night, son. Even if you did find him, you'd only end up killed yourself."

"But I can't just–"

"What you can't do is save that woman." Duggan looked at his deputy, a mixture of pity and irritation on his face. Jack Evans was a good man, if a little slow in the head. Duggan didn't want to lose him, but the fool had gone and fallen for a whore. The marshal had been a lawman long enough to have seen many a fight over a whore's love. Sometimes, it was two men that broke out in fisticuffs for a girl's affections. Other times, a man turned violent on a girl who didn't return his feeling. Either way, such affairs always ended with a fight and time spent in a jail cell. Duggan had never seen a happy ending to a man's love for a whore, and he didn't think Jack's would be the first.

Jack set his jaw. "Well, I ain't just going to leave her, sir. If you ain't going to do your duty, then I'll do it my own self."

"That's your business, then," Duggan said. "But if you do plan on saving that woman, go prepared. This ain't like cracking some drunk over the head and hauling him off to jail."

"Don't you worry, marshal," Jack said, drawing his pistol and giving it a spin. "I ain't stupid."

Duggan opened his mouth to reply, but his deputy had already slammed the door. The marshal stared after him for a moment, then sighed and looked at Sanchez, who met his gaze with fearful eyes.

"Well, deputy," Duggan said, clapping him on the shoulder, "looks like it's just you and me tonight."

When Washington Jones came to himself, his mouth was full of blood. The taste filled him with a strange new excitement. Opening his eyes, he saw a figure standing before him. The man's wrist was in Wash's mouth, leaking blood from a deep cut.

When Glava saw awareness in his disciple, he pulled his arm away. "Welcome to your new life, my child."

"Where am I?"

"Where you died," the vampire replied. "Where you have now been reborn as a true master of the night."

Wash ran a hand along his neck, feeling the small wounds there, and the memories of the afternoon returned. "You killed me, didn't you?"

"And gave you new life." Glava held out his injured arm, and Wash watched in amazement as the gash closed in on itself, vanishing within a matter of moments. "This power is now yours, along with many others. You are a new man, Washington Jones, one that need not fear the trappings of mortality."

A thrill ran through Wash's body as his mind worked to understand it. "So you're saying I can't be killed no more? Not by anything?"

The vampire's hand snatched the bowie knife from Wash's belt with the speed of a striking snake, yet Wash found he could follow it along every inch of its journey, as if Glava were casually reaching for a match. The elder vampire twirled the blade in his hands for a moment. Then, with Wash's blue eyes still watching the blade, Glava plunged the knife into his disciple's chest.

Wash felt the impact and looked down. The knife handle protruded from his ribs. He could feel the blade in his body, but the sensation was nothing more than a slight irritation. After a few moments, he reached up and pulled the blade free. It came out clean, and a small trickle of blood oozed from the wound. The skin soon closed in on itself, leaving behind no trace of the wound.

Wash looked up at Glava in amazement. "Did that just happen?"

"You are not blind," Glava said, "though you are still an idiot." His golden eyes flashed in the dim light for a moment before he turned toward the door. "Come. It is time for your first feeding."

SEVENTEEN

Cora pulled her hat down over her brow. The afternoon sun gleamed on the golden cross crowning the church's steeple, hurting her eyes. Despite sleeping through the night and most of the morning's train ride into Denver, she'd kept her head down through the streets, trying to hide from both her hangover and her growing dread.

Her boots clapped against the stone steps, bringing her up to the wooden doors. Closing her eyes, she gave a deep sigh, trying to exhale her panic and despair with the white cloud of breath that poured from her lips. It didn't work. Her hand paused on the door handle for a moment before she opened it and escaped into the darkness of the vestibule.

The thick carpet muffled her footsteps as she approached the altar and knelt before the crucifix. Closing her eyes, she savored the silence of this place of worship, willing it into her turbulent soul. After a few minutes, the throbbing in her head subsided, leaving her alone with her panic.

"Cora? Is that you?"

She turned her head and saw Father Baez approaching. "Yeah, it's me, Father. Forgive me, but I think I forgot to cross myself when I entered today."

A smile spread beneath his white beard. "I do believe the good Lord can find it in His heart, my dear. Now tell me, what brings you to my door?"

"Well," Cora said, "I got me a bit of a problem, and I heard tell you can give me some answers."

"I'll do what I can," Father Baez said, offering her a hand. "Come, sit and we'll talk."

He led her over to a pew. Cora sat down, wringing her hands despite herself. She looked at them for a few minutes, trying to find enough courage to speak. Taking a deep breath, she looked up into the priest's kind eyes. She needed the answers he could provide, no matter what they might be.

"Well, Father," she began, "I had me a run-in with a vampire yesterday, and he said something funny. About Ben." The priest's face grew grave, and Cora noticed. "So you do know something, then?"

Father Baez looked at the crucifix without answering. After a few moments, he nodded and turned back to her. "If I can help you in any way, I will."

Cora nodded. Trying to keep her voice steady, she told the priest about her two encounters with Fodor Glava. She recounted as best she could his exact words about Ben and Father Baez himself. When she finished, the priest leaned back in the pew, stroking his white beard.

"His words took you by surprise?" he asked.

"Course they did," Cora said, looking at him like he was crazy. "My Ben ain't been killed by no vampire, at least not that I know about." She paused, looking down at her hands again. "Truth is, that's the other reason I came calling on you today, Father. See, Ben didn't come back to the hotel last night, and that's got me awful worried. It ain't like him to just disappear like that."

"You were expecting him to come into your hotel room?" Father Baez asked. Cora nodded. "When was the last time you saw him?"

"Yesterday afternoon," Cora said. "Why?"

The priest looked at the crucifix again. His eyes betrayed a deep concern, but he remained silent. Cora watched his face, her fingers working at her belt. In the silence, her thoughts began running wild again. Father Baez wasn't reassuring her the way she thought he would. There were no words of comfort, no gentle laugh dismissing her worries. Candles winked on the altar, and the face of the blessed virgin looked down on them from a window.

Father Baez continued to look at the dying savior, his eyes wandering over the cloth draped around its arms. Finally, he roused himself and looked at her, his face filled with sorrow. "I've been trying to think of the best way to say this, and I've decided that our Lord's advice is best: the truth shall set you free." He took a deep breath. "Cora, my child, your husband Benjamin Oglesby has been dead for ten years."

Cora blinked.

A gale of laughter erupted from her lips. "That's

plumb crazy, Father. Like I said, he was with me just yesterday. It may be that he was killed last night, but I know he ain't been dead no ten years."

Father Baez offered her a sad smile. "I can't explain that to you, and I don't intend to try. All I know is that I conducted a funeral mass for your husband ten years ago and laid him to rest in the old church's cemetery."

"But that ain't right," Cora said. "That Fodor Glava feller said that he killed my Ben, so if he did, then Ben ain't been laid to rest. He'd be…" She trailed off, unable to voice the thought.

"He was," Father Baez said, his smile disappearing. "Your husband was killed by a vampire, this one you call Fodor Glava. His body was reanimated as the unholy undead, one of the vampire's minions."

"Right," Cora said, "so you can't have laid him to rest. That means he ain't been dead no ten years, and maybe that means he ain't dead at all."

The priest shook his head, his face lined with regret. "No, Cora. Your husband's body became a vampire, a member of the nest you destroyed. I may have laid him in the ground, but it was your silver bullet that laid him to rest. Don't you remember?"

Cora shook her head, her mouth working but unable to speak. If she had killed her husband, she would remember doing it. What she did remember was talking with him, laughing with him, and riding with him every day of those ten years. They'd put a number of monsters to rest during that time, too, which was something a dead man couldn't do. Father

Baez, for all his kindness, must have confused the story, just like Fodor Glava.

An image came into her mind: Ben's rusted pistol, lying in the bottom of their trunk amid unused bullets. She shifted her legs, uncomfortable with the thought, and felt the weight of the silver dagger in her boot. Her hand slipped down and pulled it out. The silver glimmered in the candlelight as she turned the blade over in her hands. She remembered it glimmering in the lantern's glow in the mine tunnel, Ben's fingers around its hilt.

The voice of James Townsend echoed in her ears, asking to meet her husband after a long afternoon of riding with him. The hotel clerk's confused eyes when she mentioned her husband. Ben's silence during the meeting with Lord Harcourt. Mart Duggan, asking for a description of Ben so he would know him if he saw him. She remembered now that Ben had been with her to see the marshal when she'd borrowed the gun she used to kill the wendigo. Duggan had to have seen him then, yet he couldn't recall what Ben looked like.

Cora's shoulders began shaking in quiet sobs. She felt a warm arm around her back, and she let herself fall into the priest's embrace. Her tears soaked into his vestments as the past ten years began unraveling. Ben's bright blue eyes shining as he laughed. His hand on her shoulder. His quiet concentration when he picked up a book. His grim determination as…

…they entered the vampire nest. The vampires had holed up in a large house in north Denver. It had taken the hunters nearly a week to track them; the nest never stayed in one place for long. Ben kicked the front door open, letting the afternoon sun stream into the dark interior. They entered, guns at the ready, and waited for their eyes to adjust. She could hear Ben's steady breathing next to her.

Once the darkness had retreated from their sight, they moved up a stairway along the right-hand wall. The boards creaked beneath their boots, announcing their presence, but no monsters came flying out of the shadows. The hunters went from room to room on the second floor, ensuring each was clean of undead before moving on. Boards covered the windows, letting in only thin streams of sunlight. The floor lay under a thin carpet of dust that swirled around their spurs.

They found a second staircase in a hallway attached to the main bedroom. Ben led the way down, rifle at the ready and saber on his hip. Cora kept her big Colt pointed behind them as they descended. The stairs emptied into a large kitchen. The shadows of cooking stoves lurked in the corners of the room, their fires long dead. Baskets of stale bread sat on shelves lining the walls. A door to their right opened into a pantry. In the dim light Cora could see cans of vegetables and fruit.

As they moved toward a door across the room, Ben stooped down and picked something up. He turned to his wife and handed her his find: a small hatchet. She took the handle in her free hand, then looked at him with a question in her eyes.

"We need some sunlight in here," he said, his voice just above a whisper. "Go on back upstairs and see to the windows."

"What about you?" she asked.

"I'll hold the line right here," he said. "Hurry on back so we can lick these bastards."

Cora nodded and, keeping her pistol handy, made her way back up to the second floor. Starting in the main bedroom, she began chopping away the boards covering the windows. The hatchet was light but still sharp, and streams of sunlight soon began filling the room. Her efforts echoed through the house, making her more than a little nervous. She kept one eye on the door, ready to drop the hatchet and open up with her pistol at the first sign of a vampire, but nothing came. Moving from room to room, Cora worked as fast as she could. Soon, the upper floor was awash in late afternoon sunlight.

When she finished, she made her way back down to the kitchen, dropping the hatchet by the bottom of the staircase. "All set up there," she said.

Ben was gone.

Her Colt's hammer clicked in the stillness. She gave the room a thorough sweep with her eyes before moving from her place next to the stairs. The kitchen was silent. Lowering her gaze to the floor, she checked for any sign of a struggle. The carpet of dust remained undisturbed save for two sets of tracks leading toward the far door. She knelt down next to them and took a closer look. One set belonged to Ben's boots, and the other had been made by a pair of smaller shoes.

A thrill ran through her as she began following the tracks. She didn't know how someone could have survived in a vampire nest, but they must have heard her racket upstairs and come looking. Perhaps a butler had been trapped or away when the vampires attacked, or perhaps it was a drifter taking advantage of the abandoned house. Either way, Ben must have taken him outside as soon as he appeared.

Keeping her eyes on the trail, she followed it out of the kitchen and through the central hallway of the house. The fresh sunlight pouring from the second story gave the house a glow like deep twilight. The tracks led her to a closed door near the front of the house. Cora stared at the door in confusion. If Ben had found a survivor, he would have taken him outside to keep him safe, so why did his tracks lead deeper into the house? She reached out and pulled the door open. The groaning of its hinges seemed to screech in the silent house, making her wince. Behind it, a staircase descended into the darkness of the house's underbelly.

Before Cora could give the mystery much thought, a wail echoed from somewhere in the basement. The barrel of her gun gleamed in the dim light as she pointed it into the shadows. Moments passed, but nothing came rushing up the stairs. Her own breathing filled the silence. Cora's mind urged her forward, screaming that her husband was down there somewhere, but her instincts held her in place. She couldn't help him if she was blind and stumbling in the dark.

After a few minutes of silence, she took a step toward the door. Her worry was overpowering her sense. Ben was down there, and if she didn't follow soon, she would be too late. The silence told her that he wasn't fighting anything, but that didn't mean he wasn't in danger. Vampires could see in the dark, and he couldn't. They were no smarter than animals, but enough of them might be able to bring him down. Her boot creaked on the top step, and she paused. Nothing. Tightening her grip on her Colt, she began making her descent.

Two steps later, a savage mass of arms, legs, and fangs slammed into her, throwing her back through the door into the hallway. The vampire's weight kept her pinned to the floor as it snarled and snapped at her. Her hands clamped around the vampire's neck, holding its fangs at bay mere inches from her face. She didn't remember dropping her gun.

Cora managed to bend her knees enough to get her heels on the ground and shove upward. She released the pale neck at the same time and threw the vampire over her head. It slammed into a nearby wall with a hiss. Collecting itself, the creature regained its bearings and sprang at her. Cora rolled out of its path, and the vampire sailed through the open doorway back into the shadows.

Drawing her silver dagger, Cora got to her feet. When the monster came charging out of the basement a second time, she drove the point into its face as it smashed into her. Smoke billowed around them as the vampire let out a final, inhuman screech and went limp. She pushed the corpse off of her. The dagger slid out of the vampire's skull with a wet, slurping sound. Clutching it in one hand, she crawled on her hands and knees toward the stairs. Her pistol lay on the top step, its barrel gleaming in the semi-darkness. She picked it up, stood, and wiped the dagger on her buckskin pants.

Before she could sheathe it, another snarl came from the shadows. She pointed both weapons toward the stairs. Small pinpoints of light winked at her. The flash from the revolver's barrel lit up the darkness like a bolt of lightning, but it vanished before she could make anything out. No screech cut through the gunshot's thunder, so she thumbed the hammer back and waited.

Then, without warning, a series of wails filled the air, followed by the pounding of many feet. Cora backed up as her heart began to race. The echoes made it difficult to determine their numbers, but it was more than a few. Glancing over her shoulder, she could make out the stream of sunlight coming through the front door. As much as she hated it, she couldn't take on the entire nest by herself. Keeping her face toward the chorus of howls, she began making her way toward the door. Hissing, gray shapes poured out from the basement door. Their savage eyes locked on her, their fangs glistening in the twilight. She jumped backward into the doorway. The vampires approached her, snarling and snapping, but they did not follow her into the sunlight. Counting three targets, Cora grinned to herself. She took aim at one of the ugly faces and squeezed the trigger.

The vampire ducked as she fired. Her bullet punched into its shoulder, and it shrieked in anger and pain. The rest scattered like roaches. Cursing, Cora pulled back the hammer and fired again, but her target had already vanished into the darkness. Gunsmoke drifted through the sunlight as she stood facing an empty hallway.

In the waning daylight, Cora's mind began racing. She glanced at the sky over her shoulder. The sun hung just above the western mountains; her time was short. The shadows inside the house still rumbled with the movements of the vampires, but they kept themselves hidden from her sight. She could charge down the basement stairs and hope to find Ben before they noticed, but she'd only have a minute or two at most. If she failed, neither of them would make it out alive. Still, she couldn't just abandon him to darkness and death.

Behind her, she heard a horse whinny. Cora pulled her hat low against the sun as she looked out at her mare. She was a new purchase, bought only a few months ago. Her last mount, a bay named St. Andrew, had been shot out from under her by a group of bandits. This new mare didn't have the stamina old Andrew had, but she had a gentler nature. Cora had taken to calling her Our Lady of Virginia.

Cora looked at her now, wondering how long it would take her to ride out to the farmhouse where she and Ben were staying. Father Baez was there, protecting the family in case they failed to root out the infestation. His help would be essential if she was going to storm the nest and rescue Ben, but she didn't want to leave her husband to be devoured by vampires.

Common sense finally won out. Cora smashed a vial of holy water on the front steps of the house, ran over to her mare, and swung up into the saddle. They hadn't bothered to tie their horses when they went in, so she turned the mare toward the eastern road and gave her a punch with her heels. Our Lady started off at a good canter, and Cora let her warm up as long as her patience allowed before breaking her out in a full gallop. The house shrank behind her, its whitewashed walls glowing in the sunlight.

As she rode, Cora kept replaying the scenario in the kitchen over and over in her mind, trying to figure out exactly what might have happened. The tracks she found in the dust showed no sign of a fight, so Ben hadn't been jumped by a vampire. If she had read the signs right, there was someone else still alive in the nest. How they had managed to hide from the vampires was beyond her, but maybe they knew of a secret place protected with holy water or garlic. If that was the case, maybe they'd hidden there with Ben when she'd drawn the nest's attention. All they had to do was wait for her to return with Father Baez. Cora whispered a prayer as she urged Our Lady forward into the approaching night.

By the time she flipped Our Lady's reins over a low-hanging branch in the farmhouse's front yard, the sun had already slipped behind the mountains. She glanced at the sky as she ran across the yard, cursing the evening stars for their eager arrival. Every minute that passed put Ben and his companion in greater danger.

Cora crashed through the door of the house, hollering for Father Baez before she cleared the entryway. The priest emerged from the kitchen a moment later. Behind him, she could see the worried faces of the farmer and his wife.

"What is it, Mrs Oglesby?" Father Baez asked.

"You got to come quick, Father," Cora said. "Ben's trapped down in the nest someplace, and I can't get him out by myself."

"Calm down, my dear, and tell me what happened."

The priest motioned for her to join them in the kitchen, but she remained where she was, her hands on her hips. She recounted the events at the abandoned house, adding her theory about the mysterious survivor's hiding place. When she finished, Father Baez stroked his salt-and-pepper beard.

"A troubling situation, certainly."

"Right," Cora said with a nod. She took a few steps toward the door, then looked back over her shoulder at the priest. "Well, what are you waiting for?"

"I'm afraid I can't just abandon this family," Father Baez said. "The sun has already set, and they would be vulnerable if we both left."

"But we're leaving to whip the vampires," Cora said. "Once we do, they'll be safe as a pair of bear cubs with their ma."

"We may kill some of them, yes," the priest replied, "but there would be no guarantee that we would get all of them. This house is the closest to the nest, and the vampires have already attacked it the past two nights. You and Ben were able to fend off the attacks, yes, but these people can't hope to fight the undead by themselves."

"They watched us do it enough to get the idea," Cora said, shifting her weight and glancing through the front door. They were wasting time that Ben might not have to waste. If Father Baez wouldn't leave, she would have to go back alone, and the odds would be against her.

"I'm sorry, Mrs Oglesby, but I can't come with you," Father Baez said. "My place is here."

Cora looked into his dark eyes, gauging his resolve. Finally, she nodded. "All right, then, I'm going back by myself."

Surprise filled the priest's face. "You can't be serious. Nobody can hope to survive a vampire nest after nightfall."

"Maybe I'm just that crazy," Cora said. "All I know is I ain't leaving Ben in that nest by his lonesome." Without waiting for a reply, she marched down the hall toward the door. Near the entryway, a staircase led to the second story of the house. Cora took the steps two at a time, then threw open the door to the guest room where she and Ben were staying. She pulled their traveling trunk from its place in the corner, undid the latches, and began digging through their supplies. She grabbed a spare crucifix and tucked it into her belt. A few more vials of holy water, a handful of garlic cloves, and she was ready.

She snapped the clasps closed and shoved the trunk back toward the corner. Dropping the vials and cloves into her belt pouch, she turned and thundered back down the stairs. The outside air was cool on her face. She grabbed the mare's reins and swung into the saddle.

As she turned Our Lady toward the road, a shape darted through the evening shadows toward the farmhouse door. More figures appeared, following the first with frightening speed. In the dim light, Cora could just make out the stooped forms of men on all fours. Before she could draw her pistol, they disappeared into the house.

Screams and shouts began echoing from the interior. Cursing, Cora jumped out of the saddle and landed running. She drew her revolver as her boots pounded up the porch stairs and into the house. One of the vampires crouched in the hallway, hissing at something through the kitchen door. The big Colt's thunder filled the entryway. Charging through the cloud of smoke, Cora took aim at the vampire's head and fired again. The gray lips fell silent, and she rounded the corner into the kitchen, revolver at the ready.

Father Baez stood a few paces back from the doorway, pointing a crucifix toward her. Behind him, the farmer and his wife stood with their backs to her, crosses pointing outward. Two small children clung to the woman's dress, their frightened eyes peering out from the protective ring of adults.

"By the grace of God," Father Baez said, crossing himself.

"I'm here, Father," she said. "Stay sharp. There's more vampires about."

Father Baez nodded, his eyes searching the ceiling while Cora loaded fresh rounds into her revolver. The pounding of running feet began shaking the walls, the sound moving from over their heads toward the stairs. The clicking of the Colt's hammer was lost amid the cacophony, but the big gun's roar deafened them all when she opened up on the first monster that charged through the doorway. The silver bullet punched through the creature's skull, blowing it backward into the body of its fallen comrade.

Behind her, she heard a shout from the farmer. She whirled around in time to see another vampire standing near the kitchen table, hissing at the raised crosses. Yelling at them to get down, she took aim at the creature's chest. The couple dropped to the floor, the mother grabbing her children and pulling them down with her. Another flame erupted from the revolver's barrel, and the vampire sprawled across the table, limbs dangling.

The rumble of the gunshots faded, and the house fell into an uneasy silence. Sobs came from the youngest child, a girl no older than five, as she hid her face in her mother's dress. Father Baez placed a comforting hand on her shoulder. The farmer stood up, eyes searching every corner of the kitchen as he raised his cross.

Cora's pulse pounded in her ears. She caught Father Baez's eye and nodded. The priest returned the nod, fingering his crucifix. Turning on her heel, she stepped into the hallway. Her free hand pulled the crucifix from her belt as she approached the staircase.

Pointing the holy symbol toward the top, she began her ascent.

Something stirred in the guest room. Cora pointed the crucifix toward the sound, followed by the revolver's barrel. Nudging the door open with her foot, she interrupted another vampire as it was nosing through the sheets on the bed. Its blue eyes locked on her as a hiss escaped its teeth. Cora's breath caught in her throat. The creature's face was gray and lifeless, but she recognized it. Another rush of air hissed out from beneath the vampire's familiar brown mustache as it bared short white teeth at her.

Teeth that had once belonged to her husband.

Cora backed into the hallway, shaking her head in disbelief. The monster inhabiting Ben's body followed her, using his arms and legs to creep along the floor in a half-crouch. It was still wearing Ben's buckskin pants and button-up shirt, but his riding boots and hat were gone. Cora's foot slipped off the top step, and she almost fell head-over-heels down the stairs. Regaining her balance, she brought her gun back up and pointed the barrel at her husband's face, but she couldn't pull the trigger.

"Ben," she whispered. "Ben, please stop."

The creature didn't listen. Ben's graying knuckles came to rest on the top step as Cora backed down the stairs. Tears burned in her eyes, blurring her vision.

"Ben, it's me," she said. "Don't do this, please."

Cora reached the bottom of the stairs and continued backing out the front door. The savage hunger in her husband's eyes hypnotized her, stopping her from pulling the trigger. She couldn't shoot him. No matter what was inside him now, it was still his body, his face. She couldn't kill him.

Her boot stepped on air where the porch ended, and she fell backward. The vampire lunged. Cora brought the crucifix up at the last moment, and the wicked face she loved twisted in pain. Ben's body backed away, beating the air with his arms.

"Cora? Are you OK?"

Father Baez's voice echoed from the kitchen. The vampire turned and sprinted toward him with the agility of a mountain cat. Cora pulled herself to her feet and ran after it as the priest retreated into the kitchen. She brought her Colt up again, but couldn't bring herself to fire before the vampire disappeared around the corner.

Running after them, Cora entered the kitchen in time to see her husband's fingers clamped around the priest's collar. Father Baez beat against the vampire with his wrinkled hands, but the creature didn't flinch. Teeth bared, the head crowned with Ben's hair lowered itself toward the old man's neck.

Cora kicked the vampire in the ribs as hard as she could and knocked it off balance. Before it could right itself, she kicked again, the toe of her boot smashing into Ben's face. She shoved the crucifix into his undead eyes as a scream welled up inside her. The vampire recoiled from the holy symbol, cowering against the cabinets. Cora kicked it again. It hissed and snapped at her with Ben's teeth. Squeezing her eyes shut against the oncoming tears, she brought her Colt up and pulled the trigger.

The scream exploded from her lungs. She pulled the hammer back and fired again.

The big revolver fell from her limp hand as she collapsed to her knees, her scream breaking down into sobs. A warm hand touched her shoulder, but she shrugged it off. She struggled to her feet and staggered down the hall in a near run. Her boots stumbled at the porch steps, but she managed to keep them under her until she made it to where Our Lady stood. The mare staggered as Cora crashed into her side. She pulled herself into the saddle and gave Our Lady her heels. Her vision swam in the growing darkness, and she squinted through it to point the mare down the right road.

The night air dried the tears from her cheeks as she rode. Cora gave Our Lady her head, unable to focus on anything aside from staying in the saddle. In her mind, she kept repeating the same desperate creed, the words falling into rhythm with the horse's hooves. She hadn't just killed her husband. She hadn't just shot him in the head. She hadn't. She hadn't.

Our Lady soon caught wind of Ben's horse and changed her course. Her easy gallop came to rest next to the other mare, who still stood faithfully outside the abandoned house. Cora rubbed her eyes with the back of her hand and dismounted. The front door of the vampire nest yawned open before her like the mouth to Hell itself. Whispering a desperate prayer, Cora plunged headlong into the darkness.

Pale shafts of light from the windows cut through the darkness. Cora's footsteps echoed through the house as she made her way to the basement entrance. Pausing at the door, she took a deep breath, staring down into the absolute blackness. In the shadows, she thought she saw Ben's dead eyes staring back at her. His pale face floated like a phantom in the darkness, his mouth still curled in a savage, animal snarl.

She shook her head to clear the image, her hand reaching for her revolver. Only when her fingers closed on air did she remember that she left it lying on the kitchen floor of the farmhouse. She pulled out her rosary instead, her knuckles white around the wooden beads. At the same time, her other hand pulled the silver dagger from its soft leather sheath. Another breath left her lungs as a prayer, and she began her descent.

The darkness closed in around her, forcing her to take one step at a time. Holding the rosary in front of her, she felt her way forward. Her fingers touched cold earth at the bottom of the stairs. She turned to her right and took a cautious step forward. Meeting no resistance, she took another. The air beneath the house was cold and stale, and the scent of death seemed to seep from the walls. Her eyes strained against the absolute blackness. Swaths of color flowed across her vision like gleeful phantoms.

In the stillness of the basement, the memories of the farmhouse wrapped around her mind with crushing black fingers: the hideous hissing of Ben's breath through his teeth, the inhuman hunger in his eyes, the gray shade of his face. That wasn't really him, she told herself. Her mind had been playing tricks on her. Ben wouldn't have threatened her like that, even if he had been turned. His gentle soul would have prevailed over the vampiric curse. No, Ben had to be down here somewhere, hiding with the other survivor.

Her foot struck a metal object, sending it skittering across the floor. She followed the sound, patting the ground with each step until she felt something beneath her boot. She knelt down and reached forward, the rosary dangling from her wrist. Her fingers closed around a cold piece of metal. A sword hilt. Sheathing her dagger, she picked it up in both hands, feeling the length of the blade with her fingers. It was Ben's saber.

"So that's where I dropped that."

A small scream escaped her lips as she whirled around in the darkness, holding the saber out in front of her. Without thinking, she began backing toward where she remembered the stairs to be.

"Where are you going?" the voice asked, and she paused. When it spoke this time, she heard it more clearly.

"Ben?" she asked. "Ben, is that you?"

"Sure is," the voice replied. "Can't you tell?"

"Where are you? I can't see you." Cora felt a shock of excitement run through her like a gunshot. "Why are you still here?"

"I was waiting for you, darlin'."

Cora allowed herself a short laugh. "Well, no point in waiting, then. Let's find us some matches and kerosene and send this place to hell along with any of them bloodsuckers that might still be around."

Without waiting for his answer, she turned and began walking toward the faint hint of moonlight shining in the darkness. Her spurs jingled in the still air of this house of death, singing out her relief. She hadn't shot her husband. Just as she'd thought, he had been in hiding, waiting for her to kill the rest of the vampires and come rescue him.

At the bottom of the stairs, she turned and looked behind her. "You coming?"

Ben made no reply. She strained her eyes in the dim light, hoping to see his face emerge from the shadows. It never came.

"Hey!" she called. "You still there?"

Something rustled in the darkness. Leaning forward, she searched for his face, a faint smile coming to her lips. A heartbeat later, a dark shape flew out of the shadows. It struck her in the temple, knocking her into the dirt wall. Stunned, she made a feeble attempt to pull herself up, but before she could get her boots under her, another blow rained down on her skull. Darkness flooded her mind, and she remembered nothing more.

Cora lifted her head from the priest's shoulder. Her eyes were red and swollen from crying. She took a deep breath, drawing fresh air into her lungs. Looking at Father Baez, she offered a sheepish smile.

"I'm so sorry, Cora," he said. "I know the memories are painful."

She shook her head, confused. "I don't get it, Father. I could have sworn Ben was with me all these years. Why, I saw him just yesterday, and he seemed as real as you do now."

"I wish I could explain it," Father Baez said.

"But I saw him that night, too," Cora said. "Or I heard him, anyway. He was in the basement of that house."

Father Baez shook his head. "I'm sorry, my dear. I examined the body in the farmer's kitchen, and it was your husband. I'm sure of it."

Another sob shuddered through her body as she nodded. Wrapping her arms around herself, she sat for a few minutes in silence, thinking about the memories she had just regained. She didn't want to believe them, but she couldn't deny the truth. Father Baez would not lie to her, and her memories fit with what Fodor Glava had said.

"I still don't get one thing," she said. "If what I remember now is the way it happened, how did I get out of that house alive? I remember getting hit over the head, and I must have blacked out."

A glimmer crept into the priest's dark eyes. "I followed you to the house that night," he said.

"What?" Cora asked. "What about that family?"

"I decided they would be safe," Father Baez said. "You had killed the vampires, and I figured any that remained would follow you. I prepared a lantern, tucked my crucifix into my belt, borrowed one of their horses, and set out for the nest."

"Did you see what hit me?"

The priest nodded. "When I arrived at the house, I heard you speaking to someone in the basement. It took me a few moments to find the right door, but when I did, I saw a figure crouching at the bottom of the stairs. I called out, and the man turned and looked at me. I'll never forget his face."

The priest paused, taking a deep breath. "He looked like any other man, even handsome, but his eyes were aflame with an unholy presence. They shone like gold medallions as he grinned at me. Without waiting for him to speak, I raised my crucifix and began quoting scripture. The man flinched, baring his teeth at me before running back into the shadows. When he did, I made my way down the stairs and found you lying on the floor, bleeding from your head."

"How did you carry me out?" Cora asked. "You ain't exactly built like a bull."

"I was a good deal younger then," the priest said, shrugging. "I crushed a garlic clove and spread it on the ground to keep the vampire from returning, then I dragged you back up the stairs and outside."

"And the vampire didn't follow you?"

"If he did, I didn't see him," Father Baez said.

Without warning, a fresh wave of sorrow washed over Cora. She lowered her head, but no more tears came. In their place, a dull ache spread behind her eyes. She wanted to curl up on the pew next to the priest and never move again. Everything was wrong. Her Ben was dead, and she was the one that killed him. She had pointed her gun in his face and pulled the trigger. It didn't matter that he was a vampire. Maybe she could have saved him somehow, but she didn't even try. She just shot him like a dog, snuffing out his life forever.

She couldn't take this. Standing to her feet, she began making her way back up the aisle.

"Where are you going, Cora?" Father Baez asked, rising from the pew.

"I got to find me a bottle," Cora said. "Ain't no way I can handle this on my own."

"Whiskey won't help, my dear," Father Baez said. "Please, stay with me and mourn your husband with dignity and grace." He tried to get in front of her, but she was walking too fast. "I will take you to his grave, and you can honor his memory there."

"I ain't fit to honor his memory," Cora said. "Not when I'm the one that shot him."

"He was already dead, Cora," Father Baez said. "You were purging the demon from his flesh so he could rest in peace. You saved him from the damnation of a false immortality."

"Ain't never saved nobody by shooting them in the face, Father." She reached the door and turned to look at him with empty, bloodshot eyes. "You should have left me there to die with him."

Before the priest could reply, Cora pulled open the door and stepped into the cold afternoon sunlight. Father Baez watched her disappear into the traffic on the street, sorrow filling his heart.

"Blessed Mary, bring thy comfort to Cora," he said. "Blessed Son, be Thou her strength and her light. Guide her back to Your way." He pulled the door closed.

EIGHTEEN

Wash Jones stood in front of the Pioneer saloon, his blue eyes glowing in the evening light. He watched the miners, the businessmen, and the whores shuffle through the saloon's door, feeling the warmth of their blood in his teeth. Each one glowed with a new vitality that his mortal eyes had never seen. Better yet, that vitality existed for the one reason of satisfying his hunger.

Even as he stood exposed to the winter night of a mountain town, Wash felt no cold. The freezing air felt as comfortable as a firelit room had in his previous life. Ever since Fodor Glava had awakened him to his eternal life, his true life, Wash had never stopped marveling at the new power and perceptions coursing through his body. His eyes pierced the deepest shadows, and his arms could easily heft a horse and throw it across the street. He truly possessed the power of a god, and he loved every second of it.

Wash felt a presence lingering near him. Turning his head, he saw a young whore leaning against a hitching rail, watching him. Her face was plain and her figure bony, but Wash no longer lusted after such things. The blood in her veins flowed hot and sweet.

"You look awful lonely out here," she said.

"Care to relieve me of that?" he asked with a grin, his fingers twitching.

She smiled and took his arm, and he led her into the saloon. Patrons filled the room, laughing, drinking, and arguing over cards. Somewhere in the room, the piano tinkled away at a melody, its notes lost beneath the din. Wash stood in the doorway for a moment, taking in the sounds of life, and his grin widened. Glava had promised him that they would soon rule this town as kings, dictating who would live and who would die to feed their hunger. Mere humans, so weak and ignorant, served no other purpose to him now.

His whore tugged at his arm, urging him toward the stairs. The heat from her body drove him mad with desire. Watching her slim figure ahead of him, he trembled with anticipation at the thought of his first kill. Glava had taken him to feed the night before, but this would be his first time alone with his victim. The elder vampire had also told him of how the bodies of his victims would rise again to serve him, an unquestioning army to eliminate his enemies and bring him fresh meals. Skinny though she was, the whore would make a fine slave, the first of many.

She led him into an empty bedroom, and he closed the door behind them. The bed was unmade and the sheets dirty, but he didn't mind. They wouldn't be in use for long.

The whore turned to him. "So, you got your money?"

"Let me see what I'm buying first," Wash said.

"Fair enough," she said, her pale arms reaching down and pulling her dress up over her head. Her cotton undergarments were stained from many months of use. They fell to her mid-thigh, leaving her knees and lower legs exposed. Holding her hands out, she gave a quick turn, allowing him to get a good look at her. "Well?"

Wash didn't reply as his hands fished around in his pocket, jingling the coins inside. His eyes burned with desire. She noticed, and a grin spread across her face. Slipping her shift off of one shoulder, she approached him, swinging her slim hips.

With a cry of desire, he rushed at her, pushing her backward onto the bed. His hand clamped down on her mouth to stifle her scream. He savored the feeling of her warm body squirming beneath him for a moment. She was fighting with all of her strength, but it took little effort to keep her pinned. He grinned at her, baring his fangs, and watched terror fill her eyes. Her screams emerged as pitiful squeaks from beneath his hand, and he laughed.

Then the hunger overtook him, and he sank his teeth into her neck. The taste of his first kill flooded his mouth, filling every fiber of his being with pleasure. Her vitality flowed into him, and he could feel his body being reborn, tingling with sweetness and warmth. The whore's final breath ebbed out over his fingers, and still he drank.

When her body had given up the last of her blood, Wash stood to his feet. He ran his tongue along his mouth, collecting the stray drops that lingered on his lips. He grinned. This new life was going to be perfect. He could kill whoever he wanted, turn them into his slaves, and bring himself to the heights of delight whenever he wished. He looked down at the whore's body. She was but the first of many, and it was time to add to that count.

"I am glad to see you have no reservations about killing."

Wash turned to see Glava's golden eyes gleaming at him from the shadows. "I didn't in life, and I ain't got no reason to change now." He offered his sire a bloody grin. "Hell, if I'd known that being undead was such a thrill, I'd have found one of you vampires to make me into one a long time ago."

"You would not be what you are now," Glava said. "Your fate would be like hers."

Wash looked at the corpse on the bed. "So why am I different now?"

"Because my needs are different," Glava said. "This town is overflowing with degenerates and hedonists of every trade, each looking for quick riches, quick pleasures, and quick thrills. They are easy to tempt and easy to trick, so I have all the necessary ingredients to build myself an army."

"Sweet, ain't it?" Wash said. "Why, the two of us will be unstoppable. Them damn lawmen ain't got what it takes to bring us down now."

"I did not turn you so you might have your petty

vengeance," Glava said. "You are what you are because I have need of another *nosferatu* at my side if I am to defeat the hunter."

"The hunter? Who's that?"

Glava's eyes burned with hatred. "Cora Oglesby."

"That's right," Wash said. "I owe her one, too. What was it she did to you?"

"She destroyed my fledgling army ten years ago," Glava said, "and with it my most promising acolyte."

"Your what, now?"

"My apprentice," Glava said. "Had she not killed his mortal form, he would be the one at my right hand, not you."

"Guess that's good for me, then," Wash said. "Who was he?"

"Her very own husband," Glava said. "I took a calculated risk when I should not have. Years ago, she and her husband hunted our kind together. The two of them separated in my nest, and I saw my chance. Assuming the guise of the family's late butler, I lured him to me and fed on his lifeblood. He rose again a short while later."

Glava's gaze took on a distant look. "I should have made him *nosferatu* then, but I felt it would have been too hasty. The honor of a vampiric rebirth does not always appeal to some when their souls are first restored, and so it would have been with Benjamin Oglesby. He was a religious man, wholly dedicated to his self-righteous cause of hunting our kind. Had I restored his soul to him that night, he might have attempted to rejoin his wife, or even destroyed himself out of loathing.

"To make his transition easier, I attempted to kill Cora using his soulless body. She had fled my nest when confronted with my *vrykolakas*, and I figured she would quickly fall without her husband at her side. My army followed her to a nearby farmhouse, but when they attacked, she and a local priest managed to destroy them. She even brought herself to shoot her own husband in the head, something I had not believed any mortal woman could do. Soon afterward, she and the priest came to my nest, and I was forced to retreat from that place and wait for a more opportune time. I slept for many years, rebuilding my strength, letting the poisons of age and loneliness seep into her bones.

"But now," Glava said, turning his golden gaze back on his apprentice, "now my waiting is over. I have a powerful base here, and a new apprentice to train in the ways of the night. Now, I have broken her mind, and her days are numbered."

"You broke her mind?" Wash asked. "How'd you manage that?"

Glava allowed himself a short laugh. "Her mortal mind was feebler than I knew. Somehow, she had come to believe her husband was still alive. When I summoned his familiar, she became hysterical, and I nearly consumed her." A brief contortion passed over his face as he remembered the burning of the holy water. "She managed to escape again, but her mind is weak, and I know where she has gone."

Wash grinned, and his fingers flexed in anticipation. "Where's that?"

"To the priest who fought with her ten years ago," Glava said. "While she is with him, we have little chance of success, but she will leave there soon and return here."

"How do you know that?"

"That is her way, to return," Glava said. "Just as she did ten years ago, so will she now. Her mind is weak, but her nature is unchanged. She is tenacious to a fault. This time, it will be her undoing."

"Good," Wash said. "How long till she gets back?"

"She will crawl into a bottle for a day or two until she loses herself to her rage. When she does, she will return to us, drunk and blinded by anger, and we will take her."

"What will we do till then?"

"We will attend to other business." Glava motioned with his arm. "Come. Once it is concluded, we will slake our lust with the blood of these fools."

The elder vampire walked out the door, and his apprentice followed. Glava's dark hair seemed to absorb the light of the hallway as they made their way toward the saloon. "I had the misfortune of being disturbed while obtaining my meal last night," Glava said. "Worse, the intruder was a member of the local law. Much as I prefer to remain subtle, this unfortunate event has alerted the lawgivers to our presence."

"That ain't no problem," Wash said as his boots began thumping down the stairs. "We should just go kill the lot and settle it right now."

"You have much to learn of subtlety," Glava said. "In this case, however, your solution is almost practical."

Reaching the main room, the vampire paused for a moment and looked back at Wash Jones. "We will eliminate them, but we must keep up appearances lest we draw even more attention to ourselves."

"What's that mean?" Wash asked. Despite his recent meal, he still felt a strong desire to claim another victim, and the heat of human blood in the room fought for his attention.

"It means you will learn the first of the many abilities that I have given you." Before Glava could continue, a shout rang out from the bar. Both vampires looked over to see a young man staring at them, his face twisted with rage.

"You!" the man yelled, pointing his finger at Glava. "You're the one that killed my Annabelle."

"And who might you be?" Glava asked.

"Deputy Jack Evans, and I'm going to put you in your grave right now for what you done."

"You are a number of years too late for that, good sir," Glava replied, turning to leave. Wash stood where he was, eyes wide as Jack Evans pulled his revolver and took aim. Gamblers and miners dove for cover behind the tables.

The slug hit Glava between the shoulder blades and exploded from his chest, burying itself in the door. Turning, Glava looked down at the hole in his chest. "Unpleasant," he said, his golden eyes regarding the deputy. Silence and blue smoke filled the air between them. After a moment, he looked at his apprentice and motioned with a gloved hand. "Come, Mr Jones."

The vampire opened the door and stepped out into the night. Wash followed, keenly aware of the eyes watching them depart. Looking over his shoulder, he offered the room a big grin before leaving. Jack Evans still stood at the bar with his gun raised, dumbfounded.

"You see the unwelcome attention we are prone to attract," Glava said when Wash caught up. "Not only do the people in that bar now know we are something more than we appear, but I shall also need to have this suit tailored."

"Why not just buy a new one?" Wash asked. "If you ain't got no money, just kill a rich man and take his."

"A man's dress is an important component of his presence, be he human or vampire," Glava replied, "and I don't much care for your American fashions."

Behind them, the door to the Pioneer flew open, and Jack Evans stumbled into the street. After a moment of confusion, he caught sight of the two men walking toward the marshal's station. Coaxing his drunken legs into a run, he took after them, his revolver still in his hand. It went off before he could take aim, and the bullet soared over the vampires' heads. They both turned to face him. Jack skidded to a halt a few yards from them, his vision swimming. He took aim at Glava, but before he could pull the trigger, a gloved hand clamped down on his wrist and twisted. There was a snapping sound.

"Your persistence is admirable, but also irritating," Glava said, twisting the arm further. Jack cried out in pain. Around them, people stopped to watch the scene unfold.

Another twist brought the deputy to his knees. "You were fond of the whore, were you?" Glava asked. Jack managed a nod, the fire in his eyes replaced by tears. The vampire looked up at his apprentice, a sadistic smile on his lips. "Then perhaps you should be reunited."

Glava's free hand grabbed a fistful of Jack's shirt and hauled him to his feet. With a shove, he began marching the deputy back toward the saloon. Behind him, Wash picked up Jack's fallen pistol and stuck it in his belt. He had taken two steps toward the saloon when another shout rang out. Turning, he saw a short man with a fiery red beard running toward him at full speed, a big revolver in each hand.

Glava turned as well, Jack's shirt still firmly in his grip. The man stopped a few feet from them, aiming one pistol at each vampire. "Just where do you boys think you're going with my deputy?"

"To reunite him with his whore," Glava said. "You must be the local marshal."

"Mart Duggan," the marshal replied. "I have it on good authority that his whore is dead, so you best start talking sense before I put a bullet in each of you."

Glava looked at Wash. "Might you care to handle this situation, Mr Jones? I am so looking forward to bringing these two lovers back together."

The vampire turned and began walking with his captive again. Duggan took careful aim at the dark hair and pulled back the hammer. Before he could fire, Wash Jones appeared in front of him and knocked the pistol from his grip. Without thinking, the marshal swung his other revolver toward those grinning blue eyes. He made contact, the barrel smashing into Wash's temple, but the vampire absorbed the blow without taking a step. Wash reached up and tore the second pistol from Duggan's hand. He tossed it aside, then wrapped his fingers around the marshal's neck and pulled him close.

"I never liked lawmen," Wash said. He shoved Duggan backward, sending him sprawling in the snow. The impact jarred the marshal's bones, sending spikes of pain through his body. Before he could recover, Wash Jones stood over him, blue eyes alight with pleasure. The vampire bent down, grabbed two fistfuls of Duggan's shirt, and pulled him to his feet.

"You should know, marshal, that you ain't the first lawman I've done in," Wash said, "but you're the first I aim to make my slave." His grin widened, revealing his fangs. "Why, I reckon you ought to be honored by that. You get to live forever in the cause of serving a higher being."

"I already do," Duggan said.

Wash laughed in his face. He placed a cold hand on the marshal's forehead, pushing his chin up. Duggan's neck pulsed with the blood flowing beneath it. Wash took a moment to prepare himself for the bliss to come, then lowered his face to the lawman's neck.

Before his fangs could pierce the marshal's skin, a wave of nausea hit Wash like a flash flood. The strength evaporated from his limbs. Confused, he dropped the marshal in the snow and backed away. After a few steps, the sensation subsided. Regaining his bearings,

Wash made to charge back toward the marshal when the nausea hit him again. He crumpled to the ground, holding his stomach, pale face twisted in pain and surprise. His immortal body was above disease and even death. Nothing should be able to cause any pain to him now, yet here he was, lying helpless in the snow. His stomach heaved, trying to vomit out its contents, but nothing came.

Boots crunched in the snow near his head. Through his agony, he looked up at the form of Mart Duggan standing over him, a crucifix in his outstretched hand. The sight of the holy symbol made Wash's stomach give another lurch, and he rolled away from the marshal.

"Ain't so big now, are you?" Duggan said, kicking the vampire's back. "Go on, boy. Make me your slave. Clap me in chains and drag me away."

Wash groaned in reply and began crawling through the snow. The marshal followed him for a few paces, keeping the crucifix pointed at his back. People were openly staring at the strange spectacle now, but Duggan paid them no heed. He kept his eyes on the retreating monster, his face full of cautious satisfaction. He was driving the vampire away, but he didn't know how to kill it. He needed Cora's help for that, and God only knew where she was.

Duggan gave Wash Jones one last kick in the ribs. "Go on and get yourself out of my town. I ain't likely to be so forgiving next time."

Wash swayed with the impact, but he kept crawling. After a few yards, the nausea started to fade. He rose on shaky legs and took a step. The strength began returning to his limbs. A few more steps, and he felt strong enough to turn and glare at the lawman. Mart Duggan was still pointing that horrible cross at him. Wash winced in pain and turned away. Let the lawman think he'd won. He and Glava would soon prove who ran this town.

The effects of the crucifix had all but disappeared by the time Wash made it back to the Pioneer. Ignoring the stares he drew when he entered, he climbed the stairs and made his way to the storage room where Glava had hidden the first whore's body. As he approached, his keen ears could hear shouts and growls coming from behind the closed door, and he grinned.

Glava looked up when Wash entered. "Ah, Mr Jones, you have arrived just in time. Please, take a seat and enjoy the unfolding drama."

He motioned toward the far corner of the room, where Jack Evans cowered behind a crate. The deputy cradled his broken wrist, whimpering in terror. Above him, crouched on the crate like a cat about to pounce, was Annabelle Rose. She bared her teeth and snarled at her former lover. Blonde locks still framed her face, but her naked body had faded to the ashen gray of the dead.

After a few moments, Glava stood and approached the deputy. "You see, Mr Evans, it does not do to make spectacles of those that wish to remain unnoticed." The vampire smiled at the feral prostitute. "I so often forget how beautiful your human love affairs can be. The very body you coveted so shall be your death. I imagine you long dreamed of her flesh being the last thing you felt on this earth, so perhaps you will find pleasure in this dream coming to pass."

Glava glanced at Wash as the *vrykolakas* pounced on the deputy. She buried her face in his neck, her arms wrapping around his body with a passion greater than any lover's. Together, the two *nosferatu* watched the life fade from Jack Evans. His screams ebbed into pitiful whimpers as Annabelle drained his body, slurping and sucking with the fervor of a wild animal. After a few minutes, her face emerged from the bloody spectacle and peered at them. Streaks of red ran down her neck as her eyes looked to Glava for his next command. The *nosferatu* smiled at her and pointed toward another corner of the room. She crawled over to it and sat down, licking the blood from her arms.

Glava turned back to Wash. "You see how useful the *vrykolakas* can be."

"You got a mess of them handy?" Wash asked. "Why?"

Wash looked down at his boots. "That fool marshal pulled a cross on me. I couldn't go nowhere near him without going all weak and shaky."

Glava's golden eyes blazed. He cracked Wash across the cheek with the back of his hand. "You fool! How could you have let that happen? Why did you not snap his neck at once when I told you to kill him?"

"I wanted to drink him and make him a slave," Wash said. "Ain't that what we're supposed to do?"

"Only if we can succeed," Glava said, "which is clearly beyond your grasp." The elder vampire waved his hand, dismissing him. "Return to your whoring and increase your strength. I will see to the problem you have created."

Glava stormed out of the room and down the hallway, reaching out for his servant *vrykolakas* with his mind. Just north of town, hidden in an abandoned building, the remaining monsters from the mine stirred. Hearing their master's summons, they crawled from their shelter and sprinted toward town as one. Glava could feel the snow crunch beneath their hands and feet. Through their ears, he could hear the startled screams of the townsfolk as they charged into the streets of Leadville.

The *nosferatu* descended the stairs and exited through the Pioneer's front door. Behind him, he could hear surprised shouts from the saloon. The cries spread through the traffic on the street as the naked prostitute emerged to her master, snarling like a rabid dog. Women screamed and men hollered, their voices creating a cacophony of fear in the cold night air. Despite his fury, Glava allowed himself a small smile. Though he preferred to work in secret, the chorus of terror from these mortals was not without merit. It was but the prelude to the symphony he would conduct in this small town. Let all who beheld him tremble and cower, for he was Fodor Glava, a god of blood and death made flesh.

Up the street, Mart Duggan and a frightened Mexican deputy stood outside the marshal's station, preparing to investigate the commotion. When the marshal saw Glava approach, he cursed and raised his crucifix. Glava stopped a safe distance from the symbol and smiled, his golden eyes flashing in the night.

"You seem alarmed, marshal," Glava said.

Duggan kept the crucifix held aloft. Annabelle growled in reply, and the marshal's eyes darted toward her with a hint of fear. "This ain't nothing in this town. Why, compared to a full-blown miners' riot, the two of you ain't nothing but donkey piss."

Behind the marshal, Deputy Sanchez cried out as half a dozen vampires came loping up the street from the opposite direction, driving a herd of terrified townsfolk before them. He raised the small golden crucifix he kept around his neck, an "Our Father" in Spanish tumbling out of his mouth. The *vrykolakas* stopped up a few yards short of him, pacing and snarling like a pack of wolves. Inhuman fangs glistened in their almost-human faces.

"You are outnumbered and outmatched, marshal," Glava continued, his voice calm. "Look around you. None of the people you have risked your life to protect are willing to return the favor."

Duggan glaced to either side, and his heart sank. Sure enough, the townsfolk had all but disappeared from the streets. Frightened faces peered out of the windows lining the road, watching the terrifying scene unfold. Behind him, he could hear the frantic prayers of his deputy, but it was just the two of them against an army of creatures he'd only heard about in children's stories. Duggan whispered a prayer himself as he stared into the vampire's golden eyes. He always knew that being marshal in such a rowdy town might well be his death, but he never imagined it playing out like this.

"I've spent four years protecting the people of this town," he said aloud, drawing his big Colt. "I ain't about to stand down now. I don't care if you're some fairy-tale monster with the strength of a thousand men. I don't see nothing but a swell-headed son of a bitch just like any other I've whipped, and you ain't getting me without a fight."

Glava clapped his hands together. "Such an in-domitable spirit. I have a mind to make you my new apprentice and tie that addle-witted Washington Jones to a rock for the noonday sun." As he spoke, the vampires in front of Sanchez spread out, forming a large semi-circle around the desperate lawmen. The deputy's prayers grew louder as he tried to keep his crucifix pointed at all of the snarling faces at once. They began closing in on him, their fangs gnashing together in anticipation. At the same time, Annabelle Rose began circling to Duggan's left, her eyes fixed on his crucifix. The marshal began alternating the crucifix between her and her master, panic swelling in his chest.

He was going to die.

Duggan watched the naked woman continue to cir-cle him, knuckles crunching in the snow. Out of the corner of his eye, he thought he saw the golden-eyed man make a move. He spun toward him, cross held high. The *nosferatu* simply gazed back at him.

Behind him, the woman let out a howl and charged. He brought the holy symbol back around, but it was too late. She was already in the air, hands outstretched, flying toward him with murder in her eyes.

The monster jerked to one side in mid-air as if kicked, and fell in a heap beside him. Duggan stared in disbelief at the smoking hole in her side as she struggled to her feet. The crack of a rifle echoed from somewhere behind the elder vampire, followed by a loud curse. Looking up, he saw the golden eyes vanish in a whirl of dark hair. The *nosferatu* dodged to the left as another shot rang out. The bullet punched a hole in the snarling woman's skull. Pale limbs flailed in the snow, and her final howl ended in a choking gurgle. Looking up the street, Duggan could make out a small figure in a wide-brimmed hat.

Cora Oglesby trained her Winchester on the glowing golden eyes, her rosary dangling from her left hand. Behind her, Our Lady stood in the street, her breath streaming into the night air.

"Well, now, if it ain't my old friend Mr Fodor Glava," she said, chambering a round. "Nice to see you showing your real face to the world for a change."

Glava's eyes burned with hatred. "Welcome back, widow. I hope you are prepared to join your husband in hell."

"That ain't no kind of greeting, now," Cora said. Her boots crunched through the snow toward the vampire. "And here I was hoping for an apology."

Before Glava could answer, Cora's hand dropped to her belt. She pulled out her revolver and tossed it over to Mart Duggan. "Here, marshal. You lick them spooks behind you while me and Mr Glava here have ourselves a nice chat."

Keeping a wary eye on the vampire, Duggan picked up the revolver. He whispered an order to his frightened deputy and the two men traded places. Sanchez's frightened brown eyes locked on Fodor Glava while the marshal raised pistol and crucifix at the nearest *vrykolakas*. The Colt's roar echoed off of the surrounding buildings, and the monster collapsed. The rest of the *vrykolakas* began backing away from the marshal.

Glava could feel the terror rising in his minions. He longed to charge at this hateful woman and snap her neck, but the rosary in her hand held him at bay. In his mind, he screamed for Wash Jones to come to his aid. The apprentice heard the master's call, rising from the bed of a fresh kill, and a grin returned to the master's face. Even with their holy symbols and holy weapons, Cora Oglesby and her little marshal could not hope to withstand both *nosferatu* at once.

The grin vanished from Glava's face a moment later as pain and confusion exploded through the minds of his *vrykolakas*. Through their eyes, he could see a line of men on horseback galloping up the street. Their leader held a large cross in his raised hand. The lesser vampires panicked, turning back the way they had come only to cower before Mart Duggan's upraised crucifix. Their combined terror and pain flooded Glava's mind, threatening to overwhelm his hold on them. Forgetting himself, his golden eyes slid closed as he attempted to tighten his grip on them.

A moment later, he heard the crack of Cora's rifle. He dodged to the left, but the chaos in his mind slowed his reflexes. The silver bullet caught him just below the shoulder, tearing another hole in the breast of his suit. Searing pain flooded his body, and his mind shook loose of the *vrykolakas*. He could hear the Colt's booming voice as the marshal cut down his army, but he no longer felt their pain. Blinded by his own suffering, he stumbled and nearly fell. The hunter's rifle cracked again, and pain sliced through his leg.

Fodor Glava fell to his knees, unable to understand the waves of pain flowing through his immortal body. Behind him, the revolver's echoes vanished beneath the thundering of horses. The ground beneath him shook, and he forced his eyes open. No fewer than half a dozen mounted men surrounded him, all with crosses raised. The holy symbols wracked his body with fire, sapping what strength remained in him.

The horses began shuffling as the group parted, clearing the way for someone to come through. The golden eyes closed for a moment as Glava reached out one last, desperate time for his apprentice. He could feel Wash Jones nearby; he could see the group of men on horseback through his eyes. He could also sense the man's fear. Glava burned Wash's mind, commanding him to take the group in the back, to create a distraction, to do anything at all, but the former gunman remained where he stood. The elder vampire watched in despair as Wash finally took to his heels, holy terror lending speed to his flight.

Glava opened his eyes at the sound of approaching boots. Raising his head, he stared into the cold brown eyes of the hunter. Mart Duggan stood beside her, his raised crucifix sending more waves of crippling pain through the vampire's body. Cora Oglesby held only her saber. Around them, the night was silent, as if the rest of the world had ceased to exist. Not even the stamping of a horse's hoof disturbed the frigid air as vampire and hunter regarded each other.

"How the mighty are fallen," Cora finally said.

"Just like your husband," Glava replied, managing a sneer through his pain. "Did you say those same words to him as you shot him in the face?"

"Wasn't no need," Cora said. "He wouldn't have heard me if I had, not with his soul trapped inside your filthy body."

"Where he has served me for ten years," the vampire said. "If you kill me now, his soul will be forever lost to this world. You will never see his face again."

Cora drew her arm back and slapped him across the cheek with the flat of her blade. Glava tumbled sideways, landing face-first in the packed snow. "I ain't about to let him suffer just to give my own selfish self peace of mind." She knelt down, grabbed a fistful of Glava's hair, and jerked him upright. She pressed the point of her sword into the vampire's suit just above his heart.

"This is for my Ben."

Cora slid the saber through his chest in one fluid motion even as Glava opened his mouth. His reply became a hellish wail, thin and piercing, that filled the empty streets with the voice of the damned. The men on horseback clapped their hands over their ears, and Mart Duggan winced and turned his head, but Cora Oglesby never flinched. She kept the sacred blade in her hand as the vampire's body writhed around it. Smoke burst forth from Glava's mouth and nose, rising in a great cloud above their heads. As it rose, the cries of a thousand liberated souls filled the air. Their voices grew fainter as the smoke, caught in the breath of a night breeze, melted into the stars. When the last voice had faded into the distance, the golden glow was gone from Glava's eyes.

Planting a boot on the vampire's shoulder, Cora pulled the saber out of the lifeless corpse. The blade shimmered in the moonlight as she brought it down once more. She wiped it clean on the hem of Glava's suit, slid the blade home, and turned to face the cluster of men. They all stared at her open-mouthed, faces frozen in amazement. Even Mart Duggan's blue eyes were wide in his pale face.

A grin blossomed across her lips. "Why the long faces, boys?" Kicking back with her heel, she drove a silver spur into the dead vampire's side. "Ain't got nothing to worry about no more." She held out her hand toward the marshal, and he handed her the spent revolver. She slipped the silver barrel back into her holster and pressed her way through the crowd of horses to where her own mare stood waiting. The two lawmen followed, quiet prayers still falling from Sanchez's lips.

Cora climbed into the saddle and looked down at them, her grin never wavering. "Go on home, you two. Get some sleep for a change." She tapped Our Lady's sides with her heels and walked the mare back to the group of men on horseback. James Townsend sat atop his big carriage horse, the cross in his hand all but forgotten.

"My God, Cora," he said when she rode up next to him.

"Why is your jaw hanging?" she asked. "Ain't that what you and Harcourt wanted?"

"Yes, but to have witnessed such an event…" James said, his empty hand groping for words. "The scholars at Oxford will never believe my account of this."

"Don't forget to talk up your part in it," she said. "If you boys hadn't been awake when I came calling tonight, I might have had to do all the work myself."

James let out a small chuckle. "I will be hard-pressed to convince them of my credentials as a vampire killer."

Cora shrugged. "I'm sure you'll bring them around." She held up a hand to halt his reply. "Before you get to all that writing and talking, though, I do hope you'll join me for one last ride. I'm of a mind to call on Lord Harcourt tonight and settle up about my payment."

EPILOGUE

A steady wind rolled down from the slopes of the foothills and out across the plains, making the tall grasses bend and sigh. It was not a warm wind bearing with it the gentle promise of spring, but a cold, fierce wind filled with bony fingers that pulled and poked and pierced. It swept between the silent gravestones and tugged at the thick buffalo coat of the lone figure standing amid them. The figure seemed to take no notice of the cold wind or the bright afternoon sun as it stood, head bowed, before a gray stone cross. In the distance, a pair of saddled horses huddled together against the cold. A small man stood between them, his black robes flowing out beneath his white beard.

The wind pulled Cora's tears across her cheeks and froze them in place, but she didn't turn away from the gravestone at her feet. It was small and simple, a stone cross etched with the name of the dead man and his years of life. Ten years of wind and rain and snow and sun had already begun wearing down the edges of the letters, making them smooth. Strands of yellow grass emerged from the blanket of snow, teasing the stone arms and playing with the hem of her coat.

BENJAMIN ABRAHAM OGLESBY
1843—1873

Cora read the words over and over, her brown eyes tracing each letter as if carving them anew into the stone. Her breathing was uneven, drawing the cold wind down into her body only to return it to the prairie in quiet sobs. She didn't know how long she had stood at the foot of her husband's grave, but she knew it could never be long enough. The words on the stone were colder than any winter wind, covering her heart with a frost that would never melt.

"Well," she said, her voice thick, "I never thought I'd wake up one day to find you here."

The wind whistled around her, carrying her words away from her lips as soon as she spoke them.

"I hope you won't mind that I didn't stop by sooner, but I guess I was in a bad way about you dying. Didn't want to believe it, so I just kept saying it wasn't so until you came back to me." She sniffed, offering the headstone a small smile. "We still had us some good times, even if you wasn't really there."

Memories of his kind eyes and warm smile welled up in her, bringing fresh tears to her eyes. She didn't brush them off or turn her head; she had never hidden her sorrow from him in life and would not start now. The wave passed after a few moments, and she opened her eyes again.

"Even after Father Baez told me you was resting here, I couldn't make myself come. I couldn't face you until I knew that I'd settled up with your killer." She smiled again, feeling the frozen tears crack on her cheeks. "I licked that bastard good for you. Ran him through with your sword after me and some fellers cornered him like the dog he was. James says killing him freed you to go on up to the good Lord at long last. Once you're sainted, Father Baez says he'll talk with the Pope himself about making you the patron of vampire hunters. There ain't never been one before, so there's room, and it's fitting that it should be you."

She patted her breast pocket with a gloved hand. "Got me the bounty they put on that vampire's head. There's plenty there to open a print shop, just like you wanted. Ain't settled on where I'll put it yet, but I'm thinking about going back home and setting up where your pa's old shop was. Don't know if they'd take me as I am, though; I ain't exactly no lady."

A gust of wind filled in the silence as she trailed off. She could feel the icy fingers weaving their way under her coat, and she shivered, sinking back into her memories. After a few minutes, she roused herself, reached into her belt pouch, and pulled out a familiar silver dagger. She ran her fingers over the soft leather sheath, then tied the dangling rawhide strips into a loop. Then she knelt down and hung the dagger on the stone cross.

"Here's this back. Sorry I can't put it down there with you, but the soil's frozen up this time of year. I'll come by when it warms up again and bury it then if that's all right." She paused, thinking back on the memories that had so recently returned to her. "Maybe if you'd had it with you that night, things would be different now. Only the good Lord could say for sure."

She kissed her fingers and touched them to the chiseled letters. Her hand lingered there, tracing each letter in turn. Another gust of wind swirled around her. After a moment, she sighed and rose to her feet.

"I best be getting on," she said. "Won't do to keep poor Father Baez out here in the cold, old as he is. I'll stop by and tell you where it is I decided to put our print shop once I get it figured out, but I expect you'll see me before then, too." She pulled her coat closer around her, then raised her hand and tipped her hat to the silent grave. "Take care of yourself, now."

Her boots crunched in the snow as she turned and started walking back to the waiting priest. Father Baez offered her the reins with a kind smile. She returned it, her tears still frozen on her cheeks, and climbed into Our Lady of Virginia's saddle. The priest followed suit, turning his small horse away from the cemetery. Together, they rode down the small hill toward the city, and Cora did not look back.

The wind continued to play with the long grass growing around the cold stone cross. Ben's silver dagger rocked against the granite, swaying with the ebb and flow of the air. The sun drifted down toward the mountains, and the shadow of the cross stretched out eastward, following his beloved wife's footsteps, reaching out with unmoving arms toward the place where she had stood.

Acknowledgments

Many thanks to my friend and fellow scribbler Matt Carman, who invited me to try NaNoWriMo with him and gave me the heads-up about Angry Robot's Open Door Month. Thanks also to Amanda Rutter for offering my manuscript up to the Robot Overlords and to the Anxious Appliances for sharing the mind-shredding anxiety with me.

Thanks to Melissa Gardner for being the first one to finish this book, to Nancy Gerardi for insisting that it could be a Broadway musical, and to my parents for encouraging my love of books from an early age. Finally, thanks to all the friends and family who caught typos, suggested improvements, discussed ideas, and listened to my frustrations.

THIS IS MIRIAM BLACK...
SHE KNOWS WHEN YOU'LL DIE

"Trailer-park tension, horrified hilarity, and sheer terror mixed with deft characterization and razor plotting. I literally could not put it down."
LILITH SAINTCROW

BLACKBIRDS

CHUCK WENDIG

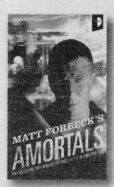

SELL THE DOG
Grab the complete Angry Robot catalog

DAN ABNETT
- [ ] Embedded
- [ ] Triumff: Her Majesty's Hero

GUY ADAMS
- [ ] The World House
- [ ] Restoration

JO ANDERTON
- [ ] Debris
- [ ] Suited

MADELINE ASHBY
- [ ] vN

LEE BATTERSBY
- [ ] The Corpse-Rat King

LAUREN BEUKES
- [ ] Moxyland
- [ ] Zoo City

THOMAS BLACKTHORNE
- [ ] Edge
- [ ] Point

MAURICE BROADDUS
- [ ] The Knights of Breton Court

ADAM CHRISTOPHER
- [ ] Empire State
- [ ] Seven Wonders

PETER CROWTHER
- [ ] Darkness Falling

ALIETTE DE BODARD
- [ ] Obsidian & Blood

MATT FORBECK
- [ ] Amortals
- [ ] Carpathia
- [ ] Vegas Knights

JUSTIN GUSTAINIS
- [ ] Hard Spell
- [ ] Evil Dark

GUY HALEY
- [ ] Reality 36
- [ ] Omega Point

COLIN HARVEY
- [ ] Damage Time
- [ ] Winter Song

CHRIS F HOLM
- [ ] Dead Harvest

MATTHEW HUGHES
- [ ] The Damned Busters
- [ ] Costume Not Included

TRENT JAMIESON
- [ ] Roil
- [ ] Night's Engines

K W JETER
- [ ] Infernal Devices
- [ ] Morlock Night

PAUL S KEMP
- [ ] The Hammer & the Blade

J ROBERT KING
- [ ] Angel of Death
- [ ] Death's Disciples

ANNE LYLE
- [ ] The Alchemist of Souls

GARY McMAHON
- [ ] Pretty Little Dead Things
- [ ] Dead Bad Things

ANDY REMIC
- [ ] The Clockwork Vampire Chronicles

CHRIS ROBERSON
- [ ] Book of Secrets

MIKE SHEVDON
- [ ] Sixty-One Nails
- [ ] The Road to Bedlam
- [ ] Strangeness & Charm

DAVID TALLERMAN
- [ ] Giant Thief

GAV THORPE
- [ ] The Crown of the Blood
- [ ] The Crown of the Conqueror
- [ ] The Crown of the Usurper

LAVIE TIDHAR
- [ ] The Bookman
- [ ] Camera Obscura
- [ ] The Great Game

TIM WAGGONER
- [ ] The Nekropolis Archives

KAARON WARREN
- [ ] Mistification
- [ ] Slights
- [ ] Walking the Tree

CHUCK WENDIG
- [ ] Blackbirds
- [ ] Mockingbird

IAN WHATES
- [ ] City of Dreams & Nightmare
- [ ] City of Hope & Despair
- [ ] City of Light & Shadow